A *New York Times* bestse... has written over nin... for Mills & Boon. Christi... BOOKreviews Reviewer... nominated six times for the *RITA*™ Award. She lives in Oregon with her family. Visit Christine at christinerimmer.com

USA TODAY bestselling author **Jules Bennett** has penned more than fifty novels during her short career. She's married to her high school sweetheart, has two active girls, and is a former salon owner. Jules can be found on Twitter, Facebook (Fan Page), and her website julesbennett.com. She holds competitions via these three outlets with each release and loves to hear from readers!

Patricia Thayer was born in Muncie, Indiana, the second of eight children. She attended Ball State University before heading to California. A longtime member of RWA, Patricia has authored fifty books. She's been nominated for the Prestige *RITA*™ award and winner of the RT Reviewer's Choice award. She loves travelling with her husband, Steve, calling it research. When she wants some time with her guy, they escape to their mountain cabin and sit on the deck and let the world race by.

Indecent Proposals

Indecent Proposals:
The Holiday Wedding

CHRISTINE RIMMER

JULES BENNETT

PATRICIA THAYER

MILLS & BOON

First Published in Great Britain 2022
By Mills & Boon, an imprint of HarperCollins*Publishers,* Ltd
1 London Bridge Street, London, SE1 9GF

www.harpercollins.co.uk

HarperCollins*Publishers*
1st Floor, Watermarque Building,
Ringsend Road, Dublin 4, Ireland

INDECENT PROPOSALS: THE HOLIDAY WEDDING
© 2022 Harlequin Enterprises ULC.

Married Till Christmas © 2017 Christine Rimmer
Scandalous Engagement © 2020 Jules Bennett
Single Dad's Holiday Wedding © 2012 Patricia Wright

ISBN: 978-0-263-31792-3

MARRIED TILL CHRISTMAS

CHRISTINE RIMMER

For my family, with all my love.

Chapter One

"God, you are beautiful. That red hair, those big green eyes. That amazing body. And those lips. Baby, those lips were made for a man to bite. Can I tell you a secret?"

Nell Bravo had a one-word answer for that one. "No."

But the handsome guy in the expensive suit wasn't listening. He leaned extra close, breathing Booker's Rye—and no, he wasn't really drunk, only buzzed enough to get pushy. "I don't usually go for tattoos on a woman." He eyed the half sleeve of bright ink that swirled over her left arm from shoulder to elbow. "But, in your case, I'm definitely making an exception. I'd like to jump you right here at the bar."

Nell considered summoning the energy to be offended, but that would be faking it. She'd never minded the brash approach, not as long as she was interested. Too bad she just wasn't—and hadn't been for a long time now.

Except for one man.

One man who managed to show up every time she turned around lately, a guy she was not letting close to her ever again, thank you very much—and that did it. That finished it. She'd had enough of the handsome fellow in the pricey suit.

Not only did he refuse to take a hint, he'd gone and made her think of the one person she wanted nothing to do with.

Ever again.

Not even in her mind.

Somewhere behind her, bells and whistles went off as a lucky slot player hit a jackpot. Nell grabbed her clutch, whipped out a twenty and slid it under her cocktail napkin for the bartender. "That's it for me."

"Whoa now," said the guy beside her, whose name was Ron. "Put your money away."

"Great to meet you, Ron," she lied. "I've got your card and I'll be in touch." He owned Ron's Custom Tile, with five stores in the Bay Area and Los Angeles. Her company, Bravo Construction, ordered a lot of tile. Maybe they could have done some business. Probably not now, though. Ron was just way too interested in looking down her dress. "Good night." She spun on her stool, lowered her Jimmy Choos to the floor and set off for the lobby area and the elevator up to her room.

But Ron was no quitter. "Hold on a minute." He was right behind her. "Baby, don't go…"

Nell stopped in her tracks. When she turned, he almost plowed into her. "Look." She pinned him with her coldest stare. "I don't know how much clearer I can make this. I'm not interested in being jumped by you—right there at the bar, or anywhere in else in this hotel. Good night, Ron."

He started to speak again, but she didn't hang around to hear it. Instead, she took off, moving faster now, weaving her way past the rows of whizzing, dinging slot machines and on to the never-ending main casino floor. She flew past the gaming tables and more bars and restaurants, her high heels tapping hard over polished floors, ears tuned for the sound of Ron's footsteps behind her.

Yep. The idiot was following her.

So what? He wasn't going to catch her. She kept going, never once looking back.

Finally, she reached the blue-lit hotel lobby with its glittering waterfall wall and swirling peacock-colored carpet. As she veered by the concierge desk, she slipped her key card from her clutch.

Entering the marble-lined bank of elevators at last, she pushed the button to go up.

Unfortunately, no car was available.

Crap. Okay, she could just keep on going out the other end of the bay and circle back around, hoping to lose Ron in the process.

Or simply wait.

Screw it. She waited, which gave Ron the chance to catch up with her. When he reached her, she glanced the other way. Maybe ignoring him would do the trick.

Not so much. He grabbed her arm and pulled her around to face him. "Now, just a damn minute here."

"Ron. You don't look all that handsome with that mean scowl on your face."

"I just want to—"

"No, Ron. I said no."

"There's no need to be rude, Nell." He spoke through clenched teeth and he still had a death grip on her arm.

Nell felt a burning need to give Ron the sharp knee in the family jewels he very much deserved. But she kept her cool. "Seriously, Ron? This is going nowhere good. It's a casino, in case you didn't notice." She pointed at the camera mounted up where the wall met the ceiling. "The eye-in-the-sky sees all. I only need to let out a scream and your evening will be downgraded from bad to a whole lot worse."

His grip on her arm loosened. Before she could congratulate herself for some smooth handling of an iffy situation, she noticed that Ron's narrowed eyes had widened and shifted upward toward something behind her.

Yanking her arm free, she turned.

Not possible. "Deck?" It couldn't be.

Oh, but it was. Declan McGrath, all six foot four and two-hundred-plus muscled-up pounds of him, right here in Vegas. At *her* hotel.

"What a coincidence running into you here," said Deck in that rough, low, wonderful voice of his.

Nell rolled her eyes so hard she almost fell over. "Coincidence, my ass. Don't even try to tell me you're here for the Worldwide Hard Surfaces Trade Show."

"Okay, I won't." The corners of his mouth inched upward in the slow, delicious smile that used to make her life worth living. Years and years ago. Back when she was young and trusting, before he'd dumped her flat—twice. "God, Sparky. You do look good."

She gave him the same look she'd been giving Ron—a look of ice and steel. "How many times do I have to say it? Don't call me Sparky."

"I just can't help myself."

"You don't *want* to help yourself."

"That's right. I never give up. And we both know it's just a matter of time until you give in and give me a break."

"You're delusional."

"I prefer to call it thinking positive."

"Hold on just a damn minute," Ron piped up from behind her. "What the hell is going on here?"

Nell turned to tell the tile man—again—to get lost.

But Deck stepped around her and took Ron's arm.

Ron flailed. "What the hell, man? Let go of my arm."

"In a minute." Deck glanced back to pin Nell with a look. "Do. Not. Move." And then he pulled Ron down to the other end of the enclosure and whispered something in his ear. Ron paled.

The nearest elevator dinged and the doors slid open. Several people filed out. Nell watched them go, thinking that she should get on and get away before Deck came back.

But then again, no. Just no. She'd been walking away from Deck for months now. Enough of that. This time he'd finally gone too far.

Following her to Vegas? Who *did* that?

She wasn't surrendering the field this time. Not until she'd treated him to a very large piece of her mind. And maybe the kick in the cojones she'd almost given Ron.

More elevator cars arrived and more people spilled out as Deck whispered in Ron's ear.

"Got it," said Ron, blond head bobbing. "Loud and clear."

"Fair enough." Deck let go of his arm.

Ron backed away with both hands up. "But hey, like I said, she's not wearing a ring."

"A ring?" Nell demanded. Not that either man was listening.

"She's naughty like that sometimes," Deck said with a so-what shrug. "Now get lost." Ron didn't argue. He took off. Nell leaned against the marble wall, her arms crossed over her chest, as Deck turned her way again. "Good," he said. "You're still here."

Where to even start with him? "You've got to leave me alone, Deck."

He came toward her, so big and solid, all lazy male grace, in jeans that hugged his hard legs and an olive-green shirt that made his hazel eyes gleam so damn bright—chameleon eyes, she used to call them. They seemed different colors depending on his mood and the light. He'd rolled his sleeves to his elbows, showing off strong forearms, all muscled and veiny, dusted with sandy-colored hair.

It just wasn't fair. No man should be allowed to look that amazing. She wrapped her arms tighter around herself to keep her grabby hands from reaching out and squeezing those rock-hard muscles of his.

Because, she bleakly reminded herself, squeezing Deck's muscles—or any other part of him, for that matter—was a big, fat never-again.

He kept on coming. She had to put up a hand. "That's close enough."

"I love that red dress. You should wear red all the time."

"I know, I know. Goes with my hair, blah, blah, blah. Did you tell Ron we're married?"

He smirked. "Worked, didn't it?"

"Except, well, doesn't that make me the kind of woman who takes off her wedding ring and goes trolling for a hot date with a stranger?"

Deck snorted. "Ron? Hot?"

"Well, theoretically speaking—and Ron's hotness or lack thereof? Totally not the issue here."

"Sparky," he chided. "You would never cheat, I know that. The thing with Ron was only to make me jealous."

Two elevators opened at the same time. People got off and others got on.

She waited till the doors slid shut to say, "There *was* no thing with Ron. And what do you mean, make you jealous? I had no idea you were in Vegas, and even if I'd known you'd followed me here, I would have zero desire to make you jealous."

"But you did make me jealous. And I forgive you. You're a high-spirited woman, always have been. You've got to have your fun."

Where was this going? Somehow, once again with him, she was failing to make the point that he should give up chasing after her because she was never getting caught—not by him. No way. "I think it's just possible that you've finally completely lost your mind."

He slapped both big hands against his chest. "Go ahead. Hurt me. Call me names. I can take it."

More elevator doors opened. If she ducked into one, he would probably just follow her. Dropping her key card into her clutch, she drew away from the wall and started walking backward. Deck came after her. They ended up facing off by a potted ficus plant around the corner from the constant flow of people going up and down floors.

"What now, Nellie?" he asked, his voice so gentle suddenly, the intimate sound tugging on a tender place inside her, a place she used to be so certain he had killed stone dead all those years ago.

Why wouldn't it die? This...*feeling* she had for him, this stupid, impossible yearning for a man who had turned his back on her twice after promising she would always be the only one for him?

He just stood there now, close enough to reach out and touch, waiting for her to make her next move. Oh, she just ached to open her mouth and yell at him to leave her alone, get the hell away from her. But yelling would not only bring security running, it would be admitting that he was actually getting to her.

Which he was. And which he knew already. She could see that in his gleaming, watchful eyes.

It was bad enough that he knew. Losing her temper over it would only prove how powerfully he affected her. "Who told you I would be here?"

"Have dinner with me and we can talk about that." He took a step closer.

"Forget dinner." She stepped back. The ficus tree was right behind her. A trailing branch brushed her shoulder. "And I already know the answer to my question. Garrett told you I was here, am I right?" Her brother and partner in Bravo Construction *liked* Deck, damn it. Plus, there was the big, high-end house Deck had hired BC to build. Generally speaking, it was good business for Garrett to help an important client get what he wanted—but not when what he wanted was another chance with Nell. Garrett had no right to take a customer's side against his business partner, who also happened to be his own flesh and blood. "I'm going to kill Garrett."

Deck stuck his hands in his pockets. She read the move as an attempt to look easygoing and harmless. As if. "It wasn't Garrett," he said.

"Then who?"

"Your mother told me."

Now Nell *really* wanted to start yelling. Willow Bravo had turned into a matchmaking nightmare over the past couple of years. She'd become obsessed with seeing her children married and settled down. At least until now Willow had shown the good sense to leave Nell out of all that crap.

But, one by one, Willow's other four grown children had found marital bliss. That meant only Nell remained single and Willow just couldn't let well enough alone.

"You pumped my mother for information about me?" Nell kept her voice low, but barely.

"Whoa. Settle down."

"That's just plain wrong."

"True," he said with zero remorse. "When it comes to you, I'll do whatever I have to do. But I didn't go to your mother. *She* called *me*. She said she hasn't forgotten how much you loved me once."

Nell pressed her lips together and expelled an outraged breath through her nose. "Admit it. She called you after you let her know that you've been trying to get something going with me."

"Think about it, Nellie." He looked way too pleased with himself. "How could she *not* know that I've been chasing you?"

He had a point.

In recent months, Deck had made himself famous in their hometown of Justice Creek with his relentless pursuit of her. He'd started his campaign to get her attention by going to the places she went—her brother Quinn's fitness center, her half sister Elise's bakery for coffee early in the morning and her friend Rye McKellan's pub. His constant presence at McKellan's had really annoyed her. She not only liked to hang out there—she lived above the pub in the loft next door to Rye's.

After a month or so of turning up just about everywhere she went, he'd called her and asked her straight out for a date.

She'd said, "Absolutely not and do not call me again."

He hadn't called again. But he *had* shown up at Bravo Construction to ask her to build his new house. She'd handed him over to Garrett.

Then he'd begun showering her with flowers and gifts. She'd refused to accept them. He'd hired a sky-writer to blaze their names in a heart across the Colorado sky. She'd pretended not to notice.

Every time he would come up with a new way to get her attention, she would shut him right down. She'd never imagined he'd follow her all the way to Sin City.

Yet, here he was again.

"I'll be having a serious talk with my mother," she

said. "And you should be ashamed of yourself, pumping her for information about my whereabouts when I have told you repeatedly that once was more than enough when it comes to you—I mean, twice when you count how you came back to me after breaking up with me, only to break up with me all over again."

"I'll say it once more. I didn't pump your mother for information. She called me and volunteered it. And as for me dumping you, that was more than a decade ago. It was high school. We were only kids. I was messed up and not ready. We're different people now."

"No, we're not. I'm still the girl who would have taken a bullet for your sorry ass. And you're the guy who fooled me twice. That's two times too many." And yet, here she was, backed up against a ficus tree, arguing with him when there was supposed to be nothing she had to say to him.

And he still wouldn't give it up. "If you won't have dinner with me, how about a drink? We can discuss how much you despise me in comfort—and in depth."

"I never said I despise you," she muttered grudgingly. Was she weakening? Oh, all right. Maybe a little. She added more firmly, "You just need to catch a flight back to Justice Creek and leave me the hell alone."

"One drink, Nell." The man had some kind of radar. He knew he was getting to her. "One drink won't kill you. And I get it. You don't want to be seen out with me. You don't want anyone to imagine you might be thinking of giving me another chance."

"Because I'm not."

"But look at it this way." He lowered his already velvety tone even more, down to an intimate, just-you-

and-me growl. "This is Vegas and you've heard what they say about Vegas. No one ever has to know…"

It was a really bad idea and she needed to walk away.

But she just couldn't help comparing him to Ron the tile man—to every man she met, as a matter of fact. He wasn't the guy for her, but he was kind of her gold standard of what a man should be—well, aside from the way he'd smashed her heart to bits two times running.

No, she couldn't trust him. But he was hot and funny and smart. He was that perfect combination, the one she couldn't resist: a big, down-to-earth blue-collar guy with a really sharp brain. And he'd been after her for months now.

Okay, it made her feel like a fool to admit it, but lately she'd been having these crazy urges to go ahead and let him catch her.

She wouldn't, of course. He would never catch her again.

But it was Friday night in Vegas, and going back to her room seemed beyond depressing. Friday night in the second week of November and she was alone when all of her siblings were happily married—half siblings, too—and there were four of those.

She was the only single Bravo left in Justice Creek. Too soon, it would be Thanksgiving and then it would be Christmas, with all those family get-togethers where everyone would be coupled up but her. Even her aggravating widowed mother was getting remarried.

And, one of these days, Nell wanted to be married, too.

Unfortunately, only once in her life had she found a

guy who really made it happen for her. That guy was standing in front of her now. And he just wouldn't let it go. He kept coming after her. With him constantly popping up every time she turned around, how was she supposed to stop comparing every guy she met to him?

It just wasn't right. It needed to stop.

But running away from him had gotten her nowhere.

"One drink, Nellie," he said again, his voice a rough-tender temptation, his eyes eating her up and, at the same time, daring her to look away.

What could it hurt, really? Maybe she would actually get through to him at last.

Maybe tonight he would finally get the message. They could speak reasonably to each other and she could convince him to give up the chase. Come to think of it, she hadn't tried talking to him civilly, woman to man, yet. And walking away time after time just wasn't cutting it.

She sucked in a slow breath. "One drink."

For about half a second, he looked totally stunned, the way he had all those years and years ago, when she'd taken the desk in front of him the first day of sophomore English and then turned around and grinned at him. He'd gaped at her, his expression one of complete shock. But only for a moment. Then he'd looked away. She remembered staring at the side view of his Adam's apple, thinking he was hot, even though one of his battered sneakers had a hole in the toe, his shirt screamed hand-me-down and his hair looked like he'd cut it himself.

He was lean and rangy then, his shoulders broad

but not thick, more hungry-looking, like some wild animal, always ready to run. It had taken her weeks to get him to talk to her. And by then, she was a goner. She'd just known he was the guy for her.

Wrong.

The grown-up Deck had lost the stunned look. Once again, he was supremely confident, totally at ease. He said, "Well, all right then, Nellie. I know just the place."

Chapter Two

Declan McGrath had done what he set out to do. He'd created the success he'd always wanted.

This year, his company, Justice Creek Barrels, had made number 245 on the Inc. 5000 list of America's fastest-growing companies. The broke nobody from the wrong side of town had officially arrived.

He had it all. Except Nell, who was stubborn, full of pride and unwilling to let go of the past and admit that they belonged together.

Didn't matter, though. She could keep on refusing him. He wouldn't give up.

And, one way or another, she would finally be his.

This, tonight, was a big step. She'd actually said yes to him, even if it was only for a drink. He had to go carefully with her, he reminded himself. If he got too eager, pushed too fast, she'd be off like a shot.

Still, as he led her to a quiet corner booth at the casino/hotel's most secluded bar, he had a really hard time suppressing a hot shout of triumph. Or at the very least, a fist pump or two.

She slid into the booth on one side and he took the other. The light overhead brought out the deep, gorgeous red of her hair. Her eyes, green as a secret jungle lagoon, watched him warily.

God, she was beautiful. Even more so than when she used to love him. And back then she'd been the most beautiful girl in the world. All the guys had wanted a chance with her.

But she'd only wanted him.

He'd thrown her away. Sometimes even a smart guy made really bad choices.

It had taken him eleven years and a failed marriage to face the truth that he was one of those guys. He didn't love easy, but when he finally did, that was it. *She* was it, the one for him. For four never-ending months now, he'd been actively pursuing her. In all that time, she'd never given so much as a fraction of an inch.

Until tonight.

Her mother had been right. He'd needed to get her away from Justice Creek and all the reminders of how bad he'd messed up with her back in the day. Vegas was the perfect place to finally get going on the rest of their lives together.

Now, if he could just keep from blowing this…

Nell tried to figure out where to begin with him as the waitress came, took their orders and returned with their drinks.

When the waitress left the table for the second time, Nell took a sip of her cosmo and jumped in. "Why me—and why won't you take a hint that I'm just not interested?"

He stared into his single malt, neat, as if the answer to her question waited in the smoky amber depths. "I don't believe you're not interested. You just don't trust me."

"Duh." She poured on the sarcasm and made a big show of tapping a finger against her chin. "Let me think. I wonder why?"

"How many times do I need to say that I messed up? I messed up twice. I'm so damn sorry and I need you to forgive me. You're the best thing that ever happened to me. And..." He shook his head. "Fine. I get it. I smashed your heart to tiny, bloody bits. How many ways can I say I was wrong?"

Okay. He was kind of getting to her. For a second there, she'd almost reached across the table and touched his clenched fist. She so had to watch herself. Gently she suggested, "How about this? I accept your apology. It was years ago and we need to move on."

He slanted her a sideways look, dark brows showing glints of auburn in the light from above. "Yeah?"

"Yeah."

"So then we can try again?"

Should she have known that would be his next question? Yeah, probably. "I didn't say that."

"I want another chance."

"Well, that's not happening."

"Yes, it is. And when it does, I'm not letting you go. This time it's going to be forever."

She almost grinned. Because that was another thing

about Deck. Not only did he have big arms, broad shoulders and a giant brain.

He was cocky. Very, very cocky.

And she was enjoying herself far too much. It really was a whole lot of fun to argue with him. It always had been. And the most fun of all was finally being the one in the position of power.

Back when they'd been together, he was the poor kid and she was a Bravo—one of the Bastard Bravos, as everybody had called her mother's children behind their backs. But a Bravo, nonetheless. Her dad had had lots of money and he'd taken care of his kids, whether he'd had them by his wife or by her mother, who was his mistress at the time. Nell always had the right clothes and a certain bold confidence that made her popular. She hadn't been happy at home by any stretch, but guys had wanted to go out with her and girls had kind of envied her.

And all she'd ever wanted was Deck. So, really, he'd had all the power then.

Now, for some reason she didn't really understand, he'd decided he just *had* to get another chance with her. Now, she was the one saying no. Payback was a bitch, all right. Not to mention downright delicious.

He finally took a slow sip of his Scotch. "Look. It almost killed me to lose you. But I couldn't afford you then. You have to know that. I had things to do, stuff to make happen." His eyes were brown in this light, brown and soft and so sincere. "I had nothing to give you then."

"I wanted nothing from you and *you* know that. Nothing but your love."

He looked away. She stared at the side view of his

Adam's apple. Just like old times. "Come on, Nellie. I had too much to prove. It would never have worked then."

He was probably right. "And it's not going to work now." She leaned across the table toward him, held his gaze steady on and concentrated on trying really hard to get through to him. "I don't trust you. I *can't* trust you. It's not that I hate you. I don't. I don't *despise* you. I just want you to let it go. Leave me be and move on."

He drank more Scotch. "Have dinner with me." She opened her mouth to say no, but then he reached out and covered her hand with his. The words backed up in her throat. "Just dinner." His grip was hot and a little bit rough, and it felt unbelievably right.

How could that be? Words and breaths and even her heart felt all tangled up together in the base of her throat, all tied in hot, sweet, hurtful knots. She opened her mouth to tell him no and he slid his thumb under her fingers, into the vulnerable secret center of her palm, and squeezed, just a little.

Impossibly, she squeezed back. The light from above caught in his eyes, burned in them.

She swallowed, hard. "It would…only be dinner."

The flame in his eyes leaped higher. Dear, sweet Lord, had she really said that? She needed to take it back this instant. She pulled free.

He didn't try to hold on, just slid his hand back to his side of the table and said in a neutral tone, "Only dinner. That's good."

And she couldn't help thinking that, really, what could it hurt? Here, in this glittery, sprawling desert city where nobody knew them? It could be a good way, a *graceful* way, to finally say goodbye.

* * *

He took her to the hotel's French restaurant, Quatre Trèfles. The food was wonderful and there were several courses, different wines offered with each new dish.

Nell drank sparingly. She planned a full day at the trade show tomorrow and didn't want to be hungover. Plus, she needed all her wits about her when dealing with the impossible man across the white-clothed table from her.

Deck looked so good by candlelight. It burnished his thick brown hair and brought out the wicked gleam in his eyes. She had to watch herself around him, she really did. She wanted to handle this goodbye evening with grace.

There was actual chitchat. He asked how she'd gotten into business with Garrett. She explained that after two years at Colorado State, she'd had enough of college. Garrett was doing pretty well building houses. She'd started out working for him. They got along well together.

She laughed. "He's always calling me a pain in his ass."

"But he couldn't get along without you."

"You've got that right. A few years back, he wanted to start building spec houses. I put in some of my inheritance for that and we became partners."

Deck talked about his barrel business, which he'd started eight years ago in the garage of the house he'd been living in then. At the time, he'd tended bar at Teddy's Bar on East Central Street. Essentially, Justice Creek Barrels found and sold whiskey and wine barrels to winemakers, breweries and distilleries. His company also made barrel furniture and other custom barrel-based gadgets and knickknacks. In the time he'd been building JC Barrels, he'd also managed to get a business degree, taking classes online and at State.

She asked about his sister, Marty. "I heard she got married."

"Yeah. His name's Hank Jackson. He's a good guy."

"I'm glad."

"They live in Colorado Springs. And as of three weeks ago, I'm an uncle."

"Wow." Nell remembered Deck's younger sister as too thin and painfully shy, one of those girls who seemed to want to be invisible. "A boy or a girl?"

"Little boy."

"Have you seen him?"

He nodded. "Hank called me when Marty went into labor. I drove straight to the hospital."

"You were there for the birth?" For some reason, the thought of him jumping in his big, black Lexus SUV and racing to be there for his nephew's birth did a number on her heartstrings.

"Well, I sat in the waiting room for four hours, until the baby was born. Eventually, they let me in to see them. Marty was exhausted, but she was smiling. And I got to hold the baby. They named him Henry, after Hank."

"Give Marty my best?"

"Sure."

"And, um, your dad?" Keith McGrath had been a major issue between them, when it all went to hell. Maybe she shouldn't have mentioned him, but avoiding the subject would have felt like cowardice on her part. Plus, the whole point of spending this evening with him was to let the past go.

"I don't see him often." Deck's voice lacked inflection. He sounded careful. Too careful. "But he's all right. He manages an apartment complex in Fort Collins, does a little carpentry on the side. He's, uh, been doing pretty well the past couple of years."

"Excellent." She allowed herself a small sip of wine.

Deck regarded her distantly for several uncomfortable seconds—and then he changed the subject, which was fine with her. Great, as a matter of fact. It was only an evening they were sharing, not the rest of their lives. Yes, she wanted to talk honestly, but they didn't need to get into anything too messy.

After dinner, they gambled a little.

And then, around ten, he suggested, "Take a walk outside with me?"

She wanted to, she really did. But it was too cold out and, really, she ought to just tell him good-night. "It's windy and in the forties out there and my jacket is upstairs."

"No problem. We'll go up, get our coats. You can put on some walking shoes if you want to."

She let him take her arm and lead her to the elevators.

They went up to her floor first. She let him in her room, because to make him wait in the hallway would have been as good as admitting she felt awkward being with him in a room with a bed. It only took a moment anyway, to change into flats and grab her coat.

They got back on the elevator. He had a suite on the penthouse floor. She stood in the living area and gazed out over the waterfall lagoon below and the lights of the strip farther out as he disappeared into the bedroom.

"What do you see down there?"

She turned and gave him a smile. "Bright lights." He'd thrown on a gorgeous leather jacket and she couldn't help remembering his hand-me-down shirts and beat-up Vans with the holes in them back when they were kids.

Down on the main floor, they went out the lobby entrance, under the porte cochere and around the famous waterfalls and the minilake out front. As they strolled under the palm trees, she buttoned up her coat against the wind.

And when he took her hand?

She let him. Because this was a real goodbye at last, and it felt good to be with him finally in this friendly, easy way. If touching him still thrilled her more than it should, well, so what?

She wouldn't act on that thrill. She was only enjoying a last, companionable evening with an old flame, making peace with the past, ending things gracefully.

At a little after midnight, he took her back to her room. He didn't try to kiss her at her door. Which was great. A kiss would be too intimate and she would have ducked away.

With a whispered "Goodbye, Deck," she went in and shut the door.

The next day, she half expected to find him waiting in the hallway outside her room when she went down for breakfast.

He wasn't. And she was *not* disappointed. Last night had been perfect. She'd had a great evening with him; however, it really was over between them and had been for eleven years. He must be on his way home by now.

After breakfast, she went to the trade show and spent the morning watching installation demonstrations and connecting with granite, marble, tile, concrete and quartz composite distributors. At around eleven, she met up with Sherry Tisbeau, who lived in Seattle and worked with her husband, Zach. Tisbeau Development built condos mostly. Nell had struck up a friendship with Sherry a few years back. They'd met in LA at Build Expo USA. This trip, Sherry had brought along Alice Bates, the Tisbeau office manager.

At half past noon, just as Sherry was suggesting they ought to go get some lunch, Nell spotted a guy who looked like Deck. He lounged against the wall by a granite dealer's booth about twenty feet away, a glossy brochure in front of his face. Her pulse started racing and her stomach got quivery.

As she gulped and stared, he lowered the brochure, revealing that gorgeous, dangerous slow smile. Every nerve in her body went on red alert. It felt amazing. Invigorating. And scary, too.

She knew she was in trouble and somehow didn't even care.

She turned to Sherry. "Listen. I see an old friend and I need to spend some time with him. I'm going to have to take a rain check on lunch."

Sherry gave her a hug and reminded her to keep in touch. A moment later, the two women were gone and Deck stood at her side.

She met those eyes and felt as light as a sunbeam,

fizzy as a just-opened bottle of Dom Pérignon. It had to stop. She needed to remind him that they'd said goodbye last night. And then she needed to leave. If she hurried she could catch up with Sherry and Alice.

About then, she noticed the lanyard around his neck and the official trade-show badge hanging from it.

"You stole someone's badge," she accused.

His grin only deepened, revealing that dimple on the left side of his mouth. "They wouldn't let me in here without one." Way back when, she used to watch for it, that dimple. She used to hope for it. It only appeared when he let himself relax. He rarely relaxed back then. He was constantly on guard.

How completely things had changed.

He took the badge between his fingers. "But then, luckily, I found this one on the floor outside—and it's not stealing if I found it on the floor."

Just turn and leave him standing here. Walk away and don't look back.

But she didn't budge. Instead, she opened her mouth and something stupid came out. "We're here in Vegas. Stuff happens in Vegas and that stuff is meaningless. That's all this is."

He gave her the lifted eyebrow. "Meaningless, you mean?"

"That's right. It's just for now. Nothing more. Nothing changes when we go home. I have my life, you have yours."

For way too many glorious seconds, they simply regarded each other. She had that sense she used to get with him, when they were together so long ago. The sense that they were the only two people on the planet.

Finally, he asked, "Hungry?"

She slipped her arm in his. It felt absolutely right there. "Starved."

She never returned to the convention floor.

They had lunch and then they played the slots. She had a great time.

Was she being an idiot?

Oh, absolutely. She knew she shouldn't give the guy an inch.

But he was so much fun—a lot more than he used be, now that'd he'd found the success he'd always craved. There was an easiness about him now, a confidence that made him even more attractive than before, if that was possible. She liked just being with him.

And why shouldn't she indulge herself? Just a little. Just for this short time that they were both here in Vegas.

She got lucky and won a thousand-dollar jackpot. She collected her winnings.

Then he suggested a couple's visit to the hotel spa, of all things. No way she was passing up an offer like that.

They took mud baths side by side and he told her all about the things you could make with a barrel, everything from cuff links to wall clocks, chandeliers to yard art. They got massages, their two tables pushed together. It was intimate in the most relaxing, luxurious sort of way. And she went ahead and allowed herself to love every minute of it.

After that, they had facials, then mani-pedis. Somehow, he looked manlier than ever, sitting in that pedicure chair as a sexy blonde took an emery board to his toes.

It was a little past six when he left her at the door to her room.

"I'll be back for you at seven thirty," he said in a tone that teased and warned simultaneously. "Be ready."

She was ready, all right. In her favorite short black dress, sleeveless and curve-hugging with a cutaway back, her red hair pinned up on one side by a rhinestone comb, wearing killer black heels with red soles. His eyes darkened when she opened the door to him, and his gaze moved down her body, stirring up sparks. He wore a gorgeous graphite suit and she wondered how she'd gotten here, about to spend an evening that could only be called romantic with the penniless, dark, damaged boy she used to love, the boy who'd grown up to run his own company and look completely at ease in the kind of suit you couldn't buy off a rack.

She grabbed her beaded clutch and her metallic Betsey Johnson wrap and off they went.

Down at the lobby entrance, beneath the porte cochere, he had a car waiting. She sat beside him on the plush leather seat and stared out the tinted side window as they rolled by one giant pleasure palace after another, the bright lights melting into each other, gold, green, red, purple, blue. Eventually, the driver turned down a side street and stopped in front of modest-looking restaurant with a red-and-white-striped awning over the door.

Inside, they sat beneath a stained glass ceiling with chandeliers shaped like stars. They had champagne and caviar, lobster bisque and the best filet mignon she'd ever tasted, the meat melting like butter on her tongue.

Okay, yeah. It was dangerous, doing this with him. Every moment she spent near him she could feel herself giving in to him, the sharp edges she used to protect herself leaving her, morphing into vulnerable softness that invited his touch.

He leaned across the table and so did she. She shouldn't have, but she was full of a happy, giddy sort of longing—to savor every minute, to get closer.

And closer.

And then he touched her, so lightly, a brush of his index finger across the back of her hand, over the bones of her wrist, up her forearm, drawing the nerves with him, making a trail of pleasured sensation along her skin. She shivered, a hot kind of shiver, the kind that promised forbidden delights to come.

"It really can't happen," she whispered.

"Why not?" That voice of his, sweet and rough, was like raw molasses pouring out.

She was in trouble. Worse, she was loving it. "A thousand reasons. It's over. You know it. It's been over for years."

"Nellie." His finger at her elbow, sliding higher, over the bright tattoo that covered the evidence of what he had been to her. "It doesn't feel over. *That's* what I know. And you know it, too, whatever lies you think you have to tell yourself."

She caught his hand, gently pushed it away. She sipped more champagne and treated her taste buds to another wonderful bite of buttery steak. "This is like some kind of dream. And I really need to wake up."

A moment later, he somehow had her hand in his.

He turned it over, smoothed open her fingers and pressed those warm, soft lips of his into the heart of her palm, his breath like a brand on her skin, his beard scruff tickling just a little. "Remember that first time?"

"Oh, God. In a tent." They'd been seventeen. It was the summer between their junior and senior years, and they'd hiked up into the National Forest, to Ice Castle Falls, pitching the patched-up tent he'd brought in the center of a clear spot, a miniature meadow not far from the falls.

She'd told her mother that she was going camping with a group of kids. Willow might have been Frank Bravo's accomplice in cheating on his wife Sondra for more than two decades, but when it came to her daughters, she had certain rules. No overnights with a boy as long as Nell was underage. So she'd lied and said she was sharing a tent with Shonda Hurly, a friend from school. Deck hadn't needed to make up stories about his plans. His father had a lot of stuff going on and pretty much let Deck do what he wanted.

Across the table, still holding her open palm in his hand, Deck said, "I couldn't believe I got so lucky, to spend a whole night with you."

"Too bad about the ants." She laughed and he laughed with her. And then the laughter faded. They watched each other across the table, the tender old memory fresh and new between them. They'd gotten down to their underwear before they realized they'd pitched the tent on an anthill. "I did a lot of shrieking, as I recall."

"They were all over you."

She'd slithered out of the tent, twisting and turning

in the moonlight in her white cotton panties and sports bra, madly slapping ants away. Deck had followed her out. He'd put his hands on her shoulders and told her to stand still. And she had. She'd stilled—for him. And he had run his hands all over her, starting with her hair, her neck, her shoulders and on down, until all the ants were gone and there was only his tender, wonderful touch.

Then he'd gathered her close to him, pressed his lips to her temple, her forehead, her mouth. She'd kissed him back, twining her arms around his neck, whispering of her love.

It was chilly up there in the mountains at night, even in summer. So they shook out their clothes and put them back on and moved the tent to the other side of the cleared space.

And then they'd crawled back inside, wrapped their arms around each other—and been each other's first time. She remembered it as awkward and intense. And beautiful, too.

Even later, after he'd stomped all over her heart, she couldn't quite bring herself to regret choosing him for her first.

The car was waiting out in front when they left the restaurant.

She felt so soft and pliant by then, her mind a happy haze from the champagne and the wonderful food, the sweet, shared memories—and Deck. Laughing with her. Touching her. Reminding her of just how good it used to be.

When he pulled her down across his lap, she let him. She kicked off her shoes, folded her legs on the seat and gazed up at his wonderful face as the bright lights flowed over him, turning his skin from gold to red to blue. He smelled of some dark spice, familiar in the deepest way. She could ride like this forever, her head in his lap, wrapped in the scent of him.

In no time, the car glided in beneath the porte cochere at their hotel. She sat up, smoothed her hair and slipped her shoes back on.

Inside, he took her hand and she let him. He led her straight to the elevators. They went up. She made no objection when the car kept right on gliding upward past her floor.

At the door to his suite, she hesitated. "We're going to have to…" That was as far as she got, because his arms went around her.

"Listen," he said.

"What?"

And then he kissed her for the first time in over a decade.

She couldn't suppress the low, pleasured hum that escaped her as his lips met hers. He just felt so good. And, well, she wanted it, that kiss, wanted those strong arms around her. So she didn't push him away.

On the contrary, she pulled him closer, sliding her hands up that hard chest of his, up and over his thick shoulders to clasp around his big neck. He tasted of the cinnamon in the coffee they'd had after dinner— hot and wet and so very right.

Her wrap slithered to the rug at their feet and she hardly noticed it was gone.

He was…bigger. Broader. More encompassing than before. She'd known that already. After all, she had eyes. But there was something so much more immediate about *feeling* it, about having him hold her, surround her. His body gave off waves of heat. That hadn't changed. And he smelled even better than she remembered—of that unnameable, too-tempting spice and also faintly of some no doubt ridiculously expensive cologne.

"We have to talk," she blurted out anxiously when he finally lifted his head.

"That's a bad idea." His hands brushed up and down her arms and she knew he was soothing her, settling her to his will. The ploy should have annoyed her, *would* have annoyed her if only his touch didn't set her on fire.

How long had it been since she'd felt this way, like she might burst out of her skin with longing? Like if she didn't make love with this guy tonight, she just might crumple to the floor in a swoon of unsatisfied lust, of thwarted desire?

Too long. Forever. A lifetime, at least.

Not for eleven years, if she let herself be painfully honest about it. Deck just…did it for her in a big way.

No other guy even came close.

Not that she would ever tell *him* that.

Somehow, she made her lips form the words that had to be said first. "We need to set boundaries."

A couple of swear words escaped him.

She put the tips of her fingers to those wonderful lips. He stuck out his tongue and licked them. She almost gave it all up right then, grabbed him close again, kissed him hard and long, demanded he take her to his bed right this minute.

But no. Things had to be said. Though she shouldn't be doing this, right now her yearning exceeded her need for self-protection by an alarming degree. She just couldn't resist him tonight.

But they needed a clear agreement as to how it would be. "We talk first."

"Nellie—"

"We talk first or I'll say good-night."

"You can't go now."

"Watch me." She tried to step back.

He only held on. But at least her insistence had gotten through to him. He gave in to her demand with a reluctant nod. "All right. We'll talk."

Bending, he picked up her wrap and handed it to her. She took it gingerly, draping the filmy, glittery fabric over her arm as he turned away to run his key card past the reader. The green light flashed.

He pushed open the door.

Chapter Three

He led her into the sitting area. "Drink?"

"No, thanks." She set her wrap over the back of the sofa and smoothed it with nervous hands. Everything felt strange suddenly. She shouldn't be here.

There was no excuse for her to be here, to give in to him in this massive, impossible, stupid way.

He took off his suit jacket, tossed it over a chair and loosened his beautiful blue tie. His shirt was a gorgeous, lustrous light gray and his watch was a Blancpain. She knew because her father used to have one and she had wanted that watch so bad. She would have worn it proudly if he'd only left it to her. He hadn't. He'd left it to her half brother Darius, the oldest of the nine of them, which she'd eventually let herself admit was fair.

"What?" He gazed at her with equal parts desire and impatience.

She kept the sofa between them, resting her hands on the back of it. "I need your agreement that this isn't going anywhere, that it's just for now, for while we're here in Vegas."

He dropped into a big white chair. Spreading his knees wide, he rested his arms on the chair arms, like some barbarian king holding court. "How many times do we have to go over this?"

"Until I'm sure that you agree and understand my, er, terms."

"Your terms." He seemed to taste the words and to find them not the least to his liking. "We don't need terms. Just do what you think you have to do. I'll do the same."

She was suddenly absurdly glad for the fat sofa between them, as if it was any kind of real barrier, as if it could actually protect her from what she would do with him here tonight. "I just don't want you to get any ideas about how things could change when we go home. They won't. When we're home, I'm not getting near you. I'm going to pretend that tonight never happened." She waited, expecting some sort of response from him.

Sprawled back in the chair, he just stared at her. She felt her skin heating, her resolve weakening. It was absurd—*she* was absurd. But something had happened since last night, when she'd given in enough to have a drink and dinner with him. Something had happened as she'd spent the afternoon and evening with him today. She'd had the advantage before.

But that advantage was gone. She really ought to miss it more.

And still he said nothing.

Oldest tactic in the book: the one who speaks first loses.

She spoke. "Yeah, okay. I want you, Deck. I want you a lot. And I'm starting to get that this is something we just need to do. We need to get it out of our systems, find closure between us once and for all…"

Dear God. What was the matter with her, spouting all this tired psychobabble? Talking about "getting it out of our systems," like sex was a juice cleanse. And "finding closure," as though closure was something a person could misplace.

Those phrases were meaningless, really. Just the stuff people said when they were about to do something stupid.

And facing him now across the nonbarrier of the sofa, she knew absolutely that having a Vegas fling with Deck was a giant bowl of stupid with several spoonfuls of trouble sprinkled on top.

But she was going to do it anyway, whether she could get him to agree to her terms or not. She was going to do it because she couldn't bear not to. Because she was almost thirty and he was the only man she'd ever been in love with. Because one thing had not changed: when he touched her, it all felt perfectly, exactly right.

He said, "I want you, too, Nellie. I always have."

Bitterness rose in her. *Too bad that didn't stop you from throwing me away.*

Then he held out his hand to her. His eyes were soft and yearning, wanting her the way she wanted him.

And in the space of an instant, her bitterness turned achingly sweet. She couldn't scoot around that sofa and grab on to him fast enough.

His fingers closed around hers and he gave a tug, bringing her up flush between his spread knees. Already, he was hard for her, the ridge of his arousal obvious beneath his fly. The sight of it thrilled her, almost had her dropping to her knees to get closer, to make short work of his belt and his zipper, set him free to her eager touch, her hungry mouth.

He brought her hand to his lips, licked the bumps of her knuckles, causing havoc inside her, bringing up goose bumps along her arms. "I have a request."

"Yeah?" It came out on a hungry hitch of breath.

"Take everything off. I want to see all of you. I've waited so long…"

Breathless moments later, she stood before him wearing nothing but the rhinestone comb.

"Nellie," he said, low and dark and wonderfully rough. "You are more beautiful even than I remember. That shouldn't be possible. But you are." He commanded, "Bend down here."

She bent from the waist. It felt like heaven, to bend to him, to give in to him. For now, for tonight and tomorrow, she had no need to resist him. She would have this night and tomorrow. Then on Monday, she would go home and set about pretending that none of it had happened.

Did that make her a liar and a coward and a fool?

Absolutely.

Her hair brushed his cheek. He framed her face with his strong hands. "Kiss me."

She didn't have to be told twice. Their lips met in a kiss that burned her down to her core. His tongue came invading. She welcomed the tender assault on her senses. He made her belly quiver. Without even touching them, he made her nipples ache and tighten.

As he kissed her, he slid the comb from her hair and dropped it to the little table by the chair. Freed, the red waves fell around them. He speared his spread fingers up into the thick mass of it, rubbing it into her scalp as though bringing up a lather, then closing those big fingers into fists, pulling a little, drawing her mouth even closer, sealing their lips together hard and fast, dipping his tongue in deeper.

When he finally loosened his hold on her, she had to remind herself to breathe. Lifting away a little, she stared down him, dazed with want. He gazed back at her, pupils dilated, black holes she could get lost in, never to be found.

They were both breathing hard. She felt herself falling into him, wrapping herself in his heat and his hunger that so perfectly matched her own, vanishing into him, though neither of them had moved.

"You won't get away, Nellie," he whispered. "I won't blow it this time. You and me. That's how it's supposed to be."

"Don't go there." She made her voice as low and rough as his. "Or I am leaving."

They glared at each other, a battle of wills.

And then he gave her that slow, dangerous grin.

Suddenly, they were both laughing.

His hands clasped her waist and he came up out of the chair. She gasped at the speed of the move, canting back, making room for him—and let out a shriek of surprise as he boosted her high and laid her over his shoulder. "Deck!"

But he wasn't listening. He put his hand on her bare

bottom, spreading his fingers, holding her where he wanted her. "Steady. I've got you."

And then he was moving, headed for the open bedroom door.

He laid her down on the turned-back bed. "Don't you dare move."

She only chuckled, grinning up at him, bringing her arms up and sliding them under the pillow beneath her head.

His eyes blazed down at her and he muttered a string of dark, delicious promises—of what he would do to her, how much he wanted her, all the ways he was going to drive her wonderfully, totally insane. And then he got out of his clothes, tossing them every which way, over a shoulder, in the general direction of the bedside chair. He threw that fancy watch at the nightstand. It dropped to the carpet. He just left it there.

When he came down to her she grabbed him close, her mind and heart and body ready, so ready, to be with him. There was no past or future tonight.

There was only right now.

And then he was kissing her, a thousand kisses or maybe a million. He said he needed to put his mouth on every single inch of her body.

She indulged him that. Gleefully, eagerly, she braced her hands on his shoulders and pushed him lower, murmuring huskily, "Wait. I think you missed a spot. Oh! Yes. There…"

Was it as good as she'd imagined it might be in her forbidden, delicious fantasies?

Better. So much better.

There was time for teasing. And there was time for overwhelming, intense kisses, for his big fingers inside her, playing her so well that she shattered in the space between two ragged breaths.

And, after that, he only played her some more, adding his wonderful mouth to the equation, until she was crying out, clutching his head, begging him, "Please, please, Deck. Please make it now. Oh, yes. Like that..."

After the third time he carried her to the peak, tumbling over, she took charge, pushing him to his back, worshipping every hard, glorious inch of his body the way he'd done to hers. She traced the tendons and veins on those big arms of his, bit the hard, high bulge of his biceps, followed the crisp trail of hair across his broad chest.

And on down.

She wrapped both hands around him and lowered her mouth to him. Somehow, for a little while, he held his natural inclination to take control in check. She savored every second of having all the power, taking him deep, relaxing her throat.

Taking him deeper still.

In the end, he couldn't help himself. He had to take the lead, even in her pleasuring of him. He cradled her head between his big hands, holding her still for him.

She relaxed into it, letting him do what he wanted with her. It was glorious, so good. And at the last second he did let go, he let it happen, let himself go over. She looked up at him on his knees above her, his big head thrown back, a long, deep groan rolling from his throat.

She drank every drop of him. He tasted like the ocean, salty and rich.

Then he pulled her up to him, into his arms, settling her close to him in the tangle of sheets and blankets. He stroked her hair, traced the bumps of her spine, rested his broad hand in the naked curve of her waist.

Did she sleep for a little? It seemed she must have.

There were dreams, of the two of them, in the good times, years ago. Laughing together by a campfire, sharing a whole conversation in a glance across a classroom, walking the hallways at Justice Creek High, his arm across her shoulders, his body pressed just right along her side.

Invincible. That was how she'd felt with him. That as long as they were together, nothing could beat them. They ruled their private world of two.

He never knew what might happen at home. His father always had some big plan in the works that never seemed to pan out. Deck had never talked about it much, but Nell knew things hadn't been easy for him and Marty. The way Nell understood it, Keith McGrath loved his family, but he was just always distracted. He couldn't seem to get a job and hold on to it. The McGrath family struggled constantly just to get by.

Nell's issues weren't nearly so bad. But it was no fun, what went on in her family. When her dad's first wife died, he'd married her mother and moved Willow into the house he'd built for wife number one. Nell had still been living at home then, so she'd moved, too. It was awful, going home to the house that had belonged to her father's first wife, to her resentful half sister Elise and Elise's best friend, Tracy, who had been taken in by Elise's mom years before, when Tracy's parents died suddenly. Elise always acted so prissy and ladylike. However, being ladylike didn't stop her from coming up with new ways to torture Nell. It was a war in the Bravo mansion back in those days, a war in which Nell fought just as dirty as Elise.

But sometimes, even though you don't believe it could ever happen when life is crappy, things do get better. It had for Elise and Nell. Now, she and Elise were tight. They would do anything for each other. Too bad they didn't know back then how it would all work out.

It was the same with loving Deck, really. She'd been so happy with him in high school. Looking back, she was glad she hadn't known how it would turn out with him. She'd had no clue that he would shatter her poor heart and that it would take her forever to recover from losing him.

Like that ancient Garth Brooks song that her mother used to love, where life was a dance and if you'd known ahead of time how bad a loss was going to be, you might have just said no to whatever was destined to break your heart.

But if you said no to love, you would miss the dance.

And, really, now that she was over it, over *him*, she could let herself admit that the dance of their young love had been pretty damn spectacular.

She could honestly say now, at last, after all these years, that she wouldn't have missed loving Deck for the world.

As for this brief, thoroughly magical reunion they

were sharing? No way would she have wanted to miss this, either.

She tipped her head back to look at him.

His eyes were open, watching, waiting.

She offered her mouth and he took it.

The magic began again.

And when he got the condom from the bedside drawer, she took it from him, rolling it down over him. He rose above her, his eyes gleaming almost golden in the light from the lamp.

He came into her and she took him, deep and true. She wrapped her whole body around him and they moved together, in perfect rhythm, all the way to the top of the world and over into free fall.

She called his name, among other things. She had no idea what crazy words came out of her mouth as her body pulsed around him.

All she knew was that it was perfect, this moment. This last dance together with the boy she'd once loved beyond all reason.

He wasn't that boy anymore. And she was no longer the girl who had given her heart and trusted him not to break it.

Which was fine. As it should be.

And this, tonight, was just what she'd needed, a Las Vegas fling with the grown-up Deck McGrath.

In the gray light of the next morning, he reached for her. She melted into him. They made love, sweet and slow.

After the loving, they ordered room service. They had breakfast in bed and then made love again. They took a long bath. Together.

And made love again.

More than half the day had passed and all they'd done was eat breakfast and take a bath—oh, and the lovemaking. Lots and lots of lovemaking. She was dizzy with it, swept away into a beautiful, sensual dream, a private fantasy, a lush, secret world containing just the two of them.

By late afternoon, he let her go down to her room. But only long enough to shower, put on a little makeup and get dressed. He was at her door a half an hour after she'd left his suite.

He started kissing her. No surprise where that led.

Finally, they both agreed they needed to get out, have some dinner. The big bed would be right there waiting for them when they returned.

She put her dress back on. He ordered a car and off they went to an Italian place he knew about. The food was wonderful and there was a really nice Chianti. Maybe she had a little more of that than she should have.

They got back in the limo.

Deck shut the privacy screen between them and the driver. They glided up and down the strip, making love. Even through the tinted windows, the bright lights reached them and played a symphony of color across their naked skin.

There was champagne. Dom Pérignon.

"When did you order champagne?" she asked, sitting there naked, feeling satisfied, shimmery all over, somehow. It was really quite wonderful.

He said, "You are so beautiful, Sparky. Bold and strong and so damn smart. More than any man deserves in this life. There is no one, *no one*, like you."

His words poured over her. They made her feel special. Treasured. Loved.

He never did answer about the champagne, not that she really cared. He popped the cork and gently pushed her down onto the seat so he could pour the bubbly treat on her belly. He sipped it from her navel. She wove her fingers in his hair and sighed in delight.

He said more thrilling things, lots of them, whispering them against her bare skin—that he loved her, that she was and always had been the only woman for him.

She took what he said as part of the fantasy he was weaving around her. No, they weren't real, his vows of love and forever. She didn't believe them.

But they sure sounded good. They went down just right with the champagne, with the feel of his hot, hard body pressing close, with the endless pleasure he gave.

It was paradise, pure and simple, to be held in his arms.

When the limo slowed and glided to a stop, she opened her eyes and asked, "Where are we?"

He chuckled. "Put your dress back on. We'll go check it out."

"An adventure?" That sounded delightful.

"That's right. Nell and Deck's big adventure." He helped her back into her clothes. Once she was dressed again, she sat there grinning like a fool as he put on his shirt, his boxer briefs and his pants. She wasn't really drunk, just...kind of high. High on pure pleasure, on sexual satisfaction.

He was fully dressed now. He held up her coat and she put it on.

Dazed, happy, glowing all over, she let him help her from the car.

They were at the Clark County Marriage License Bureau, of all things. That made her laugh. "Oh, you are kidding me."

He took her hand. "Come on, let's go inside, just for fun."

"But…it's nine o'clock on Sunday night."

"Sparky, this is Vegas. They almost never close." He gazed down at her expectantly.

She thought about how much she was loving this, every minute of this night, the two of them together, kind of hazy from the alcohol, loose and easy all over from the beautiful lovemaking. What a great way to feel. She was ready for anything.

"All right," she said. "Let's go inside."

She followed him in.

After that, well, whatever he suggested, she couldn't say yes fast enough. She let him take a number and when their turn came, she whipped out her driver's license and signed where the clerk pointed. It was all very simple. Smooth and easy as you please.

When they returned to the limo, they had a marriage license.

Really, why was she doing this? She wasn't that drunk. She didn't understand herself. She ought to…

But then he started kissing her again. And it was a game they were playing. Delicious. Thrilling. In a way, the whole thing was like a dream, *her* dream, from so long ago, the dream that didn't come true.

Somehow, impossibly, it was coming true tonight.

It wasn't that far to the wedding chapel—well, it was more of a wedding complex, really, a series of pink stucco buildings and a parking lot dotted with palm trees and spiky succulents. The limo slid to a stop and Deck pulled a small velvet box from his pocket.

Inside was a gorgeous ring. He slipped it on her finger, a perfect fit, and she thought, *He's got this all planned.*

That should have alarmed her, right?

Definitely.

But the ring was so beautiful, with a large square-cut diamond, smaller diamonds glittering along the platinum band. And everything just felt…right somehow. Tonight, she was living the teenage fantasy she'd once believed in so passionately—the fantasy of her and Deck and happily-ever-after.

The years between then and now had somehow folded in on themselves. He'd never taken a buzz saw to her heart, never married someone else.

Her life with him, the love he'd always promised her. Their own personal forever…

It was coming true at last.

The chapel complex had it all, everything two people needed to say "I do," Vegas style.

The woman in the lobby area greeted Deck by name. "Mr. McGrath." She practically cooed at him. "Welcome to Now and Forever." She aimed a thousand-watt smile at Nell. "And it's a delight to meet your beautiful bride." The woman took Deck's black credit card and sent him to the men's boutique to rent a tux.

Another woman came for Nell. "I'm Anita. And I'm so glad you've come to us for your special night. Follow me."

In the bride's boutique, Nell chose her dress. It was perfect, that dress, with a low back and lace sleeves— a mermaid dress, clinging to her body all the way to her knees and then opening out in a fishtail of lace and glittering beads. A seamstress quickly pinned and tucked at the waist and down over her hips, creating a perfect fit. And then she whisked the dress away to alter it on the spot.

Nell chose shoes with rhinestone bows and open toes. The dress had a built-in bra, but Anita offered an adorable pair of lacy satin tap pants that would look so sexy when the dress came off. Nell said yes.

She put on the pretty tap pants and the perfect shoes. As Anita helped her into the altered dress, a clear thought came swimming up through the sensual haze created by thrilling lovemaking, good champagne and a long-held secret fantasy at last coming true.

She really ought to pay her share—after all, she'd always been a girl who carried her own weight. "I want to pay for my part of this," she instructed Anita.

Anita laughed. "Oh, no. That will never do. Mr. McGrath was very clear that he will be taking care of everything."

"But I—"

"Let a man feel like a man," Anita suggested in a coaxing whisper, as if Nell would be doing Deck a favor to let him run up a giant bill.

Nell wanted to argue. But to argue would kind of ruin the fantasy, wouldn't it?

She let it go. If he wanted to spend his money, who was she to put the brakes on? "Fair enough, then."

"Excellent." Anita beamed. "Personal items—the shoes and the lingerie—are only for purchase. The dress, though, is up to you. It's offered for rental. But if you love it, Mr. McGrath said to tell you it's yours."

Mr. McGrath. She knew he must be eating this up, the poor boy who half the time didn't know where his next meal would come from, grown into a man who could whip out his credit card and buy out some Vegas wedding boutique.

She stared at her reflection in the full-length mirror. Oh, she did love the dress. "It seems kind of extravagant…"

"Honey, it's your wedding dress." Anita knelt to adjust the frothy fishtail hem. "It's a once-in-a-lifetime thing and if you love the dress, you should have it."

Nell smiled at her reflection, a smile that trembled only a little. "Well, all right then. I'm going to keep it."

"That's the spirit." Anita had her veil ready. It was full-length. Because, hey, might as well live this fantasy for all it was worth. Anita pinned it in place with a rhinestone band.

Nell decided on a bouquet of red roses and white lilies, all festive and Christmassy. Why not? It would be Christmas soon. She chose a red rose and red Christmas berries for Deck's boutonniere. Another saleslady appeared and rushed off to take it to him.

Anita settled Nell's veil over her face and led her to the Gardenia Chapel, where the starkly simple altar had tall silver candlesticks on either side and a silver wall behind it, a wall draped in a shining curtain of crystal beads. The wedding march played, and Nell walked down the aisle to where Deck, in a tux, stood with the pastor, waiting for her, his bride.

She knew a moment's stark panic. Really, what was she doing here in this silver chapel dressed as a bride?

But Deck was waiting. And she wanted to be with him. Her heart settled into a happier rhythm and, slowly, her eyes on him through the white film of her veil, she went to him. He watched her come, his mouth curved in that dangerous smile, his eyes full of equal parts heat and tenderness.

Anita was right there to hold her bouquet. Deck took her hands and they said their wedding vows. Of course he had a wedding ring for her, a thick band with diamonds in a braided pattern. He slipped it into place next to her spectacular engagement diamond.

Finally, reverently, he lifted her veil and kissed her. She sighed against his parted lips, deep in this wedding dream, together with her only love.

At last.

They signed more papers. Deck would receive their marriage certificate in the mail within ten days. She started to ask why it wasn't going to her place.

Then again, what did it matter really? Deck could handle logistics. He'd certainly done a great job of it so far. Right now was magic time, and thinking too hard about anything just seemed like a bad idea.

A photographer appeared to take pictures. She kissed Deck again for the camera and wished that this perfect fantasy might never end.

He had more champagne waiting in the limo. She had a glass, just to keep the fizzy, happy feeling going.

Back at his suite at the hotel, he helped her out of her wedding finery. They made love for hours.

Finally, he pulled her in close and traced the tattoo hidden among the dragonflies and flowers on her left arm: his name.

She'd been just seventeen when she'd had it written on her skin, *Declan*, in the symbol for infinity. She'd gone all the way to Denver to do it and used a fake ID. Because she loved him and he loved her and their love was forever.

Until it wasn't.

After the second time he dumped her, she'd had it camouflaged with a half-sleeve of ink because she couldn't stand to look at it anymore. The tattoo artist she went to that time had been a genius. She'd woven Deck's name into a complex, brightly colored design. Now his name looked like just part of the filigree pattern in a dragonfly's wing. Nobody could see it.

Except Deck. He knew where to look. He always had.

Deck pulled up the covers. She snuggled into the shelter of his cradling arms, closed her eyes and let herself drift off to sleep.

When she woke, there was a sliver of gray daylight showing between the drawn curtains.

Morning already. She felt a moment's regret. Today she had to go home.

Deck slept beside her, his eyes closed, his face easy in slumber. She watched him for a moment, her heart welling with something a lot like happiness. When she turned her head to check the clock, she saw it was ten after eight.

She felt…satisfied. Every inch of her body well-used. A little sore, maybe, but in a good way. She was also a bit hungover from the champagne, but not too bad.

Her flight would take off at 11:15 a.m. She should get up, go back to her room, have a shower, get her things together.

But something was bothering her, a sense of dread

kind of pushing at the corners of her consciousness. She stared up at the ceiling, starting to frown.

There was definitely something…

Something she'd done that she probably shouldn't have.

Something…

Wait a minute.

Images from the night before flashed through her mind.

The Italian place. She'd had a little too much Chianti, hadn't she? And then, in the limo, sailing along the strip, making love. Drinking champagne.

But the champagne was no excuse. She hadn't been *that* drunk. She'd been perfectly cognizant of everything that occurred.

She'd *let* it happen, been nothing short of complicit in what had gone down.

When, out of nowhere, they'd stopped at the place to get a marriage license, what had she done? Followed him in like a lamb to the slaughter.

And when he'd whipped the ring out of his pocket, had she said, "Declan Keallach McGrath, you hold on just a minute here? What is that ring doing in your pocket? What do you think you're trying to pull? No way am I falling for this crazy scheme"?

No, she had not.

She had said nothing.

Nothing at all.

Instead, she'd let him take her hand and slip that ring on her finger. And then she'd clung to him like a happy little barnacle to the hull of a ship, offering her mouth up to him, kissing him like she would never get enough of him as they rolled on down the strip to that wedding place called Now and Forever.

Now and Forever…

Oh. My. God.

The mermaid wedding dress. The flowers. The Gardenia Chapel. The ring…

The one he'd had ready and waiting in his pocket.

Reluctantly, already knowing what she would find, already feeling the unbelievable truth wrapped around her finger, she pushed back the covers enough to raise her left hand to eye level.

Diamonds. Sparkling furiously at her.

Sweet Lord in heaven.

What had she done?

Chapter Four

A long string of crude words escaped her. She muttered them in a low, angry whisper.

And Deck? He remained sound asleep, looking perfectly relaxed and not the least bit guilty, though he had seduced her in the worst kind of way.

Seduced her into marriage. The dirty, rotten creep.

How dare he lie there peacefully sleeping at a time like this?

"Deck!" She grabbed his giant shoulder and shoved at it, hard. "Wake up, Deck. Now!"

He made grumbly, sleepy noises and opened one eye. "Nellie. Sweetheart." He smiled at her drowsily. "C'mere." He reached for her.

Oh, no way.

She kicked free of the covers and leaped from the bed. "Keep your hands to yourself."

He gave her that killer smile and a long, slow, hungry look.

She realized she was naked. "Don't you *even* look at me like that." Snatching up her pillow, she pressed it to her torso, smashing it close with both arms. It wasn't much, but at least it covered the crucial bits. "We need to talk."

"Talk?"

"What? Is there an echo in here? You heard what I said."

He sat up, the sheet falling away from his broad, lightly furred chest and corrugated abs. Lazy and unconcerned, he stretched and yawned. She clutched her pillow tighter and waited for him to stop showing off all those muscles as if nothing was wrong.

"Okay," he said finally, shoving his own pillow behind him, leaning back against it and lacing his hands on his head. "What's the problem?"

"What's the problem?" she shrieked.

He let his hands drop. "You're shouting."

She made herself speak more quietly. "Everything, Deck. It's *all* the problem," she insisted in a low, angry growl. "We agreed on a Las Vegas fling. We agreed that it would be over and done by the time we went home, that *when* we went home, you would stop chasing after me, that you would go your way and leave me to go mine. We *agreed*. You said you were fine with it."

He looked at her tenderly. *Tenderly*, damn it. "Think back, Nellie. I was never fine with it."

"But you *agreed* to it."

He answered so quietly. "No."

"Yes." She held on to her temper by a very thin

thread. "You agreed and I trusted you and all that time you were busy planning our…wedding? Who does that? Who *thinks* like that? How can you keep insisting that it wasn't the way it actually was?" She held up her ring finger and shook it at him good and hard. "Never in a hundred thousand years did we ever agree to *this*."

"Now, Sparky…"

"Uh-uh. Don't you do that. You don't get to call me Sparky at a time like this."

"Can you just look at things reasonably, please?"

"Oh, cute." Her blood felt like it was literally boiling. "Now you're lecturing me about being reasonable. After what you did."

"Come on. Get honest. You were there. You signed the license, you put on my ring, chose your dress and decided on the flowers. You walked down the aisle to me and you said, 'I do.' It's not like I drugged you and married you against your will."

Okay, fine. He was right. Kind of.

Except that he wasn't. Except that he'd planned it. He'd played her so well.

She raked her sleep-scrambled hair back off her forehead and launched into a fresh attack. "Oh, yes, it *is* like you drugged me. You know that it is. You followed me here to Vegas and you turned on the charm. And when I couldn't resist you, you said you understood that it was only a fling—or if you didn't actually *say* it, you sure did imply the hell out of it. Then you lulled me with champagne and loved me all up and down the strip and then you took me to that chapel and I…well, I…" Her fury devolved into sputters.

Because there is no excuse for my own behavior.

That was the real problem. That was what made her the maddest of all. She *had* gone along with it, relished every moment of it. She'd been complicit in everything they did.

Her fury redoubled. In sheer frustration, she raised her pillow and bopped him a good one on his big, stubborn head. When he only blinked and stared at her, she hit him again.

"Hey! Cut it out." He snatched it away from her, leaving her standing there naked *and* empty-handed.

She let out a low moan of total exasperation and wrapped her arms around herself. "This is so wrong. I have no words for how wrong this is, Deck."

"Listen." He stuck her pillow behind him, too. "I know you're scared. But you don't have to be. Because it's going to be all right—better than all right." His eyes were all melty, all tender and hopeful. "We'll work it out, you'll see. Nellie, you know in your heart that this is what we both want. This is what we should have done all those years ago. Because you were right about us and I get it now. I had to go more than a decade without you. I even married the wrong woman. She knew I didn't love her the way that I should. She knew there was someone else. And that someone else was you—always, Nellie. You. I want a family, with you. Because we're *it* for each other, made for each other. We *need* to be married. We need to go home and start working on our life together."

She didn't know what to feel. Her damn, stupid heart ached to believe him, that she was his only one, that he only wanted her and only ever had. That it really could work, the two of them together now, when it had ended so painfully all those years ago.

She ached for…all of it. For him. And for her. Even for his ex-wife, disappointed in her marriage and in her love. She longed to ask him to tell her more.

But it just wasn't right, what he'd done, what had happened. This was no way to make a marriage, and they needed to face that. "It's not the end of the world." She made her voice even and reasonable this time. "I can put off my flight home and we'll pull ourselves together, get dressed and go find a lawyer, or whatever. We'll get a quickie divorce and that will be that."

"But, Sparky," Deck replied so very gently, "I can't do that."

"What do you mean, you can't? There's no *can't*. Just say yes and let's go."

"Uh-uh. I mean it. I can't."

"Why not?"

"Two reasons. One, I love you. And two, I don't want a divorce."

She face-palmed at that one. And then she fisted her hands at her sides and groaned at the ceiling. "All of a sudden, you *love* me."

He just sat there, looking infuriatingly droolworthy with his bed-messy hair and his scruffy, square jaw, his broad, muscled chest and that mouth that could kiss her like no other mouth ever had. He just sat there and said, "I've always loved you."

She had nothing to hit him with. Damn it. "Well." She spoke through clenched teeth. "And didn't you have some really painful ways of showing it."

"Nell. Come on." He reached out a hand. She ducked back from his touch. "Settle down. Let's discuss this reasonably, like two grown adults."

"Apparently, you haven't been listening to what I've

been saying. I'm not discussing jack with you. But I do have a question."

"Anything. Just ask."

She flashed her ring finger at him again. "How long have you had these?"

"Nellie..."

"Just answer the question, please."

He coughed into his hand. "A few months."

A human volcano, that's what she felt like. A human volcano about to blow. "You planned this whole thing, didn't you? You had it all arranged. At Now and Forever, they knew we were coming."

"If you would only take a few deep breaths and—"

"No, Deck. Just no."

"I don't want a divorce."

"You said that. I heard you. But that's just too bad, isn't it? Because *I* do want a divorce. And you don't get to be married to me if I don't want to be married to you."

"Well, now, wait a minute. I think you're kind of wrong there."

"Oh, really? How's that?"

"Because we *are* married. And before I even consider a divorce, I want you to give me—give *us*—a little time to see if we can make it work."

"I cannot even begin to express to you all the ways that is *not* going to happen." She cast a quick glance around the room, looking for her clothes—not the rhinestone shoes, sexy tap pants and white mermaid gown thrown in an explosion of beads and lace across the bedside chair. Uh-uh. The others. She needed the dress, shoes and underwear she'd had on when they left the hotel last night. When she didn't see them, she marched around the end of the bed and headed for the door to the sitting room.

"Where are you going?" he asked her bare retreating backside.

She just kept moving right on through the open door.

Her dress and underwear were in a wad on the sofa, her shoes beneath the coffee table. She grabbed her panties, put them on, wiggled into the bra and pulled the wrinkled dress over her head, reaching back, catching the zipper and managing to tug it closed without too much trouble. She was straightening the skirt when he appeared in the doorway to the bedroom.

Still naked. Still everything she'd ever wanted in a man. Except for the awful way he'd hurt her in the past. And the heedless, overbearing way he'd manipulated her last night.

"Talk to me, Nellie," he said in that gentle tone that made her want to break things—preferably over his big, fat head.

She put on her shoes. "Forget it." She grabbed her purse. "I want a divorce."

"Look. Just…don't go. Let's talk this out." He looked so sincere. It made the ache inside her intensify all over again.

But they weren't getting anywhere and he was far too tempting—not to mention overwhelming.

Space. She needed some of that and she needed it right now.

She took off his beautiful, perfect diamond rings,

set them carefully on the coffee table and stood tall to face him. "Admit it. You tricked me."

"Sparky…"

"Uh-uh. Just no. I'm going home. I can't deal with you now. At this moment, I only want to kill you in a thousand gruesome, painful ways."

"I didn't know what else to do, how to get through to you. Every time I made a move, you would cut me right off. I've tried, tried for years, to forget you, to move on. But it's just not happening. And you can lie to me all you want, Nellie. But we both know it's the same for you." He looked at her directly, without pretense, standing there naked and unashamed in the doorway.

The thing was, she believed him. And she *had* been complicit. No matter how skillfully he'd seduced her into it, when the preacher asked the big question, she had willingly, joyfully even, said, "I do." And yeah, he had it right about her. She'd never really gotten over him. No other guy compared.

Which meant that if she stayed, who knew what she might let him talk her into next?

She had to…protect herself. She had to get away, think, decide what *she* wanted to do.

Last night, he'd sapped her will and her good sense. Not to mention somehow miraculously gotten her to forget her pride and her absolute determination never to let him rule her again.

The man had told her what she wanted and seduced her into agreeing with him.

Yeah. Seduction. That's what this was. A seduction that had lasted the whole weekend. It had started with a drink and dinner on Friday night, and culminated in a diamond ring, a white dress and a walk down the aisle.

He'd taken her over.

Well, he wasn't taking her over today. Uh-uh.

She snatched up her tiny, jeweled purse and walked out the door.

Chapter Five

Hours later, Nell pulled her F-150 XLT pickup into her covered parking space in the lot behind McKellan's Pub on Marmot Drive in Justice Creek.

Ryan McKellan, who owned the bar and had the loft next to hers, came out the rear door and went around to the hatch at the rear of the camper shell to meet her. She popped the latch and he hauled out her bags for her.

"Good trip?" Rye asked, as she shut the hatch and locked the doors.

"Words fail me."

Rye was a longtime friend and knew her well. "Bad?" He held out his arms.

She stepped into the hug gratefully. "I'll say this much. It's good to be home."

When he let her go, he asked, "Whatever it is, we're

here and we're ready to listen." *We* meant Rye and his fiancée, Meg Cartwell, who tended the bar in McKellan's and shared his loft with him. The two were getting married in mid-December.

"Thanks. I may hold you to it. Right now, though, I need to get my stuff upstairs and call Ma."

"Calling your mother the minute you get home. That can't be good."

"You have no idea."

An hour later, Nell marched up the wide front steps of the Bravo mansion and between the ostentatious white pillars. It was a week and a half before Thanksgiving and there was already a giant Christmas wreath on the front door.

Her mother must have warned Estrella Watson that Nell was coming. The longtime housekeeper pulled the door open before Nell got a chance to knock. "Nell! Welcome." Estrella was a complete sweetheart. She'd been running the mansion for almost forty years, since way back when Frank Bravo built it for his first wife, Sondra. That Estrella got along so well with Willow Bravo was a mystery to everyone in the family. "How have you been?" she asked.

"It's a very long story and you really don't need to hear it," Nell grumbled, and then added more warmly, "Always good to see you, Estrella."

"Come in, come in. Your mother's expecting you." Estrella ushered her into the grand entry hall, which was already decked from floor to vaulted ceiling in greenery, lights and shiny glass ornaments. Nell shed her coat and Estrella took it from her.

"Everything's looking seriously festive around here."

"I know it's strange to decorate for Christmas before it's even Thanksgiving, but your mother said it was all right, so I got an early start this year." The housekeeper's expression turned wistful. "I love getting the house ready for the holidays and I just couldn't wait to do it up right one more time." Estrella had given her notice months ago and would retire in January.

Willow was remarrying in December—the Saturday after Rye and Meg—and moving to Southern California with her groom, Griffin Masters. She'd signed the mansion and its contents over to Nell's half siblings, Sondra's children, which only seemed right and fair to everyone, given that Frank Bravo had built the mansion for Sondra.

Still, Willow's generous gesture had taken both the siblings and half siblings by surprise. *Generous* and *fair* had not been words anyone would have used to describe anything Willow did—up till now.

"Darling." Willow appeared in the doorway to the front sitting room. She wore a white cashmere sweater and perfectly tailored wool pants, her blond hair short and shining around her still-beautiful, heart-shaped face. "Isn't this a lovely surprise? I'm so glad I was home when you called."

"Ma."

"Don't scowl so, Nellie. You'll get frown lines. Nice trip to Vegas?" Did she look smug? Willow had no shame, whether she was stealing Sondra Bravo's husband—or manipulating her children. "Come on into the library. I'll mix you a martini."

After what had happened the night before, the last thing Nell wanted was a drink. "I'll take coffee."

"I'll bring it right in," said Estrella.

"To the library, my love." With a sweep of one slender hand, Willow gestured Nell ahead of her.

They went through the sitting room to the library beyond. In addition to the glass-fronted built-in bookcases that lined the walls, there was a lit-up tree in the corner and a fire in the ornate, greenery-bedecked fireplace.

Nell took a seat on one of the two damask sofas in the center of the room as Willow, at the fancy glass-topped drink cart, whipped up a martini. "Is Griffin here?" She would just as soon not yell at Willow in front of her fiancé if that could possibly be avoided—not that she *would* yell.

Uh-uh. She was not letting her temper run away with her, no matter how crazy Willow made her.

Her mother granted her a radiant smile. "Griff is off at that shop of Carter's." Carter was the oldest of Nell's four full siblings. He built custom cars for a living. "Carter's customizing a Bentley for him, of all things. You know men and their cars. He'll be back by dinnertime." Gently, Willow stirred her drink, then put on the strainer and strained it into an antique crystal cocktail glass. She speared an olive on a toothpick and lovingly dipped it into the glass.

Estrella appeared with the coffee. She set down the tray on the coffee table in front of Nell and bustled off.

Willow sat in a wing chair and enjoyed a slow sip of her drink. "Delicious. Now, tell me all about your trip to Sin City. Some trade show, as I recall?"

Nell took her time pouring coffee from the silver service, adding cream and one cube of sugar. "You know why I'm here, Ma. Don't play innocent. It's just not you. Deck admitted you're the one who told him where to find me."

Another delicate sip from the beautiful stemmed glass. "I happen to like Declan. More important, *you* like him—you *more* than like him. You're smart and strong and loving, my darling. But you're also prideful and stubborn and slow to forgive. I just wanted to give you a little nudge, that's all."

"Stay out of my life, Ma."

"Look at it this way. Soon I'll be living in California. You won't have to worry about me interfering in your life. If you choose to throw away what you long for the most, well, at least I won't have to be here to watch you doing it."

Nell reminded herself again that she would not, under any circumstances, lose her temper. "You know that I don't want anything to do with him."

"Darling. Stop lying. He's the one for you and the sooner you stop pretending he's not, the happier both of you will be."

Nell stared down at her untouched coffee and shook her head. "Why did I come here? What was the point? You know that telling him where to find me was wrong, but you did it, anyway."

"And I would do it again." Willow raised her martini high. "To love. And happiness." Another tiny sip. "Now. Tell me how it went. I'm guessing it was glorious. Just you and the man you've always loved, alone together in Las Vegas."

Denials rose to her lips. She bit them back. They would only make her sound defensive, give her mother more chances to call her a liar. "How about this, Ma? *You* tell *me* that you're sorry."

"Why? We both know I'm not."

"But you should be. Because you were wrong to tell him where I was."

"I don't care if I was wrong. Sometimes we have to do wrong to make things right."

"Even your platitudes are twisted, you know that?"

"Yes, well. We all know that I've never let other people's ideas of right and wrong determine how I live my life. I do what I need to do. Yes, I have been wrong, *terribly* so. I realize that. But this—my telling Declan where to find you? That wasn't wrong. That was creating an opportunity. For you and for the man who loves you to finally reach out to each other. It was your chance to begin to heal a wound that's been festering for much too long, keeping you both from the happiness you so richly deserve." Turquoise eyes glittering, she set down her drink, crossed her legs and leaned in. "Now, confess. You spent some time with him, didn't you?"

"I'm not telling you anything about my private business. Not ever again."

Willow just smiled. "Meaning you *did* spend some time with him and he's starting to get through to you."

"I never said that."

"Darling, you didn't have to. It's written all over your beautiful face."

Mondays were usually a little slow at McKellan's. As a rule, Ryan and Meg took Monday nights off.

Meg, who had wildly curling light brown hair, a lush figure and the kind of smile that could light up a room, knocked on Nell's door at a little after seven. "Hungry? I made lasagna."

"I'm in." She followed Rye's fiancé to the other loft, accepted ice water in lieu of wine and sat down to Caesar salad, plenty of hot garlic bread and Meg's amazing four-cheese lasagna.

"So what happened in Vegas?" Rye asked.

Nell must have made a face because Meg chided, "Rye. Maybe she doesn't want to get into it."

Rye reached over and gave Nell's shoulder a squeeze. "Come on. You can tell us. We'll keep your secrets."

Nell realized she really did want to talk about it with someone she could trust. "I'm not ready to tell the family yet." Which was silly, and she knew it. Her sisters could be counted on to keep her secrets to themselves.

But she'd grown extra close to Meg and Rye the past couple of months. Maybe it was being next-door neighbors. Or maybe it was Meg, who had that bartender's talent for listening and accepting, for saying the right thing just when a girl needed to hear it.

Meg said, "Only if you want to tell us. Nobody's putting you on the spot."

"Speak for yourself." Rye made a silly face at Meg and she swatted at him. They were so cute together, Nell could hardly stand it.

Somehow, that kind of did it, watching Rye and Meg being happy together. Somehow, that made up her mind for her. "Ma told Deck where to find me in Vegas."

Rye groaned in her behalf. "And he showed up there?"

"What do you think?"

Rye grunted. "He showed up."

"Yes, he did. I was really mad at first, but then, I

went ahead and agreed to have a drink with him. And then we had dinner and then, well..."

"Wow." Rye put down his fork and sat back in his chair. "You had a thing with Deck in Vegas?"

"It was more than a thing."

Meg reached over and clasped her arm, a steadying, comforting sort of gesture.

Rye asked gingerly, "More? In what way?"

And she just went ahead and said it. "I married him last night."

The silence at that table was absolutely deafening.

Finally Rye asked, "But...why? How?"

So she told them. Everything—well, not all the naughty bits, but the basics. That they'd spent Saturday and Sunday nights together and on Sunday night, he'd taken her to a chapel, where she'd walked down the aisle to him.

Meg went ahead and stated the obvious. "But...he's not here with you now."

"I had a fight with him this morning."

Rye asked, "A fight over...?"

"He planned the whole thing. He set me up and I fell for it. Saturday night, we agreed on a final fling, agreed it would be over as soon as we left Las Vegas. But then *last* night, when we got married, he had the rings already—he'd had them for months, he admitted to me this morning. We went to the chapel supposedly on the fly, but they were expecting him. And then this morning, when I put it all together, realized he'd totally tricked me and demanded an immediate divorce, he said no. He said not until we at least try to make it work. So I walked out on him. I came home." For some reason, she felt almost ashamed to admit that.

Meg asked in a near whisper, "Has he called? Tried to get in touch with you?"

"I have no idea. I turned off my phone."

Meg asked so softly, "Do you want him to try to reach you?"

"Oh, God." She put her hands over her eyes, as though by hiding her face she could hide from the awful truth. "Yes," she confessed, dropping her hands and staring miserably down at them. "Damn it to hell. Yes. For months I just wanted him to leave me alone. But…slowly, he's been doing it, reeling me in. And now, well, I can't help myself. I don't want him to stop."

Nell stayed with her friends until around eleven. They offered hugs and reassurances—that she was not alone, that people got suddenly married in Vegas all the time.

They promised her it would all work out and advised her to give herself time to think about what she really wanted and what her next step should be. When she left, they reminded her that they were there for her whenever she needed them.

At her place, she turned on the phone. Deck had left two voice mails.

One that afternoon: "Pick up the phone, Sparky. We have to talk about this—damn it, Nell. Come *on*."

And one just a couple of hours ago: "I'm not giving up. We're going to work this out. Call me. Now."

She almost called him back, but stopped herself in mid-dial.

* * *

The next morning, as she was catching up on paperwork at Bravo Construction, she heard his voice in the outer office.

"I'm here to see Nell," he said, bold as only he could be. "She's expecting me."

Her assistant, Ruby, knew the drill. "Sorry, Deck. You know it's not happening—wait! You can't... Stop!"

But he was Deck and he didn't stop. Her door swung open and there he was, looking altogether too doable in jeans, a white shirt and a gray tweed blazer that emphasized his big shoulders and narrow waist.

Ruby called from behind him, "I tried!"

"Thanks, Ruby, I'll deal with it."

He stepped in and shut the door.

She closed the lid on her laptop so that she could glare at him unobstructed. "You're in my place of business. I did not invite you here and I want you to go."

He flipped back the sides of the blazer and braced his hands on his hips. "When will you talk to me?"

"Soon."

"When is soon? I need a date, a time and a place."

"Not now. You just said it. Time and place, Deck. This is neither."

"When?" The guy just wouldn't give up.

Her heart raced, her breath came hard and her pulse fluttered madly in her throat. She wanted to kill him—or else grab him and kiss him and beg him to swear to her that everything would be all right. "I need a week."

He turned around, stalked to the window and then stalked right back. "A week from today."

"That's what I said. Next Tuesday. My place. Seven p.m. Until then, will you please just leave me alone?"

His eyes burned through her for an endless count of ten. And then, finally, he muttered, "You got it." He strode to the door and yanked it open. "See you then."

And he was gone.

After rising to shut the door again, she returned to her desk and called her half brother James at Calder and Bravo, Attorneys-at-Law.

At two that afternoon, James's secretary ushered Nell into his office.

James got up for a hug, then he offered her one of the guest chairs. She took it and he settled in behind his desk. He said his wife, Addie, was doing just great and his adorable one-year-old stepdaughter was growing like a weed.

Then James asked, "So what can I help you with?"

She felt suddenly wary, though James was a good guy and totally trustworthy. "It's a legal thing. I need to know you can keep it confidential. It's...a little embarrassing and I don't feel like getting into it with the family."

James nodded, his blue eyes sincere. "I understand your concern. And as your lawyer, I will always observe strict confidentiality. Whatever you tell me, it won't leave this room."

So she told him that she'd married Deck in Vegas on the spur of the moment. "It was a mistake. And now I want a divorce."

James asked, "Are you sure?"

Okay, maybe she wasn't. But she had to do something, make a move. Take a stand. "Yes."

"How does Declan feel about it?"

"He says no—or he has up till now, anyway. He says he wants us at least to try to make it work."

James explained that he would get the paperwork together for her and help her fill it out. "Then I'll file your divorce petition with the court and arrange to have Declan served."

It sounded so complicated. "We've only been married for two days. Does it have to be a big deal? I don't want anything from him. Can't I just…fill the thing out and give it to him?"

"It's best to have a process server handle it. You are, however, allowed to mail his copy to him with a paper he can fill out and send to the court—but that's only going to work if the two of you are in agreement about ending the marriage. You just told me *he* wants to work it out."

"But *I* don't. It was a mistake, okay? He has to realize that and accept it. Doesn't he?" She felt like an idiot as she asked the question. Deck had been chasing her for months. And so far he'd shown no indication that he would give up—especially not now that he'd managed to lure her to the altar.

James looked at her patiently. "If you think he might contest the divorce or drag his feet or try to make things difficult, you really need to have him served. You need a legal record *that* he's been served. Then it will be his turn to respond, to accept or reject your terms, to add his own."

"You make it sound like it could drag on forever."

"Unfortunately, that does happen sometimes."

"It's all so…" She sought the word and sighed when it came to her. "It's sad, James. Sad and complex."

"Divorce tends to be that way."

She stood up.

He gave her a gentle smile. "I'm getting the feeling you want to think about it some more?"

"Yeah. I guess I do."

Deck wasn't at all happy about the way things were working out with Nell—or, more specifically, *not* working out.

At least he had a company to run, something to help him keep his mind off the infuriating woman he'd always loved, who swore she didn't want to be married to him.

Deck kept good and busy all day. He found five hundred rum barrels in the Dominican Republic, barrels that he already had standing orders for. Rum barrels were the hot thing for craft brewers, who wanted their beers to have complexity. Rum barrels gave specialty beers the wild, funky flavors craft-beer makers loved.

He had a long meeting with his CFO and another with the shop manager. Then he caught up with the sales team.

At six, he called it a day and went to Prime Sports and Fitness across Central Street from McKellan's. The gym was owned and run by Nell's brother Quinn. Deck spent a half hour on the elliptical and then worked out with weights, keeping watch the whole time for Nell, who had a membership, too. She never showed.

He saw Quinn, though. Nell's brother offered to spot him on his bench press. Quinn seemed the same as always—calm, quiet and helpful. If he knew that

Deck had married his sister night before last, he didn't let on.

The next day, Deck bumped into Clara Ames, Nell's half sister, on Central Street. Clara stopped to chat for a minute. She wanted to order some barrel wine racks for the restaurant she owned. They agreed she would come in to see him Thursday afternoon. As she waved and walked away, he was almost positive Nell hadn't told her what had happened in Vegas. The next day, when she ordered a dozen barrel wine racks and never said a word about Nell, or even so much as looked at him funny, he was certain she had no idea that he and Nell were married.

Saturday, he stopped in at Bravo Catering and Bakery for coffee and a blueberry muffin. Elise Walsh, Nell's other half sister, owned the place. That morning, Elise was working the register. She seemed the same as always, friendly but not overly so. He would bet she didn't know about him and Nell, either.

He couldn't resist wandering over to the flower shop, Bloom, next door, which Nell's sister Jody owned. Jody greeted him warmly. He bought a giant bouquet containing what looked like every flower known to man and then he suggested, "How about you send these to Nell?"

Jody laughed. "Nice try." He'd had Jody send Nell flowers one time, four months before. Nell had told her sister not to let him do that again.

He left the flower shop grinning. His guess? Nell hadn't told anyone in her family that she'd married him in Vegas.

Should that bother him? Probably.

But he couldn't help thinking that he might use the information to his advantage.

A better man would do no such thing.

But he'd never claimed to be any kind of saint. His mother had always been frail and unhappy. Lurline McGrath didn't have a lot of time for him or his sister. She was either sick or working herself into an early grave trying to pay back his father's debts. She'd died when he was eleven and Marty was eight, leaving them at the mercy of dear old Dad, who wasn't a bad man, just an irresponsible one. Keith McGrath always had a big plan to get rich—and inevitably ended up empty-handed and in debt to whoever he'd borrowed from last.

Deck had grown up determined *not* to end up like his father. He'd fought hard to make it on his own terms *and* always paid back what he owed. He was no saint, though. Sometimes he played it a little bit shady in order to get what he wanted.

And now that he'd finally gotten Nell all the way to the altar, he wasn't letting her get away without a fight. Yeah, he'd manipulated her to get her to marry him. But no way would she have said "I do" if deep down she didn't want what he wanted.

He only needed to find a way to convince her that she didn't really want a divorce. He needed time with her, damn it. And if he had to threaten to tell her secrets to her sisters to get that time, he would do it.

At JC Barrels, he gave the flowers to his top sales rep, Eden. Eden put them in a vase made of barrel staves and set them on a barrel table near the front door.

Then he called Garrett Bravo, Nell's partner at

Bravo Construction. They had a nice, long talk about the progress of the house Bravo Construction was building for him. By the end of that call, Deck was absolutely certain that Nell's brother had no clue she had married him in Vegas.

That night, he almost went to McKellan's. He liked it there. They had the best local beer on tap and the burgers were great. But Nell might be there. After all, she lived upstairs. She wouldn't like it if she ran into him. And he didn't want to do anything that might make her change her mind about their meeting Tuesday evening.

Somehow, he got through Saturday night. And Sunday. And Monday.

And then it was Tuesday at last.

When he knocked on her door, she pulled it open so fast he knew she'd been waiting on the other side. She wore yoga pants and a giant black sweatshirt with In Memory of When I Cared printed on the front. There were shadows beneath her jewel-green eyes, and she was just close enough when she pulled back the door that the well-remembered scent of her came to him, clean and tempting at once.

"You want something?" she asked. "Coffee? A beer?"

Just you. "I'm good."

The living area was all one space, ultramodern, with a contemporary gas fireplace, a sofa, coffee table and armchairs near the tall windows that looked toward the mountains to the west. She gestured in the general direction of the sleek, low couch. "Have a seat."

He went where she pointed.

She took the chair across from him, drew her stocking feet up and tucked them to the side. "I was thinking that I would have the divorce papers here and ready for you."

If he tried to kiss her, would she punch him? "I don't want a divorce, Nellie."

She made a halfhearted attempt at an eye roll. "You have made that unbearably clear." And then she sighed. "I went to see my brother James at his law office. He explained how a divorce is a lot more complicated than just filling out some forms and handing them to you. Long story short, I told him I would need to think about it some more."

Deck kept his expression noncommittal, but disappointment dragged on him. She'd actually seen a lawyer about a divorce. Also, the lawyer she'd gone to was James, her half brother. Who else had she told? Threatening to out their marriage to her family wouldn't do him much good if everyone already knew. "I take it you've told your family that we got married?"

She shook her head. "Just James. He's sworn to secrecy, because I went to see him as my lawyer. And Rye and Meg, I told them. But they promised to keep it to themselves."

Did that mean he could put his evil plan back in play? "So then, you really *don't* want your family to know."

She narrowed her eyes at him. "You're up to something. I can smell it. Just tell me. What are you doing, Deck?"

He surprised himself and came right out with it. "I was thinking that unless you agree to my terms, I would maybe threaten to tell everyone that you married me last weekend."

She groaned. "Dear God. You're going in for emotional blackmail now? What is the matter with you?"

"I never claimed to be perfect. And I want to stay married to you. I'll do whatever's necessary to make that happen. I think I've made that pretty clear."

"So your big plan is if I don't do this your way, you're going to bust me as a total idiot to my family?"

"I didn't say that."

"But it's what you meant—and you know what?" She threw up both hands. "Do it. You tell them. Tell my sisters and my brothers and my totally annoying matchmaking mother that we're married. See how that goes over when *I* admit that, yeah, I screwed up, drank too much champagne and ended up saying 'I do' with you in Vegas. See how that works out for you when I go on to explain that I don't *want* to be married to you and as soon as you wake up and smell the Starbucks, we're getting divorced."

This really was not going the way that he'd imagined it. He tried coaxingly, "There was a time when you begged to be married to me."

"Please. I was eighteen and madly in love. What did I know? I went home every night to the house my mother stole from Sondra. My half sister was waiting there to torture me, taking scissors to my favorite clothes, putting black hair dye in my shampoo. You were my true love, the best thing that ever happened to me, the one who finally understood me, the guy who would stick by me forever, the one who made everything right. Or so I thought until you kicked me to the curb twice. So, yeah, before you ruined everything between us I wanted to marry you and I made no secret of it."

For about the hundredth time, he tried to make her see it from his point of view. "We weren't even out of high school. I was flat broke. You were a Bravo. I couldn't come up to that, okay?"

"I told you not to worry about money. I told you I would take care of you."

"Nellie. By now, at least, you have to know me better than that."

She fiddled with a loose thread on one of her socks, looking anywhere but at him. "I hurt your pride." Her voice was softer now. "I get it. It's what you said the other night in Vegas. You had things to prove." She sent him a sideways glance. "And then I went behind your back and loaned your dad that money."

Good old Keith. He knew a chicken ripe for plucking when he saw one. He'd talked her out of five thousand dollars, said he needed it right away to keep a roof over their heads—and it should be just between the two of them because Deck was too proud to borrow money and didn't need to know. Nell had kept that secret from him for weeks. And then finally, she'd broken down and confessed everything. She'd cried and begged him not to be mad at her, because she only wanted to help. He'd realized right then that he had to call a halt with her. She just didn't get it, didn't understand how completely she'd stepped over the line. She just couldn't see that all he felt was shame when she told him—shame, like sharp, bloody teeth, gnawing away at his self-respect.

Now, so many years later, he watched her shift in her chair, lowering her legs and then drawing them up again on the other side. Now, all he wanted was to get closer to her.

But how the hell to make that happen?

He said, "All giving him that money did was make it impossible for me to stay with you."

"I didn't care about the money."

"But, Nellie, *I* did. I couldn't see then that you were only trying to help. All I saw was that it couldn't work with us, that no way was I getting married to a rich girl before I'd made it on my own—a rich girl I owed money to."

"It wasn't your debt."

"Yeah, it was. You gave him that money for my sake."

She folded her hands, looked down at them and then back up at him. Her soft lips trembled slightly. He wanted to comfort her, but he knew she'd only push him away. She said, "So you dumped me."

He nodded. "Even though it practically killed me to do it."

"Oh, and that's supposed to somehow make what you did to me okay?"

"I didn't say that. What I'm saying is that you weren't the only one hurt by what happened."

"Can you just not confuse the issue, please? *You* dumped *me*. *You* made that choice. If it hurt you to do it, well, how is that in any way my fault?"

"I didn't say it was your fault."

"Great. So stop making excuses for yourself. You dumped me. And then you turned right around and dumped me again…"

It was only the truth. He couldn't deny it. He'd walked away from her in the spring of their senior year.

And when she'd come after him again that summer, he ached so bad from the loss of her, he took her for a ride in his rattletrap pickup—so they could talk.

There'd been no talking. He drove out to a deserted spot where they used to go to be alone. He'd barely turned the engine off before they were all over each other.

It was so wrong that he did that, made love to her when he knew he wouldn't stay.

It had been raining when he started kissing her, a sudden summer thunderstorm, the raindrops beating at the roof and the windshield, making a hollow, empty, furious sort of sound.

Afterward, Nell had pulled on her cutoffs and zipped them up. She'd straightened her bra and tugged her shirt back down. And then she'd glanced his way at exactly the moment he was sliding her a guilty look.

Their eyes met and held.

That did it. She *knew*. She got it. What had just happened was only a moment of weakness for him, not the fresh start she'd been begging him for.

That time, there was no begging. That time, she got mad. *You dirty, rotten bastard. How could you?*

He'd said all the stuff a guy says when it's over— that it wasn't going to work, that he was really sorry and he would take her home.

She'd called him worse things than a rotten bastard then. *Forget it*, she'd screamed at him. *I don't need you to drive me. I don't need you for anything, not ever again. I'm out of here.* And she'd shoved open her door and jumped out. She was drenched to the skin in the space of a minute.

He'd reached across the seat to roll down the hand-crank passenger window. *Come on, Nellie. Don't do this. Get back in the damn truck.*

But she only stood there, the rain pouring down her face, sheeting over her hair. And she'd yelled in the window at him, *Go, damn you, Declan! Just go!*

He couldn't just go. He couldn't be with her anymore, but he had to make sure she was safe, at least. So he had sat there and waited for her to stop acting crazy and get in the pickup again.

She didn't budge, just took out her phone, turned her back to him and made a call. And then she'd started walking, trudging through the mud, hunched against the downpour.

He'd followed her out to the two-lane highway, where he drove at a snail's pace along the shoulder behind her, waiting for her to finally give up and let him take her home.

But she didn't give up. Not Nell. She just slogged along, never pausing, never once looking back.

He'd known for certain then. This really was the end. She wouldn't be coming after him again. He'd lost her forever this time.

Which was good, he'd told himself. It was right. It was what he needed, for her to leave him. Because it couldn't work with them. They were worlds and worlds apart.

Finally her brother Carter had appeared out of the rain in a souped-up canary yellow Plymouth Roadrunner. Nell got in the car and Carter hit the gas.

Deck didn't ease the pickup out into traffic again until the yellow car had disappeared around the next curve.

Two years later, he'd sent her a check, with interest, for the money his father had "borrowed." Nell had cashed the check and that was that—they were done.

Or so Deck had told himself at the time.

But then, well, the years went by. And he never really got over her. There was no one else who could even compare to her. Now and then he would see her—on the street, in a store. Always from a distance. Both of them took great care not to get close.

He always felt that tug of yearning just at the sight of her shining red hair, at the confident set of her shoulders, the sweet upward tilt of her chin. Not that he ever planned to do a damn thing about it. He knew she'd never let him near her again.

Six years after that day in the pickup, he and Kristy Brice started going out. A year later, they moved in together and a year after that, they were married.

Bad idea. Kristy tried her best to make the marriage work, but no woman wants to be a man's second choice. A year after they got married, Kristy said she knew he didn't love her and she was through being second best, that he'd always kept some part of himself separate from her and that he'd said another woman's name in his sleep more than once. When he wouldn't talk about it with her, Kristy went to her friends. They'd told her the old stories about him and Nell.

Then Kristy came at him with what she'd learned from her girls. "You still love Nell Bravo," she accused.

Hearing his wife say it right out loud like that had finally done the trick. Kristy had shocked him into realizing it was true.

He'd never really let Nell go. Not in the deepest part of himself.

Kristy divorced him. He felt regret that he'd hurt her, that he'd failed her as a husband. He'd gotten it all wrong, he knew that. It took him another year and a half to admit to himself that he not only still loved Nell, he wanted her back—that he would do whatever he had to do to make her give him one more chance. He really was trying to fix what he'd broken.

Unfortunately, Nell refused to get with the program. "It's too late, Deck."

"No. It's not."

"You have to let it go."

He really was losing her all over again. It was all going down for the third time. He'd never get this close again and he couldn't lose her now. He had to do something to stop the end from happening.

But what?

An idea came to him—half-baked, a little weak, but what else did he have?

He went with it. "Give me till Christmas. If you don't feel differently by then, if you still think it can't ever work, I'll see my lawyer on December twenty-sixth. I'll make it happen fast. You'll get served by the first week after New Year's."

"Uh-uh. No. You won't change my mind—not in a month, not ever." As she spoke, she drew herself up in the chair and lifted her chin high. Her mouth trembled slightly, though. Did that mean it was all false bravado?

Or was that only wishful thinking on his part?

Didn't matter. He was not giving up. "Just until Christmas. Give me—give *us*—that much of a chance."

Nell couldn't afford to be tempted by his proposition. It was a bad idea to indulge him in any way. She'd messed up big in Vegas. Now she needed to hold the line with him. "How can I ever trust you to do what you say you will?"

"I swear it, Nellie. If you still want a divorce on the day after Christmas, you've got it."

She was weakening and she knew it.

And, really, how *could* she? Hadn't he hurt her enough before? How could she even consider giving him another chance to stomp on her heart? "This is all wrong."

"No, it's not."

"It didn't work when we were kids and it's not going to work now."

"Damn it, Nellie." He stood up so fast she had to swallow a gasp. And then he came out from behind the barrier of the coffee table. She braced as he came closer. "A chance, that's all. I just want a chance with you. I know I messed up all those years ago. I know I hurt you—and then I turned right around and did it again. But, Nellie, I had nothing and it seemed to me that you had it all. I needed to prove that I could make it on my own, without anyone's help. I just... No way was I going to end up doing to you what my dad did to my mom, no way could I be the loser you married who ruined your life. I loved you and I wanted you, but it wasn't enough. I knew that I would only drag you down. So, yeah, I walked away from you. I'm sorry, so sorry. But, Nellie, I have paid. Because I lost you and you were what mattered most."

She stared up at him as he loomed above her. He had his hands stuffed in his pockets and his eyes were full of longing. And pain, too.

It hurt so bad to see *him* hurting. She could barely

keep herself in that chair. She wanted to reach up to him, gather him close, shower him with soothing kisses, promise him it was all going to be okay.

She ached to comfort him—because she still cared. She still cared way too much.

The inescapable truth came clear to her, finally.

If she really was done with him, she wouldn't be here right now. If she'd really had enough of him, no amount of good champagne and hot, sexy loving would have had her walking down the aisle to him.

Nell stared up at the man who had chased her relentlessly for months now, the man she'd sworn for years she would never so much as speak to again—and faced the truth at last.

She wanted another chance, too.

Chapter Six

Deck said, "Okay. I admit it. I don't have the first clue how to give you the love you deserve. I'm pushy and I want things my way and I'm not always as patient as I probably ought to be. Maybe if we'd stayed together for all these years, I would have learned by now. I'm bad at love, I know that. But I do want to learn, Nellie. I want to learn with you."

Her heart kind of twisted. Really, did he think *she* could somehow teach *him*? Did she know any more about this love-and-forever thing than he did?

Maybe not.

But she certainly hadn't found love and forever *without* him.

And she wanted that. Wanted forever with the right man. Could that really be Deck?

Her fast-beating heart seemed to think so.

Yeah, she did fear that the third time around with him would *not* be the charm. But she was going there, anyway. She'd tried running away from her feelings for him. Tried it for years.

And yet, here she was, married to him. Staring up at the face that still haunted her dreams, daring to hope that maybe this time they would make it work.

"Sparky," he whispered prayerfully. "Say you'll give me—give *us*—this last chance."

She gulped hard. And nodded.

His gaze flared hot. "Was that a yes?"

Her heart seemed to have lodged hard in her throat. She managed a desperate little whimper of sound and nodded again.

He looked down at her like he could eat her right up. "Yeah?"

And, finally, the words came. "We'll, um, give it till Christmas to see if there's any hope that this marriage might work. But I want you to—"

"Come here." He reached down, clasped her wrist and hauled her up from the chair.

"Deck, wait, I..."

Of course he didn't wait. Instead, he stole the words from her lips by wrapping her tight in his powerful arms and slamming his mouth down on hers.

She gave it up. Her conditions could wait. It felt too good, the taste of his mouth, his body hard against her, the scent of him, clean with a hint of spice, filling her head. "Deck..."

"More." He breathed the demand against her parted lips.

She kissed him back, kissed him slow and sweet and achingly deep. Kissed him *more*.

But then he started tugging on her sweatshirt. "I want this off you."

"Wait."

"Uh-uh."

She pushed her shirt back down and then pressed her hands to his chest. "Not so fast."

His eyes were a smoky gray now, full of sexy promises she couldn't wait for him to keep. "You just said yes. We have to celebrate. Where's your bed, damn it?"

"First, you need to hear me out."

He muttered something low and grumpy followed by a gruff "What, then?"

"First of all, we're going to be married. *Really* married. And that means we're going to be together, *live* together."

"Works for me." He tried to grab her close again.

She kept her arms braced on his chest. "Here. At my place."

He scowled and looked around. "It's nice," he finally said grudgingly.

"And yet somehow you don't look happy about the idea of living here."

"Because we should live at my house. Yeah, it's a rental until my new house is finished. But it's great. You'll love it. It's bigger than this and there's land around it. We can hike up into the forest, visit Ice Castle Falls just like old times."

"We can stay here and still go hiking."

"McKellan's is open till two. What about the noise?"

"Oh, please. I ran the build on this loft. The sound-proofing is state-of-the-art—and don't think I don't know what you're doing. It's called control and you have to have it."

He only shrugged. "Letting other people run things is way overrated." With that, he scooped her up in his arms, turned around until he had his back to her chair and then dropped into it, taking her down with him.

Again, he tried to kiss her, but she didn't allow it. She managed to slip her fingers between his lips and hers. "We'll compromise and spend weekends at your place."

"Agreed—can I have my kiss now?"

"There's more."

"Kiss me first." His lips brushed her fingertips.

With a sigh, she let her hand drop and offered her mouth to him. He took it. For a sweet, endless moment, she surrendered to the pleasure he brought, let herself revel in the wet glide of his clever tongue, in the taste of him, hot and just a little bit minty, in the sheer deliciousness of simply being held by him.

Then she pushed at his chest again. "And we *are* telling my family."

That caught him by surprise. "You mean my evil plan to threaten you with telling all never even had a chance?"

"Not a prayer. I've been keeping what happened in Vegas to myself for a week now and I don't want to do that anymore. It just creates…distance, you know? Distance from the people I care about. If we're doing this, we are putting it all right out there—that you followed me to Vegas and I couldn't resist you."

He gave her a lazy grin. "Well, I can't say I mind the sound of that."

"Good. Because I plan to confess everything, that

I gave in to your killer charm and married you in a gorgeous silver wedding chapel. We're going to tell them the truth and then deal with any possible family fallout up front and honestly. None of it will be a secret. Not even the fact that it might not last past Christmas." She bent close for another kiss.

He caught her face between his hands. The playful, happy light had left his eyes. "Slow down."

She couldn't resist taunting him. Just a little. "Not a fan of telling it like it is?"

"I'm all for honesty."

"Yet you don't look too happy about telling everyone the simple truth."

"I just mean we don't have go crazy on this whole honesty thing."

"Well, *I* meant what I said. If we're doing it, we're owning it."

He spent several seconds glaring at her before his hard look softened. "Full disclosure. You sure, Nellie?" He stroked a finger down her cheek and along the side of her throat.

She sighed in pleasure at the simple touch. "Full disclosure, absolutely. And did I mention there will be endless holiday family events? They're pretty much constant from Thanksgiving to New Year's around here. Including two weddings—my mother's to Griff, and Rye and Meg's. As my husband, you will be expected to go with me to all of them."

"Yes." He said it with feeling. "I give in. Anything, Nell. However you want it."

"And there's your sister, too." She laid her palm against his cheek, felt his heat and the pleasant prickle of his beard scruff. "I want us to drive to Colorado

Springs, to visit her and her husband, bring some gifts for the baby."

"You got it."

"And, Deck, we need to talk about your dad."

The light left his eyes and his face turned blank. "What about him?"

"We need to get together with him. We need to tell him we're married and working on making the marriage a forever thing."

"That's completely unnecessary."

"He's your dad."

"I don't want you having anything to do with him."

"He's your *dad*."

"You keep saying that."

"Because it's true. I'm not just pretending he doesn't exist. Plus, you need to know that you can trust me around him, that I'm not going to be taken in by him again."

"I already know that."

"Great. Then we'll go visit him. Together. Or he can come here."

Now he wouldn't look at her. "You're being unreasonable."

She slid off his lap and stood staring down at him, wondering how she was going to get through to him. "Deck…"

He looked up at her then. "It's not your damn call, Nell. *You* make choices about *your* family and *I'll* decide about *mine*."

"But you keep track of him, don't you, and you see him now and again?"

"So?"

"I'm guessing you help him out when he gets in trouble?"

"You were always way too damn smart, you know that?"

"So that's a yes, then? You do keep an eye on him and you do help him out now and then."

"Because I'm a controlling SOB and we *both* know that. For some reason I don't understand and refuse to examine deeply, I feel responsible for him, for the messes he gets into and the people he screws over. I send him money to help him get by because it's the right thing to do—and because maybe the money I send will mean one less poor fool he takes advantage of. But that's it. I don't see him all that often and I don't want you around him."

She wanted to give in. But that just felt wrong to her, like they would be leaving a big barrier between them, a scary question from the past, still unanswered. "We're grown-ups now. He can't hurt us. He only has power over us if we give it to him."

"Pretty words." He got up and walked around her to the island that marked off the kitchen area. When he faced her again, he had one word for her. "No."

Should she give it up? She really wished she could make him understand. "Your dad was…a big thing… between us. He's why you left me, Deck—okay, maybe not all of it. But he was the final straw. A very big final straw."

"That's in the past."

"And that's why I want us to go see him together. I want us to have a new memory of dealing with him, one where we are together, united, one where we can be kind to him and include him, while, at the same time, there's no way he can touch what we have."

Deck gripped the counter behind him and leaned back against the island. The muscles of his broad chest and shoulders popped into sharp relief as they stretched the fabric of his knit shirt. "I don't need a new memory of dealing with my father."

"But I do."

He looked down at his boots and then slanted his glance up to her again. "Give it up, Nellie. I agreed to all of your other conditions. Just not this one. Let this one go."

"I don't know if I can."

His square jaw hardened. "So the deal's off if I won't take you to the old man?"

She didn't want it to be off. Now that she'd said yes, she had hope, burning like a bright flame inside her. She wanted to see if just maybe they had a future together, after all. She wanted that a lot. "Will you at least think about it? Please?"

"Nellie..." His rough, low voice raised a pleasured shiver down the backs of her knees, sent a buzz of need vibrating along her spine.

She tried again. "Think about it."

"Is it a deal breaker?"

"Do you have to have all the answers right this minute?"

He watched her from across the open space, his gaze dark, calculating. Then he asked again, "Is it a deal breaker?"

"If you just have to know now, then yes. I want us to see your dad together. Please."

The silence stretched between them. He refused

to give in on the subject of his dad and she had made her point. There was nothing more to say about it right now.

Finally, he pushed off the counter and stalked toward her, his hot gaze never leaving her face. She hardly knew what she felt—relief, frustration, growing desire?

When he stood before her again, she could feel the heat of him.

All the other emotions faded to gray. There was only desire—vivid, immediate. Only the pull between them, the wonder of wanting him so very much, of knowing that when he touched her, she would be all his.

Again. At last.

"Give me your hand, Sparky." She held it out. A slow grin tugged the corner of his mouth and that dimple appeared, the one that told her he felt good, easy in this moment. "Not that hand."

She giggled like some silly kid and gave him her left hand. He dug in a pocket and came up with diamonds. "You brought my rings." He slipped them both on her ring finger. They looked so beautiful. She couldn't help smiling dreamily down at them. "I do love them. I…kind of missed them."

He raised her fingers to his lips and kissed the tips of them, one by one. "Good. I have your dress and your shoes and those sexy satin shorts, too."

She glanced up into his waiting eyes. "It was extravagant of me to ask for that dress. It's not something I'll ever have a chance to wear again."

"Maybe in forty years, when we renew our vows?"

She laughed. "That is not the kind of dress I'm going to wear when I'm seventy."

"Or maybe our daughter will wear it for *her* wedding."

Could they really be those people—the ones with children who grew up and had weddings of their own? The ones who were still together as senior citizens? She put her hand on his chest, felt his heartbeat, strong and steady, beneath her palm. "I want this to work, Deck. I honestly do."

"It *will* work." He bent closer.

She lifted her face to him. The night to come shimmered in the air between them—*all* the nights. A lifetime of nights, she fervently hoped.

As his mouth covered hers, he scooped her high in his arms.

In her bedroom, he took a strip of condoms from his pocket before tossing his jeans to a chair.

She said, "I'm on the pill."

"Yeah?" The dimple appeared in the corner of his mouth and his eyes gleamed blue-green in the light from the bedside lamp.

"Yeah."

He volunteered, "I've always used condoms and, except for you and me in Las Vegas, I haven't been with anyone since the last time I was tested. It always came back negative."

"Me, too. On all counts."

He tossed the condoms over his shoulder. She whipped back the covers and he grabbed her around her waist, taking her down to the sheets with him.

They tumbled together, laughing and kissing, peeling off the last of their clothing.

The kisses got longer, deeper, wetter, the hunger building, the heat flaring higher.

She was on fire for him, so crazy, so eager. No one had ever felt the way he did in her arms, so big and hard and exactly right. The rightness mattered the most. The way he could thrill her and still make her feel that sense of belonging, of coming home. She wrapped her legs around him and he came into her, filling her in a hard, hot glide, pushing deeper still.

Surging up to meet him, she moaned way too loudly at the sheer glory of it. His name was the only word she knew and she chanted it, "Deck, Deck, Deck," over and over, until the sound of it felt like his heart beating under her touch, so strong and deep and sure.

He took her to the peak and on over it. Once, and again and again after that.

Later, they got up and went back out to the main room, Deck in his boxer briefs and Nell in her black sweatshirt and warm socks. They ate rocky-road ice cream straight from the carton, sharing the spoon, and then ended up on the sofa making love again, eventually falling asleep curled up tight with each other.

She woke well past midnight as he lifted her from the sofa and carried her back to the bed, where he set her on the edge of the mattress and helped her out of her sweatshirt. Then he eased her down to her pillow and pulled off her socks.

"Come to bed," she grumbled. And he did, wrapping himself around her, settling the covers up over them, nice and cozy. "Marriage isn't half bad," she murmured, as sleep crept up on her again.

He cupped her breast in one hand and nuzzled her neck. "Good night, Mrs. McGrath."

Mrs. McGrath. "Not bad at all…"

Rye called her cell at six thirty the next morning. With a sleepy groan, she untangled herself from Deck and grabbed the phone off the nightstand. "This better be good."

"That big Lexus LX of Deck's is down in the parking lot. Thought I should find out if you need rescuing."

The man in question yawned, scratched his cheek and then tried to reach for her.

She laughed and batted his hand away. "Too late. There's no rescuing me now. I've surrendered to the inevitable."

Deck mouthed, *Who is it?*

She whispered, "Rye."

Rye asked, "So what you're telling me is that he's with you and you're good with it?"

"That's right."

"Giving marriage a try, after all?"

Deck tried to tickle her. She swatted the rock-hard bulge of his shoulder and said to Rye, "Yes, we are. He'll be moving in here, so don't freak out if you see him entering my loft."

"As long as he's welcome there."

"He is. I'm giving him a key and the alarm code."

"Must be true love, after all."

"Well, we *are* married."

"All righty, then." She could hear the grin in Rye's voice. "You can go back to…whatever it was you were doing."

"Thanks, Rye." She ended the call.

Deck reached over and snatched the phone from her hand. She screeched in protest and a wrestling match ensued, one that ended with the phone on the floor somewhere and Deck making love to her again, a satisfying outcome for both of them.

A little while later, she brewed them coffee and scrambled some eggs and explained that she would talk to her sisters and her cousin Rory today. "Ideally, we can all five meet for lunch or something. If not, I'll find a way to get with each of them separately and explain everything."

He set down his coffee cup, his expression suddenly guarded. "Explain that we're married, you mean?"

"Yeah." She studied his face across the table. He didn't look happy. "You okay?"

"Fine." He didn't seem fine. He seemed like something was bugging him.

"Tomorrow's Thanksgiving," she said.

"I know what day tomorrow is."

He definitely had something on his mind. She considered prodding him again as to what. But no. When he was ready to share, she had no doubt he would. "Oh, and just so we're on the same page, dinner will be at Clara's. We'll need to be there at two. Is JC Barrels closed tomorrow?"

"Yeah."

"Can you bring whatever things you need back here tonight?"

"Sure."

"We'll spend tomorrow together and go to Clara's from here."

"Works for me." He ate a bite of eggs. "So why not just handle it tomorrow?"

"Handle what?"

"Telling your sisters. Everyone will be there at dinner tomorrow, right? We can tell them all then."

Men were kind of dense sometimes. "Except for my sisters. They need to know today."

He tipped his head to the side, studying her, like a burglar seeking points of entry into a house with a state-of-the-art alarm system. "For some reason, your sisters have to know before everyone else?"

"Yes, they do."

"And your mother? What about her?"

"God, no. We can tell her Thursday. She and Griff are coming to Clara's for dinner, too. It's a first and we're all feeling good about it. Ma's kind of the last family outlier to come back into the fold. Until this year, she's always begged off on the family Thanksgiving. She was feeling guilty, we all think, and rightfully so, after what she did to Sondra."

"Wait a minute. You can wait till tomorrow to tell your mom, but your sisters have to know *now*?"

And this is a big deal to you, why? she thought, but decided not to ask. For the sake of their new marriage, she tried for diplomacy. "It's about closeness. I'm close to my sisters. They're my girls, you know? They support me in whatever I do in life, no question. And they need to know from me, privately, before everyone else, that I'm married. It's bad enough I told Rye, Meg and James first. But today, I will explain everything to my sisters and they will be fine with it."

"Nellie, that makes no sense."

"Not to you, maybe."

"Just wait until tomorrow."

"Yeah, well." She ate a bite of toast, chewing it slowly, then enjoying a nice sip of coffee, after which she set her cup down with care. "That's not gonna happen."

"I want us to do it together."

It all came unpleasantly clear to her then. "So that you can control what gets said, am I right?"

He flashed her a look—annoyed, but maybe just a little abashed, too. Being Deck, he went with annoyed. "You're pissing me off."

"Welcome to married life. It's called compromise, Deck. And we're both going to be doing a lot of it— oh, and as for your fabled need for control? You'll have to let some of that go, I'm afraid. I promise to be patient with you. But, as for my sisters, I'm telling them today."

"I just might have to break into your closet and cut up some of your clothes." Elise narrowed her eyes and tried to sound threatening.

Nell was sitting next to her, so she threw an arm around her and planted a big kiss on her cheek. "Please don't hurt me, Leesie. I'm sorry I didn't tell you first."

Clara, Jody and their cousin Rory all laughed.

By some minor miracle, Nell's sisters and Rory had all been able to make it to lunch at the Sylvan Inn, a cozy restaurant just outside the town limits where the food was good and the atmosphere friendly. It was kind of the go-to lunch place for the five of them—and their sisters-in-law, too, on occasion. They tended to congregate here when important news needed sharing, when big decisions had to be made or life events required that they celebrate together.

Rory said, "Those rings are gorgeous." And everyone sighed in total agreement.

Then Jody said, "I have to ask…"

Nell nodded. "Yeah?"

"Well, you love the guy, right?"

"I do love him." Nell said it out loud and realized she hadn't said those all-important words to Deck, not this time around. She needed to remedy that, preferably soon.

"So then," said Jody, "why keep the option open for an after-Christmas divorce?"

Nell ate a French fry. "If you knew how hard it was for us to even get to this point, trust me, you wouldn't have to ask."

Clara frowned. "Jody's question is valid, though. I mean, now that you're married and you've come to realize that the love is there with him, why not go all in on it? Leaving the door open to divorce takes the focus off making it work."

Nell gave a slow nod. "I get that. I do. But *he's* the one who suggested we try it till Christmas."

Rory said, "He only did it to get you to give the marriage a chance, right?"

"Yeah. And I *want* to give it a chance. But I don't want him running all over me. I mean, the guy is relentless."

"We noticed." Elise got dreamy eyed. "I like that in a man." Everybody laughed. They all knew Leesie was thinking of her husband, Jed, who could give Deck some serious competition when it came to relentlessness.

Jody said, "So what you're telling us is, you're just not willing to give up the divorce option yet."

It was only the truth. "That's right."

Jody prompted, "Because…?"

"He… Well, he hurt me so deep when we were kids. And he did it twice. And I vowed to myself *never again*. I'm not all the way back from that yet. And he did manipulate me in Vegas—no, I wouldn't have married him if I didn't still want him, still *love* him. But he seduced me to the chapel, he truly did. And, as I said, Deck's the one who suggested the Christmas deadline in the first place, though I know he's not happy about it."

"Because he *loves* you." Jody hit her own forehead with the heel of her hand. "And he wants to stay married to you."

"I know. And he's made it painfully clear that he's not looking forward to having everyone know it could be over by New Year's."

"I get why he feels that way," said Clara. "I mean, really. Think about, Nellie. Nobody has to know that you're keeping your options open. It's not their business."

Elise grinned. "Well, except us. *We* have to know. We're your sisters and we have to have all the facts in order to give you the best advice when you need it."

Nell admitted, "Deck *would* be relieved if we didn't have to tell everyone that we made a deal to reevaluate our marriage on the day after Christmas."

Rory said, "Which means that if you just keep that part of it to yourselves, he'll appreciate that you considered his feelings in the matter."

"True. And he would also see that I'm willing to compromise to make things work between us."

"So...?" Jody made the word about five syllables long.

Nell gave it up. "So, all right then, tomorrow we'll tell the family that we got married in Vegas and we're deliriously happy together. And as for the rest of it, they don't need to know."

That night, Nell and Deck went down to McKellan's for burgers. Deck played pool in the back room with Rye for a while. Meg was behind the bar. Nell kept her company between customers.

Later, upstairs, Nell couldn't wait to get her new husband out of his clothes. They kissed their way to the bedroom, shedding clothing as they went. And when they got there, they fell to the bed together in a tangle of seeking hands and eager, endless kisses. They made love fast and hard and hungry—at first.

The second time was even better. They lay on their sides, joined, moving together slow and lazy and endlessly deep. She felt him all through her. He was branded on her heart, the one she'd loved and lost and somehow miraculously found again.

Afterward, he held her close, his breath warm against her cheek, his finger tracing his name among the flowers and dragonflies inked on her skin.

She said, "I saw Garrett this afternoon at the office."

"Let me guess. You told him we got married."

She waved her ring finger at him. Even with the bedside lamp turned down low, all those diamonds caught the light and glittered. "Well, I *was* wearing these…"

"What did you say to him?"

"Just that we got married in Vegas."

"What about full disclosure?"

"I didn't get into any of that."

"And when you told him we're married, Garrett said…?"

"Something along the lines of 'What the hell, Nellie?'"

"That's understandable."

"Yeah, given that I've been insisting for months that I wanted zero to do with you ever again. Not to mention, I've seen him practically daily since we got back from Las Vegas and never said a word about the wedding till today. But then he gave me a hug and said he was glad for us and he knew we'd be happy together. So that worked out."

"Well, all right, then. And how did it go with your sisters?"

"It was great and they were amazing."

He made a low, gruff sound. "Can you maybe be just a little more specific?"

She pulled away to her own pillow, plumping it a little, then snuggled down with a sigh. "They're happy for us—and about the full-disclosure thing? I've been rethinking that."

"You have?" He watched her face closely, as if scanning for clues.

She nodded. "I've been thinking about it and I've realized you're right. I mean, why tell people we're married and then turn right around and announce that it could end after Christmas? They won't know whether to congratulate us or say how sorry they are that it might not work out."

Something happened in his eyes—a softening. Or maybe just relief. "Yeah?"

"Yeah."

He reached out and guided a loose curl behind her ear. "I think I really like being married to you."

She was tempted to indulge in a little lecture on the topic of compromise, maybe get on him again about the two of them going to see his dad—but then, it didn't all have to be one long negotiation. Sometimes you just did what the other person wanted because giving in made you both happy.

And she did feel happy now. Really happy. Just to be lying here in her bed with him, the way married people do.

Instead of launching into a lecture, she asked softly, "So tomorrow at dinner, you want to be the one to make the announcement?"

"I do, yeah." His fingers eased under the veil of her hair. He rubbed the back of her neck, and she sighed in pleasure just to feel his touch. When he gave a tug, she moved in close to him again. He pressed those warm, supple lips to her temple. "Anything specific you want me to say?"

"Nope. It's all yours."

"You trust me, huh?"

Did she? Well, she was definitely working on that, and now was not the time to play it too cautious. Now, she needed to give her all for this life they'd agreed to try to build together.

She tipped her head back enough for a slow, tender kiss. And she whispered, with feeling, "Yes, Deck. I trust you. I do."

Chapter Seven

As soon as they got in the door of Clara Bravo Ames's rambling old Victorian house the next day, Deck knew that his announcement of their sudden marriage would only be a formality. Not only had Nell already told her sisters, her cousin, her brothers James and Garrett, and Ryan and Meg, she was wearing her rings. Females of the species seemed to have radar for sparkly rings—even little girls.

Deck had barely had time to hand Clara the excellent bottle of Zinfandel he'd brought before Darius Bravo's eight-year-old stepdaughter, Sylvie, came flying down the stairs with Quinn Bravo's seven-year-old, Annabelle, right behind her.

"Hi, Aunt Nell!" Sylvie chirped.

"Hey, Sylvie. Annabelle. Love those dresses." Both girls were done up in velvet jumpers with lace-collared, puff-sleeved shirts underneath and bright bows in their hair.

Sylvie grabbed Nell's hand and squealed in delight. "Aunt Nellie, these rings are bee-ootiful!"

Nell gazed down at her fondly. "Thanks. I love them, too."

"Did you get *married*?" Sylvie's big eyes widened even more as she shifted her gaze from Nell to Deck. "Is this your *husband*?"

"Why, yes, honey. He is. This is Declan, but we all call him Deck." Nell wrapped her hand around his arm and grinned up at him, causing the usual tangle of heady sensations—happiness, frustration that he could still lose her, an ever-present undercurrent of desire.

It had always been like this for him, with her. He wanted her so much, the feeling overwhelmed him. For a guy who liked to have things under control, she was kind of a bad choice. And not only because nobody told Nell Bravo what to do.

From that first day in sophomore English class, when she'd turned around in her chair and blown his mind straight out the top of his head with nothing more than a smile, she was everything. He couldn't keep his cool with her. He lost all objectivity.

It hadn't been like that with Kristy. His first wife had seemed so much more his type. She'd been willing to let him make most of the decisions. She was gentle and sweet and understanding. Kristy had been perfect.

She just wasn't Nell. He'd had to face the bleak fact that Nell owned whatever shriveled sliver of a heart he had. So he'd managed the impossible and earned himself another chance with her.

He was not going to blow it this time.

Sylvie chattered away. "My teacher, Miss Delshire, just got married. She's *Mrs.* Ankerly now. And she has pretty rings, too—but not as pretty as yours."

"Let me see, let me see!" demanded Annabelle, who was not only Quinn's daughter, but also Sylvie's BFF.

Deck knew them all, every Bravo in Justice Creek, including kids, dogs, cats, whatever. When he'd mounted his months-long campaign to win Nell back, he'd made it his business to learn everything he could about everyone in her family.

"Aunt Nell! They're so pretty!" Annabelle cried.

Then the two girls put their heads together. Sylvie whispered something and they both giggled, apparently delighted. When they pulled apart, they gazed up at him solemnly.

"Are you our uncle now?" asked Sylvie.

"Yes, he is," said Nell.

"Nice to meetcha, Uncle Deck," the two said, pretty much in unison. One and then the other, the girls offered him their soft little hands. He gave each one a careful shake.

Giggling again, they ran back up the stairs.

"This way." The doorbell was ringing as Nell pulled him into a large bedroom off the entry hall, where coats and wool scarves were piled high on the bed.

"Come here." He guided her around in front of him, took off her pink wool hat and tossed it onto the bed.

She gave a low chuckle as he unwound her pink scarf. Her eyes were as clear and green as perfect emeralds right then, and her cheeks were rosy from the cold outside. And then there was the incomparable sweet scent of her. She took him by the collar of his coat and pulled him closer, whispering, "I can do that myself, you know."

He tossed the scarf on the pile of outerwear somewhere in the general vicinity of the hat. "But I love helping you out of your clothes."

Her lush mouth was right there, too tempting to resist. He captured those soft lips. She sighed and opened for him. As always, she tasted every bit as good as she smelled.

"Well, I have to say, this is very encouraging," said a woman's voice from somewhere close behind him.

Nell stiffened in his arms. Reluctantly, he released her and turned to face Willow and her fiancé, Griffin Masters. They must have just arrived. Both were pink cheeked from the cold outside and wearing heavy coats.

"Happy Thanksgiving, Ma," Nell said with a slightly forced little smile. She nodded at Willow's fiancé as she unbuttoned her coat. "Hey, Griff."

Griffin, a tall, white-haired guy, still handsome and fit at around sixty, said, "Good to see you, Nell." He turned to Deck. "Declan, right? I think we met at McKellan's once."

Deck clasped the other man's hand and opened his mouth to say something cordial and generic. But before he got the words out, Willow gasped.

"Nellie!" she cried as Nell tossed her coat onto the pile. "Is that a *wedding* ring?"

Nell made a low, impatient sound. "Ma. Will you settle down?"

"But…you didn't say a word. I can't believe you're…" Willow sent a wild-eyed glance at Deck. "I mean that you two finally…" Willow was actually sputtering and, from everything Deck had heard about her, she never sputtered. Then she seemed to shake herself. She braced her hands on her hips. "All right. Let me see that ring. Let me see it this instant."

"Ma, come on. You're acting really strange."

"Give me your hand."

Nell gave in and held it out.

Willow grabbed it with a long, dramatic sigh. "Beautiful. Just beautiful." She hauled Nell close and hugged her tight. "Oh, darling. At last. I'm so happy for you, because I know you've found *your* happiness. And that is all I want for my children."

Nell met Deck's eyes over her mother's shoulder. Her gorgeous face showed him everything. Her mom drove her crazy, but the love was there, too. "Thanks, Ma."

Willow took Nell by the shoulders. "When?" She shot a confused glance over Nell's shoulder at Deck. "How?"

"In Las Vegas," said Nell. "Deck swept me off my feet."

"Las Vegas! But that was a week and a half ago."

Nellie got that narrow-eyed, don't-mess-with-me look. "That's right. And your point is?"

"But I had no clue. What is going on?"

"Nothing."

"That's not true. You were already married when you came over to get on my case for telling Deck where to—"

"So?" Nell's lip curled, but not in a smile. Deck read her like an all-caps text. She was about to say something to her mother that she would later regret.

Deck saved her from herself by clasping Willow's arm. "Hey. Don't I get a hug, too?"

Willow blinked—and took the hint. "Oh, yes, you do." He pulled her close. She whispered, "Well done," before he let her go. And when Griffin moved behind her to help her off with her coat, she faced her daughter with her usual serene smile. "However it all came together, I am so happy for you, my darling. I know the two of you are going to have a splendid life because you are and always have been so very right for each other. And I wish you all the joy in the world."

"Thanks, Ma," Nell replied, equally gracious now. "I'm glad you're here, you and Griff. It's nice to have the whole family together for Thanksgiving."

An hour and a half later, they sat down to dinner.

To accommodate so many Bravos, Clara had brought in two extra tables and arranged the seating in a U shape, with an extra table a few feet away for the kids. There was turkey and ham and just about every side dish imaginable. Dalton, Clara's husband, said a short, simple grace after which they all settled in to eat too much and drink really nice wine.

By then, there was no one in the family who didn't already know that Nell had married him in Vegas and he'd moved in with her at her loft. He didn't really need to make a speech about it.

Still, it felt right to say something. After the big meal was over and the coffee and pumpkin pie had been served, he tapped his spoon on his water glass, picked up the last of his wine and pushed back his chair. A hush settled over the table—except for Jody's baby, Marybeth, who slapped her little hands on her high-chair tray and let out a string of cheerful nonsense syllables.

Deck winked at the baby. "Exactly, Marybeth. I couldn't have said it better myself." A ripple of laughter flowed around the table. Deck said, "By now, I doubt there's a single person in this room who doesn't already know that a miracle happened in Las Vegas Sunday before last." He glanced down at Nell beside him. Her eyes shone clear green and those lush lips curved up in a hint of a grin. "Nell said yes. And I rushed her right to the altar before she could change her mind." He raised his glass. "To all of you at this table, thank you for putting up with me the last few months. I know it wasn't easy." There was more laughter. "And I'm sure many of you have wondered when I would finally give up the chase. But the thing is, I couldn't. Because there is only one woman for me. I know I blew it so bad before—twice. But this time, I promise you, I'm going to get this right. Nellie, here's to you." Her smile went full-out and she blushed the most perfect shade of pink. "Thank you for making me the happiest man alive." He drank the last of his wine and sat down again as the Bravos around him laughed and applauded.

Nellie leaned close and gave him a sweet, swift kiss. He was right where he wanted to be, at her side.

Now, if they could only make it last past Christmas.

That weekend, he took her to visit the new house her company was building for him. The exterior walls were up and finished, the roof on, windows and doors installed.

Outside a light snow was falling as they walked through the framed-out, wall-less rooms wearing their heavy coats, hats, boots and warm gloves. He described some of the planned finishes and the rustic chandelier he'd already chosen for the two-story entry.

"Anything you want to add or change," he coaxed, "just say it and consider it done." He was kind of hoping she might make a few suggestions. That would mean she could see herself living here.

She said only that she thought what he had planned sounded perfect.

In the wide-open space that would soon be the kitchen, she asked, "So, last I heard from Garrett, we're on schedule for completion in March, right?" Her breath plumed in the icy air.

He perched on a paint-spattered sawhorse and pulled her up nice and close. "Yeah. Move-in ready second week of March, barring any number of possible holdups."

"Shh. Never say that out loud. Talk about tempting fate." She swayed toward him and he hooked his gloved hands at the small of her back. Even through her down coat, he felt her soft breasts and the perfect inward curve of her waist. She tipped that pretty chin up to him. "I like it here. It has a very open feel."

He kissed the tip of her nose. "Are you saying you think we should just forget about putting in actual walls?"

She laughed. The sound reached down inside him and warmed him up better than a nice, cozy fire. And then she said sincerely, "I think it's going to be beautiful."

Will you be moving in here with me? he thought, but didn't let himself ask. Again he reminded himself that there would be plenty of time to work it all out once they got through Christmas and made it past the deadline.

The deadline.

It bugged him more with every hour that went by. Why had he even offered it? He wanted to renegotiate— more than renegotiate. He wanted to make it go away.

But every time he got close to asking her to forget the damn deadline, he would remind himself that he'd be better off to chill a little, put his focus on making the next month a good one, giving her a holiday season to remember and several weeks' worth of marriage she couldn't bear to walk away from.

If he could manage that, December twenty-six would take care of itself.

That night he took her out to dinner at a nice little place called Mirabelle's. From there, they went on to his 4000-square-foot rented house on two acres of wooded land a couple of miles from town.

She set her overnight bag on his king-size platform bed in the master suite and whistled in approval. "This place is gorgeous. If I didn't know how fabulous your new house is going to be, I would wonder why you didn't just buy this one."

"I'm extravagant," he confessed, and dragged her down across the bed with him.

She stroked her fingertips lightly into the hair at his temple and traced the shape of his ear. It felt so good— her touch, her scent, her body just barely brushing along his. "You worked hard for it." She gave him a light, sweet peck of a kiss. "Might as well enjoy it."

He went ahead and busted himself. "I probably would have bought this one. But the goal was to get close to you. Hiring you to build my house seemed like a surefire way to get a little face time, at least."

"And then I just handed you off to Garrett."

"Really pissed me off."

"But you went ahead with the new house, anyway."

"Yeah, well. By then I'd hired an architect and he'd come up with the design. It was everything I'd asked for—and more. I fell in love with it and I wanted it."

She dipped her head even closer and brushed a kiss against the side of his throat, her lips so soft, just right. Like everything about her. "Because you demand the best, right?"

"You bet I do."

"*We're* the best—Garrett and me. So you got your house and we got your business. Everybody wins."

He captured her mouth—and right then his phone, which he'd dropped on the nightstand next to the bed, started playing a series of beeping sounds.

She pulled back. "R2-D2?"

"It's my sister. She always loved *Star Wars*, so…"

"Cute." She gave him that grin, the one that made him want to help her out of her clothes.

He sat up and grabbed the phone. "Marty. Hey."

"Hey, Deck…" She sounded strange. Apprehensive, maybe?

"What's happened?" he demanded. Nell, still stretched out across the bed, frowned up at him, looking worried now.

At Marty's end of the line, the baby cried. "Hold on a minute." Her voice retreated and he heard her soothing little Henry. "It's okay, sweetie. It's okay…" He realized about then that he hadn't told his sister that he'd married Nell. As he considered how to break the news, Marty came back on the phone. "Deck, I got a call from the hospital in Fort Collins."

He knew then. *Keith McGrath strikes again.* "Dad."

"He fell down some concrete stairs at that apartment complex he manages." A litany of bad words bounced through his brain. Marty went on, "They took him to Fort Collins Memorial."

"Is he dead?" Okay, that was a little too cold and abrupt. Nell's eyes widened in alarm. He brushed a hand down her arm to soothe her.

"No, Deck," his sister said in a chiding tone. "He's not dead."

Nell's frown had only deepened. He stretched out on his side facing her again and mouthed, *He's okay*, though he really didn't know yet what condition Keith was in.

Marty said, "He's got a bump on the head and some bruising. They're keeping him overnight for observation, but he's conscious. He gave them my number as next of kin." The baby fussed some more. He heard her making soft, cooing noises to settle him down.

Deck got the picture. Either he went or Marty would. He sat up for the second time and swung his legs over the edge of the bed. Nell sat up, too. She scooted in close to him.

She would want to go with him.

No way. He wanted her nowhere near his father. Keith McGrath had supposedly changed his ways the last couple of years, but Deck wasn't about to give him another chance to mess things up with Nellie.

Marty said, "Hank's going to drive me up there."

Not happening. "You're three hours away with a baby to take care of. I'm closer. I'll go."

"But I—"

"Don't argue. I'll leave right away." He felt Nell shift beside him but didn't look at her. "I'll call you from the hospital as soon as I've got the whole story."

He heard Hank's voice on Marty's end, though he couldn't make out the words.

Marty said, "Okay."

Deck wasn't sure which of them she was talking to. "Couple of hours, tops," he promised, "and I'll have more information for you. I'm sure he's going to be fine." Because one way or another, Keith always made it through to mess up again.

"Be gentle with him, Deck. I mean it. He fell and hurt himself. He's doing his best now, staying out of trouble. And he's getting old."

"I will be gentle," he parroted, gritting his teeth a little.

"And call me as soon as you know what's going on."

"Got it. Will do." He ended the call.

Nell's hand settled over his. He realized he still hadn't told Marty they were married. But that was the least of his problems right now.

Five minutes ago, life had seemed just about perfect. Now he had an hour-plus drive ahead of him, and his dad to deal with at the end of it.

He twined his fingers with Nell's, turned to meet her waiting eyes and told her straight out, "My dad's been hurt. I'm not sure of the details, but he fell down some stairs. He's at the hospital in Fort Collins and I have to drive up there and take care of whatever needs doing."

She watched his face closely, worry darkening her eyes to bottle green. "But is he okay?"

"I think so. He's a little banged up, Marty said, and he hit his head. But he's going to be all right."

The tension between her brows eased a little. "That's good."

"Yeah." The word had kind of a bitter taste in his mouth.

"Well, then." She squeezed his hand and started to stand. "Let's get going." He didn't move. After a second, she sank back down beside him. "What's going on? Talk to me."

He caught her face between his hands. "Listen…"

Her gaze searched his. And she knew. "Uh-uh. You're not leaving me here. I'm going with you, Deck." Her voice was satin over steel.

"No. That's no good. Just let me handle this and we can—"

"Stop." She ducked from his touch and stood. "This is what I was talking about. This is where you don't let me in."

He rose, too. "Look. I have to get going. We can hash it all out when I get back."

"The whole point of being married is that we support each other, that we're *there* for each other."

"That's fine. I get it. I do. But, right now, I have to go."

"It's not fine in the least." She let out a hard huff of breath. "You're shutting me out, blowing me off."

"How many ways can I say it, Nell?" His voice was colder than he'd meant it to be. But why wouldn't she take a damn hint? "We will talk this over later."

A low growl of frustration escaped her. She glared at him for a hot count of five. Then she wrapped her arms around herself, whirled and stalked to the floor-to-ceiling windows that dominated the room. During the day, they offered a gorgeous view of the mountains. Now, though, they showed only a dark reflection of the bedroom and the ghostly shadow of the moon outside. For a moment, she simply stood there, staring at the shadows in the window. Then she spun back to face him. "I'm not happy with this."

Would she be long gone when he got back?

Bet on it.

Would he really blame her if she left? No. But he couldn't stand the thought of her near his father. And he knew where to find her if she walked out.

He would make it all up to her. Somehow. After he finished dealing with Keith. "I promise you," he said as gently as he could. "I'll make this as quick as I can."

"How quick you make it isn't the issue."

"Nellie. Come on. I can't deal with this now. I have to go."

She turned to the dark window again, leaving him staring at her rigid back. He didn't know what to say to make it better. The only way to do that would be to give in and take her with him.

Not going to happen.

He stuck his phone in his pocket and headed for the door.

Chapter Eight

Nell bit her lip to keep from calling after him.

She stared blindly out the dark window, keeping her arms wrapped tightly around herself as a way to hold herself in place, to keep from racing down the stairs after him, yelling at him to stop being an idiot and let her the hell in, let her support him when he needed her, let her *be* there for him as a wife should.

Marriage.

She had no idea how to do it. But she'd lived through a lot of yelling and carrying on between her mother and father when she was little—no, Ma and her dad weren't married at the time, but they'd shared a house whenever he wasn't with Sondra. And they had a family together. And the way they went at each other, well, even a little girl could tell that was no way to say *I love you*.

So, terrific.

Deck was leaving without her. She didn't have to like it, but she pretty much had to accept it. He didn't want her with him because he didn't want her near his troublemaking father. And that made no sense at all to her. Hadn't he noticed that they were all grown-ups now? She, at least, was fully capable of not letting one poor old man mess with her head.

Deck, though? Apparently not so much.

She stood very still, listening, and heard a door close downstairs. A few minutes later, faintly, she heard him drive away. About then, she realized she'd ridden out here with him and didn't have her truck.

Very bad words did an angry dance through her brain. Because, yeah, she was mad enough at him right then to want to be long gone when he got back.

It was after ten at night. No way would she call up someone in the family to come to her rescue. Maybe an Uber.

She got out her phone—and then just didn't have the heart to call for that car. Instead, she plunked the phone on the nightstand next to a framed picture of her and Deck at the Gardenia Chapel. They were standing in front of that curtain of shimmery crystal beads, she in her white mermaid gown and he in his rented tux. They looked deliriously happy. Sex and champagne will do that to people.

When she'd first spotted it there on the nightstand, she'd been touched that he'd thought to have it framed, that he'd put it by his bed.

Now, she felt sorely tempted to grab it and slap it facedown and not even care if she ended up cracking the glass.

But no. Her husband might be an idiot when it came

to his father, but that didn't give her a free pass to bust up his stuff.

She returned to the window again.

Outside, it had started to snow. She watched the snowflakes blow against the glass and her fury calmed a little, enough that she couldn't help hoping that Deck would drive carefully and that his dad really would be all right.

It was snowing steadily when Deck parked in the lot at Fort Collins Memorial.

Flipping up the collar of his heavy winter jacket, he jogged to the entrance. The wide glass doors slid open automatically. The woman at the front desk said he should have a seat in the waiting area, that the doctor who had treated Keith would come to speak with him soon.

He took a chair and called Marty to let her know he'd made it to the hospital and would call her back as soon as he'd consulted with the doctors and had a chance to see Keith. When he hung up with Marty, he thought about calling Nell. But a phone call wouldn't fix anything, and they could be interrupted at any moment.

However, he *had* left her stranded at his house. Yeah, he wanted to keep her there, to have her waiting for him when he got back so he could make it all up to her.

Somehow.

But trapping her at his house was just plain wrong, and he supposed he'd been a big enough douche to her tonight already.

Plus, the lack of a vehicle wouldn't keep Nell anywhere she didn't want to be. One way or another, if she wanted to leave, she would go.

So he settled on a quick text in which he provided the alarm code for the house, explained where to find the extra house key and the key to the Land Rover in the garage.

She texted back, Thank you. My best to your dad. Drive safe.

Civil. Innocuous, even. Still, her current frustration with him came through loud and clear.

He started a reply. I'm sorry. I just...

It was as far as he got. Explaining himself by text wasn't going to cut it. Better to leave it alone for now.

He put the phone away and wished he were anywhere but there. The minutes ticked by as he watched the lady at the desk hang tinsel and shiny little ornaments on a two-foot fake tree she'd set up on one end of the long counter. She hummed happily along to piped-in holiday tunes. Not even December yet and already Pentatonix sang "White Christmas" everywhere he went.

"White Christmas," my ass, he thought, completely Scrooge-like and unrepentant about it. It had better not get too damn white out there or he'd have trouble driving home.

"Declan McGrath?" A woman in blue scrubs beckoned him. He got up and went to her. "I'm Dr. Farris. Your father is resting comfortably. He's going to be fine. He has a concussion, some bruising and various minor contusions."

"What happened?"

"He tripped over a mop bucket he was taking down a flight of stairs."

Oh, I'll just bet. "Right."

A tiny frown crinkled the space between the doctor's dark eyebrows. Okay, he'd sounded pretty damn cynical. Probably because he was. Keith McGrath had fallen down stairs before. Somehow, that always happened when people he owed money to got tired of waiting for him to pay up.

Dr. Farris asked, "Are you implying there's something more sinister going on here? Do you somehow suspect that your father has been attacked? I did examine him. And I'm telling you honestly that his injuries *are* consistent with a fall."

Deck got the message. She was the doctor. She would be the one to know if Keith's injuries had been caused by something other than a fall. And he really should stop assuming the worst—at least until he'd checked on Keith and found out if he'd been up to his old tricks. Deck shook his head. "No. Sorry. I'm sure you're right."

The doctor regarded him sharply for several seconds and then went on, "Your father is coherent and resting comfortably. Barring any unforeseen complications, we're expecting to release him tomorrow."

"I would like to see him now."

"Of course. This way." She led him through a set of heavy doors and down two intersecting hallways to a room across from a nurses' station. The door was shut. When she pushed it open, the room beyond was dark. Dr. Farris turned back to Deck and whispered, "He's sleeping."

"It's all right. I'll just go in and wait."

The doctor left and Deck entered the shadowed room. He took off his coat, draped it over the bedside chair and sat down. As his eyes adjusted, he watched the sleeping man on the bed and listened to the soft sounds made by the various machines.

Keith, who'd grown thin and wiry as he aged, lay on his back, his face with its crooked beak of a nose turned away, a bandage in his gray hair. He'd banged up an elbow and had a scrape on one arm.

Eventually, he turned his head and opened his eyes. "Declan." He gave a dry little chuckle. "What a surprise."

"You had them call Marty," Deck accused.

"She's nicer to me than you. Marty still loves her old dad."

"She's got a newborn, Dad. Have a little damn consideration."

Keith made a snorting sound—and then flinched. "Hurts like a son of a bitch. They won't give me anything but Tylenol because it's my head." He shut his eyes. A sigh escaped him. "I know what you're thinking. You're wrong. I wrestled a damn mop bucket on concrete stairs. The bucket won."

Deck found himself buying that story now. People Keith ripped off tended to do more damage to his face. "Okay."

His dad opened his eyes again. He stared at Deck, his thin mouth set. Defiant.

"Dad. Go back to sleep."

"You just gonna sit there and watch me?"

"Go to sleep."

Keith let out another tired sigh, but said nothing more. A few minutes later, his eyes drifted shut.

When Deck was sure he'd gone back to sleep, he went out to the waiting area, called Marty and reported that Keith was doing great and they would be checking him out of the hospital in the morning. She said she would be there. He insisted that there was no point in her driving all the way to Fort Collins. He would take care of Keith, make sure the old man had everything he needed.

Marty came, anyway.

The next morning, right after the day-shift doctor had told Keith he could go home, she arrived with Hank and the baby. She handed the baby to her husband and bent over the bed to give the old man a kiss. "How you doin', Dad?"

"Everything hurts," Keith grumbled. "Even my hair." Fondly, Marty patted his shoulder. He asked, "How's my girl?"

"I'm fine, Dad. Never better."

"Let me see my handsome grandson." Hank brought the baby close again and Keith said what a good-looking kid he was.

Deck stood by the window and watched the old man interact with Marty and her family. Really, Keith seemed like your average, everyday granddad, a little goofy for the grandbaby and straight up fond of his daughter. Deck knew he probably ought to give the old man a break now and then. Keith had been behaving himself for a couple of years now, keeping his nose clean since that last stint at Buena Vista for check kiting.

Still, Deck just didn't trust him. He doubted that

he ever would. Maybe, though, he could at least make an effort to be nicer to the guy.

As for bringing Nellie to see him...

His gut knotted up just thinking about it. Uh-uh. He didn't want her anywhere near him. Yeah, okay, he might as well be honest with himself, at least. He might as well admit that he wasn't rational about this. What harm, really, could his dad do to Nellie? No way would she be taken in by Keith a second time.

It was just that Keith had played his smarmy, low-down tricks on her, convinced her what a good guy he was and that all he needed was a few thousand bucks to turn everything around. It generally worked on people when Keith pulled that crap, mostly because Keith believed it himself. And it had worked on Nellie. Keith had shamed Deck to the core, messing with Nellie like that. That betrayal had cut deeper than all the other ways the old man had screwed up as a father.

Deck had never been able to forgive Keith for taking Nellie's money. He doubted he ever would.

Marty, tired circles under her big brown eyes and her butterscotch hair pinned up in a messy bun, came toward him. "Hey, sourpuss, give your little sister a hug."

He pulled her close. She smelled of milk and baby lotion. "You didn't need to come," he whispered in her ear.

"Too late. Already here—now come on, let's get Dad back home."

Marty and Hank drove Keith back to his apartment at the complex he managed.

Deck stayed behind to make sure the hospital bill

came to him. Outside, the snow had stopped. It hadn't piled up much. The roads would be clear. He couldn't wait to get home, find Nellie wherever she'd run off to and make it up with her.

But it wouldn't be right to leave Marty to handle everything on her own.

So he went to Keith's place to help get him settled in. Keith comanaged the building, working with a couple, Dale and Ginny Hill, who had the apartment next to his. The Hills promised they would look in on him and that they could manage fine around the building while he recovered.

Ginny patted Keith's shoulder downright fondly. "You'll be back in your workshop in no time."

Keith nodded. "That's my plan, Gin." He had a shed on the property where he made children's furniture, toys and planter boxes that he sold at local farmers markets and craft fairs.

Marty walked Deck out to his car when he left. As she stood there shivering in the cold, he realized he'd yet to tell her about him and Nellie.

"Hop in," he said. "I'll turn on the heater."

She climbed in on the passenger side. He got the heat going and tried to figure out how to break the big news. "A couple of things…"

"Don't start, okay?" Frowning, she fiddled with her hair, pulling a bobby pin out of her bun and sticking it back in again. "I really do think he just fell down the stairs."

"It's not about that."

Marty gave him the side-eye. "So…you believe it really was just an accident?"

"Yeah."

And his sister smiled full out. "Hallelujah. He *believes*."

"It's hardly a miracle."

"Maybe not to you."

He gave her a look of infinite patience and said, "We both know if he's having trouble managing on his own, he's most likely to call you. And you'll be calling him constantly, checking on him."

She made a wrap-it-up motion with her hand. "So, and…?"

"He seems to be doing pretty well at the moment. But if you think he needs a nurse or something, let me know, okay? I'll find him one."

"Aw." Her eyes got suspiciously dewy.

"What are you making cooing sounds about now?"

"Well, it's just, I know you're not past all your issues with him, but you're good to him, anyway. It's one of the many things I love about you."

He reached across and pulled her close for a quick half hug. When he let her go, she grabbed for the door handle. "Oh, and, Marty, one other thing…" She waited, her eyes expectant. "I got married two weeks ago."

Marty's mouth dropped open. And then she reached across the console and punched him in the shoulder.

"Hey! Knock it off."

She put her hands to her head as though in fear her brain might explode. "What is the *matter* with you? You run your own company, you're a big, fat success. To do that, you *have* to have a pretty good idea of how to deal with people. But when it comes to the ones who love you, you have your head right up your butt. Two weeks you've been married and not a single word to your own sister?"

He winced. "Sorry. You're right. I should have called."

"Oh, you bet you should have. Who is she? Do I know her?"

"It's Nell."

Her eyes got as wide as bar coasters. "Bravo?" At his nod, she burst out, "Seriously? Nell? After all these years? I can't believe she'd ever have anything to do with you again. I mean, I was three years behind you in school, but everybody knows how you wrecked her when you dumped her flat."

"I was an idiot."

"Yes, you were. You *loved* that girl."

"Yeah. And after it didn't work out with Kristy, I finally had to face the fact that I'd never gotten over Nell."

"And she actually gave you another chance?"

"Well, I was pretty persistent." Understatement of the decade, not that he really wanted to get into how long and how hard he'd had to keep after Nell to get her to give him a break. Marty would probably have a good laugh about that.

His little sister used to be so shy and quiet. But since she'd met Hank and things started working out for her, she'd grown more confident, more willing to speak up about whatever she had on her mind. Most of the time, Deck thought that was great.

Right this minute, though? Not exactly.

Marty stared out the windshield, eyes far away. "Nell Bravo. Wow. Just wow. I mean, never in a million years…" Her voice wandered off, which was fine with him. He didn't need a long detour down memory lane. Marty's bun bounced as she turned his way again. "Tell me all about it."

"Uh. We got married in Vegas. It was sudden. We're still kind of, you know, working stuff out."

"What stuff?"

Stuff like whether or not we'll be together by New Years. "God, you are nosy."

She bopped him on the shoulder again. "Bring her to see us—or we'll come to you."

"Well, I was kind of working my way around to that. Nell wants to get together with you, too. Maybe next weekend? You've got the baby, so we'll come down there. I'll check with her and give you a call."

"Okay, now I'm starting to feel kind of happy. You and Nell." Marty's smile bloomed wide. "Don't you just love it how sometimes in life, things work out exactly as they should, after all?"

Marty stood waving and grinning as he drove away.

Deck pulled the Lexus out of the apartment complex lot, went around the block and parked on the next street over. He needed to call Nell and he was nervous about it. Even on a hands-free call, he wouldn't be paying the road enough attention, so he pulled over before he took out his phone.

Did he expect her to answer?

Not really.

Shocked the hell out of him when she picked up on the first ring. "About time you called."

His heart performed some impossible feat in the cage of his chest. Just the sound of her voice did a number on him. Was he a hopeless fool in love? Yeah, and likely to remain so no matter what happened on December twenty-six. "Hey, Sparky."

She made a low, grumbling sound. "I probably shouldn't even be speaking to you."

But she *was*. And that eased the knot in his gut a little, loosened the band of tension around his chest. Suddenly he could breathe again. "Where are you?"

"Oh, no," she scoffed. "I picked up the phone, which we both know is more than you deserve after the way you left. I think that entitles me to get my questions answered first. We can start with the one you just asked me. Where are you?"

He could see her as though she were right there in the car with him—green eyes flashing, that mouth of hers just begging for a scorching-hot kiss. Longing sizzled through him. "I'm still in Fort Collins, but I'm about to head home."

"Your dad? How is he?"

"He's a little banged up, but it looks like he'll be okay. They released him from the hospital and he's back at his apartment now."

"Well. I'm so glad he's all right." She must have realized her tone had softened, because she added more sharply, "But I'm *not* happy in the least about the way you walked out on me."

"I'm sorry."

She let several seconds crawl by before she spoke. "When are we going *together* to see your dad?"

Never. "Can we talk about that later?"

Another silence. And then she conceded with a tired little sigh. "I suppose."

At least she was letting it go for the time being. He relaxed in his seat a little. "Marty and Hank drove up, too. They brought the baby. I told her we got married. She's happy for us. She wants us all to get together. I was thinking we could drive down to Colorado Springs for a visit. A day trip, next weekend maybe— you don't have to decide now. Think it over."

"It should be doable." Her voice was soft again.

He couldn't stop himself from asking, "So then, have you forgiven me?"

"Don't push it, Declan. Come home. We'll talk some more."

He grinned. It felt damn good. "Home meaning…?"

"I'm at your house."

The gray day seemed blindingly bright all of a sudden, full of promise and hope. "Stay right there. I'm on my way."

She greeted him at the door in a long purple sweater, black leggings and soft boots, her red hair sleek on her shoulders. He didn't think he'd ever seen anything as beautiful as Nellie making herself right at home in his house.

She frowned up at him. "You look exhausted."

"It was a long night. I slept in a chair in his hospital room."

Her expression softened. "You're a good son."

"I only went because Marty would have gone if I didn't—and then she drove up anyway, even though I told her she didn't need to."

"A good son *and* a good brother."

He stepped forward and she stepped back. So much for a hello hug, damn it. He shut the door behind him and put on his sad face. "Don't I get a welcome-home kiss for being so good to my dad and my sister?"

She tipped her head to the side and her hair tumbled down her left shoulder, fire red, shining so bright. He couldn't wait to get his hands in it. "Hmm. There's still the little problem of how you took off without me."

"Please?" He tried to look contrite—not for refusing to take her to see his dad. He would say no to that again in a heartbeat. But for having to run off and leave her alone. He did feel regret for that.

"You have no shame." She tried to look severe, but didn't quite pull it off.

He reached for her.

She let him catch her and couldn't hide her smile when he lowered his mouth to hers. He took his time with that kiss, reveling in the simple reality of having his arms around her again. She tasted like apples and coffee, like everything good.

He let her go with reluctance and took off his coat and gloves. "Smells great in here."

"I made minestrone soup," she said. "Hungry?"

The thought of her puttering around his kitchen worked for him in a very big way.

She'd stayed.

He'd been in the wrong and he knew it. And she had to suspect he wasn't going to change. Not on the subject of the old man, anyway.

And still…she'd stayed.

"Sparky." He pulled her close again and kissed her some more. She twined her arms around his neck. He lifted her off the floor and she wrapped her legs around him, too. He turned for the stairs leading up to his bedroom.

But she broke the kiss and put her hand against the side of his face. "When was the last time you ate?"

"I had some eggs at the hospital this morning."

"You need to eat." She smoothed the collar of his shirt in a proprietary way that pleased him to no end.

But there were more important things in the world than soup. "What I need is to take you upstairs, peel off all your clothes and show you what a good husband I can be."

"First, you should eat." She squirmed a little. "Put me down." He gave up and let her go. She grabbed his hand. "Come on. Soup."

She led him into the kitchen, where she pushed him into a chair and filled a couple of bowls with that terrific-smelling soup. There was crusty bread and sweet butter, too. She took the chair across from him and they ate in silence for a few minutes.

"I wanted to go with you last night for *you*, Deck," she said finally.

He ate more bread. It was a much better use of his mouth than answering her, because he wasn't going to say what she wanted to hear.

She took a thoughtful sip from her water glass. "It goes both ways, you know. You don't only take care of me. I take care of you, too. I can't do that if you won't let me—and I know. You were too proud to let me take care of you when we were kids. I can see now how you felt you *couldn't* take care of me and you hated that. But what's the point of finding each other again if we just reverse roles? It has to be both of us, each for the other. That's the only way it can really work."

Her skin was the most gorgeous shade of milky white that turned the prettiest pale pink when she blushed or got turned on. He didn't think he would ever tire of just looking at her. He watched her hand as she set down her water. Slim and white, that hand. But he knew it had rough spots—on her palms and at the joints of her fingers—from building things. He really liked the rub of that slight roughness against his skin.

And what were they arguing about? Right. Taking care of each other. "Sparky, you're here now. You stayed. You made soup. That's taking care of me."

She ate a bite of bread and took a spoonful of soup before she said, "Please just think about taking me to see him. We don't have to stay long or anything." She gazed across at him, so hopeful, so sweet.

And as far as his dad went, they were at exactly the same place they'd ended up the first time they'd had this discussion, the day before Thanksgiving, when she'd finally agreed to give their marriage a real try.

"All right. I'll do that," he lied—and waited for her to call him on it.

She simply shook her head in in a weary sort of way and concentrated on finishing her soup.

He knew a strange, frantic sort of feeling, that she was only playing him along. Yeah, she was being gentle with these ongoing requests to meet up with Keith.

But she wasn't giving it up.

No, she hadn't laid down any real ultimatums on the subject. Still, he definitely felt the pressure from her. The fact that she wouldn't just give it up and leave it alone had him trying to gauge how important a visit with Keith was to her.

Important enough to be a deal killer on the day after Christmas?

No. She'd never draw that kind of a line about it.

Would she?

Uh-uh. He was reading way too much into it.

Maybe if she kept after him about it in the weeks to come, he would start to worry.

But one way or another, he'd steer her away from Keith—and still end up married to her when Christmas was over.

As of now, well, why get all tied up in knots about it? Better just not to think about it, to put it completely out of his mind.

Chapter Nine

After he finished his soup, she dragged him into the living room, where she had boxes full of Christmas decorations all ready and waiting, along with a big fake tree for him to assemble.

She explained, "I put the soup in the slow cooker this morning and then I went looking for your Christmas decorations. I checked the closets, the attic and out in the garage. Didn't find any."

"That's probably because I don't have any," he muttered. *Because I don't need any.*

She elbowed him in the ribs. "Don't you dare get grinchy on me."

"Wouldn't dream of it—so you bought all this junk today?"

"Junk?" she mimicked pointedly.

"Ahem. Let me try that again."

"Please do."

"So today you bought all these *gorgeous* decorations and this tree that I'm certain will look terrific over there in the front window?"

"Yes, I did," she announced with pride. "I took your Land Rover out and I went shopping. One of the guys at the Christmas Store loaded the tree box into the car for me. But getting it in here by myself took some planning. After you called and said you were on your way home, I took the tree out of the box and dragged it in here in sections."

"You could've just waited for me."

"I know." She gave him her sweetest smile. "But I wanted to get going on it. I thought we could put this tree up today and do the one at the loft tomorrow night."

"We need trees at both places?" Wasn't one way more than enough?

Not to Nell, it wasn't. "No, we don't *need* them. We *want* them."

"Ah. Good to know."

She slanted him a pouty glance. "Or maybe you're too tired to decorate? Would you rather go upstairs, get some sleep?"

He hooked his arm around her neck and pulled her close enough breathe in the almond scent of her shampoo and press his mouth to the smooth skin of her forehead. "If we go to bed, it won't be for sleep."

"I didn't say *we*, Mr. Scrooge. Whatever you decide to do, I'll be down here decorating."

So that pretty much settled that. If he couldn't give her a visit to his dad, the least he could do was help her with the damn tree.

It took several hours. But, really, it was almost worth all the work. That night, they had a fire in the fireplace and the tree all lit up in the front window. His big rented house had never felt so much like a home.

The next night they were back at her place with another tree to decorate. She had one of those retro aluminum trees for the loft. He stuck the branches in the fat tube that served as a trunk and mounted it on the stand. All the decorations were aqua blue. Nellie had a color wheel that she put on the floor at the base of the tree and it turned slowly, bathing the shiny branches in alternating bands of different-colored light.

"Pretty, huh?" she asked, when they stood back to admire their evening's work.

"Spectacular," he replied drily. "And how come you didn't warn me that when a man gets married he's automatically signing up for a whole bunch of holiday decorating?"

"Are you complaining?"

"Me? No way."

"Good. Because Thursday, we're going to out to Rory and Walker's ranch for their annual family decorating party."

Thursday night at Rory and Walker's, all the Bravos and their husbands and wives were there.

Everyone pitched in to wind garland over every banister and railing in sight. They piled greenery on the mantel and put up those little Christmas villages and miniature snowy scenes on just about every available flat surface. All while an endless succession of Christmas records on actual vinyl played from Walker's old-school stereo system.

Deck decided that it wasn't half-bad. There was hot chocolate. And beer and drinks for anyone who wanted liquor.

And a whole bunch of wedding presents for him and Nellie. Apparently, the Bravos *had* to throw a party whenever one of them got married. With two more family weddings coming up in the next few weeks, opportunities were limited to celebrate an unexpected Vegas marriage.

So Rory had declared that the decorating party would be in honor of Deck and Nell. Elise had brought a wedding cake, three tiers done up to look like a stack of Christmas presents, complete with fancy frosting bows and shiny sugar ornaments. Deck and Nellie cut the cake and smeared frosting on each other's faces. They shared sugary kisses as Rory, who was a professional photographer, took shot after shot.

Much later, at the loft, they opened their wedding gifts, which were mostly household goods, fancy tablecloths and serving pieces, vases and candlesticks, all that stuff married people used now and then, for special occasions. Deck pictured Nell dressing up the table for a dinner party in some distant, happy, hazy future, imagined himself sitting down to eat with friends and family around them, glancing down the full table at Nellie, his wife.

It was so far beyond what he'd known growing up. They'd never had a damn tablecloth on their rickety kitchen table, let alone silver candlesticks and a big, smiling family.

But he would have all that now. And with the woman he'd wanted since the moment he set eyes on her. He should be happy. Proud of himself to have come this far, gotten this close to having everything he'd ever imagined in his wildest dreams.

And he *was* happy. Just with a few raggedy spots around the edges. Because it wasn't a done deal until they got out to the other side of Christmas together.

Nell set down a giant glass vase from Jody and nudged him with her shoulder. "You're wearing your grim face."

What was it about women? They took one look at a guy's face and saw way more than any man ever wanted them to know.

He wrapped his arm around her and nuzzled her ear. "I was just thinking, *Wow, that is one big-ass vase.*"

She let out a little snort of laughter—and then asked softly, "Not gonna talk about it, huh?"

I hate that damn agreement and I wish we'd never made it. How hard was that to say?

Really hard.

He could hit the jackpot. She might answer, *I hate it, too. Let's pretend you never suggested it. Let's call this a done deal and stay married forever and ever.*

Or he could end up making things worse. She might say she wasn't ready to put the agreement aside and then proceed to tell him why—including how she wasn't giving up on that visit with Keith and if he kept refusing to take her to see his dad, she would refuse to stay married to him.

Bottom line? He didn't know what she would say.

Uh-uh. Better just to let it play out, stop being such a weenie about it. One way or another, he would find a way to keep her with him when the holidays were through.

* * *

Saturday, they did Rocky Mountain Christmas, Justice Creek's annual holiday shopping fair on Central Street. Deck enjoyed it. Nellie bought presents for just about everyone in her family and Hank and Marty, too. As for Henry, he got the most stuff of all. Nell bought toddler toys and blue pajamas, onesies and booties and a mobile for Henry's crib. That night, she wrapped everything to take to Marty's house the next day.

It was snowing Sunday morning, but it had tapered off by noon when they left for Colorado Springs.

At Marty's, Nellie put the gifts she'd bought under Marty's tree. They had dinner. After the meal, Hank turned on the game in the living room. Nellie asked to hold Henry. She sat on the sofa with him and he went to sleep in her arms.

Marty pulled Deck into the kitchen, supposedly to help with loading the dishwasher, but really to report that Keith was doing fine and already back at work playing fix-it man around his apartment complex.

"Great," said Deck, ready for talk of Keith to be over and done. "Glad he's feeling better."

Marty was watching him way too closely. "You haven't even told him that you and Nell got married, have you?"

"Why does this feel like the beginning a lecture?"

Marty braced a hand on the counter by the sink and scowled at him. "He's your father, Deck." At least she kept her voice low so Nellie wouldn't hear. "He'll be happy for you."

"Can you just stay out of it?"

"Look. I get it. I know you've still got issues on your issues when it comes to him. And I was there. I remember what he did, hitting Nell up for a 'loan' that you had to pay back. I understand why you don't trust him. But I feel like a liar every time I talk to him. It's big news that his son got married. It's something he should know."

Did he get that? Yeah, maybe. A little.

He blew out a hard breath. "I'll call him tomorrow and tell him. I should check on him, anyway."

Marty smiled then. "Thank you." She tipped her head toward the living room. "You did good, big brother. Nell's a total keeper."

"Yeah. She's all that and then some." *And now if I can just manage not to screw it up.*

Deck called his dad from his office at JC Barrels the next morning and got voice mail. "Hey, Dad. Marty says you're doing fine, already working again, so that's good. Listen, can you give me a call when you get a minute?" He hung up and felt antsy for an hour and a half.

Until Keith called him back.

"What's up?" the old man asked.

Deck rose from his desk and shut the door. "It's like this. I got married to Nell Bravo. It was a few weeks ago—before you fell down the stairs. Marty got after me to tell you. So, well, now you know."

The silence at the other end of the line went on for a while. Finally, Keith said, "Congratulations. I'm happy for you."

"Thanks." The word tasted like sawdust in his mouth.

"She's a good girl, that Nell."

Stay the hell away from her. "She's not a girl anymore."

"You pay her back that money I took off her?"

"I did."

"I figured you would."

"Yeah, well. That's all. I'll talk to you—"

But Keith wasn't finished. "How you and your sister turned out so good, I got no clue. I'm grateful every damn day for the both of you, and that is a plain fact."

"Dad, you don't have to—"

"All I'm sayin' is, it's a comfort, that's all, to know that in spite of what a mess I made, you two will be okay."

What the hell was he supposed to say to that? It wasn't that he couldn't forgive Keith. It was just that he still didn't trust him and didn't know if he ever could. "Well, I just wanted you to know I got married. Give me a call if you need anything."

"Declan?"

"What?"

"You gonna bring that sweet girl around to see your old dad, let me apologize for taking her money back in the day?"

Not a chance. "Doubtful."

Keith took a moment to let that sink in. "Well. You be happy together, you and Nell. She was always the one for you."

Okay, he just couldn't let that remark stand. "If you knew that, why'd you mess with her?"

"What can I tell you? I had the devil on my tail back in those days. I made one bad choice after another, until it got so that bad choices seemed like the only kind there were."

"Well, you can't really blame me, can you, if I have trouble trusting you?"

"No, Declan. I can't blame you. I *don't* blame you. Not one bit."

Nell spent that morning at a reno she was supervising for her brother Quinn up in Haltersham Heights. Quinn's passion was his gym, Prime Sports and Fitness, but he flipped houses for profit and he used Bravo Construction to do the work.

When it got close to lunchtime, Nell called Meg. "Where are you?"

"At the loft going crazy."

Nell laughed. "That's a pretty normal state for a bride five days before her wedding. How 'bout lunch?"

"Yes! Please! Now!"

"Twenty minutes, the Sylvan Inn?"

"You're on."

They got a deuce in the corner and the biggest gossip in Justice Creek, Monique Hightower, as their waitress. Monique sashayed over, her blond curls bouncing. "Happy Holidays! Nell Bravo, where have you been? A demolition site?"

Nell wore work clothes and boots, but so did more than one man in the place. "Count your blessings, Monique. At least I washed off the construction dust. How are you?"

"Terrific. I hear congratulations are in order."

"Thanks."

"I mean, really. You and Declan? After all these years. I seem to recall you once said you wouldn't spit on him if he was on fire in the street."

Nell smiled sweet and slow. "Believe it or not, Monique. Sometimes true love does win out."

Monique handed them menus, rattled off the specials—and then turned on Meg, "So the wedding is Saturday, or so I heard?"

"That's right."

"You and Ryan and your whirlwind romance. I hope you'll be very happy."

"Yes, we are. Thank you so much."

The less of Monique the better, as far as Nell was concerned. "You know what? I'm ready to order now."

Meg agreed that she was, too. They ordered sandwiches and coffee and handed the menus back. Monique bustled away.

Meg leaned across the table and whispered, "I have no idea how she keeps her job."

"Sometimes I wonder, too. But then again, what would the inn be without Monique here to drive us all crazy?"

"You're right. And at least she didn't ask what *Clara* thinks about me and Rye." Clara and Rye were lifelong BFFs. They'd even almost gotten married once—at Christmastime three years before. Many people in town believed that Ryan McKellan would always be in love with Clara, who had married Dalton Ames the summer after that almost-wedding to Rye.

Monique appeared with their coffees.

As soon as she was gone, Nell reached across the table and fondly patted Meg's arm. "You get that crap a lot, people giving you innuendo about Rye and Clara?"

Meg only shrugged and dribbled cream into her cup. "Now and then."

"It *is* just crap, you know. Rye loves Clara. But he's *in love* with you."

Meg sipped her coffee and answered easily, "I know."

Nell felt the tears rise—the good kind. She sniffled and waved her hand in front of her face. "I love it— that you love him, that he loves you. That you two just went for it and it's working out so right."

"Yeah," Meg agreed quietly. "He's the man for me. I love Rye, I'm *in* love with Rye. And I trust him."

"Trust..." Nell felt an ache, a bittersweet yearning in the center of her chest as she thought of Deck, of the marriage they were trying to build. Did they have trust, really, between them? He didn't trust her around his dad. And she didn't quite trust him enough to give up the option for an after-Christmas divorce.

Meg fake coughed into her hand and muttered, "Warning. Monique. Closing in behind you."

And then the waitress was there. "Here we go." She slid their full plates in front of them. "Now, what else can I get you?"

"We're set," said Meg. With a giant smile, Monique whirled and bounced away. Once she was busy at another table, Meg asked, "Now what were you about to say?"

Nell picked up a triangle of her BLT. "I was just thinking about Deck and me, that's all. How we seem to be doing everything backward. I mean, we get married on the fly and then we negotiate whether or not to try to make it work."

"But do you trust him?"

"To be true to me? Absolutely."

Gently Meg coaxed, "So what you're really saying is that there are other ways trust is lacking between you?"

"Exactly. I had a few issues growing up. He had it a thousand times worse than I did. We fell so hard for each other in high school. And then everything went wrong. Now, trust is sort of a work in progress with us."

"But you *are* in love with him and he's in love with you. You're it for each other."

Nell poked a stray piece of bacon back into her sandwich. "That wasn't a question, was it?"

"Nope. I know a couple in love when I see one." She picked up a section of her grilled ham and cheese. They ate in companionable silence for a few minutes.

Then Nell asked, "So how was the trip to Oregon?" Ryan and Meg had flown back to Valentine Bay, Meg's hometown in the Pacific Northwest, on Thanksgiving weekend.

"It went well. My parents love Rye. And he got along great with Aislinn and Keely." Aislinn Bravo and Keely Ostergard were Meg's two lifelong BFFs.

Nell said, "I can't wait to meet my cousin." Nell's dad and Aislinn's father had been brothers, though they'd lost touch over the years.

"Won't be long now. Aislinn and Keely are driving in Thursday." The two would share maid-of-honor duties at the wedding. "They threw us a combination wedding shower and bachelor/bachelorette party at the Lighthouse Café, my favorite restaurant back home."

"You miss Oregon?"

"Now and then." Meg sounded just a little bit wistful. "But I love Justice Creek. I'm happy here—and my parents are coming in tonight." She glanced away. "They're staying with us at the loft."

Nell leaned a little closer across their small table. "And…?"

"I love my mom."

"But…?"

Meg groaned. "But she thinks she knows everything and she won't stop with the well-meaning advice. I wanted to get them a room at the Haltersham." The century-old luxury hotel was by far the best in town. "But my mom looked so hurt when I suggested it. So she and Dad are staying with us."

Nell had an easy fix for that one. "Have them stay at my place."

Meg started right in protesting. "No, Nellie. I didn't mean—"

"Don't argue. It's perfect. They'll be right there with you—just not right on *top* of you."

Meg set down her half-eaten section of sandwich. "I was just whining a little, not hinting. We'll be fine."

"I know you weren't hinting. But I *am* offering—scratch that. I'm *insisting*. We'll just stay at Deck's. Better for you, no problem for me. Deck and I are going back and forth between our two places anyway until we figure out where to settle in the end." And didn't that sound reasonable, even if it wasn't the whole story? Now Nell was the one glancing away. She frowned down at her French fries and wondered if that showed lack of trust, too, somehow—that they couldn't even agree on one place to live? Or was she just suddenly oversensitive on the subject of trust?

Marriage. Sometimes it seemed like a lot more trouble than it could possibly be worth.

"Something wrong with your French fries?" asked Meg.

"Not a thing." Nell picked one up and popped it in her mouth. "Your parents. My place. It's the perfect solution to your problem."

After lunch Nell drove home to her loft to pack what she'd need for several nights at Deck's. She tossed her bags in the back seat of her crew cab and went on into the office at Bravo Construction, where she called the cleaning service she used occasionally. They would send someone over right away to change the sheets and spiff things up at the loft for Meg's mom and dad.

Then she called Deck. "Got a minute?"

"For you, a lifetime."

Well, that made her feel all melty inside. "I might just need to keep you around, McGrath."

"Works for me because I'm going nowhere." His rough, low voice caused a slow burn in her lady parts.

"You are a very dangerous man."

"No, just determined."

And relentless. "Um. Where was I...?"

"About to suggest a little afternoon phone sex? Or wait. Where are you? I'll come there."

"Oh, I'll just bet you would." She had that ache again. And not only for sex with him. For *everything* with him. "But I, um, I called to say I offered the loft to Meg's parents. They'll be here this evening, stay through the wedding Saturday and fly back out to Oregon Sunday. Any problem with us moving over to your house tonight for the rest of the week?"

"As if you even need to ask."

"I didn't think you'd mind too much," she muttered wryly. He was such a caveman. And he wanted her in *his* cave.

"You know…" All of a sudden, his voice had turned way too casual. "We could simplify everything if you just moved to my place permanently."

Why did saying yes to that tempt and terrify her simultaneously? "Not ready to do that yet."

"Yet." His voice was rough again. She wanted to rub herself against it. "Meaning you will be, eventually."

I think so, yes. She should say it out loud.

But her trust?

As of right now, it wasn't quite there, and she wasn't letting him push her too fast. "We need to get groceries."

If it bothered him that she'd changed the subject, he didn't let on. "I'll pick you up at the loft. We can stop at the store on the way back to the house."

"Deck. I need my truck—you know, to go to work, get around. Because this is the twenty-first century, and women have lives and jobs of their own."

"You can have the Land Rover."

"Thank you, but I want my *own* car."

"You sound about twelve. About twelve and sticking out your tongue at me. Makes me want to give you a spanking."

"I believe I am mildly offended."

"Only mildly? Good. I can work with that. This could be hot."

"Hold that thought. Until tonight."

"Spoilsport."

She laughed. It felt so good, teasing him. Making

simple plans with him—to stay at his house, to stop on the way home for groceries.

And as for having him as her partner in life...

Warmth flooded through her. She wanted that. Wanted *him*.

So why was she hesitating? Why not just throw out the damn agreement and go all the way, promise him forever and get to work on the rest of their lives?

"Sparky? Still with me?"

She put all the tough questions away and answered, "Right here. Get whatever you need from the loft and meet me at Safeway. Five thirty. Customer-service desk."

"I'll be there."

And he was.

They grabbed a cart and rolled up and down the aisles like your average married couple out getting the groceries on a weekday evening.

She bought a holiday centerpiece of roses, pine-cones, holly and amaryllis as the store PA system played Christmas tunes. To "The Little Drummer Boy" and "Santa Baby," they argued about what to have for dinner. And they forgot the eggs. She had to run back for them after they'd already unloaded everything onto the checkout belt.

She followed him home and—yep, she'd started calling his place home in her head. So that was another little step toward forever, wasn't it?

It had started snowing again. By the time they reached the house, it was coming down pretty steadily.

Deck pulled his car into the garage, got out and ran back to her in the driveway. She rolled her window down.

He said, "I'll move the Land Rover and you can pull in."

"Thank you." She tipped her head out the window, offering a kiss for his thoughtfulness. He met her halfway and she reveled in the cold bite of snowflakes on his soft, warm lips.

Inside, he turned up the heat and she turned on the tree. They put the groceries away. He made *pasta e fagioli*. They sat down at the breakfast-nook table with the soup, a bottle of wine and a loaf of French bread.

It was all so homey and comfortable and natural. She was happy, in his warm house with the snow falling outside, her festive centerpiece on the table.

And with Deck.

Deck, whom she'd lost so long ago. The man she'd put behind her for good.

And yet here she sat at his table. She slept in his bed.

Deck. Her husband.

Of all the impossible, terrifying, wonderful things.

"Have I got soup on my nose?" He had on that crooked smile she loved so much—a little bit rueful, a whole lot sexy. "You're staring at me."

I love you, Deck. I always did. I never stopped.

It felt good to think it. It felt *real*. She should let it out, say the words, share her growing acceptance of him in her life, share her joy in the happiness they'd found together since those wild nights in Las Vegas.

She opened her mouth to say it, *I love you*.

But then she had a sudden flashing vision of her younger self, drenched to the skin in a hard summer rainstorm, trudging through the mud, arms around her middle, huddled into herself, letting herself cry now that he couldn't see her doing it. Because he was behind her in his ancient pickup, following her even though she'd told him to go, even though all she wanted was to get away from him. All she wanted was never to set eyes on him.

Not ever again.

That long-ago summer day had broken her. That day had shown her that there was no hope for her with him. She had to be done with him.

She couldn't love him anymore. They were finished. Forever. She'd given him everything, all she had, keeping nothing back. He'd thrown her away, anyway.

A girl had to learn a lesson from that. From heartbreak like that, a girl learned to be more careful, to keep a closer watch on her vulnerable heart.

Now, she met his eyes directly across the table and answered his question. "Your nose is clean." *But I am not ready yet to give you everything I have again.*

Life was so painful and strange. At eighteen, she'd been eager to take on forever with him. But he'd walked away. And now he finally wanted everything with her.

She couldn't do it, couldn't give herself completely. She just didn't trust him. Not all the way—and really, he didn't completely trust her, either. If he did, they would be going together to visit his dad.

"Don't," Deck said in a low growl. "Don't go away. Don't shut me out." He knew her so well, knew she'd retreated into her doubts, left him sitting there at the table, across from her but alone.

"I'm right here," she lied. It wasn't constructive, behaving this way. Far from it.

And he wasn't having it. "Uh-uh," he said. "No

freaking way." He slid his napkin in by his bowl, shoved back his chair and rose to loom over the table. "If you're going to run off inside your head, the least you can do is tell me why."

She pushed her bowl away.

"Say it," he commanded.

She lifted her hands—and then let them drop limply. "Look. I want to trust you."

"But you don't." The words dropped into the space between them, heavy as stones.

She confessed, "No. I don't fully trust you not to hurt me again, just like you don't trust me not to mess up with your dad somehow."

"What will convince you that I know I screwed everything up and all I want now is a lifetime to prove to you that it will never happen again?"

"Time, I think. I just need time."

"Nellie." He spoke so patiently, standing there across the table from her, not the least bit cocky for once. "That's what we're doing. Giving it time—and as far as my dad goes, it's *him* I don't trust, not you."

Anger shivered through her. "Oh, please. What's he gonna do? He can only manipulate me if I let him. And I'm not going to let him."

His burning gaze dropped then. He stared down at his almost-empty bowl as though wondering how it had gotten there. "I'm just…" The sentence wandered off.

Impatiently, she finished for him. "Not ready?" When he didn't look up, she added, "Well, neither am I. And however it all shakes out, it's good, you know? You and me, this Christmastime together. I'm glad for it. I really am."

He did lift his head then. His gaze caught hers, held it fast. "You and me, Nellie. That's all I want."

I want that, too.

But she didn't say it. She couldn't give him what they both wanted yet. She just wasn't ready to take that next step.

"You and me, Nellie," he repeated, his voice rougher, more demanding. "You need to get used to it. You need to admit it. You're mine and I'm yours. Even the way I messed up when we were kids hasn't changed that. Eleven years apart, and here we are, right where we were always meant to be."

She didn't argue. It sounded so good. She wished...

But all she could give him was, "I hope you're right."

With a low oath, he came for her.

She waited for him, her gaze never wavering, every nerve tingling, her skin supersensitized, sudden, sweet heat blooming low in her belly.

Okay, maybe he *had* seduced her to the altar, and maybe they each had issues they hadn't resolved yet. Who could say what would happen on the day after Christmas?

But right this minute, they shared what she'd given up all hope of ever having with him. Right this minute, they had each other, in a warm, safe place, a tree in the front window, the snow drifting down outside.

When he reached her, she rose to meet him. And when he pulled her close she tipped her head up, eager for his kiss.

Deck's kiss.

Nothing like it.

A perfect, ever-deepening kiss.

A kiss that swept her away to a lush, carnal world where doubts melted like snowflakes on warm skin.

He framed her face in those big hands and he claimed her with his soft lips and his seeking tongue. It was so good, the feel of his hands on her, the taste of him, the heat of his breath, the forceful way he took her mouth. She swayed against him.

He grabbed her up and lifted her right off the floor.

Hooking her ankles at the base of his spine, she plastered her body hard and tight against him. He wrapped her up in those giant arms of his and kissed her all the way to the living room. At the fireplace, he eased her down onto her feet again and went to work getting her out of her clothes.

He had her naked in a minute and he tossed his own clothes on top of hers in a tangled pile. And then he kicked it all out of the way and took her down to the soft rug in front of the fire.

"Come closer," she whispered.

"I'm right here." He licked the outer shell of her ear, tracing the curve of it all the way down to her earlobe, which he bit—gently at first.

And then harder.

She moaned and nuzzled closer still, licking a trail up the thick, beard-bristled column of his throat, over his square jaw and then catching the corner of his mouth in a hungry little kiss. He turned into that kiss, fully claiming her lips all over again.

They rolled and she was on top.

She took advantage of the dominant position, sliding off him to kneel at his side, pressing kisses down the center of his deep, strong chest. Following the tempting trail of hair along his rocklike belly, she moved on down to where he was waiting, hard and proud, for her to curl her eager fingers around him, lick the salty tip of him.

And slowly take him deep in her throat.

Rising onto his knees, he held her head in his hands, wrapped her hair around his fingers, said dark, dirty, sexy things as she drove him toward the peak— and over.

She swallowed every drop.

And then, with a final rough groan of satisfaction, he pulled her back down with him and cuddled her close to his side. The fire kept them warm until he'd recovered enough to start all over again, tipping her chin up with a finger, settling his hot mouth on hers.

She moaned at the sheer wonder of it. His scent of dark spice was all around her, and she gave herself up to the joy that he brought.

"Nellie…" He kissed her name onto her lips.

And then he rolled her under him. He wouldn't let her up until she'd lost herself completely to the touch of his knowing hands and the wet, hot demand of his skilled, seeking kiss.

She was limp and pliant as a happy rag doll when he picked her up and set her down on top of him. For a little while, she used him as a giant, hot, hard pillow, her legs draped to either side of him, her head cradled on his chest. She listened to his heartbeat.

And she thought that this, right now, was happiness, the two of them naked and satisfied together, in front of a cozy fire.

The future? Who needed it?

This, right now, was everything.

He combed her tangled hair with lazy fingers. A knowing chuckle escaped her as she felt him, tucked against the core of her, rising once more.

"It's so crazy, what you do to me." He pulled her up so he could catch her lower lip between his teeth, so he could whisper a dark command, "Take me, Nellie. Do it now."

No problem. She was wet and so ready. With an easy roll of her hips, she had him where she wanted him.

Whispering impossible sexual promises, he slid those hands down over the twin curves of her bottom, his wonderful fingers gliding in, finding the liquid heart of her. Spreading her wider, he surged up into her, filling her completely in one hard, high stroke.

They groaned in unison then, as she pressed down and he pushed up. Finding the rhythm, they rocked together toward a glorious explosion of bliss.

He went over first, his arms banded so tight around her. "I love you, love you forever, Nellie," he vowed as he came.

Her finish took fire from his. The words of love filled her head.

And I love you, Deck. Always. You're the one, the only one. There's never been anyone who means what you do to me. So many years without you. I don't know how I did it. I don't know how I'll bear it if we don't make it work this time…

She wanted to say it, to tell him everything. Her heart cried for her to confess it all.

Why not? Every word was true.

Yet she held the words back.

She just wasn't ready to go that far. Some still-wounded part of her didn't quite trust him enough.

Chapter Ten

The next day they woke to a clear sky and a foot and a half of snow on the ground.

They stood on the front porch in their pajamas and heavy socks, sipping their morning coffee, blinking against the glare of the sun reflected off that wide, sparkly blanket of white.

Deck took a slow sip of coffee. "Looks like a snow day to me."

Shivering a little against the cold, she sidled up closer to the warmth of his body. "It's just so beautiful."

He wrapped an arm around her and brushed a kiss into her hair. "Come on back inside..."

In the house, he turned on the big screen over the fireplace and they learned that the schools and most Justice Creek businesses were calling it a snow day, too.

Before they sat down to eggs and toast, Deck sent a group email to everyone who worked for him, letting them know that Justice Creek Barrels officially had the day off. Nell called Garrett, who agreed that Bravo Construction would be closed, as well. And then she called Meg to make sure her parents had arrived before the storm.

"They got in safe and sound late yesterday as planned," Meg reassured her.

After breakfast, they put on their snow gear and Deck led her out to the big shed in the back. He had a pair of snowmobiles in there, all gassed up and ready to ride.

They spent a half hour buzzing around the property as she familiarized herself with the controls. When she felt comfortable going farther afield, they headed up the twisting road behind the house and eventually into the forest, where the snow wasn't deep enough to ride.

When they had to stop, he suggested they leave the machines and continue on foot for a while.

They started climbing, weaving their way through the tall, dark trees, moving higher up the mountain. Eventually, they emerged onto a lookout point.

Far below, Justice Creek was picture-postcard perfect, like one of those Christmas village scenes at Walker and Rory's holiday decorating party.

Deck, at her back, wrapped his arms around her and rested his chin on her shoulder. He rubbed his rough cheek against her soft one. "It's a beautiful little town."

"I wouldn't live anywhere else." She turned her head back to him and they shared a quick kiss.

The clouds had gathered again. Snowflakes drifted down out of the gray sky.

"Ready to head home?" He pressed his cold lips to the bit of bare skin between her wool hat and her thick scarf.

Reluctantly she nodded. They started back down.

By the time they reached the house, the snow had stopped again. They put the snowmobiles away and shoveled snow for a while. The shoveling devolved into a snowball fight. He was merciless, firing those fat, frozen balls at her as fast as he could grab them up. She did a lot of shrieking and ducking behind trees, leaping out now and then to get him a good one, preferably right in the face.

They even made a snowman. He was a little lopsided, with sticks for arms and a tipped-up row of coffee beans for a smile.

Late in the afternoon, they went back to bed and made love for hours, getting up only for sandwiches and soup. And then heading right back to bed again.

It was a good day, lazy and easy and fun. They didn't talk of the future, of what would happen after Christmas. There was only the two of them, together right now and happy to be so. She wished it would never end.

The next day, real life intruded. The sky and the roads were clear, and they both went to work.

Friday, the day before Rye and Meg's wedding, Nell had lunch with her sisters and Rory at the Sylvan Inn. Meg came, too, and brought her two best friends from Oregon.

Keely Ostergard owned an art gallery in Valentine Bay. Aislinn Bravo, who was slim and delicate, with big, haunted eyes, looked European, somehow. Both boyish and sophisticated, Aislinn resembled some glamorous French actress—Marion Cotillard. Or Audrey Tautou.

Aislinn and Rory had a lot in common. Aislinn loved the tiny principality called Montedoro on the Mediterranean coast where Rory had been born and raised. Aislinn, as it turned out, had been born there, too, when her pregnant mother gave birth earlier than expected during a visit to the villa of a Montedoran count.

While Rory and Aislinn shared stories of Montedoro, Nell leaned close to Meg and asked how it was going with the visit from the parents.

Meg laughed and whispered, "Let me put it this way. The wedding's tomorrow and I can't wait—and not only to be Ryan McKellan's bride."

Saturday in the early evening, Meg married Rye in a tiny log church up in the National Forest. She wore a cream-colored lace dress and a winter crown woven of small white flowers, lacy cedar branches and red berries. She had only Keely and Aislinn as her attendants. Walker stood up as his brother's best man.

In the front row, Meg's mother cried through the ceremony. Mostly, she cried softly, but now and then a sob or a sudden snort would get away from her. When Meg's dad tried to hush her, she moaned, "I can't help it, Todd. Our little girl is all grown-up…"

After the ceremony, the guests followed the bride and groom along a lantern-lit path to the reception in a rustic, barnlike building not far from the chapel. It was all so charming and romantic. Rye and Meg had never looked happier. Nell teared up a little to think that Rye McKellan had found exactly the right woman for him at last.

The next day, Aislinn and Keely set off for the long drive home to Valentine Bay. Meg's parents drove their rental car back to Denver, where they boarded their flight to Portland.

Monday, Meg and Rye were leaving for their Christmas honeymoon in Hawaii. Nell stopped by their loft in time to say goodbye and to help carry suitcases down to the car. As soon as they were gone, she went back up to her own place to see if she needed to call the cleaning people again.

The loft was spotless. Nell changed the sheets and then called Deck at JC Barrels to remind him that they had dinner at her mother's house that night. Griffin's grown children and their families would be there.

"It's at seven," she said.

"No problem. I'll be home by six at the latest. We can go together."

She found herself wondering which place he meant by "home."

"We're at my place tonight, remember, all week? Until Friday?"

A silence and then a hard sigh. "Can we just give that up? What's the point? We're comfortable at my place. And it's getting old, having to drag stuff between two houses."

He was right on both counts. She kind of wanted to give in, stay at his place, eliminate the extra hassle of moving back and forth. And, more and more, she found herself thinking of his house as home, of how much she would love moving to the new house when it was completed.

But some part of her resisted, the part that still doubted, still couldn't quite trust. They'd made an agreement and she really did need what he'd offered—until Christmas—to decide finally if she could make that big leap into forever with him.

"Nellie?"

She realized she'd been quiet for too long. "I'm here. And you're right. I do like it at your place and going back and forth is extra work…"

"But?" The single word had a hard, angry edge.

"Come on, Deck. We had an agreement."

He said something vaguely obscene under his breath and then, more clearly, "Agreements change."

All of a sudden, she felt miserable. Her heart thudded uncomfortably beneath her breastbone and her stomach had tied itself into a knot. Were they about to have a fight on the phone?

She didn't want to fight with him. She *loved* him.

Even if she did still have issues with him, even if she had yet to tell him she loved him out loud. "Yes, agreements do change," she said as gently as she could manage. "But both people have to be willing to make that change."

"And you're just not." It was an accusation.

"Be reasonable. It's not fair for you to get on me for wanting to stick with the plan."

"I hate the damn plan."

Then you should never have suggested it, she thought, her own anger rising. Somehow, she kept herself from actually saying those bitter words.

A moment later, she was glad she'd kept her mouth shut, because he gave in. "All right." He sounded like a weary traveler in the middle of a long trip down an endless, winding road. "I'll be at your place at six. We'll stay there until Friday, the way we agreed."

She'd won the point.

Shouldn't she feel better about that? "We could compromise."

"How?" He sounded wary, but interested. Definitely an improvement over tired and pissed off.

"We could stay at your house for another week and then move to my place through Christmas…"

In his office at JC Barrels, Deck was silent on his end of the line. He understood that she was trying for compromise. Still, he glared at the bookcase made of wine barrels on the opposite wall.

Christmas. The deadline.

It was flying at them way too fast. Only two weeks to go now.

In two weeks, she would decide whether to stay married to him.

Or not.

"Deck?" she asked hopefully.

"I'm still here," he growled into the phone as he got up from his desk chair, crossed to the bookcase and picked up a blue geode bookend that Marty had given him several Christmases ago. It was heavy, that geode, and would make a satisfying crash if he pitched it at his office door.

Nell added hopefully, "If we did it that way, instead of moving back and forth four times, we would only have to do it once."

Carefully, without making a sound, he set the geode back on the shelf. "You're right." Plus, they'd been at his house all last week when they should have been at her place, what with Rye's parents staying at the loft. "It's more than fair."

"So...?" She sounded so sweet. And he loved her too damn much. They were so close to having it all. No way was she leaving him two weeks from tomorrow. He wouldn't allow it.

Except that he *had* made that agreement. He'd given his word. He didn't see how he could rationalize not keeping it.

And who did he think he was kidding, anyway? She was Nell. She did what she wanted and no man alive would make her stay if she was bound to go.

He needed to take her to the old man. If he did that, she would see it as proof of his trust. He could win her promise of forever that way, he knew it.

But he still didn't want her near Keith McGrath. He just didn't. He didn't give a good damn if the need to keep her away from Keith was irrational. Okay, Keith seemed to have cleaned up his act lately. Didn't matter. The old man had run one too many scams in his day. His father didn't deserve to breathe the same air as Nellie—and if Deck had any say in the matter, Keith never would.

"Hey," Nell said softly, calling him back to the here and now, where she was still waiting for his agreement as to where to stay, when.

"All right," he said. "We're at my house till next week and then your place through Christmas."

That night at the Bravo mansion, Nell was impressed with her mother's efforts to make the big family dinner fun for everyone.

The long table in the formal dining room seated

twenty-four. It wasn't big enough. Willow had brought in two more tables and Estrella, the housekeeper, had arranged them, as Clara had at Thanksgiving, in a U shape. Every seat was taken.

Willow had invited the whole Bravo family that night—her children, her stepchildren, their spouses and kids. Rory and Walker came, too. Griffin's two sons and his daughter and their families had flown up from California the day before to stay until the wedding on Saturday.

Already, Sylvie and Annabelle Bravo had made fast friends with Griffin's seven-year-old grandson, Hunter, *and* with his eight-year-old granddaughter, Nicole. The rest of Griffin and Willow's grandkids were babies—except for Clara and Dalton's two-and-a-half-year-old, Kiera.

Little Kiera spent the cocktail hour following the older kids around. More than once, her voice could be heard calling out above the laughter and chatter of so many guests, "Sylvie, Belle! Wait for me!"

Estrella had outdone herself with the Christmas decorations. A brilliantly lit tree stood in each of the downstairs rooms, presents spilling out from under them in bright, beribboned piles. Swags of greenery looped along every railing. The mantels were decked out festively, too.

Willow had even hired a singing piano player to fill the house with holiday tunes. She beamed at the chaos of everyone talking at once, of children laughing and running all over the place. She never turned a hair when Hunter wrestled with his cousin Nicole, upsetting a side table and sending an antique vase crashing to the floor.

Instead, she just waved a slender hand and called out, "It's okay! Accidents happen. Careful of the glass, now," as the mothers scooped up the apologizing children to whisk them away from the broken glass, and one of the helpers Estrella had hired for the evening rushed in with a broom.

At the dinner table, Ma's surprising new sweetness continued.

"Beautiful, Griff," she enthused, after her fiancé said grace. "Everyone, I can't tell you what it means to me to have all of you here."

Nell leaned close to Deck and whispered, "My God. I think I see an actual tear in her eye."

"Be nice," he chided. "And what's that in *your* eye?"

She swiped the moisture away, leaned close to him again and whispered out of the side of her mouth, "I have the occasional sentimental moment. My mother? Not on your life."

"She's happy with Griffin, with the whole family around her."

Nell glanced along the table at the many smiling faces and thought of all the years of family turmoil. "There was a time I would have called you crazy if you'd tried to tell me that, someday, we'd all end up here together, sharing a really nice holiday dinner before my mother remarried and gave the mansion to Sondra's children."

"She's happy," Deck said again, all soft and coaxing.

Nell surrendered to the sweetness of the moment. "Yeah. Yeah, she is."

* * *

The next day, Nell got home to Deck's house before he did. She picked up the mail from the box out by the main road, including something from Keith McGrath in a plain, business-sized envelope. In the house, she left Keith's letter with the rest of Deck's mail on the end of the kitchen counter and got busy cooking dinner.

An hour later, Deck came in from the garage still in his winter gear just as she was taking the lemon chicken out of the oven. "Smells good in here." He came up beside her and eased her hair away from her neck with a gentle swipe of his gloved hand.

And then his cold lips touched her nape.

She bumped him with a hip. "Back off. This is hot."

"Yes, ma'am." He waited until she'd set the chicken on top of the stove and then he reached for her.

She laughed as his arms went around her. "Your nose is cold."

"Kiss me, anyway."

She happily complied, sliding her hands up to meet around his neck and tipping her mouth up to meet his. When he lifted his head, she surged up again to brush one more kiss across those wonderful lips of his. "Dinner in ten minutes."

"I'll hang up my coat." He turned for the front hall—and stopped at the end of the counter to check out the mail, picking up the envelope from Keith first. "What's this?"

"From your dad."

"I see that."

She busied herself checking the rice and getting down the water glasses to fill before she took them to the breakfast-nook table. He simply stood there, frowning at that white envelope.

"You think maybe it's a bomb?" she teased, trying to sound totally offhand because she was all too aware of the tension in the way he held his shoulders, in the slight frown that creased his brow. She tried again, straight-faced this time. "Deck. Just open it."

He slanted her a look—distracted. Annoyed. "Later." He took his mail, including the unopened letter from Keith, and headed for the front of the house. When he came back, he'd gotten rid of his coat and gloves as well as the mail.

She set the bowl of steaming rice on the table—and then just had to ask, "Well, what was it?"

He gave a cool shrug. "I have no idea. I didn't open it."

She considered what else she might say on the subject, but couldn't come up with anything especially helpful. Talking about Keith rarely went well.

He asked, "Want wine?"

She decided that the wisest move at this point was to just let it go. "Love some. I put a bottle of Pinot Grigio in the fridge…"

It snowed that night. And it snowed again on Wednesday and on Thursday, too.

But by Saturday, the day of Willow and Griffin's wedding and also the night of the annual Holiday Ball, the roads were clear and the world-famous Haltersham Hotel in the shadow of the Rockies, with its white stucco walls and red-tile roof, glowed with light in every window.

Willow and Griff had reserved two of the hotel's

smaller ballrooms—one for their simple marriage ceremony and one for the reception dinner.

At five that evening, Hunter Masters, the ring bearer, led the way down the aisle. Four flower girls—Sylvie, Annabelle, Nicole and Kiera—followed Hunter. Each little girl wore a red velvet dress, white tights and shiny black Mary Janes. Tiaras sparkled in their hair. The girls marched solemnly down the aisle to where Griffin and Hunter waited for the bride. Each girl carried a white basket filled with red rose petals. They scattered the petals as they went.

More than one guest whispered how well-behaved they were—even little Kiera. They were all four so beautiful and sweet and solemn, marching to the altar and taking their places on the far side of Hunter. Now and then, Kiera was seen to fidget. But she had her idols, Sylvie and Annabelle, on either side of her. They alternately soothed and shushed her. She reveled in the attention—and kept pretty quiet, too.

Then came the bride in a stunning, simple sheath of Christmas-green velvet, diamonds at her throat and sparkling in her ears. She carried a bouquet of pinecones, evergreen boughs and red winter berries.

Nell, in the first row of chairs with Deck at her side, started crying about then. It was all just so perfect and so very beautiful—and why in the world hadn't she remembered to bring tissues?

Deck wrapped his arm around her and pressed a white handkerchief into her palm. Gently, he curled her fingers over it and then dropped a kiss against her temple.

Right then, her love for him felt so huge inside her, like it could crack her ribs and burst right out of her chest. She lifted her head enough to kiss his fresh-shaved cheek and whisper, "Thank you."

Then, carefully so as not to end up with mascara smeared down her face, she dabbed at her eyes as her mother said "I do" for the second time—to a tall, handsome white-haired gentleman who seemed to make her happier than she'd ever been before.

After the ceremony, they all moved to a room across the mezzanine, where the tables were set with gold-rimmed china, gold flatware and tall candlesticks twined with Christmas greenery. Elise, the event planner of the family, had coordinated with the hotel to create Willow's wedding and this reception dinner. Nell caught her half sister's eye across the room. They grinned at each other, all the battles they'd once fought in that look, and the unbreakable friendship they shared now, as well.

It's perfect. Nell mouthed the words at her sister.

Elise, beaming, returned a slow nod.

The champagne flowed freely and just about every adult had a toast to propose as the children ran in and out between the tables, giggling and sometimes tussling with each other.

"Oh, let them play," Willow would insist whenever any parent tried to step in and settle them down. "They're just having fun…"

Eventually, dinner was served. The kids sat down—for a few minutes, at least. They drank their milk and shoveled in spoonfuls of mashed potatoes. And quickly got back up to play some more.

Once the dinner dishes had been cleared away, the staff served coffee and rolled in a four-tiered fantasy of a cake frosted in snowy white and decorated with marzipan poinsettias. Rory took pictures as Willow and her groom did the honors. They were like a couple of giddy kids, Ma and Griff, giggling and mugging for the camera as they stuffed each other's faces with cake.

Finally, Willow thanked everyone for making her wedding the happiest day of her life. It was after eight by then and the Holiday Ball was about to begin. Parents took the kids home.

Everyone else headed for the main ballroom, stopping off first in the ballroom's lobby to check out the silent auction, which occurred every year at the Holiday Ball.

This year, the auction proceeds would go to the local animal shelter, the Pet Adoption Project. The shelter had approached every business in town to donate prizes. All kinds of cool pet stuff had been the result, including a bunch of imaginative pet beds, toys and play structures. Bravo Construction had donated a catio, a fully enclosed outdoor space with cozy sheltered areas and climbing runs where pets could play outside, protected from predators and safe from the temptation to wander off. Justice Creek Barrels had donated a whiskey-barrel doghouse and a wine-barrel dog bed.

Nell stroked the curved wooden sides of the doghouse. "It's beautiful. I always wanted a dog…"

"Me, too." He ran a slow finger down the side of her throat, stirring lovely shivers as he went. "Maybe we should get one."

She almost said yes—but then she thought of the deadline. Better to wait until that was settled. "Maybe. In the New Year…"

Something flared in his eyes—frustration? Resentment that she'd yet to throw out the deadline and admit she couldn't live without him? But all he said was, "I'll hold you to it."

"A dog's a big responsibility."

"That's right. A dog is a long-term commitment." He slipped that big hand around her neck and tugged her closer. They shared a quick kiss. "What kind of dog would we get?"

"Well, we would just go to the Pet Adoption Project, find one we both like, a friendly dog, a short-haired one, I think."

"A big one?"

"Midsize."

He kissed her again. "Midsize will do." He tugged on a curl that had come loose from her updo. "I'll tell you what's beautiful, Sparky. You are. I love this dress." It was cobalt blue satin, a simple, full-length strapless sheath.

Her heart kind of stuttered inside her chest and a sweet shiver raced down her spine. She fiddled with the collar of his snowy dress shirt and those all-important three little words rose to her lips. *I love you.* She actually opened her mouth to say them.

But then he took her hand. "Let's dance."

They went through the wide, carved doors into the Haltersham's main ballroom, where the chandeliers were authentic Tiffany art glass and the windows, topped with graceful fanlights, looked out on the crescent of silvery moon suspended as if on a string above the dark mountains.

The band had a keyboardist this year. They were playing a dubstep version of "Deck the Halls." They'd turned the Tiffany lights down low and a strobe flashed on the packed dance floor. Deck pulled her onto the floor and they bopped around to the crazy beat, laughing and having a great time.

After several fast songs in a row, the band finally played a slow one. Deck gathered her close. They swayed to "All I Want for Christmas," and she wished she could capture the moment, like a scene in a snow globe, the two of them dancing. Married. Together. At the one and only Haltersham Holiday Ball.

Monday, Willow called Nell. Griff's family had already left for Southern California. Willow and her new husband were leaving the next day. They would spend Christmas in San Diego.

"Come for lunch here at the house," her mother offered—well, it was more of a summons, really. And that had Nell suspecting that Willow planned to offer some annoying bit of motherly advice.

Didn't matter, though. Not really. Nell wanted to see her mother anyway, to wish her well and say good-bye.

Willow would be in Southern California until after the holidays. She would return only to collect the few things from the mansion that she wanted to keep— and, after that, to visit now and then.

Griff wasn't there when Nell arrived, which made her even more certain that Ma wanted a private talk, just the two of them. Estrella served them chef's salads and hot homemade bread in the dining nook off the kitchen.

Willow chattered away, about how happy she was, about her fondness for Griff's family and for her own stepchildren, too. She laughed at that. "Who knew I would end up loving Sondra's children?"

Nell felt her eyes fill. Lately she seemed to tear up over everything. "Never in a million years," she agreed. "But loving your stepchildren looks good on you, Ma."

Eventually, Willow did get around to the subject of Deck. "He's a good man—and he's always been the *right* man for you. You need a guy who can keep up with you. I'm so glad you two finally got back together."

"Yeah. We're happy. Together. It's working out great." They were. And it was. And so why did she sound so limp and pitiful when she said it? She loved him, deeply. Completely. More so, if that was even possible, than she had all those years ago. And yet something within her still held out against telling him she belonged to him, against promising him all of her days, now and forever.

Ma asked, "What is it? What's holding you back, Nellie?"

Did life get any weirder? She was actually considering confiding in her mother.

And then she did it. She admitted, "I guess I'm still not completely over how bad he hurt me way back when."

Willow sipped her sparkling water. "It's understandable. I mean, at the time, you and the rest of your brothers and sisters were furious with each other and with your lives—and with me and your father, too—for a number of valid reasons. Back then, you never willingly told me what was going on with you. But even I knew that Declan had cut you to the core."

"Everybody knew."

Willow reached across and laid her hand on top of Nell's. "You sat in your room for weeks. You never washed your hair and you lived on Cheetos and Mountain Dew."

"Ma, he hurt me so bad. It was the deepest, dirtiest kind of blow—not only to my heart, but to my sense of myself as a person worth loving. And now, I just can't stop myself from wondering, what if he does it again?"

Willow gave Nell's hand a gentle squeeze before pulling away. "He won't. He's a grown man now. He's ready for a strong woman like you. Plus, look how hard he's fought to get another chance with you. That man is not going to mess it up with you again."

"How can you be sure? How can *I* be sure?"

"I'm so sorry, baby girl. I don't have the answer to that one. I'm fresh out of guarantees. But I do think that at some point, you just have to do it, go for it. You have to let yourself love full out, to open your heart wide and give the man you love your trust. Yes, that will mean you give him the way to hurt you the most. But it's also the only way to real, lasting happiness with another human being."

Chapter Eleven

Nell left the Bravo Mansion at a little after one. Her work schedule that afternoon was light, with no appointments. She called Ruby just to make certain there was nothing she needed to deal with right now.

"Nope," Ruby said. "There's nothing that can't wait till tomorrow."

"All right then, I'm taking the afternoon off."

Nell headed to Denver, where she bought Deck his Christmas present.

She got back in time to meet him at his house at six for the move to her place. They would live at the loft until Christmas, so she boxed up everything under his tree to take with them.

Stuck between a present from Marty wrapped in gold foil and another from Clara and Dalton, she found the envelope from Keith. Apparently, Deck had stuck it there the other day for reasons that made zero sense to Nell. She dropped the envelope into the box with the other gifts.

The box full of gifts was big and unwieldy, so when they got to the loft, she had Deck carry it up the stairs. She opened the door for him and ushered him in ahead of her. "Go ahead and unload it, would you?"

"Sure." He carried it over to the tree and set it down.

As he knelt to do the job, she reminded him, "That letter from your dad is in there."

"I know." He didn't look up, just kept picking up bright packages and shoving them under the sparkly aluminum tree.

"You threw it under the tree at your house?"

"That's right." He still didn't look at her.

It was probably a good time to just let it go. But that unopened letter annoyed her no end. Okay, he had problems with his father, but what if there was something important in there? "You ever plan to open it?"

He did look at her then, a swift glance tight with impatience. "I'll open it at Christmas with the rest of the presents. How 'bout that?"

"It's a present?"

"How the hell would I know? I haven't opened it yet."

She put up both hands. "Well, all right, Mr. Cranky Pants. Guess we'll find out what's in it at Christmas."

"Nellie…" At least he sounded a little bit sorry.

Not that she cared. "There's more stuff in my truck." She turned for the door again.

He was up and across the room in about a second and a half. "Hey…" He caught her arm.

"Let me go. I have things to do." But she made no move to pull away.

He slid his hand up under her hair, gathered her close and pressed his lips to the spot between her eyebrows. The tender little kiss felt good—even if she did find him totally exasperating. In a sexy, manly, irresistible kind of way.

"Sorry," he whispered. "I'm an ass."

"Yeah. Pretty much."

"Forgive me?" He tipped up her chin. "Please?"

She whispered, "Yes," as his lips met hers in a slow, sweet kiss.

It seemed to Deck that he could feel her resistance, that she still wasn't sure yet, wasn't ready to promise him the rest of their lives.

Christmas was a week away and he couldn't figure out how things would go down at the deadline. It was driving him crazy. He wanted to talk to her about it.

But what was there to say?

Are you staying with me, Nellie?

Such a damn, simple question.

Except, what if she said no?

He just needed to stop thinking about it, let it be. Enjoy her and what they had together, face her decision when the time came.

They finished bringing everything in and putting it away. She suggested they go down to McKellan's for dinner.

Later, in bed, it was as good as it had ever been. Better. Every time was better.

In the morning, she scrambled eggs for their breakfast. She made them so light and fluffy, but not too dry.

Exactly the way he liked them.

They went to work, came home. Bought groceries. Shared a meal, went to bed.

It was all so ordinary, their life together. Ordinary in the most perfect way. It was all he'd ever wanted, really, even when he'd thrown it all away. A good life with the right woman—with Nellie.

A dog, maybe, midsize with short hair, as they'd planned at the Holiday Ball. And, someday, a kid or two.

Why did time always go by so fast when you only wanted to make it slow the hell down, when you wanted every minute to last?

All of a sudden, it was five days till Christmas, then three, then two.

On Christmas Eve, Nell's half sister Elise and her husband, Jed, threw a little party at their place for family and friends. It was several couples and a few single friends, pretty much everyone in their circle who didn't have kids yet. They had dinner and then they went downstairs to Jed's man cave, where they played pool, pinball and video games. Elise's enormous cat, Mr. Wiggles, draped himself on top of a tall corner cabinet and looked down on the party through narrowed amber eyes. Elise had put a silly elf suit and hat on the big guy. That cat wore it in style.

Back at the loft, they made love by the fire. And then, a second time, in bed.

By then it was two in the morning.

Christmas Day already. Dread had curled up tight in his belly, a rattler ready to strike.

"Get some sleep," she whispered, and turned off the lamp.

"Come here." He hooked an arm around her waist and pulled her flush against him, her back to his front, spoon style. She snuggled in good and close, her perfect butt right where it would do the most good, perking him up all over again.

He nuzzled her hair. "You smell like Jordan almonds. I love Jordan almonds."

"It's my shampoo."

"It's so damn sexy…"

She took his hand and eased it up between her beautiful breasts. "I mean it," she scolded in a whisper. "Go to sleep."

He cradled one breast, pressed his nose even deeper into her fragrant hair and closed his eyes.

It was going to be all right. It had to be. If she had it in her head to leave him, she wouldn't have made love with him twice tonight, would she?

She wouldn't let him hold her like this, so close, so intimate.

So absolutely right…

"Declan. Oh, Declan…" Nell's voice, in a sweet little singsong, teased him awake.

Was that coffee he smelled?

He opened one eye to a slit—enough to see her standing over him in her flannel snowman pajamas and a giant, floppy cardigan, a steaming mug between her hands.

"Merry Christmas." She smiled down at him.

Deadline day—or more specifically, their last day before the deadline. One way or another, by tomorrow, she would decide.

And right now, she *was* smiling. So far, so good. He asked hopefully, "Is that coffee for me?"

"Yes, it is." She laughed and backed up, holding out the cup. "But you have to get up to get it."

He threw back the covers and swung his bare feet to the rug. "Gimme that."

She backed up another step, taking one hand off the coffee mug and using it to make a show of fanning herself. "Put something on. When you're naked, it's too hot in here."

He would have made a grab for her, but then she might spill the coffee and it looked scalding hot. So he got up and strolled to the bureau against the far wall. He took out a pair of sweats, his ancient waffle Henley and some heavy socks, and put them on as she stood there, watching him, a teasing smile on those lips he never could wait to kiss. She looked downright adorable. Plus, she had coffee.

Once he was dressed, she let him have the mug. He took that all-important first sip. "This might be heaven I'm in right now." He paused to sniff the air. "Is that breakfast I smell?"

She crooked a finger at him and backed toward the door. "This way…" And she led him to the main room, where the table was all set. "Here you go." She pulled out his chair for him.

"I'm liking this." He sat down and she served him. "Eggs Benedict." He couldn't resist putting out a feeler. "Okay, that does it. This needs to be a Christmas-morning tradition." He held his breath waiting for her answer.

"Merry Christmas," she said again, and leaned in

for a kiss, one he thoroughly enjoyed—even if her answer told him zero about how things would shake out.

The food was amazing. He focused on that, on enjoying every bite, on staying firmly in the damn moment, on not thinking of how if she chose to leave him, he would have to let her go because he'd given his sworn word on that, straight up.

And he couldn't go back on his damn word now.

He cleared the table. She turned on the fire and the rotating light for the tinfoil tree. She queued up the Christmas tunes, putting them on nice and low. Beyond the tall windows, the snow was coming down thick and fast.

"Time for presents!" she crowed, clapping her hands like a kid.

"You're really into this," he grumbled, because she enchanted him and maybe he would lose her tomorrow, and if that happened, he had no next move.

"Oh, yes, I am!" She grabbed his hand and towed him over to the sitting area closer to the fire and the big windows with the nice view of the mountains through the swirling snow. "Sit." She pushed him down to the sofa. "Stay." With another happy giggle, she hustled over to the tree and came back with a present. "Here you go. Open it."

It was from Marty. He untied the big purple bow and ripped off the shiny paper. Inside was a Pottery Barn box containing a three-tiered server. "Just what I always wanted," he said without a whole lot of enthusiasm.

"I love it." Nell took it from him and set it on the kitchen counter. "You can put fruit on it." *You?* Did that mean he would be using the damn server alone because she wasn't staying? Or was it just a universal-type you?

"Great idea." He set the empty box aside and went to the tree, returning with a box wrapped in silver. "This one's yours."

"Thank you." She beamed him a sweet smile.

As she opened it, he went and got the rest of the presents he'd chosen for her. There were a lot, because he wanted to give her everything, and when it came to her, he had zero restraint.

There were Louboutin boots and a Fendi bag, a fur-trimmed Prada puffer jacket and a Blancpain Quan-tième Retrograde watch set with diamonds, the face made of mother-of-pearl. There were also several lacy bits of La Perla lingerie—yeah, okay, the bras, thongs and see-through body suits were more for his pleasure than hers.

But she got all excited over them, anyway. She jumped up and announced that it was way too much and he shouldn't have—but she loved it all anyway, every one of the gifts he had chosen for her. "This watch, most of all. Oh, Deck…" She already had it on and she gazed down at it adoringly. "It's amazingly gorgeous even if it did cost too much. I love that you've got one and my dad had one. And now, so do I." She kissed him.

He kissed her back. And for a moment, he almost forgot that he could lose her tomorrow—come on, how could he lose her? In no way did she seem like she planned to go.

She wouldn't be showering him with kisses and jumping up and down over the watch he'd given her if she planned to call it off tomorrow.

Would she?

But then again…

Maybe he just had no clue what she was really thinking.

It had been that way for her, hadn't it, both times he'd left her?

He would never forget that look of pure shock on her face the first time he told her they were through. To her, it pretty much must have seemed out of nowhere. She'd confessed that she'd loaned Keith five thousand dollars.

And he'd just waited until she stopped apologizing and said, "That's it, Nell. We're finished."

She'd given him that look then—stunned. Mortally wounded. Like he'd taken a knife and shoved it straight through her heart. *But…I love you, Deck. You love me. We're forever.*

Yeah, well. None of that matters. I'm through with you. It's over. We're done. And he'd walked away—just left her standing there with her mouth hanging open.

For weeks after that, she kept showing up wherever he went, trying to get him to talk to her. He always refused.

And then nothing. For a while, she left him alone. He didn't know which was worse—her popping up everywhere or not seeing her at all.

Then came that summer afternoon, the air thick with ozone, dark clouds heavy in the sky.

He'd been working at the pizza parlor over on East Creekside Drive and found her waiting outside for him when he finished his shift that day.

"Please, Deck. I just need to talk to you. Just talk to me, that's all."

He should have said no the way he had every other time, just said no and walked away fast.

But he'd missed her so much, like there was a giant, gaping hole inside him that only she could fill. So he'd taken her for a ride out to their special place.

And when he stopped the pickup, he reached for her. She'd landed against his chest with a happy cry and she'd gazed at him so tenderly, green eyes full of hope and a fierce, bright joy. She had thought they were making up, that this was a new beginning for them.

Because no way would he make love to her only to send her away all over again. What kind of lowlife would do something like that?

She didn't understand that it was only a moment of weakness for him—not until afterward, as she was putting her clothes back together. He'd glanced at her sideways, furtive and guilty, because he felt like such a jerk.

And it had happened again. She got that look of pure shock, as though he'd struck her a killing blow. That time, the look only lasted a split second.

Then she got mad…

Now, all these long years later, on Christmas morning with the snow coming down outside, she'd never looked happier. She was humming along to "Rockin' Around the Christmas Tree" as she opened a gift from Garrett and his wife, Cami.

Deck got up and poured them more coffee.

They'd almost made it through the big pile of packages. There remained one good-sized, brightly wrapped box tied with a giant green bow—and the damn letter from Keith that he should have opened days ago. He picked the letter up off the floor and returned to his chair.

She rose, got the box and carried it back to the sofa, where she sat down again, this time with the box in her lap. "This one's for you," she said, her smile blindingly bright. "It's from me." He started to set the letter aside, but she put up a hand. "No. You go ahead. This can wait another minute."

He tore open the envelope.

Inside, he found one sheet of paper—a short note scrawled out by hand. And a check. His stomach heaved and rolled when he saw the amount.

He set the check on the little table next to his chair and read the note to himself.

Son,
I'm happy for you that you finally got back with Nell. She was always the one for you and I know that I'm more than a little to blame for the way it worked out between you and her years go.

It's been eating at me all this time, that I took money from her. Like a lot of things I've done in my life, it just wasn't right.

I know you said you paid her back, so I am paying you back. I know it isn't anywhere near all you've had to pay in your life for something that was never in any way your fault—for a simple accident of fate, having me as your old man. But this check is good in the way that I know matters to you, because I earned the money honestly, selling stuff I made with my own two hands.

You be happy. That's all I want for you.
Sincerely,
Your dad

Deck couldn't breathe suddenly.

It was too much. All of it.

A check for five thousand dollars from the old man. And this letter.

This letter that brought back too damn many ghosts of Christmas past.

And Nell, too. Nell on the sofa with a Christmas present for him, looking so beautiful, his lifelong dream come true—as tomorrow came flying at him way too damn fast.

"Deck?" she asked from across the coffee table and a thousand miles away. "Deck, what does it say? What's the matter?"

He couldn't do it. Not right this minute. He just couldn't deal. He dropped the note on the coffee table. "I need some air." And he got up and headed for the door.

His boots were there. Moving on autopilot, he pulled them on. He grabbed his heavy jacket off the peg and shrugged into it, took his keys from the little dish on the entry table and dropped them into a pocket of the coat.

"Deck! Wait…"

But he couldn't wait. Not until he had some fresh air and a moment or two to himself.

He opened the door, stepped through, pulled it shut behind him and made for the stairs—not the ones to the parking lot. The other ones that led to the door that opened onto the sidewalk in front.

Down he ran. At street level, he shoved the door wide into a wall of freezing wind and blowing snow.

The door shut and locked automatically behind him. For several seconds, he just stood there sucking in air hard and fast as wind and snow whipped around him, blowing his coat open, the snow sticking in his eyelashes, icy cold on his cheeks.

His head spun with images. The glow on her face just now, when she'd opened her presents, how bad he'd hurt her back in the day, the sad, desperate Christmases when he was a kid, especially the worst one— Marty grabbing his arm, whispering frantically, *No, Deck. Dad said to stay right here...*

It was ridiculous.

He was ridiculous.

He needed to get away for a while, get straight with himself, clear his head. Nell wouldn't stay with him, he was sure of that now. What he'd done to her in the old days, it was too wrong. She couldn't possibly forgive him. He was going to lose her again and he had no idea how to keep that from happening.

Talk about irony. He had it all now, everything he'd worked so hard for. Everything but Nellie to share it with.

Through the whirling snow, he could see his Lexus, waiting where he'd left it at the curb, across the street and down. It was still early on Christmas morning—no other vehicles, no people in sight—so he just walked in the street, moving at a slight diagonal toward his car, his mind locked on Nellie, on her beautiful face, on how he would lose her and how he *deserved* to lose her.

The big vehicle came at him from behind. He heard

tires screaming and glanced over his shoulder just in time to see the terrified face of an unknown woman through the windshield.

It happened so fast.

One second he was trudging along, arms folded across his chest against the wind, images of Nellie flooding his brain. And then, out of nowhere, he was flying through the air.

Chapter Twelve

His ass hit the windshield. He felt the weird give of the safety glass as it broke into a web of tiny pieces without actually shattering. There was a faint scream from somewhere—the woman behind the wheel, maybe.

And then he was bouncing again, up onto the roof of the vehicle. He put his hands down to break his fall and managed somehow not to crack his skull open. And then he was rolling again. Some blind instinct for self-protection surfaced. Ducking his head, drawing his knees up and in, bringing his arms up to protect his skull, he somersaulted back over the roof, whacking his left arm a good one as he went. There was a hot bloom of pain on the outside of that arm, midway between his elbow and his wrist.

But he was still rolling, over the back of the vehicle

and down to the frozen ground behind it. He landed
hard—on his ass again. The impact shot up his spine.
He let out a groan.

Stillness. The vehicle had stopped and so had he.
He sat in the middle of the street, his head down, knees
drawn up, left arm cradled against his chest. That arm
hurt like a son of a bitch.

Time got weirdly distorted. For some unmeasur-
able length of it, he just sat there, cradling his injured
arm, wind and snow whipping around him.

He heard the slam of a car door. A moment later,
someone was standing over him. "Omigod! Oh, my
Lord! Are you all right?"

He made himself look up. It was the woman he'd
seen through the windshield. "I think my arm might
be broken."

"Omigod!" she squealed again. "Oh, I'm so, so
sorry. You were just walking. In the street. I didn't
expect that. And the snow was so thick. By the time
I saw you it was too late to stop and I…" She let her
voice trail off as she knelt beside him, cell phone in
hand. And then she gasped. "Ambulance. I should get
an ambulance." She punched up three numbers and
put the phone to her ear.

And then he forgot all about her.

Because Nell was there. "Deck." She knelt on his
other side. She had on that puffy coat he'd given her
a half an hour ago. Her hand clasped his shoulder and
she asked so gently, "Where are you hurt?"

The lady from the SUV was babbling out information to whoever she'd gotten on the other end of
the line.

He just stared at Nellie. God, she amazed him. Just

looking at her made his heart hurt in the best kind of way. She had her red hair tucked under a purple wool hat and she wore those snowman pajamas shoved into a pair of winter boots. Her nose and cheeks had already turned red from the cold.

"Deck, can you hear me? Are you hurt anywhere?" Her eyebrows were all scrunched up in worry over his dumb ass.

"I'm pretty sure I broke my arm, but other than that, I think I'm all right."

"Your head…?"

"You won't believe this. I managed to fly through the air and roll over the back of an SUV and *not* hit my head—and we should probably get out of the street before another car comes along."

She unwound the wool scarf she had around her neck. When he scowled up at her in confusion that she'd suddenly decided to start taking off her clothes, she explained, "For a sling," and got right to work knotting it around his neck, creating a cradle for his bad arm.

"Nellie," he said, still stunned at the miracle of her presence when he'd already reconciled himself to the loss of her. "You're here…"

"Of course I'm here. Now, come on. Let me help you…" She took his good arm and eased it across her shoulders. "Ready?"

"Yeah."

He groaned at the effort and staggered at first, but she hauled him upward and helped him hobble to the sidewalk behind his Lexus. The lady from the SUV trailed along behind them, still talking on the phone.

"We should get you to the hospital," said Nell.

But the woman who'd run into him pulled the phone from her ear and said, "Don't move. An ambulance is on the way." As if on cue, they heard the siren in the distance.

The EMTs stabilized Deck's arm and put him in the ambulance. Nell stayed behind to talk to the guy from Justice Creek PD. The officer asked for Deck's identification, so she went back up to the loft and found it on the dresser in the bedroom. While she was there, she grabbed her purse, too.

Back downstairs, she gave the officer the license, answered his questions and got insurance information from the woman who'd run into Deck. Then, finally, she headed for Justice Creek General.

By the time she got to the emergency room, they'd already x-rayed Deck's arm and given him something for the pain. The ER doctor explained that Deck had a nightstick fracture of the ulna—the outer bone in the lower arm. It was a simple break and Deck was lucky. Most likely, no surgery would be required. The doctor performed closed "reduction," meaning he manipulated Deck's arm to realign the two broken pieces of bone, and then he put on a splint.

In a few days, when the swelling went down, Deck would visit an orthopedic specialist who would probably replace the splint with a cast. In the meantime, the doctor prescribed over-the-counter medications and ice packs applied often for thirty minutes at a stretch.

It was early afternoon when they released him. The nurse took Deck out in a wheelchair—hospital procedure, she said. Nell got her truck from the parking lot and picked him up by the front doors.

He didn't say much during the short ride home. When they got there, he seemed to have no trouble getting up the stairs, and that eased her worry for him a little. A broken arm was no fun, but it could have been so much worse.

In the loft, she wanted to put him to bed, but he insisted he was hungry and would eat at the table. He iced his arm as she heated up soup and made them grilled-cheese sandwiches.

"Feel like a nap?" she asked, when he'd finished his food.

He caught her hand as she reached down to take his empty soup bowl, and an arrow of love for him pierced straight through her heart. "Turn the fire back on." He kissed the back of her hand. "Sit with me on the couch."

She had him brace his injured arm on a pillow, draped a fresh ice pack over it and sat with him. He wrapped his good arm around her. She leaned her head on his shoulder and felt such gratitude, that he was here with her, that he was all right.

He asked, "Did you read that note my dad wrote?"

She tipped her head back enough to brush a kiss on his beard-scruffy jaw. "No. I almost did, to see what had freaked you out so bad. But then that seemed wrong. He didn't write it to me."

"I want you to read it."

That was good, right? That he would share it with her? "Okay." She picked up the single sheet of paper from the coffee table where he'd dropped it before he ran out into the snow. It only took a minute to read it. The simple, heartfelt words made her eyes blur with tears.

"I know you have...problems with him," she said. "But this is a *good* thing that he did, Deck—this letter and the money, too." She tipped her head toward the check he'd left over on the side table.

"You're right. It's a good thing." Deck pulled her close again. "It was...bad when Marty and I were kids. And after my mom died, it got even worse."

She pressed her hand against his chest. He felt so warm and solid. Safe. Here. With her. "I knew it. Though you never would talk about it."

"He never beat us or anything. He loved us, he did. He just... Every cent he got had to go into some big scheme. We were hungry a lot. And he was always gambling and borrowing. Sometimes he gambled or borrowed from guys who took it out on him with their fists when he didn't pay up. He would come home with black eyes—and worse. One time, at Christmastime, a couple of guys he owed money to came to the house."

"Oh, Deck. That's just so horrible and wrong..." She reached up and laid her hand against his cheek.

He gazed down at her, but his eyes were faraway, lost in what had happened all those years ago. "We survived. And we're a lot better off now—Marty and me and Dad, too."

"But still..."

He eased his good arm out from around her and clasped her hand instead. They twined their fingers together. "That time they came after him at the house, I was twelve. It was the year after my mom died. We had this little tree. They knocked it over, smashed up the ornaments. I was hiding with Marty in her closet and we could hear the ornaments breaking out in the living room. Marty begged me to stay put, but

I couldn't stand it. I came out screaming for them to leave my dad alone, leave *us* alone. I yelled at them to stop breaking our tree. One of them popped me a good one right in the jaw. I went down, but then I jumped back up. The guy who'd hit me laughed. And then he hit me again. My dad was begging him to stop, to leave me alone."

"That's so awful. I just can't even imagine it—and wait. What about Marty?"

"She was always smarter than me. She stayed in the closet until they were gone." He let go of her hand to smooth his palm down her hair. "And, yeah, that guy who hit me knew what he was doing. But they gave up and left before he did any permanent damage. I had a few bumps and bruises, but I was okay."

"You were just a kid. It must have been terrifying." Reaching up, she wrapped her hand around his neck and pulled him close, nose to nose. "But all that's over now. You're an amazing man and I love you. I love you so much, Deck."

He went very still then. His eyes burned into hers. "You mean it, Nellie? You're not gonna leave me tomorrow, after all?"

She tried to sniff back the tears, but they wouldn't be held in. A couple escaped and trailed down her cheeks. Tenderly, he brushed them away. She sniffed again. "Deck?"

He kissed her wet cheek. "Yeah?"

"I want you to open your present now, please."

He studied her face as though committing it to memory. "All right. I would like that."

She picked it up from the end of the sofa where

she'd dropped it when she ran out after him. "Here you go. You need help? I mean, your arm and all..."

"I think I can manage."

It took him a little while one-handed, but he got the bow off and tore the pretty paper away to reveal a white box. He removed the lid. Inside, on a fat bed of wadded-up tissue paper was another, much smaller box. She'd wrapped it in pretty paper, too. And tied it with a satin bow.

He slanted her a glance.

She said, "That's the *real* present."

He smiled then, and she saw that dimple in the corner of his mouth, the one that told her everything was good with him. "You're such a tricky girl." He untied the bow on that one and tore off the paper with his teeth. "Damn," he said, when he saw what was inside. "Nellie."

She took the velvet box from him and flipped back the lid to reveal a thick platinum band. "I mean, since we're staying married, you really need a ring. I want all the other women to know they'd better keep their hands off my man."

He breathed her name so softly then—"Nellie," like it was the only word he knew.

She leaned across him and slipped it on his left hand. "There. It looks really good, I think. Even with the splint."

"Nellie."

She lifted up enough to kiss him. He wrapped his good arm around her nice and tight. "Merry Christmas, Deck."

"I love you, Nellie."

"And I love you."

Hope and happiness shone in his eyes. "You and me, that's what you're saying, right? You and me forever?"

She nodded, kissed him again and then rested her head on his broad chest. "That's right."

His warm breath stirred her hair. "And a midsize dog, maybe kids later?"

"All of it, Deck. We're going to have all of it. I'm in it, all the way, with you. I want this marriage, want to make it work, to make a life at your side. The 'till Christmas' deal was a bad idea. I was a coward, afraid to just say yes, let's go for it. Let's make it real. I was afraid you would hurt me again, afraid to put my heart on the line. I'm not afraid anymore—scratch that. I'm terrified. But I do love you. You're the man for me and I want to share my life with you and only you."

"That's what I want, too. All of it, with you. And Nellie, I know I let you down, since we got back together. I should have trusted you more, should have taken you to see the old man like you asked me to."

She shook her head. "I pushed too hard on that, same as I tried to push you to marry me when we weren't even out of high school. I'm an impatient woman, but I'm not pushing now, Deck. Someday, when you're ready, I'm hoping you'll take me to see your dad."

"I will get to that," he said. "I swear it."

"When you're ready," she said again.

They were quiet together, watching the fire.

Then he said, "And Nellie I...well, I want you to know that I'll always regret the way I treated you before. It was so wrong, what I did to you, how bad I hurt you. Twice. I am so sorry."

"I accepted your apology that first night in Vegas, remember?"

"Yeah. I do remember. I remember everything, Nellie. Every moment with you."

"I'm glad." She pulled away enough to look at him then, to hold his gaze with hers. "And I need your promise."

"Name it. Anything."

"I need your word that whatever happens in the future, we face it together. If the barrel business goes bust and Bravo Construction goes belly-up and we're barely getting by, if there's some awful family tragedy— anything, everything, whatever goes down. Deck, we have to turn *toward* each other. We can't ever let pride or fear or grief or anger win out over the love between us, over the life we're going to build together. We can't ever walk away. Do you promise?"

"I do. I promise." And he kissed her, slow and achingly, perfectly sweet. "Merry Christmas, Sparky," he said softly when he lifted his head. "I was sure you would leave me and I got hit by a car. But here we are, together, talking midsize dogs and kids, eventually. All in all, I have to call this the best Christmas I ever had."

The following Saturday, the roads were clear. Nell woke excited for the day to come. They were going to Fort Collins to see Keith McGrath.

Deck's dad welcomed them to his small apartment at the front of the complex. Keith fussed over Deck's arm and Deck said he shouldn't worry. The break was a clean one and healing well. The cast, put on just yesterday, would be off in six to eight weeks.

"Just as long as you're going to be all right," Keith said. Then he offered a simple, straightforward apology to Nell for the way he'd behaved eleven years before.

"Apology happily accepted." Nell hugged him and said how glad she was to see him doing so well.

Keith served them lunch. Once they'd eaten, he took them along a series of paths to the back of the property and around to the far side of a large parking lot. He had a workshop there. He turned on the space heater to warm things up a little and proudly showed off the kid-sized furniture and wooden toys he made.

"Someday," he said with a shy smile, "you two might be needing a few kid-sized chairs and a table to match."

Deck put his arm around Nell. "It won't be right away. But, yeah, Dad. One of these days. And a wooden train set, too."

"Anything," Keith promised with obvious pride. "Turns out I'm pretty good at this carpentry thing. If it can be made out of wood, you just tell me what you want. I'll do my best for you."

A few minutes later, Keith took them back to his place. As they approached the door, a wiry-haired brown dog stuck his head out from under a boxwood hedge.

Keith dropped to a crouch. "All right. Come on, now." The dog wiggled over and Keith scratched him behind his ears and under his chin. "You want something to eat, boy?" The dog gave a hopeful whine. "Come on inside, then." Keith held the door open and the dog led the way in.

"He got a name?" asked Deck when they were gathered in the kitchen. He held out his hand for the mutt to sniff.

"Bailey. A tenant brought him when he moved in, snuck him in, really, because he knew the complex doesn't allow pets. I warned the guy that the dog had to go. A week later, the tenant took off—skipped out on a month's rent, left Bailey here behind." Keith got out a bowl and a bag of kibble. He put down the food and then a second bowl of water. The dog got right to work on the meal. "I'd keep him. But, like I said, no pets allowed. So far, I haven't had the heart to take him to the pound. And wouldn't you know, I just seem to find myself feeding him whenever he comes around? Which happens to be pretty much every day."

Nell crouched by the dog. Bailey stopped eating long enough to wag his tail at her and lick her palm, then went right back to gobbling kibble. She glanced up at the two men standing over her.

Keith made a thoughtful sound low in his throat. "Well, now. You two wouldn't be in the market for dog, by any chance? He's a good dog, friendly. Comes when you call, knows the basic commands…"

"You can stop pitching, Dad." Deck smiled and that special dimple appeared at the corner of his mouth.

Nell rose to stand by her husband. "What do you think?"

He brushed a kiss across her upturned lips. "Looks about midsize to me."

* * * * *

SCANDALOUS
ENGAGEMENT

JULES BENNETT

To my very best friend, Michael. Thank you for giving me the best happily-ever-after.

One

Josie Coleman flung open the front door of her beach-front home and rolled her eyes.

"I've told you for years to just come on in," she exclaimed as she stepped back. "Why do you insist on knocking?"

Her best friend, Reese Conrad, shrugged like he always did when he refused to just walk into her home, where he was always welcome. She always just walked right into *his* house when she stopped by. They didn't live far from each other on this stretch of beach in Sandpiper Cove, North Carolina. It was one of the things she treasured about the place.

"Respect," he replied in that low, gravelly tone of his.

She always asked the same question and he always gave the same one-word response. She'd also offered him a key, but he always said he didn't need one because he only stopped by when she was home.

Typically, they were either at his place, out on his yacht or traveling together when their schedules permitted.

"I thought you were out of town on a work trip." Josie walked through the spacious open layout of her living room and headed back toward the wall of open glass doors leading to her patio. "I'm having coffee if you want to join me."

"It's five o'clock in the evening."

She stopped and threw a glance over her shoulder. "What does that have to do with the love of coffee?"

He laughed and shook his head. Like he didn't know her mad love of coffee?

"I'm good," he replied as he followed her out onto the outdoor living area. "And I cut my trip short because I had seen all I needed to see."

Something crossed through his eyes, something almost…sad. Reese was usually the happiest guy she knew. He had everything—a successful career in the restaurant industry, parents who doted on him and loved him unconditionally, her as a best friend. What more could he need?

Yet something was off.

"Everything all right?" Josie asked as she settled into her lounger and curled her hands around her favorite coffee mug, the one Reese had given her last Christmas.

Reese shoved his hands in his pockets and glanced out at the horizon. It was impossible to be in a bad mood with this view, but she couldn't get a bead on what was going through his head. That was a first. They always knew each other's thoughts. They could be at a party or in a crowded room and one look at each other and they'd smile or nod, knowing exactly what the other had on their mind.

There was something to be said for the unique bond between lifelong besties.

"Honestly—"

Her shrill ringtone cut off anything he was about to admit. Josie sat her mug back on the glass table and picked up her cell, then muttered a string of curses.

"What now?" she answered, totally not in the mood for her ex-husband.

Out of the corner of her eye, she caught Reese staring at her. Reese knew the mess she'd gotten into by marrying the wrong guy on a whim. The marriage had been a mistake and she was still trying to figure out how she'd temporarily lost her mind and agreed to marry a man she didn't love.

Oh, Chris was a nice guy; he just wasn't for her, and lately he'd been trying to win her back. There was no going back.

"Listen, I'm not trying to be rude," she said now into the phone, "but it's not going to happen. We're divorced for a reason." She sat up and swung her legs to the side. "You're a great guy, but we're just not good together, Chris."

Yet he'd been calling and texting more and more. Josie could see where Chris would be confused. They'd only dated for three months before they'd up and eloped. Never in her life had she made rash choices—she prided herself on being just as regimented and predictable as her military father—yet she'd been spontaneous with one of the most important decisions of her life.

For someone normally so methodical about her life, that rush to the courthouse had been completely out of character. But Reese had just gotten engaged and that act had made her wonder if *she* should be entering the next chapter in her life as well.

Obviously, the answer had been no.

Now here they were: she was divorced and Reese had a broken engagement. Maybe they just needed to stay as they were, as they had been for years. They were happy hanging out and traveling together. Having significant others enter the mix would only mess up their perfect best-friend vibe.

But she had yet to get Chris to understand her point of view. Unfortunately, no matter how much she told him she wasn't getting back together with him, he didn't get it. Maybe if he believed there was someone else he would realize there was absolutely no room for him in her life.

"I've moved on," she blurted into the phone as she came to her feet. Josie darted her gaze to Reese, who merely raised his brows in surprise. "That's right. He's here right now, so I have to go."

Josie disconnected the call and tossed her cell onto the lounger she'd just vacated. Reese continued to stare at her, but she just sighed and shrugged.

"He's getting relentless," she defended. "I had to say something."

"So I'm your rebound guy?"

Josie smiled, feeling a tiny bit guilty for using Reese. "He doesn't know who's here, and it was the first thing

that came into my head. He has to think I've moved on
with someone else or he'll keep wasting his time trying to win me back. He has to let it go."

She crossed the patio and placed her hand on his
arm. "I'm sorry I used you as the scapegoat. Let's forget about Chris. What were you getting ready to say
before?" she asked.

"I went to Green Valley, Tennessee," he told her. "It
wasn't just about business."

Josie dropped her arm and wiggled her brows.
"Something personal? A woman?"

He hadn't dated since he'd ended things with his fiancée nearly a year ago. He'd been too busy taking over
his family's posh restaurant empire, with establishments
up and down the East Coast. Recently his father had
suffered a heart attack, which led to open-heart surgery. Reese's parents were now at some tropical resort
to celebrate his life and their new retirement.

So what had Reese been doing in Tennessee if the
trip didn't pertain to his business?

Before he could explain further, the doorbell chimed
and echoed through the house and out the patio doors.
Why did she have to keep getting interrupted when she
was just trying to get the scoop on her friend, who obviously had something serious going on?

"Sorry about that," she told him as she came to her
feet. "I'm not expecting anyone, so just give me one
second."

Josie crossed the living area to the foyer and glanced
through the sidelight. Seriously? What would it take for
Chris to get the hint?

On a frustrated sigh, Josie opened the door. Her ex

stood before her. The man was tall and strong, and always took pride in his athletic build. He wasn't unattractive. He just wasn't the right guy for her. If she could keep him in the friend zone, that would be fine, but he didn't want to accept that.

"Chris," Josie groaned. "We just hung up."

"I know, I know, but I had just pulled up to your house when I called and I only want a few minutes of your time."

Chris stared at Josie with his heart in his eyes and she wanted to tell him to go out with some dignity, for pity's sake.

"I only wanted five minutes in person," Chris explained. "That's all. Just five minutes."

"Chris, we're not doing this again. We're not meant for each other."

"But what if we are?"

Before she could respond, Reese's arm slid around her waist and he pulled her against his side.

"Everything all right, babe?"

Babe? What the hell was he doing?

She glanced from Reese to Chris and remembered what she'd said earlier. Well, damn. Looked like she'd caused a minor mess here.

Chris's eyes went from Josie, to Reese, and back again.

"Can we talk alone?" he implored.

"Say what you want," Reese stated with a smile. "My fiancée doesn't keep secrets from me. Right, lover?"

Was he out of his ever-loving mind? She didn't need his help, and he was making this uncomfortable situation an impossible one.

Engaged? That was taking things a bit far. She'd only mentioned that she'd moved on, not that she'd moved on and was ready to walk down the aisle again.

"You're marrying this guy?" Chris asked. "I always knew there was something more than friends going on with you two. Were you seeing him the entire time we were together?"

"What? No, of course not," she said defensively, wondering how she could circle around and restart this conversation with less chaos and confusion.

"As you can see, Josie is not available," Reese added with another squeeze of her hip. "We're getting ready to go out for the evening."

His hand dipped down over the curve of her hip and too many thoughts and emotions hit her at once. First, why was he being so handsy? Second, was she *enjoying* this?

She shouldn't have a rush of tingles from her best friend's touch. It wasn't like they'd never touched before.

But they'd never touched like this. Not in a faux intimate way.

And it was like something shifted between them.

He was so firm, so strong, and he smelled too damn good.

No.

She shouldn't be thinking of Reese's muscle tone and his cologne. That would only lead to trouble, right?

Yes, trouble with a big fat capital *T*.

The last time she'd let herself step outside her comfort zone, she'd found herself married to the wrong man.

Reese was her *friend*.

Her best friend.

And she needed to keep him in that zone. She liked her life nice and tidy. She liked having everything, and everyone, in their own place.

But that excellent muscle tone...

To save her sanity, Josie extracted herself from Reese and offered Chris a sympathetic smile.

"I do hope you can move on," she told him. "There's a woman out there for you. She's just not me."

Chris's expression went from disbelief, to anger, to... hell, she wasn't sure, but the man wasn't happy.

His eyes scrutinized her. "Are you sure this is what you want? I mean, you're not even wearing a ring. You deserve better. You know I treated you like a queen."

Before Josie could reply, Reese stepped forward.

"What she deserves and doesn't deserve is none of your concern anymore. You've had more than that five minutes you asked for."

Without another word, Reese stepped aside and slammed the door in Chris's face. Josie stared at the space that had just been open and couldn't believe Reese had the audacity to...to...

"Are you serious?" she exclaimed.

Reese turned and started back toward her patio as if he hadn't just acted like a complete jerk. She marched right after him. This was her house, her ex, and Reese wasn't just going to do whatever he wanted and manipulate the situation to his liking!

"Are you going to explain yourself?" she demanded as she stepped outside.

Reese shrugged and took a seat on the sofa. "Explain what? He called and you told him you were in a relationship, so when he showed up, obviously I'm the one who had to play the role."

Josie tucked her hair behind her ears and crossed her arms over her chest. In the last twenty minutes, her ex-husband had said he truly believed they could get back together and her best friend had claimed to be her fiancé. Even stalling for a few seconds trying to gather her thoughts didn't calm her mood or give her any more clarity…especially over the fact that she'd liked Reese's touch more than she should.

"Engaged seems a little over-the-top, don't you think?" she asked.

"Not really. The guy is persistent. You have to push back with people like that. Subtlety isn't something they understand."

"Oh, an engagement and slamming the door in his face were far from subtle hints."

He offered her a wink and a grin. "You're welcome."

Josie growled and clenched her fists. Reese might be her very best friend, but he could be quite infuriating at times…in an adorable kind of way. He meant well, but sometimes that alpha quality took over and common sense vanished.

"Better drink your coffee before it gets cold," he added, pointing to her forgotten mug.

Josie reached for the drink and crossed to where he sat with that smug smirk on his face.

"I really want to throw this in your face," she grumbled.

"Aw, darling. Is that anyway to treat your new fiancé? Be nice or I won't get you that ring you need."

"You know he's going to tell people what just happened," she informed him. "We're both in the public eye. How will we dodge this?"

If she had a job where people didn't recognize her or didn't know her name, Reese's engagement claim wouldn't be a big deal. But considering Reese was a billionaire mogul splashed all over the internet right now for taking over his family's empire, and she was an influencer and columnist for the country's top-selling magazine, there was no way an engagement between them would go unnoticed.

"I'm not too worried about the public." Reese shrugged. Again with that damn shrug, like this was no big deal. "Just wait and see how it plays out. He may surprise you by keeping quiet, or we may need to play it up. What kind of stone would you like in your ring?"

Josie narrowed her eyes. "I'm going to need to switch to wine for this conversation."

Ignoring his chuckle, she stepped back into her house and moved into the kitchen. From her vantage point at the wine fridge, Josie stared out at Reese, who didn't seem to mind that he'd just upended both of their lives. He simply sat in one of the sturdy wicker chairs and stared out at the horizon.

When he'd first arrived today, he'd said he needed to talk. All she'd managed to learn was that he'd been away on personal business. If it hadn't concerned a woman, then what else would it be? He didn't have much of a social life. If he went out to dinners, they were all work-related, and the majority of the time, those dinners were in his own restaurant.

The man worked like a maniac, and that was saying something coming from *Cocktails & Classy*'s most celebrated columnist. Josie never took a day off either, but at least she could work from home and only travel to the headquarters in Atlanta when she absolutely had to. Reese traveled all over, constantly on the lookout for new ways to keep his restaurants fresh and upscale.

She poured a glass of pinot and swirled the contents before heading back out. She never got tired of the ocean breeze, and she always slid open the wall of glass doors when she was home. The added outdoor living space was what had sold her on this house right after her divorce.

Now that she'd calmed down a little, Josie stepped around the coffee table and took a seat on the sofa across from Reese.

"Want to tell me why you got so territorial?" she asked.

He propped his feet on the coffee table and laced his fingers behind his head as he stared at her, since she now blocked his line of sight to the ocean.

"Besides the fact that he was the wrong man for you to marry in the first place? I was trying to help you out."

Josie took a sip and set her glass on the table before leaning forward and keeping her gaze locked on his. "I can fight my own battles."

"You shouldn't have to," he retorted.

While she appreciated the way he was always ready to protect her, she didn't need him to. His failed engagement and her failed marriage had really opened her eyes to the fact that there was no rush to move on to what was expected. Who said she had to get married right now? There was no magical age when she had to be married, and who said she had to be married at all?

But she knew Reese might want a family and a married life of his own.

The day would come when he would find the woman he wanted to spend his life with.

The thought unsettled her. Or maybe it was that Josie could still feel his fingertips along her waist and her hip. She shouldn't still be tingling in those spots, but she was—which was both confusing and frustrating.

Josie's cell buzzed on the table and she glanced to the screen at the same time Reese muttered a curse. Chris's name popped up with an unread message.

"He's still not taking the hint?" Reese asked. "I slammed the door in his face."

She didn't bother opening the text; she would deal with it later…or not.

"Maybe I should've just talked to him for a bit," she stated.

"No. Every time you talk to him, that gives him hope. You just need to cut all ties."

Reese was right, but she really hated being rude. She'd told Chris as nicely as possible that they were really over, and they'd been divorced for six months already. Wasn't that enough of a sign that she was moving on? One would think divorce would be enough "cutting ties," but Chris hadn't wanted the divorce to begin with.

"Don't worry," Reese added. "He'll get the hint once he sees us together and notices my car out front when he drives by."

Josie laughed. "It's not like you'll be here twenty-four hours a day, Reese."

His eyes flashed to hers. "Sure I will. I can work from here. It will be tricky, and I have to do some traveling still, but you're the top priority in my life right now. So which bedroom do you want me to take?"

"Bedroom?" she asked. "You mean—"

A naughty grin spread across his face that sent a curl of unwanted arousal through her.

This was her best friend…what was going on?

"I'm moving in, honey."

Two

Well, this wasn't what he'd planned when he'd arrived at Josie's house yesterday. But damn if he hadn't gotten completely sidetracked by feeling her against his side, having that curvy hip beneath his hand.

He'd always known his best friend was sexy as hell, but she'd always been his friend. Now she was his fake fiancée...how the hell was he supposed to play this out?

What had he gotten them into?

Yesterday he'd needed her advice; he'd needed her guidance and her shoulder to lean on. Not that he did that often, but his life had imploded and he had nowhere else to go.

He was still trying to process everything himself. From receiving a cryptic letter at his office while his father was recovering from heart surgery, to finding out his father wasn't his father at all…if the letter from a deceased woman was actually true.

Reese sank down on the edge of the bed in the guest bedroom of Josie's home and clutched the letter in his hands. When he'd left for Tennessee several days ago, he'd told Josie he'd be gone a week. He'd come back after two days.

Traveling from Green Valley, Tennessee, back to Sandpiper Cove, North Carolina, had only been an hour's flight. Those were the perks of owning your own plane and being your own pilot. He'd taken the time going both ways to think about all that had happened… he still didn't have a clear picture or any answers.

He'd gone to Hawkins Distillery a few days ago and met with Sam Hawkins and Nick Campbell, the two men who were supposedly Reese's half brothers. Nick's late mother had apparently wanted to leave behind a deathbed confession by distributing letters for the three men about their true paternity. She was the one who had mailed the letter to Reese.

They all shared the same father—Rusty Lockwood, billionaire mogul of Lockwood Lightning. Everyone knew the world-renowned moonshine company, but not many knew the man behind it…including Reese.

A week ago, he'd hired an investigator to dig up everything that wasn't easily accessible to the public, and Reese had also been doing his own online research. On paper, or the internet as the case may be, Rusty appeared to be a saint. The man owned the largest moonshine distillery in the world and donated thousands of dollars each year to Milestones, a charity for children with disabilities.

Unfortunately, last week, Rusty had been arrested for skimming from that same charity, and according to Sam and Nick, Rusty was the devil himself. Both guys had dealt with Rusty for years and neither one had a kind thing to say. They weren't happy with the knowledge that Rusty was their biological father.

Reese didn't know what to believe, because all of this had blown up in his face so fast and come without warning. He didn't like being blindsided by anything, especially not a revelation that meant he might have been betrayed and lied to his entire life.

The letter had arrived while his father was in the hospital, but once he was released, he and Reese's mom had gone on a relaxing vacation with the doctor's blessing and Reese didn't want to mess up their time away.

There had just been so much all at once... His father's health, the shifting responsibilities of the business, the letter claiming Reese wasn't his parents' child...

But by the time his parents got back home, Reese hoped he would have a solid plan and some much-needed answers.

Should Reese confront them? Or did he just let this knowledge go and ignore the past? What was the actual truth in all of this? There were so many questions and part of him wished he'd never learned the truth, but the other part of him wanted to know the history... *his* history.

Reese refolded the letter and sat it on the nightstand before coming to his feet. He hadn't gotten much sleep last night, mostly because this wasn't his home and he wasn't used to that cushy bed with all the pillows.

Josie might be very strict and straitlaced when it came to her fashion sense and her career, but she did love a cozy-feeling home. Granted, everything in her house was either white or gray. She really did lack color in her life, but he wouldn't change her for anything.

Especially those damn curves.

Who had known how well she'd fit intimately against his side? Just that simple gesture had conjured up a night of fantasies he shouldn't have allowed himself when it came to his best friend. Didn't he have enough going on in his life without adding an unwanted sexual attraction to Josie?

Reese rubbed a hand over his bare chest and padded from the room and down the hallway toward the kitchen. He needed coffee, because this was the time of day when it was actually acceptable to have a cup. It was too damn early, but he might as well get his day started.

He'd visited here so many times over the years, but he'd never made coffee, so he searched through her cabinets, trying to be quiet because he was positive she was still asleep. He hadn't heard a word from her this morning, and he also knew she wasn't an early riser.

He, on the other hand, had too much to do, including following up with his assistant about the RSVP to the new restaurant opening in Manhattan in two weeks.

Conrad's was moving up the East Coast and opening a big new space in New York. Reese couldn't wait to get into his favorite city. Manhattan had always been a goal of his.

He'd grown up here in Sandpiper Cove and he absolutely loved the beach. Loved it so much, he'd purchased his own private beach with his home, which was not far from Josie. His yacht was docked at the end of his own pier and he didn't want to lay his head down anywhere else.

But this new restaurant in Manhattan would be all his. He'd inherited his father's string of upscale restaurants from Miami up to Boston, but this was his first venture on his own and he had a few changes in place that he was excited to test.

"Good heavens."

Reese turned from the coffeepot to find Josie standing in the doorway, her hand over her chest, her eyes fixed on his. But his eyes immediately locked on the tiny shorts and tank she wore. The outfit left little to the imagination…and last night he'd done plenty of imagining.

"Could you put some clothes on?" she grumbled as she shuffled in.

Reese couldn't help but grin as she made her way to the cabinet and pulled down a mug. Her hair was all in disarray, like she'd had a fight with her pillow all night, and those pj's, black of course, weren't covering much, either. The simple tank dipped too low and the shorts literally covered the essentials and nothing more.

His body stirred in response.

There were some things he could control, like not telling her he'd like to strip her down and pleasure her beyond anything she'd ever known. But there were other things, like his arousal, that weren't quite so easy to hide.

Damn it. He had to get a grip. This was Josie. He couldn't risk a quick romp just because suddenly his hormones had woken up and realized she was sexier than he'd known.

They were friends…nothing more.

"You've seen me in swim trunks. This is hardly any different," he replied, taking the mug from her hands. "Go sit. I'll get this for you."

She shoved the hair from her face and went to the bench at her kitchen table. "Trunks are one thing, but boxer briefs are another. If you're staying here, put some damn pants on."

Reese poured two cups of coffee, leaving hers black to match her wardrobe and her bleak mood.

"I don't recall you being this grouchy in the mornings," he told her as he sat across from her. "I know you're more of a night owl, but this is a new side."

She curled her hands around her mug. "This is my only side before caffeine. Be quiet so I can enjoy it."

Reese sipped his hot coffee and waited on Little Miss Sunshine to perk up. Clearly, she'd had a restless night, too. He didn't even try to hide the fact that he was staring at her. She looked like a hot mess, which irritated the hell out of him because his boxer briefs were becoming more and more snug. There was going to be no hiding anything in a few minutes.

"Shouldn't you be lifting weights or jogging or going to some meeting where you fire people?" she asked around her mug.

Reese laughed. "Glad to know what you think of a day in the life of Reese Conrad."

She merely shrugged, causing one slinky shoulder strap to slip down her arm. Reese's eyes landed on that black string and he barely resisted reaching out to adjust it.

Hands to yourself.

A physical relationship would certainly change things between them, but the main question was—would they be better or worse?

Wait. What?

Why was he even letting his mind travel to that space? He needed to get control over his wayward thoughts and keep himself in check.

"You don't have to stay here, you know."

His focus shifted back to her face. She stared at him over the rim of her mug. Those dark eyes never let on to what she was truly thinking…just another way they were so alike. Both held their emotions close to their chest.

"How many times did Chris text you last night?" he asked.

Josie's eyes darted away as she mumbled something under her breath. He thought he heard a staggering number, but even one was one too many at this point. Beyond the fact that they were divorced, she'd blatantly told Chris no and Reese had mentioned they were engaged. A lie, sure, but Chris didn't know that. The man should back off.

"All the more reason for me to stay for a while," Reese replied.

Maybe his presence would keep Chris away, maybe it wouldn't. Reese really had no idea. He did know that he obviously enjoyed a round of torture before breakfast because he was in no hurry to move away from his newly appealing best friend and get going on his busy day.

Did she always sleep in something so damn…sexy?

Maybe they did need to set some clothing boundaries now that they were temporarily living together.

Their friendship was solid; it was perfect. They completed each other and there was nobody else he would trust with every aspect of his life. But he wasn't quite ready to open up about that letter. He still wasn't sure what to do with the truths it had revealed, and the strange things he was feeling since announcing their fake engagement weren't helping him figure it out.

Only a week ago, his main worry had been about his Manhattan opening and now…well, that opening was the least of his worries. He and his selected launch team had a good handle on the upcoming momentous day and Reese truly believed the opening would be nothing short of a smashing success.

"How's your father?" she asked as she set her mug down. "Still doing good?"

His father. Those two words sounded so odd now, so foreign. He had no idea how he felt about the changes in his family, except maybe a little deceived that the people he'd loved his entire life had lied to him from the beginning.

"Reese?"

He blinked and focused on Josie. "He's fine," Reese replied. "His doctor has checked on him every day since they've been gone."

"That's great. Your mom and dad have worked so hard and then for him to have heart surgery right after retiring—he deserves some downtime."

Which was one of the reasons Reese had been holding on to this letter, this secret. When the letter came, it had been with a stack of mail that Reese hadn't gotten to immediately. He'd been so swamped with taking over the Conrad restaurants, plus working on the launch of the new one, that if something didn't seem pressing or like an emergency, he'd put it on the back burner.

Josie sighed and came to her feet, bringing his attention back to her.

"I have to finish my article before my noon deadline," she told him. "I'm just going to grab a quick shower first. Feel free to use the guest bath or head on home and get ready there. We can meet up for dinner later if you're free."

She sashayed out of the room…and that was the best way he could describe those swaying hips beneath that flimsy material. It was driving him out of his mind.

He was going to need a shower, too. A very, very cold shower to get control of this new reaction to his best friend, one he should ignore.

Reese cleaned up the few dishes in the kitchen and headed to the spare room to throw on his clothes from yesterday and head to his house for a few things.

As he moved toward his room, he heard a thump from one of the other guest bedrooms. Then a string of muttered curses followed and Reese let his curiosity get the best of him. He circled back to the nearly closed door and tapped his knuckles on the frame.

"You okay?" he called.

The door flung open and Josie seemed even more frazzled than earlier. A strand of inky black hair fell across her face and she blew it away.

"What are you doing?" he asked, trying to peek over her shoulder.

"Nothing."

Because she tried to slip out the door, Reese took it upon himself to put a hand on the wood and ease it back open.

"You know you're a terrible liar."

He stepped around her and into the room. Simple furnishings with whites and neutrals, a white rug on the hardwood, a sturdy white chair in the corner with a black-and-white-striped pillow.

"Is this where you keep all your journalism secrets?" he joked. "Cocktail recipes or dinner party themes? Am I close?"

"Funny," she mocked, crossing her arms over her chest. "I don't have secrets and even if I did, you would already know them."

The closet door was open just enough for Reese to see a slash of red. Interesting, considering he never saw her in an actual color, let alone something so vibrant.

He moved to the closet and revealed a walk-in space full of the widest variety of colorful clothes he'd ever seen. There were two rows of hanging clothes…all with tags dangling from the sleeves. Boxes of shoes lined the perimeter of the floor and the most insane number of designer handbags in all colors and patterns topped off the high shelves.

Reese glanced over his shoulder, turning his attention to Josie, who glared back at him.

"Opening a department store, Jo?"

She tipped her chin in that defiant way of hers. "No."

"What's with all the brand-new clothes?" he asked, glancing back to the closet that clearly held thousands of dollars' worth of merchandise. "And all this color? Are you giving yourself a makeover?"

Josie's eyes darted to the open room, then down for just a second, but enough for him to see her vulnerability.

"Want to talk about this?" he asked.

She shook her head. "Nothing to talk about. I come in here every morning before I get ready."

"Trying to find something to wear?"

Why was she not just saying whatever she was thinking? For someone who wore black like it was her job, she certainly had a hell of a lot of funds tied up in a brand-new, not-black wardrobe.

"I can't be her," she murmured.

What? What did that even mean? Who couldn't she be?

Forgetting the lame joke he'd been going for when he first saw this shocking surprise, Reese took a step toward her, wondering what she'd been hiding and why she seemed so sad, so…almost helpless.

She'd just told him she didn't keep any secrets, but that had clearly been a lie because all of this was obviously something she wanted to keep to herself. How long had this closet full of color been here? And who couldn't she be like?

"Jo—"

An alarm went off from somewhere in the house. Josie immediately turned from the room. Confused as to what had just happened and what the annoying noise was, Reese followed her. He was tempted to grab something from the newly discovered closet to throw over her excuse for pajamas to conceal that dark skin of hers.

Granted, he wasn't covered much, either, but she was a temptation he was having a difficult time resisting.

There was only so much a man could take, but the risk of taking what he suddenly wanted was too much. Their friendship was too special, too perfect the way it was. He couldn't afford for his life to get any messier.

Reese found Josie back in the kitchen tapping away on her phone and thankfully killing that annoying alarm.

"Sorry," she stated with a smile. "That was my reminder to check my planner."

Reese stared at her as she continued to scroll. "You need a reminder to check your schedule? Isn't that just a given?"

Her eyes darted to his and for the briefest of seconds, that heavy-lidded gaze dipped to his chest. Well, well, well. Even with the caffeine and a somewhat better mood, she wasn't immune to his nakedness.

So now what? There was a sudden sexual pull that confused him, intrigued him...challenged him.

"I have an alarm to remind me about nearly everything," she informed him, setting her cell back on the table and turning to face him fully. "A reminder to drink all my water, feed my plants, check in with my new assistant because she seems a little overwhelmed at times, and—"

Reese held up a hand. "I get it. I knew you were structured, but I had no idea it was to this extent."

Josie smiled. "I can set up your phone so you are more organized with various reminders if you want."

"I've got it all up here," he said, tapping his head. "And my assistant is on everything before I can even think, so I'm good. I wouldn't know what to do with that annoying alarm going off all the time."

"Oh, I have different alarms for different reminders," she countered with a scoff. "I can't have one alarm, Reese. That wouldn't make any sense."

"Of course," he mumbled, then shrugged. "What was I thinking? I guess it's true that you never really know someone until you live with them."

Josie shook her head as she rolled her eyes. "We're not living together. You can go to your place at any time."

"You coming with me?" he asked.

"I'm good here, and Chris is going to be a nonissue," she stated with more confidence than she should have.

Why would Chris give up? Reese sure as hell wouldn't. Josie's ex had had the best woman in the world and he'd let her slip away.

"I'm really going to get a shower now," she told him. "I'm already behind on my morning routine."

As Josie started to pass, Reese took a step to block her. Her hands flew up and flattened on his chest, those dark eyes flashing up to his.

"What's with the closet, Jo?" he asked, really needing to understand what she was hiding, because he'd seen that flash of vulnerability and hurt and he hated knowing she experienced both.

Though it was damn difficult to concentrate with their clothes nearly nonexistent and her hands on his bare skin. Reese had to respect her, respect their friendship and remain in control.

Crossing that invisible barrier into something more intimate would be a mistake. Where had this damn attraction come from? Sexy was one thing, but the ache, the *need* was frustrating.

"Don't worry about the closet," she murmured with a flashing smile. "Why don't you worry about your upcoming restaurant opening instead of me?"

Reese smoothed her hair back from her shoulder, once again torturing himself with the touch of her satiny skin.

"Oh, Conrad's Manhattan is in the forefront of my worries, but what kind of fiancé would I be if I didn't add you to the list?" he joked.

Josie laughed, just as he thought she would, but her eyes dropped to his lips a fraction of a second before she took a step back and sighed.

"You're not my fiancé, Reese. We're just friends."

She licked her lips and blinked as if those last two words were painful to say.

"Just friends," she reiterated beneath her breath as she walked away.

Reese didn't turn to watch her disappear down the hallway. He needed a minute because this morning had been so bizarre. Did Josie have stronger feelings for him than she was letting on? Would she be interested in exploring more with him? And what the hell was up with all of those colorful clothes hanging in the closet with tags?

One thing was certain: now that they were temporarily living together, Reese had to evaluate his feelings and try to figure out what the hell was truly going on between him and his best friend.

Three

Rain pelted down in sheets, right onto Reese. He seriously missed his garage for this very reason. He ran from his SUV to the porch of Josie's beachside home. The second he stepped beneath the shelter, he raked the water from his face. He was absolutely drenched and his overnight bag with dry clothes was in the car because he hadn't wanted to get that soaked as well. He'd just have to dry off and wait out the storm.

He rang the doorbell and glanced in through the sidelight. He didn't see any movement, but surely she was home. He really should've taken that key she'd offered him a long time ago, but why would he have ever had a reason to be here without her?

He rang the bell again and waited. Finally, the lock clicked and the door flew open. Josie stood before him in a black tank and a pair of black shorts, but her hair dripped water droplets onto her shoulders and face and she swiped moisture from her cheeks.

"What the hell happened to you?" he asked.

"There's a leak above my closet," she growled as she turned to race back toward the guest room. "This damn storm."

He closed the door and slid out of his wet shoes so he didn't slide on the tile leading down the hallway. Reese followed her and realized the closet in question was the one with the hoard of colorful clothes. The contents were strewn across the room. Boxes of shoes lay haphazardly along the floor; dresses were in heaps over the chair in the corner and all over the bed. Handbags littered the space around the shoes.

Good grief, there was even more than he'd first realized. How had all of this fit in that space? Granted it was a walk-in closet, but still. Josie really could open a boutique with all of this variety.

Her muttered curse filtered out from inside the closet. Reese stepped in to find her strategically moving buckets beneath the drips.

"Every time I think I have it, another area presents itself," she told him. "I do not have time for this."

"Do you have more buckets?"

She shook her head. "I have vases. There are several on the kitchen island. Just dump the flowers in the trash."

Reese raced from the room and headed to the kitchen where he came to an abrupt stop. The most obnoxious display of flowers covered her entire island. A wide variety of colors and blooms…all fresh and nothing Josie would ever purchase for herself.

No surprise to find cheesy notes attached. Reese made quick work of getting rid of the flowers, then he took armfuls of vases back to the closet.

"Want to discuss this?" Reese asked, holding a vase up and wiggling it.

"Nope."

"You have thousands of dollars' worth of flowers spread across your island."

"Not my money," she said, taking one vase at a time and looking at the ceiling for where to usefully place it. "And before you say anything else, I definitely realize Chris is an issue now."

Well, at least that was something. Chris wasn't going to just slink away. Reese truly believed the man thought he stood a chance at getting Josie back, but that wasn't happening.

"Why did you marry him to begin with?" Reese asked, his thoughts coming out before he could stop himself.

Josie reached for another vase, her dark eyes locking on his for the briefest of moments. "That's a conversation for another time."

And definitely one he would circle back to, because he'd wondered this since the moment she'd dropped the bomb that she'd eloped at the courthouse. The courthouse, for crying out loud.

Josie deserved more than a quickie wedding. He remembered her always talking about wanting a ceremony on the beach, small and intimate. Her love of the beach was just another thing they had in common…granted, he wasn't looking for marriage.

That engagement of his had been a mistake and one he'd likely have to answer for when they circled back to the topic later. Josie deserved an explanation, too.

Reese took the last two vases and looked around, but didn't see any more leaks. He sat them aside and pulled out his cell. Getting his contractor out here as soon as this storm passed was imperative, before any more damage was done.

Minutes later, he disconnected the call and focused back on Josie.

"My guy will be here as soon as he can."

Josie glanced from bucket to bucket to vase. "This place is a mess."

"Have you seen any other leaks?"

Josie's eyes widened and she pushed passed him to exit the closet. In her hurried, frantic state, he assumed that was a no. Whatever room she went into, he looked in another. It didn't take long to find that there were two other small leaks, both in Josie's bedroom.

"This is an absolute nightmare," she sighed once the other vases were in place and they'd gone back into the kitchen.

"It can all be fixed," he assured her. "My guy is the best and once this storm passes, we'll get it taken care of."

Josie pushed her hair from her face and stared at the mess of blooms and greenery. "I do feel bad putting them all in the trash."

"Then don't." Reese reached for one stem and picked it up, examining it before glancing back to Josie. "We can make smaller arrangements and take them to the cardiac unit where Dad was. We could give some to the nursing staff and some to the patients."

Josie granted him the widest, sweetest smile. "I would have never thought of that. You're sweet sometimes, you know."

Reese shrugged, not really needing compliments for just trying to find a solution to this mess.

"He had excellent care there, so maybe these would brighten their day. And I know they always have patients with no family."

"Always thinking of others." Josie reached up and rested her hand on the side of his face. "One day you're going to find the right woman. She's going to be damn lucky."

"You're the only woman who puts up with me," he joked.

She dropped her hand and glanced to the flowers. "Well, you keep up with those sweet gestures and you'll be taken in no time."

Taken. The only place he wanted to be taken was to a bed with Josie. Or here in the kitchen would work.

But Josie had everything and everyone in a particular slot, and he was in the friend zone, which hadn't been an issue…until now. The structure in her life stemmed from her retired military father. Her mother had passed away when Josie was a toddler, so she didn't remember her and Reese had never met the woman.

"I'm not looking for marriage," he stated honestly. "Being engaged was enough of a scare to make me realize I prefer being married to work. That's a relationship I can feed into and grow, not to mention control."

"Ah, yes. Control. Well, that is why you'll always be alone. Women don't want to be controlled," she scolded. "Don't you want to have someone to come home to? Someone to share everything with? Someone to grocery shop with?"

Reese laughed. "First of all, I don't grocery shop. Second, I tell you everything. And when I come home, I have a glass of bourbon. All my bases are covered."

Josie rolled her eyes. "That sounds so lonely."

"And in my defense, I'd never want to control a woman," he told her. "I know not to fight a losing battle."

"You really are a great guy," she stated again.

"Are you vying for a new position?" he asked. "We are engaged, after all."

"We're not engaged," she laughed. "Though I might need to convince Chris you were telling the truth because clearly he didn't believe us or he just doesn't care."

"Or he's an idiot, which is my vote," Reese added. "Pack a bag and come to my place."

Josie's eyes widened. "What? I'm not just coming to your place. My house is falling in, if you haven't noticed."

"Your house isn't falling in. My guy will be here to fix everything and you don't want to be here during that construction anyway." Reese reached for her and raked his thumb over her ring finger. "We need to get a ring."

Josie pulled her hand away and laughed. "Can you focus for two minutes?"

"Oh, I'm focused."

She rolled her eyes and turned her attention back to

the flowers. "Let me find some tissue paper and ribbon. I'm out of vases."

"Just gather them all up and we'll find vases at my house," he told her. "Grab a bag of whatever you need to stay the night."

"This is silly, you know." Josie started gathering the flowers. "I can stay here."

"You can, but why?" he countered, helping her gather everything. "We'll do a movie night like we used to."

She stilled and gave him a side-eye. "I get to choose the movie?" she asked.

Reese cringed. "Don't tell me."

Josie squealed and a wide grin spread across her face. "Oh, you know it."

Yeah, he did. Her all-time favorite movie was *An Affair to Remember*. She'd first introduced it to him when they were in high school and he'd absolutely hated it. Since then, any time she chose the movie, that's the one she went with. He didn't hate it now—hell, he could say the thing word for word. If she enjoyed it, that's all that mattered.

"Go pack your stuff and I'll take the flowers," he told her. "I'll meet you at my house."

"Deal."

She practically skipped from the room and Reese couldn't help but feel a niggle of worry deep in his gut. Spending more time alone with Josie had never been an issue before, but his hormones had never entered the picture before, either. At least, not like this. Now she was coming to his house for the night and Reese couldn't help but wonder how much more he could take before he snapped and crossed the line they couldn't come back from.

He was a jumble of nerves—between the mysterious closet she hadn't explained, the letter he'd received and the fact that he wanted Josie more than anything he'd ever wanted.

One night. He just needed to take this fake engagement one night at a time. Surely he could control himself for one night…right?

Josie pulled through Reese's gate and wondered how she'd let him talk her into this. Granted, she hadn't put up much of a fight. She'd been tired, worried about her roof, and she really didn't want to be present when workers started banging around and making more of a mess.

Still. Was he going to parade around in those little black boxer briefs again? True, she'd seen him in swim trunks, but that was before something had shifted in her mind with the words *my fiancé*.

That was before he'd pulled her into his side and caressed her hip like only a lover would do. There was something so possessive, so damn sexy about the way he'd taken charge. Her entire life she'd prided herself on being independent. Yet the way Reese had claimed her had done something to that friend switch and she wasn't sure she could flip it back to the way it used to be…the way it was *supposed* to be.

Ugh. This entire situation had gotten out of control so fast, she was both confused and frustrated. For someone who always had every damn thing in order and under control, her mental state was a complete mess.

Josie pulled around the circular drive and stopped right in front of the steps leading up to Reese's insanely large beach house. The man never did anything in small proportions. His house was easily four times the size of hers and he lived alone. His chef and maid came and went—they were hardly ever seen, yet the house remained immaculate and there were always fresh dishes in the refrigerator.

Reese treated his employees like family and they remained so loyal and went above and beyond to please him. He might be a billionaire mogul, but he was literally the only person she knew with a selfless heart of gold.

Josie's cell chimed just as she put her car into Park. If this was another text from Chris...

She'd totally downplayed how much he'd texted and called because she didn't want Reese to go complete Neanderthal on her...though proclaiming upcoming nuptials had been pretty caveman of him.

She opened the text, relieved to see it was from her editor, Melissa, but that relief quickly turned to dread.

Congrats on the big engagement! We just posted a blog teaser, but I want a Q&A with you and Reese ASAP! This is so exciting!

With her breath caught in her throat, Josie reread Melissa's text. Josie had confided in her assistant, Carrie, earlier that morning, more joking than anything, that Reese had claimed they were engaged and her world had been flipped upside down, but she was still getting that column in on time.

Josie had thought they were just having random chatter and now this? A teaser blog post had already gone up on the site...the site that had hundreds of thousands of hits per day. There was no pulling back from such a dramatic announcement without tarnishing the stellar reputation of not only *Cocktails & Classy*, but of her own image as well.

Josie stared at the message, unsure how to respond. She did, however, know who was responsible for this leak. As if following up with her somewhat new assistant constantly to make sure things were done properly wasn't annoying enough, now she couldn't trust her.

And here they'd thought getting rid of Chris would be the biggest issue.

Obviously, Josie's assistant would have to be dealt with first thing in the morning. Right now, though, she had one other matter to handle.

She had to actually fake an engagement to her best friend. This had gone beyond just lying to her ex. Now the public was aware of her personal life, too.

Josie hit Reply and chose her words carefully. Thankfully, she wasn't responding in person and dealing with Melissa seeing her shocked face.

Thanks. I had no idea you would find out this way. We're still processing the news, so the Q&A might have to wait.

Josie knew her fans would want the scoop, especially since she was coming off a divorce only six months ago. The outpouring of love and kindness had overwhelmed her and left her feeling a little guilty, considering she hadn't loved Chris. He'd been a nice guy who'd come along at the wrong time. Why wouldn't he just let her set him free?

She prided herself on being available to her readers and really interacting with them, so it was quite understandable that Melissa would want to share the happy news with the world. Unfortunately, the last thing Josie wanted was another public relationship…another *failed* public relationship. Because this fake engagement certainly wasn't going to last.

Josie didn't wait for a reply. She grabbed her purse and suitcase and headed up the steps to the front door. She was going to have to tell Reese about all of this and then she'd have to see how he felt about a real, fake engagement.

Good heavens, he'd probably do something stupid like really go buy her a ring. And knowing Reese, the thing wouldn't be subtle or cheap.

If only she'd kept her mouth shut earlier on the phone. But in her defense, Josie hadn't had any reason not to trust her assistant. And maybe Carrie was just chattering and not thinking when she told Melissa. Still, the lie was out there and Josie was going to have to deal with the consequences.

The front door flew open and Reese reached for her suitcase. Josie jumped back at his abrupt greeting.

"Why didn't you use the elevator?" he scolded. "I would've gotten this for you so you didn't have to lug it up the stairs."

"It wasn't a big deal," she replied as she stepped into the open foyer. "I'm quite capable of carrying my own luggage."

He muttered something about her being stubborn, but she let that roll off. She was well aware of her stubborn side and she wasn't apologetic for it.

"You ready for that movie?" he asked. "We can set up in the theater room or we can go out onto the patio."

The outdoor patio with a viewing screen was quite impressive, but she couldn't focus on the niceties of his house right now. All she could think about was how fast this fire was spreading and who else knew she and Reese were engaged.

"What's wrong?" he asked, reaching for her hand. "Chris—"

"No."

Well, he had texted, but that wasn't the problem.

"Then what is it?" Reese insisted.

Josie smiled and pulled in a deep breath. "How do you feel about picking out that engagement ring?"

Four

Well, that wasn't at all what he'd thought she'd say. She'd been upset earlier when he'd joked about a ring.

"Engagement ring?" he repeated.

Josie pulled her hand from his and sat her purse on the accent table inside the front door. Tucking her hair behind her ears, she turned to face him once again.

"It's a silly story, really," she began with a nervous laugh. "There was some harmless talk, or what I thought was harmless, on the phone with my assistant about Chris and everything that had happened and then the way you got him to leave. You know…by saying we were engaged."

Reese listened, actually rather amused at her jittery state. Something really had her ruffled.

"We talked about work and moved on," Josie added, fidgeting with her hands. "When I pulled in just now,

I got a text from my editor congratulating me on the engagement and telling me that she's got a teaser announcement on the blog site and she needs a Q&A from us. All I can figure is my assistant thought I was serious. I mean, I don't know who else would've told my editor and I guess maybe I forgot to mention this info was confidential. I'm sorry this is all just a big mess now."

Reese continued to watch as she twisted her fingers, smoothed her black dress, toyed with her hair again. The woman was a bundle of nerves ready to explode. This faux engagement was quickly getting to both of them. Likely she was stressed because her life wasn't so neat and tidy right now, the way she liked it. And for him… well, he wanted to strip his best friend and feel those curves beneath his touch and he wasn't sure what to do about those feelings. So, yeah, they had one hell of a problem he didn't have time to solve.

"Then we'll get a ring and answer some questions," he told her, shoving aside his lustful thoughts. "Is that all?"

Her eyes widened. "Is that all? That's your response? We're not getting married, Reese. I can't do this again so publicly. I'm freshly divorced from a marriage that never should've happened in the first place and you and I are both public figures. I mean, we're no royal couple, but the media will be interested in this story."

Reese wrapped his arm around her waist and guided her on into the house. As they stepped down into the sunken living area, he tried to figure out how to assure her that everything would be fine.

"Listen," he started, then stopped and turned to face

her, placing his hands on her shoulders. "We play the role. Surely we can pretend to like each other."

She glared up at him and met his crooked grin.

"Would you be serious?" she demanded.

He leaned in just a bit more. Her eyes dropped to his lips, but she pulled her gaze back up to his and held steady.

"Oh, I am serious, Jo. We can answer the questions for your editor and make an appearance at my grand opening in two weeks as a couple. We can push through all of that and then figure out what to do after." He smoothed her hair back and framed her face with his hands. "We can always say we split because we realized we were better at being friends. That's very believable because people have already seen us together as friends—they know we already have a relationship."

"But I don't want to fail at something else," she stated. "Not even fake failing."

That's what she was afraid of? Failing? Nothing about faking being in love with him. Interesting.

"You've never failed at anything," he reminded her. "Not even that marriage you ended once you realized it wasn't working. And I sure as hell am not going to let you start now. We've got this. Together."

She closed her eyes and pulled in a breath, her slender shoulders tensed beneath his hands. Reese gave her a reassuring squeeze, needing her to realize he'd never let her get hurt. He was right here by her side.

"Trust me?"

Her lids lifted as she focused on him. Those deep brown eyes staring at him were usually so good at hiding emotions, but not now. He saw the fear, the vulnerability, the concern. He had all of those, too, but he also had faith enough in their relationship that they would make it through anything...even stepping over that invisible line.

The one he'd promised himself not to cross.

Josie ultimately nodded and a wave of relief washed over him. He would care for and protect her at all costs. He could juggle his family, old and new, plus the Manhattan opening, and still make sure Josie came out of all of this unharmed.

With her eyes still locked onto his, physical need consumed Reese. He leaned in closer, never taking his focus from her. Little by little, he closed the distance until his lips were a whisper from hers.

"Wh-what are you doing?"

Barely hanging on by a thread.

"Practicing," he murmured. "We need to be believable in public."

She licked her lips, but since he'd leaned within a breath of her, her tongue brushed across his bottom lip and Reese knew she certainly hadn't meant to.

But whether she'd meant to or not didn't matter. Just that briefest touch of her tongue snapped something in him.

Reese covered her mouth, gently to give her an opportunity to back up and stop if this was something she didn't want. If she stopped, he would have to respect her decision, but now that he'd touched her in such an intimate, non-friend way, he wanted more.

So. Much. More.

Careful not to touch her anywhere else, Reese clenched his fists at his sides. The desire to reach for her, pull her even closer to get the full experience, consumed him, but he couldn't pressure her. As much as he wanted to keep kissing her, to touch her, his first priority was to make her feel secure.

He had to be patient or he'd risk everything they had.

When her lips opened beneath his, Reese took that as the proverbial green light and deepened the kiss. Delicate fingers feathered up his arm and sent shivers racing through him.

When had he last shivered during a kiss?

Never. He didn't get all giddy and shaken just from a kiss. He wasn't some hormonal teenager.

The woman was potent, more so than he ever could have imagined. When Josie let out a little sigh, Reese reluctantly pulled back.

Clenching his jaw, along with his fists, he closed his eyes and thought of anything other than how much he wanted to take her into his room and finish this.

A kiss so powerful without truly touching was only a stepping-stone to something else…and it was that something else he wanted to experience with her.

"What was that?" she murmured, her hands falling away.

Trying to lighten the intense mood, Reese smiled. "A hell of a practice kiss."

He didn't want to expose his true feelings, didn't want her to feel awkward, either. She'd just gotten here and he didn't want to send her running.

Josie took a step back and nodded. "Right. Well, you're a hell of a kisser."

Now how could his ego stay low with that type of a compliment? And how could he not want even more?

Just that simple taste had his imagination running even more rampant with endless possibilities.

"Back at ya," he stated with a grin. "I'll get your stuff into a guest room and then we can watch that movie. Which room do you want?"

"Anything with an ocean view," she told him.

Reese nodded and grabbed her suitcase, needing to get a minute to himself to get his head back on straight. As he took the luggage onto the elevator, Reese wondered how the hell he could focus on anything other than that kiss and how soon they would do it again.

Because now that he'd had one taste, he wanted another, and his drive to share more intimacies with her was stronger than ever. Judging from Josie's surprise reaction and then her response, maybe she had similar needs as well.

Focusing on all of this pent-up desire when he had so much else going on should be silly, foolish even, but all he could think about was how powerful it was and how soon he could kiss her again.

An Affair to Remember was not holding her attention and the lack of interest had nothing to do with the fact that she knew each scene word for word. No, her focus was on her still-tingling lips and the man sitting right next to her on the plush sectional sofa. There were plenty of other seats, but here he sat, right by her side.

What the hell had he been thinking, kissing her like that? Touching her with only his lips, yet her entire body had felt that touch. That little niggle of desire he'd launched earlier by claiming her as his fiancée had become something more. She ached with a need she didn't recognize. Never before had a kiss, so simple and sweet, left her wanting to rip someone's clothes off.

But Reese had pulled back and she'd been left with confusion and need.

If that was their practice kiss, she didn't know what would happen if they had to do the real thing for display...this one had felt pretty damn real.

Her cell vibrated against the table and she glanced down at the screen. But it wasn't her phone; it was his. She'd thought for sure it would be Chris again.

Reese leaned forward and grabbed his phone, stared at it for a minute, then muttered something under his breath before firing off a text.

"Everything okay?" she asked.

He shot her a smile and a nod. "Fine. Just work."

"For the Manhattan opening?"

"No, it's about some business I have in Tennessee."

Surprised, she shifted and put her feet up under her on the sofa. "Does this have anything to do with the trip you just got back from, the one you were so secretive about?"

His eyes darted from the television screen to hers. They'd decided to stay in the theater room since the weather was still nasty outside.

When he remained silent, she reached for the remote and paused the movie, instantly silencing the room. She stared at his strong hands still clutching the phone and wondered what secrets he kept locked in there.

Reese blew out a sigh and reached for her hand. The innocent, friendly gesture he'd done so many times before felt oddly different now, after that toe-curling kiss.

This was still her best friend...her best friend turned

faux fiancé. But they only had to play the game for a few weeks and then they could go back to being friends in all aspects.

She would ignore that little voice asking if being friends was all she wanted. Could she be fearless for now? Could she let Reese out of the friends box, just a little? If she was honest, she'd been wanting…something for a long while now, something different…a change. Maybe she could channel her mother's boldness, just for a while. Since none of this would last, maybe she could grab this chance to pretend to be that bold woman she so desperately wanted to be.

She had such mixed feelings about all of this. How would her heart stand up against playing his fiancée, with all the touching and lingering glances? And how would such acts change the dynamics of their entire relationship? Could they easily slide from one type of intimacy to another without any emotional damage?

She wasn't sure. And yet a part of her wanted to find out.

"I'm not purposely keeping anything from you," he finally told her as his thumb raked over the ridges of her knuckles. "Just sorting through some things. I'll fill you in when I'm ready."

Whatever it was sounded serious. Reese was always the good-time guy. The one who pulled her out of her shell and tried to get her to ditch her planner and do something, anything, spur-of-the-moment. So whatever plagued his mind, it was something big.

The way he kept stroking her hand had even more shivers pumping through her and Josie wasn't so sure staying here at his house was a great idea. At least she was not staying in the same room with him. The hour was getting late and she had to start on a new project in the morning. She was going to need a clear mind and not one filled with passionate kisses and unsettling fantasies about her bestie.

"I'm tired," she told him as she eased away and came to her feet. "I have a busy day tomorrow so I'm going to head up to my room."

Reese stood, too, instantly invading her space by his sheer size. She'd always known he was a broad guy—he did value his gym time—but she hadn't realized just how powerful and sexy he appeared until just now. Her heart beat quicker; her body tingled in ways it shouldn't from just looking at her best friend.

"Are you okay?" he asked, his brows drawn in. "If you're worried about the leaks at your place, my contractor will fix everything and you'll never know there was a problem."

Her leaks. Right. She'd honestly forgotten about that particular mess. Pretty much everything pre-kiss had slipped from her mind. Though she really should try to get back to reality because none of this—not what she was feeling, not what they were pretending—was valid.

Those few seconds of connection with Reese weren't real. He didn't want to build anything with her based on that kiss and he'd already told her this was all for show.

Fine. She could deal with that, but she still didn't know how all of this would work. She didn't have another space filed away for him. He was her rock, her very best guy, the one she could go to for anything. Shifting him somewhere else in her life would only unsettle the solid structure she strived for.

If she failed publicly at a relationship again, she worried how her reputation would hold up. She worried she'd let herself down, because she'd always prided herself on her independence and her control. Thanks to her military father and her regimented childhood, she knew no different.

"I'm not worried about the leaks," she assured him.

Reese reached up and tucked a strand of hair behind her ear, then trailed his fingertips down her jawline. Had he always been this touchy? This affectionate? Was Reese's interest recent or had she taken all of those innocent touches for granted before?

"Is it the kiss?" he asked.

Her heart caught in her throat. Leave it to him to draw out the awkwardness and make it bold and commanding.

"We're still friends," he added. "That kiss didn't have to mean anything."

Josie swallowed and went for full-on honesty as she looked him directly in his daring blue eyes. She was drowning and she had no clue how to save herself other than to just get out of the current situation.

"But it did."

Before the moment could get any more awkward or before he replied that he didn't feel anything, Josie turned and left the room. Maybe that made her a coward, but right now, she was afraid. Afraid for what would happen after two weeks of pretending, when she'd only been here two hours and already had stronger feelings than she should. The fear also stemmed from not knowing how much longer Reese could stay in that friend box she'd so carefully packed him in.

But most of all, she worried that she would never be the same because now that she'd had a hint of what Reese could bring out in her…she wanted to experience even more and that revelation would certainly keep her awake all night.

Five

"Is everything okay, son?"

Reese tightened his grip on the steering wheel as his father's voice came over the speaker in his SUV.

Son. The simplest endearment, one Reese had heard countless times over the years, yet the word only reminded him of all the lies he'd been living for nearly forty years.

Reese turned into Conrad's first location in Sandpiper Cove. This place was as old as he was and the most sought-out restaurant in the state. Many magazines and even television shows showcased Conrad's and its specialty menus and fine dining experience.

All of this belonged to Reese now because he was Martin Conrad's son…or so he'd always believed.

But even having this dynasty passed down to him, Reese wanted to build his own legacy, which was why he was getting the next phase going with his opening in New York.

"I'm fine," Reese replied, pulling into his parking spot. "I'm glad you and Mom are having a nice trip. You both deserve the getaway."

And they did. They had worked every single day for as long as Reese could remember, growing this dynasty from a meager savings account that they'd invested in an old shack. All of that blew up into something amazing and the shack remained, but took on renovation after renovation. Surrounding properties were purchased to accommodate the growth and it wasn't long before they realized they should open another restaurant and then another.

Reese was proud to be part of such a hardworking family; they had taught him so many of his core values. He'd always wanted a family of his own, children to pass this legacy down to someday.

But now? Well, now he questioned everything.

"We're having the best time," his father stated. "Wait... What, Laura?"

Reese waited while his parents held their own conversation in the background. Despite everything he'd learned from that letter, and he was still questioning the validity of revelations from a woman he'd never met, Martin and Laura had raised him. They'd loved him and provided for him, so no matter the outcome of their eventual confrontation about his biological father, they were his parents. He just wished like hell they would've trusted him enough to tell him the truth—if there was a truth to tell.

"Engaged?" his father exclaimed. "Reese, your mother

says you're engaged? She's reading that blog she loves from Josie's magazine. What, Laura? He's engaged to *Josie*? Our Josie?"

Josie had been part of his family for so long. When her father was out of town working or traveling, Josie tended to land at their house. Most holidays during their college days she had spent with them. She was like the daughter his parents never had.

Reese raked a hand over the back of his neck. Yeah, he probably should have told them about this sooner, like last night, but his mind hadn't been on the fake engagement; it had been on Josie and kissing her and her telling him that the encounter had been much more than a simple kiss. He'd wanted to know exactly what she meant by that.

But she'd walked away.

He'd stood in his theater room staring at the empty doorway long after she'd left. Obviously, he hadn't been the only one affected by the kiss and now he had to figure out what to do with this information.

Still, his parents deserved a heads-up. They truly loved Josie like their own…and they were clearly thrilled by this unexpected news.

"Son, are you still there?"

Reese pulled himself back to the call. "Yeah. I'm here. And I was going to tell you today, actually. This all happened so fast."

"Josie is such a wonderful girl," his father boasted. "Hold on, your mother wants to talk to you."

Reese swallowed and listened to the static as the phone was passed around, then he was immediately greeted with his mother's high-pitched squeal.

"Darling," she yelled. "I'm so happy for you guys, though I don't know why I had to read about it online instead of hearing the news from my own son. We will discuss that later, but for now I want to know how you feel. Are you excited? How did you propose? I saw this coming years ago. I cannot wait to throw you guys a proper engagement party."

Reese's mind whirled with one question and thought after another. His mother was always all-hands-on-deck. The woman was only "off" when she was asleep. There was no way he could let her start planning an engagement party. She would get way too wrapped up in this and right now, he couldn't share that it was a sham.

"Mom, let's not order any party decorations just yet," he stated. "Josie is swamped with work and I'm busy with the Manhattan opening. Let's get on the other side of these two weeks and then we can talk. Okay?"

Silence on the other end was all the warning he needed to know she did not like his idea.

"I promise," he quickly added. "You know how important this next opening is. I'm starting a new chapter and I need to focus solely on that. Josie completely understands."

"Of course she does," his mom agreed. "That's why the two of you are so perfect for each other. You're both workaholics."

Well, that was definitely true. Reese took after his father—well, after Martin. He devoted nearly every moment to making sure their upscale restaurants maintained the highest prestige and top-notch reputation people had come to appreciate from them.

"I've asked Josie to cover the event, too," he quickly

told her, turning the conversation toward business. "I figure since she's going as my date, and there's no one else I'd rather give an inside scoop to, this would be a win-win for everyone."

"I can't wait to see you guys," she exclaimed. "You give Josie a big hug and kiss from me."

A hug and a kiss? Sure, no problem. Everything else that came to mind? Yeah, that was the problem.

"We will see you at the opening," she told him. "Love you, Reese."

Emotions threatened to overtake him, but he tamped them down. His mother did love him, that was never in question. But at some point, he'd have to find the right words and the right time to question them.

"I love you, Mom. See you in two weeks."

After Reese hung up, he sat alone with his guilt and tried to tell himself this situation wouldn't last long. Two weeks and he and Josie would go back to being friends. Nobody had to know this had all been a sham, not even his parents.

But he would know.

Every part of him wondered how the hell he could go back to never touching her, never kissing her the way he truly wanted.

And he knew she was affected, too. He'd seen that flare in her eyes and heard that swift intake of breath.

Reese's cell chimed in his hand before he could exit his SUV. He glanced down to the screen to see a message from Josie.

Melissa wants a photo shoot along with the Q&A. She has it all scheduled for tomorrow morning at nine and is hoping to use Conrad's as the backdrop. Want me to make an excuse to postpone?

Reese stared at the message. If they kept pushing forward, how much damage would be done in the end?

But, really, what would a few pictures hurt? The Q&A wouldn't be a big deal. They knew each other better than they knew themselves at times. And the coverage might be good for his new opening, too.

No big deal. We can all meet at the restaurant.

She instantly replied back.

I'm sorry about all of this.

He blew out a sigh and hit Reply.

I'm sorry, too. We'll get through this together.

There was only one thing in his entire life he was afraid of and that was losing Josie forever. Even with everything going on around him, he couldn't lose her. The risk of seeking something more with her terrified him, but he was starting to believe that if he never tried, that would terrify him more.

What if he didn't lose her friendship? What if something magical developed? If he didn't test these new feelings, his fear of the unknown could rob him of the chance at something good.

But… Having a committed relationship really wasn't something he had the time for right now. He was just getting started on this new chapter in his career, and he needed to devote every bit of energy and time to making this next phase a success.

Not only did he demand that of himself, he also didn't want to let his parents down. They'd entrusted their dynasty to him and he'd be damned if he'd get sidetracked.

Reese shot off another reply to Josie.

See you at home tonight.

The message went before he realized how familial that sounded. He certainly wasn't ready for all of that. Maybe someday, but not now. He was too slammed with work and the fact that his personal life from all angles had taken drastic turns.

Yet he couldn't deny he liked knowing Josie would be at his house waiting on him. He'd already asked his chef to prepare Josie's favorite meal and dessert. There was a bottle of her favorite wine chilling and he intended to make this very stressful situation as relaxing as possible for both of them.

Reese stepped from his car and into the hot summer sun that was already beating down. Every single day he came to Conrad's when he was in town, but today he had the urge to blow off work and hit the beach like normal people. He wondered if Josie would ever consider doing something that spontaneous, that out of the ordinary, something that wasn't already scheduled in her planner.

Reese stepped in through the back door, disarmed the alarm and headed for the office he kept on the top floor. The second floor was for VIP guests only and that lounge area was consistently booked. But Reese kept his office on the top floor away from the noise and confusion where he could really work and continually design new ways to grow the company.

As soon as he stepped off the elevator, he pulled up Josie's text again and replied. Tomorrow was a special day and he didn't want it marred by the black cloud of deceit hanging over their heads.

Take the rest of tomorrow off after the Q&A and photo shoot. I have a surprise.

He knew what her response would be. He knew exactly what she'd send back before he even glanced at his screen. So when the phone vibrated in his hand with a new message, he laughed.

I hate surprises. I need to plan what I'm doing. It's like you don't know me.

Oh, he knew her, which was exactly why he wanted to push her beyond her comfort zone, see her live a little. They were both stressed and a day off would do them good. No, he didn't have the time to take off, but nothing was more important than Josie.

Besides, tomorrow was her birthday and he would surprise her with whatever the hell he wanted.

He didn't respond to her message; he just decided to let her think about all the possibilities he might have in store. She'd mentioned working from home today, his home, not hers since there was a crew already at her place working on the damaged roof. He'd already told his chef, Frisco, to take extra special care of Josie and to make sure she was comfortable.

Having her at his house seemed strange, yet right. Reese couldn't help but wonder how she felt being there after last night.

Reese planned on discussing that kiss with her again, finding out exactly how she felt…because he wanted more. More kisses, more touches…just more of Josie, and now that she was in his home, he had the opportunity…but should he take it?

Six

Josie finished her work, leaned back in the chair and stared at the screen. Something felt so off, but she just couldn't put her finger on it. Having an empty wineglass wasn't helping.

It grated that her entire work mode could be tilted off-balance because she'd kissed her best friend. No, he'd kissed her…she'd just enjoyed the hell out of it and still felt the tingling on her lips.

With a sigh, Josie came to her feet and closed her laptop. Thankfully, this piece on new summer cocktails wasn't due for another week. She had all the makings for an amazing article. She even had inspiration photos from the art department with oversize martini glasses filled with pale pink drinks and floating flowers. The recipes shared from various coastal restaurants around the world were in, interviews with restaurant owners were done…but she couldn't find that hook that made everything just come together in an article that didn't sound like a rookie wrote it.

Josie picked up her empty wineglass and left the office. Reese had three designated spots in his home for work and all of them faced the ocean, but she'd chosen the smallest because she preferred to be cozy and quaint…a tough feat in a house of this magnitude.

The moment she hit the top of staircase, a delicious aroma wafted up from the first floor. The chef had only made his presence known once and that was to ask her what she wanted for her lunch. Josie was so used to making her own things or grabbing something from a seaside café that she might get spoiled if she hung around Reese's house too long.

Whatever Frisco had made for dinner smelled like it was going to be divine. The hint of something with peaches hit her as well. There was no way Josie could ever be that masterful in the kitchen; her skills were relegated to her keyboard.

The second she reached the bottom of the steps, Reese walked in the front door. His eyes locked onto hers and Josie gripped the wineglass as she froze. She hadn't seen him since last night, since she fled the room after he'd kissed her. Likely he wasn't awake all night replaying that moment; at least, he didn't look haggard.

That bright blue button-up, folded up on his forearms, showed off not only his tanned skin, but also that excellent muscle tone she knew he worked hard to maintain.

Damn, that kiss had changed everything.

"Looks like you need a refill." Reese broke the silence as he nodded to her glass. "And dinner smells amazing, so this is perfect timing."

He closed the door and tossed his keys onto the accent table before crossing the foyer. Those cobalt-blue eyes locked onto hers and she would have sworn they were more intense than ever.

Yes, that kiss had changed everything.

She'd thought their dynamics had changed with his fake engagement, that first embrace at her door, but that was nothing compared to having his lips on hers. She couldn't seem to put him back in the friends-only box.

Josie had always noticed Reese's striking features and the beauty of his gaze, but she'd never *felt* it before. Josie couldn't begin to share with him what he was doing to her, not when she couldn't even explain all of this to herself.

"I just finished my article," she told him, trying to have what should be a normal conversation. "It's not where I want it, but I can't think anymore today."

Reese reached for her glass. "Let's go have dinner and you can bounce your problems off of me."

Her problems? That was quite laughable considering *he* was the problem. Well, not him physically. No, physically he was the answer, but that was the problem.

Ugh. She was such a mess with her mixed emotions and wayward thoughts. She knew what she meant, but trying to categorize all of her views was proving to be impossible. Josie didn't care for this out-of-control feeling or not being able to maintain some regulation over her own life.

"I'd rather you tell me what's going on tomorrow," she countered, coming down off that last step.

Reese laughed as he started guiding her toward the back of the house. That hand on the small of her back seemed too intimate, but just days ago that would've merely been his friendly gesture. Now she questioned everything…including these newfound emotions.

"We're doing the thing for your magazine and then I have a surprise."

Josie rolled her eyes as she came to a stop. Turning to face him, she crossed her arms over her chest.

"That thing?" she repeated. "You can't be that relaxed about an interview and photo shoot for this fake engagement."

"I'm not relaxed," he amended. "But it's scheduled and there's nothing we can do to change that."

She could call the whole thing off. She could come clean to her boss, just tell her it's a farce, but that would only damage her credibility. If she were going to reveal the truth, she should've done so right off the bat.

"Oh, my mom and dad are thrilled, by the way," Reese added.

Josie gasped. "You told your parents?"

"You know my mother reads your *Cocktails & Classy* blog every single day. I didn't think to warn them off ahead of time."

Guilt overwhelmed her. Josie closed her eyes, pulling in a much-needed deep breath. This lie was spiraling out of control faster than she could keep up. She truly loved and respected Martin and Laura Conrad. What would they think of her after she and Reese "broke up"?

"Hey," Reese said in that calming tone of his. "This

is all going to work out. We just need a couple weeks of make-believe and then we're back to being friends and nobody has to know otherwise."

Two weeks might as well be two years or two decades. With the way she was feeling right now, the end result of this charade would be that she'd possibly get intimately attached; her heart might get even more involved, because she didn't know if she'd have the willpower to put a stop to this madness.

Josie focused back on Reese. "Two weeks," she sighed. "We can do this."

The smile that spread across his face packed a punch and she forced herself to return the gesture. Who knew one kiss could cause so many emotions?

"I believe you said something about refilling my wine?"

He nodded and gestured for her to go ahead. "I had my chef make all of your favorites for dinner, so I hope you didn't have a big lunch."

Josie laughed. "He tried to feed me a five-course meal at noon."

"I told him to make sure you were well-fed and taken care of."

Taken care of. That's exactly what Reese lived for. He was always taking care of his parents, taking care of his staff of hundreds, taking care of her. He was the most selfless, giving man.

Before that kiss, those selfless traits were just part of what she'd loved about him as her friend. But now... well, she couldn't help but wonder how that generosity would carry over into the bedroom.

The instant mental image had her stilling, fantasizing for just a moment. Then she crashed back to reality as she refocused on Reese's gaze.

"I would've been fine with a banana or a smoothie," she told him. "But I appreciate it."

They stepped into the vast kitchen with views of the ocean through the windows, which stretched across the entire back wall. The sun was starting to set, casting an orange glow over the horizon and making the bright blue water sparkle like diamonds.

A million-dollar view.

Josie turned her attention to the long island and nearly gasped. "What is all of this?"

Reese laughed as he went to the wine fridge at the end of the island. "Dinner."

"For all of Sandpiper Cove?" she asked, her eyes scanning each dish.

"I told Frisco to prepare all your favorites and I gave him a list."

And from the looks of things, Reese hadn't missed a thing. There was even a little bowl of Tootsie Rolls, which made her laugh.

"How in the world did he pull off all of this?" she asked. "And the lunch he prepared was insane."

Reese shrugged. "That's why I can never let him leave me. I'd starve, and he's a magician when he's in his element."

Her eyes locked onto his. "You know we can't possibly eat all of this, right?"

"Of course not," he agreed. "Frisco always takes any extras to the homeless shelter, so I don't mind that he goes all out. I know none of this will actually go to waste."

Flowers to the hospital, food to the homeless shelter. Seriously, her best friend was not a typical jet-setting billionaire. She'd always admired his giving nature, or maybe it was that she'd just not seen him in this light before. Because the fact that he always put others first was becoming sexier and sexier.

"What's that smile for?" he asked.

She circled the island and placed a hand over his heart. "You're just remarkable. I mean, I've always known, but lately you're just proving yourself more and more."

He released the wine bottle and covered her hand with his...and that's when the memory of that kiss hit her again, hard. She shouldn't have touched him. She should've kept her distance. Because there was that look in his eyes again.

Where had this come from, this pull between them? When did he start looking at her like he wanted to rip her clothes off and have his naughty way with her?

"We need to talk about it," he murmured.

It.

As if saying the word *kiss* would somehow make this situation weirder. And as if she hadn't thought of anything else since *it* happened.

"Nothing to talk about," she told him, trying to ignore the warmth and strength between his hand and his chest.

"You can't say you weren't affected."

"I didn't say that."

He tipped his head, somehow making that penetrating stare even more potent. "It felt like more than a friendly kiss."

Way to state the obvious.

"And more than just practice," he added.

Josie's heart kicked up. They were too close, talking about things that were too intimate. No matter what she felt, what she thought she wanted, this wasn't right. She couldn't ache for her best friend in such a physical way. If that kiss changed things, she couldn't imagine how much anything more would affect this relationship.

How could she maintain control of her emotions if she let this go any further? She was already having a difficult enough time trying to cope with the current circumstances.

"We can't go there again," she told him. "I mean, you're a good kisser—"

"Good? That kiss was a hell of a lot better than just good."

She smiled. "Fine. It was pretty incredible. Still, we can't get caught up in this whole fake engagement thing and lose sight of who we really are."

His free hand came up and brushed her hair away from her face. "I haven't lost sight of anything. And I'm well aware of who we are…and what I want."

Why did that sound so dangerous in the most delicious of ways? Why was her body tingling so much from such simple touches when she'd firmly told herself not to get carried away?

Wait. Was he leaning in closer?

"Reese, what are you doing?" she whispered, though she wasn't putting up a fight.

"Testing a theory."

His mouth grazed hers like a feather. Her knees literally weakened as she leaned against him for support.

Reese continued to hold her hand against his chest, but he wrapped the other arm around her waist, urging her closer.

There was no denying the sizzle or spark or whatever the hell was vibrating between them. She'd always thought those cheesy expressions were so silly, but there was no perfect way to describe such an experience.

And kissing her best friend—again—was quite an experience.

Reese deepened the kiss, parting her lips and exploring further. She'd stop him in just a minute—she just wanted a little more.

Josie slid her hand from his and gripped each side of his face as he leaned her back a little more. That strong arm across her lower back held her firmly in place. Threading her fingers through his hair, she tilted her head to give him even more access, but those talented lips trailed across her jaw and down the column of her neck.

Any second she should end this, but it felt so damn good she couldn't muster up the strength to tell him to stop. She also couldn't remember why this was such a bad idea.

That hand behind her started shifting; a thumb slid beneath the hem of her shirt and caressed her bare skin. Josie let out a moan, then quickly bit down on her lip to quiet herself. Reese's lips continued to explore her neck, the sensitive spot behind her ear, then down into the vee of her shirt.

There were too many clothes in the way. Her body ached like it never had before and she wanted to feel his skin against hers.

"Reese," she panted, though she didn't know what she was begging for. She just knew she wanted him to keep going, to keep making her feel everything she'd deprived herself of.

An alarm echoed in the room, but Josie ignored it. She didn't want this moment to end...at least not yet.

But the insistent beeping kept going. Reese rested his forehead against her shoulder and she noted his body trembling just as much as hers...if not more.

"I have to get that," he murmured.

Get what? Her mind was still spinning and she didn't know what the noise was, but she wanted it to go away.

Reese slowly released her, holding her steady until she looked up at him and nodded. Her legs weren't quite as steady as she would've liked, so she rested a hand on the edge of the island and willed herself into a normal breathing pattern and heartbeat.

When Reese grabbed his cell from his pocket, Josie realized that hadn't been an alarm at all, but a call. Maybe the interruption was a blessing, because she still wasn't convinced she could have stopped what had been about to happen...and she was already wondering when it would happen again.

Seven

Reese cursed the caller before even looking at the screen. He needed to get in control and back to reality before answering, but he was having a difficult time with that considering he could still feel Josie's sweet body beneath his touch.

Damn it, how far would he have taken things? How far would she have allowed this to go?

Glancing down at the screen, he saw Sam Hawkins's name.

Sam Hawkins, the man who was very likely Reese's half brother and one of the men Reese had gone to see last week. The owner of Hawkins Distillery in Green Valley, Tennessee, was a pretty remarkable guy, considering he was the youngest distiller in the country.

Reese glanced to Josie, who was staring down at

the floor, her eyes wide with shock. He wasn't sure if she was shocked over their behavior or shocked over the fact that she'd enjoyed it so much—because those pants and moans and the way she'd clutched his hair were all clear indicators she'd been more than eager for things to progress.

Turning from temptation, Reese answered the call. "Hello?"

"Reese," Sam responded. "I hope this isn't a bad time."

Bad time? Reese supposed it could've been worse—like if Sam had called in about ten minutes when clothes were strewn across the floor.

He looked again at Josie, who still seemed to be trying to catch her breath. Yeah, same here. He'd only meant to see if the effect of the kiss last night had been a onetime occurrence, but the moment his lips touched hers, there had been another internal snap that he couldn't control.

"Now is fine," he replied, focusing on the sunset outside instead of the beauty before him. "I didn't expect to hear from you so soon."

"I know. Nick and I were going to give you some time to process everything," Sam stated. "Especially considering you don't know Rusty like we do, it's still a shock to discover your father at our age."

Understatement. Reese hadn't even known there was a father to discover. He thought Martin Conrad *was* his father, for nearly four decades.

"Since Rusty is home from his stint in jail for embezzling from one of our local charities, Nick and I planned on confronting him with the truth."

Reese was well aware that Rusty had been arrested for skimming funds from a charity that Lockwood Lightning endorsed and supported. From all the stories Reese had heard and from the bits and pieces of what he'd dug up online, Reese had drawn his own conclusions that he'd lucked out in life by not having Rusty Lockwood raise him as his child.

"And you want me in on that meeting?"

Reese had to choose his words carefully because he still hadn't explained everything to Josie—they'd sort of been busy pretending to be engaged, fighting a magnetic attraction—and he still wasn't sure how the hell to handle any of this.

"We don't want to pressure you, but I did want to include you," Sam told him. "All of this is still new to us as well. I wouldn't mind getting to know my half brother a little more, but that's going to be your decision."

Half brothers. Reese had grown up an only child and used to wonder how having a sibling would've changed his life. He likely would've been sharing the family business. Having someone else to lighten the load wouldn't be a bad thing. He would've had an automatic friend growing up, too, but he'd had plenty of friends even without siblings.

Friends like the one he'd just groped until she was moaning in pleasure.

Pushing aside those delicious thoughts of Josie, Reese focused on what he wanted to know about Nick and Sam. Discovering two guys who were prominent in their fields of luxury liquor and hospitality—fields surprisingly similar to his own—and who were both eager to get to know him sounded promising, and Reese found that he did want to explore these new relationships.

This whole new chapter in his life would take some time to wrap his mind around, but new ventures never scared Reese. He welcomed challenges… including kissing Josie Coleman.

Again, he shifted his focus back to the call and away from Josie.

"I could make another trip to Green Valley," he told Sam. "Why don't you tell me when would work for you guys? I'm opening a new restaurant in Manhattan next weekend. Maybe we could discuss a possible working relationship as well."

"That would be a solid start," Sam agreed. "I'll talk with Nick and text you. We plan on confronting Rusty soon, though."

Reese swallowed and wondered if tag-teaming was the answer. What good would come from all of them going to Rusty? What did Sam and Nick hope to accomplish? Did they just want to let the mogul know that his sons had all been identified?

None of them needed money and Reese certainly wasn't looking for a father figure to fill a void. He had plenty of love and affection from the amazing couple who'd raised him.

Reese really needed to talk to his own parents before he went to Rusty. He needed all of the history, no lies, no secrets. Reese needed every bit of his life revealed to him.

He needed to understand his true role when it come to Rusty Lockwood. He needed to know where he actually stood in all of his relationships and what the hell he was supposed to feel.

Because his entire world was in upheaval and he honestly had no idea what to think about any of it.

"I'll see what I can work out," Reese replied. "But I can't make promises right now."

"Understood. I'll be in touch soon."

Reese disconnected the call, held his cell at his side and continued to stare out the window. He wasn't ready to face Josie yet, not when his body was still humming from their brief, intense encounter. Their clothes had stayed on. There had barely been any skin-on-skin contact. What would happen when they finally took that next step?

Because Reese had every intention of doing just that. He'd been uncertain before, even after that first kiss, but the way she'd responded moments ago—how could he deny either of them?

There was too much passion here to ignore. There was too much pent-up desire. Who knew how long those feelings had been stirring?

They would never know what they could have if he didn't take the risk. No, he didn't want to lose her as his best friend, but what if things only got better?

When he turned, he found Josie staring straight at him. She'd clearly had time to compose herself, but that hunger was still in her eyes. Her squared shoulders and tight lips, though, were good indicators that she wasn't happy about what she was feeling.

"You're going back to Green Valley?" she asked.

Reese pocketed his phone. "That's not where I thought we'd pick up from where we just left off."

She crossed her arms and stared across the room. "Where did you think we'd pick up? Kissing? Because I'm still not sure that's a good idea."

And that's where they clearly disagreed. There wasn't a better idea, in his opinion.

"You weren't complaining a minute ago," he reminded her—just in case she'd forgotten. "In fact, you were enjoying yourself, if I recall."

Her gaze darted away for a split second before she glanced back to him. "A minute ago, I was sidetracked by, um…"

"My slick moves?" he asked with a smile.

Her eyes narrowed. "Does your ego need to be stroked? I could've kissed anyone and gotten carried away. My eyes were closed, you know, and I happen to like kissing."

Jealousy consumed him as he closed the distance between them. He had her wrapped in his arms and falling against his chest. Her hands flattened on him as her focus was directed straight at his face.

"You think you'd react that way to just anyone?" he asked, tipping her back just enough so she had to cling to him. "Don't throw other men in my face, Josie. I might prove you wrong."

"But…we're friends, Reese."

Something in him softened at her tone, which was laced with confusion—as well as curiosity and desire.

"We *are* friends," he murmured, closing the space between their lips. "Very, very good friends."

Because this was Josie, he wanted to take it slow. He wanted her to recognize this insistent attraction and come to terms with the fact that they had already crossed the friend line. They might as well fully explore this passion.

True, everything surrounding them was in total chaos. But if they didn't take the chance now when they were thrown together, then when would they?

"Reese."

His name slid through her lips as she closed her eyes and tipped her mouth to his. As if he needed any more invitation than that to claim what he so desperately ached for.

Reese wanted her out of this little black dress, he wanted her hair messed up, and he wanted to be the cause of every bit of her chaotic, sexy state.

He'd never wanted a woman so bad in his life.

Her hands came up to his shoulders; her fingertips dug in. Didn't she know? He'd never let her fall.

Reese lifted her up firmly against his body as he spun her around and sat her on the edge of the table. She eased from his kiss and locked her gaze with his. He waited for her to stop him, all the while praying she'd let him continue. Touching her was like a drug he hadn't known he was addicted to and now he couldn't get enough.

He reached up to the strap of her dress and eased it down her arm, taking her bra strap with it. Josie trembled beneath his touch and he had to force himself to keep this slow pace. She wanted him, wanted this—that much was evident in her heavy-lidded stare and flushed cheeks. Not to mention she wasn't telling him no.

Keeping his attention on hers, Reese slid the other straps down, earning him a swift intake of her breath as she raked her tongue across her lower lip. There was no way she could imagine the potent spell she held over him—he hadn't even been sure of it himself until now.

Josie shifted and braced her hands on the table behind her, quirking a brow as if daring him to stop. Damn, this woman was silently challenging him in the most delicious way.

Reese started to lean in, more than eager to get his lips on that velvety skin of hers.

"Reese," she whispered.

He stopped, his hands braced on either side of her hips.

"As much as we both want this, tell me it won't change things."

The plea in her tone, in her eyes, had Reese swallowing the truth—because things had already changed. The dynamics of their relationship had started changing the moment he knew he wanted her, which, if he was honest with himself, was years ago. She was just finally starting to catch up.

"You'll still be my best friend," he answered truthfully.

He settled his lips over hers as he grazed his hand up her bare thigh and beneath the hem of her dress. She shifted and rocked back and forth slightly to give him better access.

There was nothing he wanted more than to pleasure her right now. To pour out all of the passion he'd been storing up just for her. No woman could ever compare to Josie—which was why he refused to lose her in his life. Yes, intimacy would change things, but maybe it would make them even closer.

Reese feathered his fingertips along the seam of her

panties, earning him a soft moan and a tilt of her hips. But the moment he slid a finger beneath the silky material, he was the one eliciting a moan.

Josie leaned further back, dropping down to her elbows, but still keeping her eyes on his hand. He'd never seen a sexier sight than what was displayed before him. With her hair a mess, her dress hanging on by the curve of her breasts, those expressive eyes silently begging for more and her spread thighs, Reese didn't think he'd be able to ever have a meal at this table again without getting aroused.

As much as he wanted to roam his mouth over all of that exposed skin, he didn't want to miss one second of the desire in her expression. The moment he slid one finger over her heat, Josie's eyes fluttered closed and her mouth dropped open on a gasp.

Yes. That's what he wanted. That sweet, vulnerable reaction.

Finally, Josie eased back all the way and arched her body as she reached down and circled his wrist with her delicate fingers. Relinquishing control was not his go-to, but he was more than willing to let her guide her own pleasure.

It wasn't long before those hips pumped harder against his hand, before she cried out his name and clenched her grip a little tighter.

Reese took it all in. The passion, the need, the completely exposed way Josie let herself be consumed by her desire.

He'd never forget this moment, not for the rest of his life.

When Josie relaxed against the table and released his

wrist, Reese eased his hand away and adjusted the bottom half of her clothing. She'd gone totally limp and he couldn't help but smile. He'd never seen her so calm, not worried about a schedule or making plans for something else. She was still, quiet…and utterly breathtaking.

As much as he wanted to use her release as a stepping-stone to more, Reese gathered her in his arms and lifted her against his chest. Her head nestled against the crook of his neck like she'd done so a thousand times before.

Reese lifted her bra straps back into place and adjusted the top of her dress.

Josie's hands reached for the zipper on his pants.

"Not now," he murmured, placing a kiss on the top of her head.

Such an innocent gesture when the most erotic thoughts were swirling through his head. Just knowing she wanted to keep going was a victory he hadn't known was even possible. But she was coming off a euphoria she hadn't anticipated and he didn't want her to think he assumed or expected her to reciprocate.

Josie lifted her head, her tranquil gaze locked on his. "Why?"

He said nothing, but he also wasn't ready to just let her go. Gathering her up, he crossed to the wall of glass doors and eased one open with his foot.

"Where are we going?" she asked, looping her arms around his neck.

"You're going to sit out here and relax and I'm going to bring you food."

When he placed her on the cushioned chaise in the

outdoor living area, she simply stared up at him with her brows drawn.

"That's what you're worried about? Food?"

"Oh, I'm not worried," he corrected. "You haven't had dinner."

She blinked and then shook her head and muttered something under her breath about men being more confusing than women. That was an argument he was smart enough to walk away from.

Leaving her outside, Reese went back into the kitchen, and his gaze kept wandering to the now-empty table. Yeah, he'd never be able to eat there again without thinking of her as she'd just been, and he sure as hell wasn't about to tell his chef what had happened in his kitchen.

Reese turned back to the island, rested his hands on the edge and dropped his head between his shoulders. He just needed a minute to get control over his emotions and his arousal. Turning down her advance had been the most difficult thing he'd ever done, but he wanted the time to be right, for her to come to him because that's what she truly wanted and not because she was fuzzy-headed from a recent orgasm.

When he glanced back up, he caught her gaze staring back at him from where she remained outside. There was a vast distance between them, but he recognized so much in her eyes that he couldn't deny. Along with confusion and a hint of frustration, he still saw passion and he wondered exactly what she planned to do about it.

Eight

Josie stepped out onto the balcony off her guest room. The moonlight cast a bright, sparkling glow over the ocean. She had no clue how long she'd been standing out here letting her thoughts roll through her mind.

Chris had texted only a little while ago and she'd finally responded, telling him this was her final correspondence, she had moved on and she wished the best for him. Then she blocked his number.

She didn't know what to make of everything that had happened earlier with Reese and she couldn't worry about Chris's feelings at this point. It was her slipup on the phone with him that had started this entire ordeal and toppled her life out of control.

All of those neat, tidy boxes that had compartmentalized every aspect of her life were now completely obliterated.

From the way Reese made her feel, to the fact that she'd never felt such a rush of emotions, to the way he'd eased back when she'd reached for him. Everything was different now and she had no idea how she could juggle all of these feelings and still remain calm.

Josie crossed her arms and rubbed her hands over her skin. The breeze off the ocean washed over her, tickling her and doing nothing to dampen her arousal.

And she was still aroused. True, Reese had brought her to pleasure, but she wanted more. He'd left her wondering what else she could experience with him. What would happen if they managed to get all of their clothes off? If they were skin to skin and not worried about anything else beyond physical intimacy?

How would this change their relationship?

Not only that, if she completely let go and gave in to her desires, there would certainly be no controlling where it led. She'd never felt like she was floundering before, but that's exactly where she was right now. The decisions she should make collided with the decisions she *was* making and all of it was confusing the hell out of her.

A sickening feeling settled deep in her stomach over the possibility of losing her very best friend. She couldn't afford to be without him. She couldn't imagine even one day without texting or talking to him. He literally knew her secrets; he was her go-to for everything.

And he'd made her eyes roll back in her head and her toes curl with a few clever touches as he'd laid her out on his kitchen table.

Shivers racked her body as she recalled every talented trace of those fingertips. Who knew her best friend had such moves? And who knew she'd love it so damn much?

Dinner earlier had been strained. Josie wasn't sure if things were awkward because she was still aroused or because their relationship had shifted so far away from something she could recognize and label.

Regardless, Reese and his chef had outdone themselves with all of her favorites. She only wished she could've enjoyed them more.

Josie turned back toward her room and closed the patio doors at her back. She had to get up early and look refreshed for her Q&A and photo shoot. Considering it was well after midnight, she wasn't sure how fresh she would be able to make herself. There was only so much carefully applied concealer could do.

The silk of her chemise slid over her skin as she padded her way back to her bed. Every sensation since she'd felt Reese's touch only reminded her of how amazing he'd been. Every moment since her release, she'd ached for more and didn't know how to make that happen.

But didn't she know? She was just as much in charge of what was going on as he was.

But was she as brave? Nothing scared or worried Reese. That was the main area where they were 100 percent opposite.

In that kitchen earlier, though, they had been completely and utterly perfect.

Except for that one-off with Chris, Josie had never done something so spontaneous in her life. She made plans for everything and typically got irritated when her plans were shifted or canceled. Some might have even called her a nerd, but she preferred to be described as "structured."

Right now, though, she preferred to finish what Reese had started. Or maybe she'd started this? Regardless of who'd started what, the fact was, nothing had been finished.

And maybe she opted to break out of her perfect box because Reese made her feel things she'd never felt before. Maybe, if she was being honest with herself, she liked experiencing her reckless side with him because she knew she was safe. Reese would never let her get hurt.

Was he in his room thinking about what happened or was he fast asleep without a care? Knowing Reese, he'd fallen right to sleep, and she wasn't even a thought in his mind right now.

Well, too bad, because there was no way she could ignore this and certainly no way she could go to the Q&A and photo shoot while feeling such turmoil.

She didn't know if she was making the best decision or the biggest mistake.

There was only one way to find out.

Arousal and nerves clashed inside her as she tiptoed down the hallway toward Reese's bedroom.

This was insane, right?

She should just go back to her room, read a book or play on her phone or anything until she could push him from her mind.

But one step led to another and she found herself standing outside the double doors leading to the master suite. Josie placed her hands on the knobs and eased the doors open. Moonlight flooded the room, cascading a beam directly onto the king-size bed across from her.

She couldn't do this. She shouldn't be here.

What was she thinking? This was Reese. Her very best friend from school who had seen her at her absolute worst—when her prom date dumped her, when she had that dumb idea to get a perm and he told her she was beautiful anyway, when she broke out in hives from some new facial cleanser she'd tried for an article and he ordered in dinner so she didn't have to go out in public.

He was her rock, her support…not her lover.

Josie turned back toward the hall.

"Stay."

The word penetrated the darkness and had Josie reaching to grip the doorknob again for support. Her heart beat so fast, so hard in her chest, unlike anything she'd experienced before.

"I shouldn't be here," she murmured, still facing the darkened hall. Too late to slip out now.

"You want to be here or you would've stayed in your room."

Why was he always right?

"That doesn't mean this is a good idea," she told him.

The sheets rustled behind her and Josie pulled in a deep breath, willing herself to finish what she'd come for. This was what she wanted; this was exactly why she'd made that short trip from her room to his.

He knew full well why she'd come, so denying it now would only make her look like a fool.

Josie turned, not at all surprised to see Reese standing behind her. Bare chest with a sprinkling of hair, broad shoulders, his dark hair messed up from his pillow and those hip-hugging black boxer briefs were not helping her resolve.

"Who's to tell us this is a bad idea?" he countered in that husky tone of his.

Well, no one really, but shouldn't she be the one saying this wasn't smart? Shouldn't she insist that they were friends above all else?

Yet she'd come to his room because she wanted to forget that common sense logic and remember exactly how amazing she'd felt in his kitchen.

"Stay."

He repeated the simple command, and something just clicked in place—something she hadn't necessarily planned or given much thought to. For the first time in her life, she didn't care about her plans. She only cared about her wants.

And she wanted Reese.

Everything about this felt out of control, and yet safe at the same time.

That moment when she took a step forward, she saw Reese's shoulders relax, a smile spread across his face. There was something so intimate and arousing about the darkness, the quiet of the night and the moonlight streaming through the windows. There was no need to even pretend she didn't want to be here. It was time she owned up to exactly what she needed and not make excuses or apologies.

When this was over, there would be no room for regrets. Regrets would only lead to the downfall of their friendship, and she refused to let him slip from her life.

Josie reached for Reese and she could have sworn she heard him mutter something like "finally," but she wasn't positive. Her heart beat too fast, the thumping rhythm drowning out anything else.

All at once his hands were on her, his mouth covered hers, and he cupped her backside, lifting her against his firm body.

Every thought vanished as she let the overwhelming sensation of passion consume her. An unfamiliar feeling overcame her and all she could think was that this felt too right to be considered wrong.

Reese turned and moved them through the room, never taking his lips from hers. Josie laced her fingers behind his neck and held on as anticipation built and her body ached for so much more.

She tilted and landed softly on the comforter as Reese came down to rest on her. The weight of his body pressed her deeper into his warm bed.

The way he settled between her thighs had Josie tipping her hips, silently begging him for more. Reese's lips left hers and roamed over her jaw and down the column of her throat. She arched her back, granting him access to anything and everything he wanted.

His weight lifted off her as he eased his way down her body. Strong hands tugged at her chemise and Josie reached down to help him. She shimmied the silk up and over her head, tossing it aside without a care, leaving her only in her lace panties.

Reese came up to his knees, and in the glow of the moonlight, she didn't miss the way his heavy gaze raked over her body like this was the very first time seeing her.

He'd seen her plenty—in all kinds of outfits, in a bikini—but never like this and never so intimately. She wanted to freeze this second, to remember his

look forever. She'd never felt sexier or more beautiful than right now.

Josie lifted her knees and came up onto her elbows.
She wanted him to touch her with more than his stare.
She needed skin to skin, and she was done waiting.

In a flurry of movements, she worked off her panties
and assisted him in taking off his boxer briefs. Reese
slid off the bed for a moment and procured protection
before coming back to her.

This was really happening.

Josie should have been worried, but all she could
think of was how much she wanted him to join their
bodies, to make them one. Nothing felt weird or awkward, even though this was Reese.

Actually, she was surprised how perfect it felt.

He braced his hands on either side of her head and
leaned down to glide his lips over hers.

"Be sure," he murmured.

Josie wrapped her arms and legs around him, guiding him to exactly where she wanted him. The second
he slid into her, Josie's body bowed as she cried out.
Her fingertips dug into his shoulders and Reese immediately set a rhythm that did glorious things to her.

With his strong grip on her hips, Reese eased up and
stared down at her while he made love to her.

No. They weren't making love.

This was sex. She hadn't planned for anything more.

"Get out of your head," he told her. "Stay with me."

He eased back down, slowed his pace and smoothed
her hair away from her face. She didn't know how he
always knew what she was thinking. He was just amazing like that.

Speaking of amazing, the way he moved his body over hers, glided his lips across her skin, had her body climbing higher. Josie gripped his hair as he covered her mouth with his. Her ankles locked even tighter as her climax hit.

He didn't release her lips as he swallowed her moans. Her knees pressed against his waist as every possible emotion overcame her. The intense pleasure and utter serenity completely took over. Josie lost herself in the moment, the man.

Nothing could ever compare to this right here.

Before she could come down from her high, Reese pulled his lips from hers, pumped even harder, and she watched as his jaw clenched. Those bright blue eyes locked onto hers as his release rolled through him.

Josie had never seen a sexier sight.

This was the only side to Reese she had never seen, and she honestly hadn't known she could get turned on so much even after her body had stopped trembling.

But seeing him come undone, well, Josie figured she'd be staying the night in this bed because she wasn't finished here.

Reese eased back down, shifting to the side and gathering her in against his side.

"Stay," he whispered.

Again, such a simple word that held so much meaning, so much promise.

Josie turned, tipping her head up to his as she raked a finger across his jawline. "I'm just getting started," she whispered back.

Nine

"Who were you referring to when you said you couldn't be her?"

Reese didn't mean to break the silence with that question, but he'd been wondering for some time now and obviously Josie wasn't going to be forthcoming with the information.

Just in the past two days he'd discovered there was much more to her than he'd ever realized. Clearly, she'd held this secret, but she'd also been hiding a passion that matched his, which he hadn't even considered.

Knowing they were compatible in more ways than just as friends blew his mind.

Having Josie in his bed had been more than he'd ever imagined…and he had a hell of an imagination where she was concerned. But realizing they were so damn compatible was just another confirmation that a physical relationship had been worth the risk.

The silence stretched between them as she sat on the edge of the bed with her bare back to him. The sun hadn't even come up yet and she was trying to leave. She'd spent the night here, they'd gotten little sleep, and they had to get ready to go to this interview at his restaurant and attempt to fake an engagement.

Reese would rather stay in this bed and figure out what was really going on between them, to know what she was thinking. Physically, she was here, but he wasn't sure she was with him mentally.

"What do you mean?" she asked, glancing over her shoulder.

That long, silky black hair fell down her back and he had the strongest urge to reach up and feel those strands slide between his fingertips.

"In your closet the other day," he reminded her. "The one with the leak. Who were you referring to when you said you couldn't be like her?"

Her eyes darted down, but even from her silhouette, he could see the sadness in her expression. Reese eased closer, but didn't touch her. He still didn't know where they'd landed in this postcoital moment, and he didn't want to make things awkward. He wanted her to feel comfortable enough to answer his question.

"My mother," she murmured. "I don't remember much about her, but I do remember her always wearing bright colors. She loved blues and reds. She always had on red lipstick, too."

Reese had never met Josie's mother, and actually hadn't seen many pictures of her, either. But he did recall seeing one photo, years ago, and Josie looked exactly like her mother. The long, dark hair, the doe eyes, the petite frame and the flawless, light brown skin tone.

"I remember Dad saying that when he first met mom during his travels to the Philippines, when he first joined the army, he fell in love with her on the spot. He loved how bold and vibrant she was. She challenged him and made him work for her affection. They were so in love."

Reese wanted to erase that sorrow from her tone, but he wasn't sorry that he'd asked. This was a portion of Josie that she'd kept locked away from him. They'd been friends for so many years, yet he'd never heard her talk of her mother this way and he sure as hell hadn't had a clue that she'd kept a shrine to her in her closet in the form of unworn clothes.

"Were those clothes hers?" he asked.

"No." Josie came to her feet and slid back into her chemise before settling back down and turning to face him. "I buy them thinking I'll take the plunge one day and just step out in something bold like she always did. But I'm not her. I'm boring, predictable and more comfortable in black. Besides, that's how my readers know me—classic black. Any photo I'm in or any event I attend, I'm always in black. It's my signature look now."

She attempted a soft smile, but that sadness still remained in her eyes. Had she always had that underlying emotion? Did he just take for granted that she was okay with how her life had turned out? He couldn't imagine losing his mother, but he doubted Josie would ever feel whole with that void in her life.

He was still trying to figure out how he felt regarding

the fact that he was adopted. Now he had three parents and his world was all over the place. Even so, this was nothing like what Josie had gone through.

"You can wear whatever you want whenever you want," he informed her. "Be yourself. If that's a bright red dress, then do it."

She gave him a sideways glare, that typical Josie look when he suggested something she thought was a completely moronic idea.

"I'm serious," he urged. "There's no dress police. Maybe that could be your next article. How to revamp yourself—or some clever title you'd come up with."

Josie laughed and relief washed over him. He always wanted to hear her laugh, to see her wide smile and know she was happy.

"I wouldn't use something so trite as the word *revamp* in my title. I'm beyond college days when I was too tired to come up with something catchy."

She came to her feet again and smoothed her hair back from her face with a sigh. "Besides, I'm not getting the equivalent of an adult makeover, so this plan is irrelevant. I'm fine with who I am, I just sometimes wonder what it would be like. That's all."

Reese sat up in bed, the sheet pooled around his waist. He kept his eyes on that body he'd worshipped nearly all night. He wanted to know if she'd join him again tonight, because one night wasn't nearly enough, but he wanted to leave that next step up to her. He wasn't ready for a long-term commitment and he didn't want her to misunderstand what was happening here. It was up to her to continue what they'd started. She'd come to him once before…he had to believe she would again.

"I'm going to get ready," she told him. "If we leave early, we can swing by Rise and Grind. I haven't had an iced mocha latte in forever."

"You had one last week. I picked it up for you and brought it to your house and even delivered it into your home office."

Her brows drew in as if she were trying to remember, but then she shrugged. "Well, a week is too long."

Reese shoved the covers aside and rose. Josie's eyes immediately landed on his bare body and then darted away.

"You're not going to act embarrassed, are you?" he asked, purposely not grabbing his clothes.

"No, no." She glanced anywhere but at him. "Nothing to be embarrassed about, right? We're both adults and last night was…it was…"

Reese bit the inside of his cheek to keep from laughing at her stammering and her focus darting all around the room like she was trying to find something to land on other than him or their night together.

He rounded the bed and came up behind her. Not touching her took a considerable amount of willpower, though.

"No regrets," he told her.

Josie jumped, clearly unaware he'd moved closer.

"I don't have regrets," she stated, still without looking at him. "I have concerns."

Might as well be the same thing, but he wanted to alleviate any worries.

"Nothing we did was wrong," he told her, taking her shoulders and turning her to face him. "You know that, right?"

Her eyes caught his as she nodded. "I just don't want things to change."

"How would they change? We both had a great time, we both enjoyed it…if your moaning and panting my name were any indicators."

She rolled her eyes and smacked his bare chest, which was the exact response he wanted. He needed to lighten the mood so she didn't feel like this was anything more than what it was…sex between friends. He didn't want her worried or afraid that they couldn't still be the best of friends.

They were both on unfamiliar ground here. And he wasn't sure how the hell to even start setting boundaries. All he knew was that he wanted her on a level he'd never wanted anyone before…the rest could sort itself out later.

"We won't start comparing notes," she said with a smile. "You did your fair share of that sexy clenched-jaw thing so I know you had a good time."

"Sexy jaw thing?" he asked. He had no idea what that meant, but he'd had a good time. He decided to zero in on the fact that she'd called him sexy.

Maybe they would be right back in his bed tonight.

"Your ego needs no help from me," she told him as she took a step back. "And I need to get ready. Coffee is on you this morning."

She sashayed out, but not before tossing him another grin that punched him with a heavy dose of lust. He had no idea how this interview would go or what they'd be expected to do in the photo shoot, but none of that mattered.

Reese was already counting down the time until they came back here, and he could get to know more of that sweet body of hers.

"And if you could slide the back of your fingertips down her cheek," the photographer suggested.

Josie stilled, her palms flat against Reese's chest. He had one arm wrapped around her waist and had her flush against his body, while he used the other hand to obey the photographer's commands.

"Now lock eyes," the photographer added. "Like you're dying to kiss, but you can't."

Well, at least that part wasn't fake. With Reese this close and her hormones still in overdrive from last night, she desperately wanted to feel his lips on hers… sans an audience.

Was that normal? Should she want to strip down her best friend? She wasn't even sure what to call this new-found relationship they'd created, but she also knew if she read too much into it, she'd drive herself mad.

Maybe she just needed to create a new box, one without a label but still a nice, neat area to keep these emotions in for now—until she knew what to do with them.

"A little closer," the photographer stated as she snapped away.

She moved in closer and Josie tried not to break eye contact with Reese, but the lights and the people standing around watching were a bit unnerving.

They'd set up just inside the stunning entryway of Conrad's. With the serene waterfall wall, the suspended glass bulbs showcasing pale greenery, the place seemed simple, yet classy, and perfect for a photo where the photographer wanted to focus on the couple.

"Breathe," Reese whispered.

Her eyes held his and that desire staring back at her had her heart beating even faster. Having sex and being in the dark was one thing, but pretending to be in love with lights and cameras all around was definitely another.

Melissa stood off to the side, smiling like a mother of the bride. Guilt settled deep. All of this had started simply because she wanted her ex to move on.

One failed marriage was embarrassing enough. She didn't want to be known for another unsuccessful relationship. Perhaps she and Reese would fool everyone with these photos of a couple in love and then once they announced they were better off as friends, people would see them in public together, and everything would go back to normal.

She hoped.

"Oh, wait a minute."

Josie jerked away from Reese when her editor interrupted the clicking of the camera.

"Where's her ring?" Melissa asked. "We can't do photo shoot about the engagement without the ring."

Josie froze. The ring? Damn it, she hadn't thought that far ahead. Reese had joked about it, but that had just been him trying to annoy her in that playful way of his. They weren't actually going ring shopping. Good grief, that would be absurd, but she couldn't think of a lie right off the top of her head.

Her eyes darted back to Reese's, who was reaching into his pocket.

"Right here," he stated, producing a ruby set in a diamond band. "I cleaned it for her this morning and we were in a rush to get here, so I slipped it into my pocket."

Josie's attention volleyed between Reese's sexy grin and that ring she'd never seen before in her life. Was he serious? How in the hell did he just procure a ring—a rather impressive, expensive-looking ring—out of his pants pocket? Even Reese wasn't that powerful...was he? How had he made this happen and why hadn't he clued her in on it?

"Here you go, babe."

Reese lifted her left hand and slid the ring into place and the damn thing actually fit like it was made for her. Had he known her ring size, too?

"Let me see," exclaimed her editor.

Josie was busy examining the rock herself because this was seriously a piece of art. When her editor grabbed her hand and squealed, Josie couldn't help but laugh. She glanced back to Reese, who merely winked, as if he'd had everything under control from the start.

Again, the man took care of all the details and never acted like he was put out or tired. How did he do all of that without a planner, a spreadsheet, a personal assistant?

Okay, he had assistants, but Reese was also very hands-on. There was no way he'd send an assistant to get an engagement ring, not even a fake one.

"You two are so lucky," Melissa stated, glancing between Josie and Reese. "Okay, get back to the shoot. I just had to see what he chose and it's absolutely perfect."

Josie glanced around at the crew staring and waiting on them to continue. "Um, could Reese and I have two minutes?"

Everyone nodded and Josie grabbed Reese's hand and pulled him toward the back of the open room. There wasn't much privacy to be had, but she had to use what she could.

She turned so that Reese's broad frame blocked her from the rest of the audience.

"Where did you get this?" she whispered between gritted teeth.

Reese smiled. "I couldn't let my fiancée be without a ring. That wouldn't say much about our love, now would it?"

She narrowed her eyes at his sarcasm.

Of course he only smiled and replied, "I bought it."

He bought it. Like he'd just gone out and gotten a pair of shoes or a new cell phone. She didn't even want to know what this ring cost.

"Can you return it?"

Reese's brows drew in. "Return it? Why?"

She couldn't say much with their current lack of privacy, so she merely widened her eyes and tipped her head, knowing he could practically read her mind most times.

"It's yours, Jo. Think of it as a birthday present if that makes you feel better."

That soft tone of his had her heart melting and she firmly told her heart not to get involved. Whatever this was going on with them had to be structured or the entire faux engagement would explode in her face, taking her heart in the process.

"I'm sorry, but we still have to get to the interview," Melissa chimed in. "We do have deadlines, you know."

Yeah, Josie was well aware of deadlines—when it came to work *and* Reese.

Less than two weeks now.

Josie glanced down to the ring on her finger, the symbol of so much more than what was actually going on. There was another layer of guilt because each day that went by, she found herself deeper into this lie.

The deep red stone stared back at her and she wondered what on earth made him choose one so bold instead of a traditional diamond. She also wondered what the hell she'd do with an engagement ring once the engagement ended.

Reese lifted her hand and kissed the spot just above the ring as his eyes remained locked onto hers.

"Ready?" he asked.

Was she ready? She didn't know how to answer that because she had a feeling he wasn't talking about the pictures.

The ring weighed heavy on her hand as they went back to the crew. This farce was almost over. She only had to hang on until after the Manhattan opening and then they could go back to the way things were before... if that was even possible.

Ten

Reese had never been more relieved than when that interview was over. There were some questions he and Josie definitely had to fudge, but they'd sounded believable and that's all that mattered.

And when he'd asked her to take the rest of the day off, he'd never thought she'd actually do it. Yet here they were, leaving her house after she wanted to pick up a few things and check on the progress of the work.

Reese's crew said it would be at least another week because they'd run into some other issues they were fixing while there. Fine by Reese. He was in no hurry to get her out of his bed.

"I assume you're taking me somewhere for my birthday and it has something to do with the beach."

They both loved being outside whenever possible. Their schedules were so demanding, and nothing relaxed them quite like the gentle waves and the calming winds off the ocean.

Reese pulled out of her drive and said nothing. He wanted this evening to be all about her and he wanted her to relax without worrying about the fake engagement, the article, the renovations on her house…nothing.

He also needed a break from his thoughts and issues. Josie was always the answer when he needed some space from reality.

"I'm not telling you what the surprise is," he stated. "We already went over that."

"That was yesterday. I'm going to find out soon anyway."

"Then that's when you'll know and not a minute before."

He didn't even care that she pouted and turned her attention out the window. He'd planned a perfect birthday evening and she would love it.

"You're coming to the opening with me next weekend, right?" he asked as he turned down his private road.

"I wouldn't miss it."

"I want you to cover it, if you don't mind multitasking as my date and my journalist."

Now she glanced toward him with a smile on her face. How did her smile turn him on? It was such a simple gesture, yet packed such a lustful punch. Maybe that's why he always wanted to make her smile.

"I am quite capable of doing both," she informed him. "So my surprise is at your house?"

Laughing, Reese pulled up and waited for his gate to open. "Something like that."

She remained silent as he parked and gathered her things.

"Follow me," he ordered as he followed the path around the back of the house, leading toward his dock.

"Oh, a ride on the yacht," she exclaimed. "Fun. It's a beautiful afternoon."

A perfect day for relaxing…and maybe more. He'd planned this birthday surprise well before last night, so now he couldn't help but wonder if they'd pick back up where they'd left off.

Reese assisted her down the dock and onto the yacht. His chef stood at the entrance to the cabin and nodded as they stepped on board. Frisco wasn't just his chef, though that was his main position and what he'd been hired for, but the man did absolutely everything Reese asked and typically a little more. He was invaluable.

"Good afternoon, Reese. Miss Coleman."

"Thanks for setting everything up, Frisco." Reese slapped the man on the back. "That will be all. Take the rest of the day off."

"Thank you, sir."

Once Frisco left them, Reese gestured for Josie to step on into the cabin.

"Go change," he urged. "I'll get things ready to go."

"Don't you want to change, too?"

He took a step closer, but didn't reach for her. "Is that an invitation?"

Her eyes clouded with desire, a look that had been new to him only days ago, but now he knew it all too well. Even though they'd only spent one night together, he wanted so much more. One night was not nearly enough time to explore all things Josie.

"Isn't that why you sent Frisco away?" she asked, quirking a brow.

"I sent him away because I want to spend your birthday with you, under the sun and then the stars, out on the water, without anyone around. He's done all I needed him to do."

Her eyes raked down him in a way that he hadn't experienced before. Reese liked this side of Josie and had to admit his ego swelled a little—okay, more than a little—knowing he had a hand in drawing out her passion.

"Maybe I need help changing into my suit," she purred as she reached for the hem of her black pencil dress.

She pulled it up and over her head, tossing the garment to the side. Josie stood before him in only a matching black silky bra-and-pantie set and those little black heels. With all of that dark hair pulled back, he wanted to yank the pins out and mess it all up.

"You surprise me," he told her. "That's not something I ever thought I'd say with you."

Josie shrugged. "I may like to plan everything, but I also know what I want."

Arousal slammed into him.

"And what's that?" he asked.

With her eyes firmly set on his, she reached for the snap of his dress pants. "More of last night."

Reese shoved her hands away and wrapped his arms around her waist, hauling her up against his chest as he claimed her mouth. He needed no further permission to take what she so freely offered.

Josie locked her ankles behind his back as Reese

crossed the living quarters. The accent table on his way stopped him, though. He wasn't going to make it to the bedroom, not with the way Josie was clawing at his shirt.

She jerked his shirt up as he dropped his pants and boxer briefs to the floor. Josie laughed as he attempted to toe off his shoes and kick his clothes aside. A few random strands of her hair had fallen across her face, but he wanted her even more out of control.

Reese reached behind her and released the fastener holding her hair up. The silky strands instantly fell around her shoulders and her laugh quickly sobered as she stared up at him.

He gripped her hips and scooted her closer to the edge of the table. When he slid a finger inside her panties to pull them aside, she curled her fingers around his shoulders.

"Protection?" she asked.

He glanced toward the bedroom where he'd been heading. "In there," he nodded.

She bit down on her lip and jerked her hips against his hand. "I trust you. I just had a checkup and I'm on birth control."

Reese swallowed. Never in his life had he gone without a condom, and knowing he had the okay to do so with Josie was a hell of an unexpected turn-on.

"I'm clean," he assured her. "I'd never do anything to hurt you."

She locked her gaze with his and nodded, giving him the silent affirmation to go ahead.

Holding the thin material aside, Reese slid into her, earning him another of her slow, sultry moans.

He gritted his teeth, taking just a fraction of a moment to relish the fact that no barriers stood between them. This was a first for him.

But the urge and the overwhelming need to have her took hold again and he couldn't remain still. Josie lifted her pelvis against his, urging him on, and Reese was more than ready to comply.

Josie lifted her knees against his sides, wrapped her arms around his neck and covered his mouth. He might physically be in the dominant position, but she held all the power. He was utterly useless when it came to her, and she could do anything she wanted.

There was frantic need coming off her in waves, a feeling he couldn't quite identify, but now was not the time to analyze her every thought or motive. All he wanted was more of this reckless, unrestrained Josie.

Reese reached around and flicked open her bra. Never removing his lips from hers, he fumbled enough to get the bra off and away so he could claim handfuls of her breasts. He wanted all of her, as much as she would give, and he was so damn glad he didn't have to hide his desire anymore.

"Reese," she murmured against his lips.

Her body quickened and he slid a hand between them to touch her at her most sensitive spot, knowing it would drive her over the edge.

Her gasp against his mouth and the way her entire body tightened had him pumping even faster, working toward his own release. Josie cried out and dropped her head to that crook in his neck. Reese used his free hand to press against the small of her back, making them even more flush for the best possible experience.

That's when euphoria took over and his body started

trembling. Josie's warm breath hit the side of his neck, only adding to the shivers consuming him.

Her fingers slid through his hair as she placed a kiss on his heated skin.

Reese blew out a slow breath when his body calmed. It took another minute for him to regain the strength to pull away, but he only eased back slightly to look down at her.

"Still need help with that suit?" he asked.

"I think I need some water," she laughed. "And maybe food if that's any indication of how my birthday surprise is going to go."

Reese smiled. "That's not exactly what I had planned for your birthday, so we're both surprised."

Reese took a step back and helped her from the table. He still wore his shirt and nothing else, while she still had on her panties, which were now very askew.

Fast, frantic sex had never crossed his mind when it came to Josie. He'd always thought he'd take his time and explore every inch of her. He hadn't rushed last night, but he still hadn't taken the time he wanted. And just now? Yeah, that was the fastest sex on his record.

But he wasn't sorry.

Josie had set the pace; she had wanted him here and now. Who was he to deny her...and on her birthday no less?

Reese unbuttoned his shirt and went to pick up his other clothes strewn over the floor.

Josie slid out of her panties and gathered her things, throwing him a smile over her shoulder as she headed toward the suite.

Reese barely got to enjoy the bare view when his

cell chimed in the pocket of his pants. He shuffled the pieces in his hand until he could find the phone. Clutching everything under his arm, he glanced to the screen and contemplated letting it go to voice mail. He really didn't want any interruptions, but his parents couldn't just be ignored.

And he was going to have to tell them what he'd found. They were going to be at his new opening, but he needed to talk to them before that. His big night in Manhattan certainly wasn't the time to tell them he was aware of the adoption and knew who his biological father was.

With a sigh, he slid his finger over the screen.

"Hey," he answered. "Still enjoying the mountains?"

"Hi, sweetheart," his mother answered in that smiling tone she had. "We are actually heading back home. We're on our way to the airport now."

"Home?" he questioned. "I thought you were only coming to New York next weekend. Are you guys okay?"

"We're fine," she assured him. "You know how your dad is. He just feels useless if he's not doing something productive."

"He retired," Reese reminded her. "He's supposed to be useless right now, relaxing in some amazing location that will give you guys all the drinks and massages you want."

His mother laughed. "Sounds good to me, but I think he misses you. I mean, I do, too, but he worries you're taking on too much and he just wants to support you and be there if you need advice."

Reese pinched the bridge of his nose and closed his eyes. "I've been doing this my whole life. I've got it covered."

"I tried to tell him that, but you have to remember he doesn't know what to do with his days right now. Just, maybe give him a little piddly job or, I don't know, ask his opinion on something?"

There were a million things involved in running a successful chain of upscale restaurants, and that was before adding in a brand-new opening. Reese could no doubt find something for his father.

Josie came back through wearing a one-piece black bathing suit that shouldn't have his body revving up again, but…well, it did.

"I'll see what I can do," Reese told his mother without taking his eyes off Josie. "Could you and Dad come to the house tomorrow?"

"I'm sure we can. Everything all right?"

Reese tore his eyes from Josie. He hadn't meant to just blurt out that he needed to see them, but now that he had, he'd follow through. As uncomfortable as this conversation was going to be, he wanted the truth.

"I'm fine," he assured her. "I just have something I don't want to discuss over the phone."

"Well, I'm intrigued. We'll be there around one if that works for you."

"I'll have Frisco prepare lunch. Have a safe flight. Love you, Mom."

He hung up and clutched his cell at his side. Should he just leave this letter alone? He and his parents had a great relationship; there was no reason to pull all of this past out in the open.

But he had two half brothers that he wanted to pursue a relationship with and he had to be honest with his parents about the events that had happened since they'd been gone.

"Are you skinny-dipping or putting on trunks?"

Josie's question pulled him back to the moment. He glanced toward the glass doors overlooking the sparkling ocean and back to the woman who expected him to follow through on this birthday celebration.

She deserved it all, and he wasn't going to let this unexpected bomb in his personal life affect her day.

"Do you have a preference?" he asked with a wink.

She merely laughed and shook her head. "You sounded serious with your mom. If this fake engagement is getting to be too much, you can go ahead and tell her the truth."

"What? No, that's not it." He sat his clothes down on the curved sofa and pulled on his boxer briefs. "I just have something to discuss with them that I don't want to wait on since they're coming home early."

Josie tipped her head, her ponytail sliding over one shoulder. "Is it the restaurant opening? You haven't acted like you're worried about it."

"I'm not," he assured her truthfully. "My team is on it and I was just up there. I know that night will be perfect."

Her brows drew in. "Oh, I didn't know there was something else bothering you. I just assume if something is wrong that you know I'm always here to listen."

Well, now he felt like a jerk.

Reese stepped forward, wanting to console her, but selfishly wanting his hands back on her body. He found the more he was with her, the more difficult it was to keep his distance...especially now that he knew exactly how she felt and how she trembled beneath his touch.

"I do tell you everything," he assured her. "You're my best friend, Jo. Let's just enjoy your day and talk tomorrow. Deal?"

He really needed to talk to his parents before he opened up to her. He owed them that much, giving them the courtesy of explaining their side and listening to what they had to say.

Josie reached up and patted his cheek. "Ignore me. You don't owe me an explanation. I just want you to know I'm here anytime."

His settled his hands on the dip in her waist and pulled her closer. "I'm well aware you're here. But today, let me pamper you. Now go out and lounge on the sundeck. I'll get changed and we'll take off. I'll join you in a bit."

She looked like she wanted to say more, but she nodded and stepped away. When she hit the steps leading up, she turned back.

"Hurry. I need someone to rub sunscreen on my back."

That was an invitation he couldn't ignore. For now, he was just going to focus on Josie. He wasn't going to think about the father he'd never met, telling his parents he knew the truth and he certainly wasn't going to think about the way the words *best friends* sounded wrong when he'd said them because they were more.

He just had to figure out how the hell to keep both of them from getting hurt when this all went back to platonic, because after he had his opening in Manhattan when they needed to be seen arm in arm, they would have to face reality.

And the reality was…all of this was temporary.

Eleven

Josie barely recognized herself. First, she'd ditched work, then she'd lain around the yacht letting Reese ply her with mai tais, and now she was enjoying a candlelight dinner on the deck with the full moon shining down on them.

She had to admit this birthday was turning out to be pretty awesome.

"You're going to spoil me," she told him as she reached for her wineglass.

Reese sat his napkin on the table and leaned back in his chair. "It's your birthday. I'm supposed to spoil you."

Josie didn't mean just today or in this moment. She meant in general. Reese had always been the one to comfort her, to make sure she was happy, to have her back at all times.

Hence the faux engagement.

But the undercurrent in this relationship had shifted and she was discovering that it was difficult to find her footing. She should feel guilty for wanting more sex, for enjoying it as much as she was, because there would come a time when they had to revert back to being just friends. They couldn't go on this way forever. At some point, Reese might want to find someone and settle down and have a family. That's how he was raised; that's all he knew—family and business.

Oh, she knew he dated and jet-setted around with multiple women, but none of those relationships lasted and he'd never claimed to have been in love before. He'd also never acted like he wanted to marry anytime soon, which had made that engagement months ago all the more shocking, but Josie knew the day would come. Reese's genetic makeup was that of a family man, of heritage and legacy. Those were just traits ingrained in him.

She, on the other hand, knew nothing of that type of commitment or long-term bond and the idea terrified her. Her family had been ripped apart, and then the emotional walls went up. Reese had been the only one she'd firmly clung to.

She was proud of herself, though. She'd stepped out of her comfort zone and been bold enough to take what she wanted. But how did she go back to what she'd been once everything was done? When they didn't need to show their faces to the public and they could just be Reese and Josie, best friends? Was that even possible?

So, sex was good. It was great, in fact. Josie figured she'd just enjoy herself, enjoy this bit of freedom she'd never allowed herself to have, and hope nobody got hurt in the end because she still needed that rock her best friend provided. She always had.

Josie glanced down to the ring on her finger and couldn't deny how much she loved the sparkling piece. The oval ruby surrounded by twinkling diamonds. She'd never given an engagement ring much thought before.

"Looks good on you."

She turned her attention to Reese, who nodded toward her hand. "I knew a ruby would look good on you."

"You were just dying to get some color on me," she laughed. "It's beautiful, but you know I can't keep this."

"Sure you can. I told you, consider it your birthday gift, but for now the public can believe it's your engagement ring."

"Reese—"

He reached across the table and grabbed her hand, stroking his thumb over the stone. "A friend can't buy another friend a nice birthday gift?"

She didn't know why every time he threw out the word *friend* she felt a little…off. Josie couldn't quite find the right word for how the word made her feel, but it certainly wasn't settled.

She hated disruption in her life. She'd grown up with a very regimented, standoffish father, and all of that rearing had carried over into her adult life. Everything had changed after her mother passed because, looking back, Josie realized that it was her mother who had been doting and loving, while her father demanded structure and obedience.

Josie still craved that safe zone, the comfort of knowing every aspect of her life was in the proper place.

"I got you something else," he said, hopping up from the table.

"I don't need anything else," she laughed. "The cruise, the dinner, the ring. I'm good, Reese."

He smiled down at her. "Trust me, this was not expensive, but I couldn't resist."

Now she was intrigued. She waited while he stepped down into the cabin and then came back holding a small, narrow box that was so small there was no bow. Just simple wrapping.

"It's really not much," he repeated, handing the gift over. "But I hope you'll put it to good use."

She took the gift, but kept her eyes on him. "It's too small to be a sex toy."

Reese laughed. "I'm all the sex toy you need right now."

Right now.

Josie let the words wash over her. She tried to brush them aside, but they wiggled their way right past the giddiness that consumed her and hit her heart. The simple term took hold, threatening to penetrate and cause pain.

She refused to let their current situation hurt her or damage their friendship.

Ignoring thoughts of the future, Josie tore the paper and discovered her present.

"A tube of red lipstick?"

She glanced up to Reese, who stood there smiling.

"I figure if you're not comfortable wearing the clothes, maybe we could ease you into the color."

She stared at the name brand and was actually impressed he'd known what to purchase. "I'm not sure bright red lips would be easing into wearing color."

"Just try it," he told her. "Don't let fear win, Jo. That's all this is. Fear. It's a tube of lipstick. I'm not asking you to skydive."

Josie took the cosmetic from the box and slid the lid off. Turning the base, she stared at the vibrant shade and wondered how the hell she could pull that off. Her makeup regimen consisted of mascara, black of course, and sometimes a sheer gloss if she wanted to be extra.

"Listen," he told her as he pulled his chair around the table and next to hers. He grabbed her hands and set the tube on the table. "I'm not trying to make you into someone you're not. I'm not trying to make you uncomfortable, but you have all of this inside of you. If you want to channel your mother or pay tribute to her in some way, then do it. Do it for you, and who gives a damn what other people think."

She stared into those bright blue eyes and wondered how she'd never gotten lost in them before. How had she never noticed just how remarkable Reese was? Not just to look at, because she'd known for years how hot he was, but he was her friend…right? She shouldn't have had lustful thoughts.

Yet now she did.

They'd been intimate a handful of times and she already had enough fantasies to last a lifetime.

Beyond his looks, though, there was that heart of gold. He dominated everything around him, but not in an asshole kind of way. Yes, he demanded respect, but his loyal circle of friends and employees loved him and would do anything for him. That was the sign of a true leader.

"Why did we never date when we were younger?"

she asked before she could stop herself, because they weren't even dating now.

His brows drew in as he released her hands and sat back in his chair. "I asked you out."

Confused, Josie racked her brain, but drew a blank. "You did? When?"

"In college," he told her as if she should remember. "I was helping you move from the dorm into your first apartment and I asked you out."

She recalled when he'd helped her. They thought they'd never get her hand-me-down couch up that flight of stairs to the second floor. They'd laughed, argued, shared a horrible pizza for dinner.

Oh yeah. That's when he'd asked her.

"I thought you were joking," she finally stated, but caught the sober look on his face. "You were serious?"

Reese didn't smile. He didn't make a move as he continued to stare back at her. "I'd never been more serious."

Oh. Well.

What did she do with that information?

She couldn't exactly go back in time, but if she could, would she have said yes? Josie had never thought of Reese as more than a friend until recently, but the word *more* was such a blanket term. It could be applied to anything.

She didn't know how to reply to his statement, but he had clearly thought about this over the years because he hadn't forgotten the moment. Obviously, there had been a bigger impact on him than her.

What exactly did that mean? Surely he didn't want to take this beyond best friend territory…did he?

"Reese, I—"

He leaned forward and cut her words off with a kiss. She melted into his powerful touch, completely forgetting anything she needed to say.

"No more talking," he murmured against her lips. "I want you wearing nothing but that ring and the moonlight."

Shivers raced through her at his sexy command. Anything they needed to discuss or work out with this relationship could be done later, because Reese was stripping her clothes off and she had a feeling she was about to get another birthday present.

"I discovered I'm adopted."

Josie's gasp over the warm night air seemed to echo.

It was well past midnight, so technically her birthday was over. They were on their way back to his place, fully dressed, and he found he couldn't keep the news from her any longer. The only people who knew that he knew the truth were strangers. Reese needed her advice and her shoulder to lean on. That was the main thing he valued about their relationship. Even when he was trying to be strong, to put up a front of steel, he could let his guard down around her and she never criticized or judged him.

He'd wanted to tell his parents first. He really thought he owed them that. But the other part of him needed Josie's advice on how to handle such a delicate situation. There was nobody he trusted more with this secret.

"Adopted?" she repeated. "Reese, how... I mean, who told you? Are you sure?"

He guided the yacht toward his dock. In the distance,

his three-story beachfront home lit up the shoreline. He always loved this time of night when the water was calm and quiet. He needed a stillness in however he could manage to gain one, in order to keep his sanity.

"I'm pretty certain," he told her, still keeping his eye on the dock. "I also found out I have two half brothers in Green Valley, Tennessee."

"That was the reason for your trip."

He nodded as he felt her come up beside him. The wind whipped her hair, sending strands drifting over his bare arm.

"Who are your birth parents?" she asked.

Reese shrugged. "I received a letter from a woman who I found out was my half brother's mom. She was dying and before she passed, she sent three letters. Even her son didn't know who his father was growing up, but she wanted to clear the air, I guess. Anyway, I don't know about my birth mother, but my biological father is Rusty Lockwood."

"Lockwood," she murmured. "As in, Lockwood Lightning?"

"Yeah."

"Wow." Josie laid her delicate hand on his arm for support. "Have you met him?"

Reese slowed the engine as he neared the dock. "No, but I've not heard pleasant things about him and in my own research, I've read some disturbing news. He's certainly no comparison to Martin Conrad."

The gentle squeeze from her touch had a bit of his anxiety sliding away.

"Nobody is Martin Conrad," she agreed. "Do your parents know you found this out?"

"No. That's what I want to talk to them about tomorrow."

He still didn't know how to approach the topic other than just showing them the letter and giving them a chance to explain.

"Do you…um, do you need me there?" she asked, her tone low, uncertain. "I mean, I don't want to step over the line and make you uncomfortable, but if you need someone—"

Reese reached up and slid his hand over hers as he glanced her way for a brief moment. "I want you there."

She seemed to exhale a breath and her body relaxed against his. "I don't even know what to say, but I'll do whatever I can for you."

He knew she would. He knew no matter what decision he made, she would stand by him.

"I'm going to Green Valley in a few days." He steered the ship expertly between the docks. "I'd like you to come with me if you can get away."

"I'll make the time, and I can always work on the road," she told him. "Or are we taking the jet?"

"It's going to be a quick trip," he stated, killing the engine. "We'll fly to save time."

She nodded and smiled. "Tell me when to be ready and I'll be there."

Once the yacht was secure and he'd assisted her off the dock, Reese blocked her path to head back to the house. He framed her face with his hands and leaned closer.

"You said I would spoil you, but I think it's the other way around," he murmured against her mouth. "Maybe I'm the one getting spoiled because I don't deserve all I want to take from you."

Reese wrapped his arms around her, pulling her against his chest and claiming her lips. He didn't want to talk, didn't want to think, didn't want to consider tomorrow or even the day after that. Right now, he wanted to take Jo back to his bedroom and show her just how much he ached for her.

Because their two weeks were slowly coming to an end, and he wasn't quite ready to let this physical relationship go. And maybe there was more, maybe there was something beyond the physical. Reese wasn't sure if he was getting the friendship bond confused with something more or not…he only prayed nobody got hurt in the end.

Twelve

"Darling, you look so happy."

Reese cringed when his mother wrapped her arms around him and then stepped back to examine him and Josie, who stood at his side.

"I cannot tell you how thrilled I am that the two of you are together," she went on. "I've known for years you were the one for my son."

Josie's eyes darted to his, but Reese merely smiled. He had bigger things to deal with right now than this fake engagement. He was about to crush the two people who loved him more than anything, who'd raised him like their own, who'd given him the life he lived today.

But they all deserved for the secrets to come out so they could move forward. He'd had time to deal with the truth. He knew his parents were good people and they likely had done what they thought was in his best interest.

"Can we at least get inside before you start smothering them?" Martin asked as he stepped into the foyer.

Reese stared at the man he'd always thought of as his father. He'd never given it much thought, but other than the fact that they were both tall with broad shoulders, there were no other similarities.

Laura reached for Josie and wrapped her arms around her, too. Reese hated the guilt that layered in with his anxiety. He'd never held on to this many secrets at one time in his life.

Between the engagement and the news about his biological father, Reese had to get something out in the open before he drove himself mad. The only saving grace in all of this was that Josie was finally in his bed, where he'd wanted her for longer than he cared to admit. Granted, now he didn't know how to take a step back with her into that friend territory. He honestly wasn't sure he wanted to, but they'd agreed that after his opening, they would make an announcement that they were better off as friends and call off this fake engagement.

What did it say about him that he wasn't ready for that announcement?

"Oh, my word, that ring is gorgeous," his mother declared, holding Josie's hand. "So unique and perfect."

"It's really beautiful," Josie stated, but Reese didn't miss the tightness in her tone. "Why don't you guys come on in? Frisco set up lunch out on the back deck."

Reese was thankful Josie took over and turned the attention away from the engagement, but that meant the next topic was another he didn't want to get into.

Lunch flew by with chatter and laughter, but Reese knew time was ticking and he'd have to just pull the letter from his pocket and share.

Josie's fingertip drew a pattern over the condensation on her water glass and he knew she was feeling all the nerves as well. He met her gaze and she offered him a reassuring smile.

"I'm glad to see you guys," Reese started. "But there's something I need to discuss."

His mother sat back in her seat and shifted her attention. "Yes, you have me intrigued. Is this about New York? You're not moving, are you?"

Reese shook his head. "I love it here and I'm fine with traveling wherever I need."

"Is something wrong, son?" his father asked, resting his elbows on the arms of the dining chair.

Reese reached into his pocket and pulled out the letter. He passed it to his father.

"I received this right after you were released from the hospital and I didn't want to bring it up," he added. "And then I wanted you guys to enjoy your trip, so I kept it to myself until I could sort things out."

Martin Conrad's eyes darted from Reese down to the folded letter. He opened the paper and started reading. It didn't take long for the color to drain from his face.

"Martin, what is it?"

His father remained silent as he finished reading, but ultimately he handed the letter across the table.

Reese's heart beat so hard, so fast, but he tried to remain calm. This was the best move in the long run; there would just be some painful hurdles to overcome.

Surprisingly, his mother didn't get upset. She squared

her shoulders and placed the letter on the table, running her fingertip along the creases in a vain attempt to smooth it out.

Her dark brown eyes finally came up to his.

"I want you to know we did everything we could to make the best decision at the time," she told him. "We went through an agency, but the birth parents wanted to remain anonymous."

"That's when we decided not to tell you about the adoption because we had no more information to give," his father added. "You were our son from day one. Blood didn't matter."

No, it didn't. These were his parents and there had never been any doubt the lengths they would go to to make him happy and show their love.

"Do you hate us?" his mother finally asked. "I don't think I could stand it if you were upset with us. We just wanted to give you the best life."

Reese scooted his chair back and went around to his mom. "Never," he said, leaning down to wrap his arms around her. "I could never hate either of you. I just didn't want to keep this from you. I may always wonder why you didn't tell me before, but I respect that you have your reasons. I've never been a parent or in your shoes, so I can't judge."

"Well, now you have the birth father's name," his dad chimed in. "Have you reached out to him?"

Reese straightened, but kept his hand on his mother's shoulder. "No. I wouldn't have done that before talking to you. I did go to Green Valley, Tennessee, though. I've met with my half brothers. Nick Campbell and Sam Hawkins."

"Sam Hawkins," his dad murmured. "He's the son of Rusty Lockwood, too?"

Reese nodded. "And Nick is a major investor and renovator. He's opening a resort this fall in the Smoky Mountains. A project his late mom started."

"Sounds like all the boys turned out well," his mom said. "I don't know Rusty, other than through the Lockwood Lightning name."

Reese glanced to Josie, who had given her silent support this entire time. He wasn't sure what all to get into regarding Rusty, but he knew he didn't want to think about it right now. He'd let the secret out; that had been his main goal.

"I plan on going back to Green Valley," Reese added. "Sam and Nick want to confront Rusty. All of us together."

His mother inhaled sharply and glanced up at him. He saw the fear in her eyes, but she remained strong. Two of the strongest women he'd ever known both had their eyes on him.

"I only want to meet him, maybe see if he knows the name of the woman who gave birth to me."

Now Laura Conrad's eyes did well up. The last thing he wanted was to cause her pain.

"I may not do anything with the information," he assured her. "I honestly don't know. All I know is this is still new to me and you guys have had years to process. I'm asking you to trust me to do what is right for me now."

Martin came to his feet and eased around the patio table. "Of course we trust you, son. You do what you think is best. We'll support you."

Reese nodded, worried if he said too much, emotions would clog his throat and overcome him. This delicate situation demanded control.

His father reached out and wrapped his arms around Reese. Patting his back, Reese took the embrace, this one meaning so much more than any in the past.

"Will you keep us posted on what you find?" his mother asked.

Reese turned back to face her and smiled. "Of course. Josie and I are going to Tennessee in a couple of days. I'm not sure how long we'll be there, so we may just go on to New York from there."

His mom came to her feet and opened her arms. He gathered her in, recognizing as always how petite yet resilient she was.

"I hope you find what you're looking for," she whispered. "I just don't want this to change us."

He eased back and held on to her slender shoulders. "You guys are my parents. Nothing can change that."

Over his mother's shoulder, Reese caught Josie swiping a tear. He didn't even think of the emotional impact this would have on her. Having a distant relationship with her father and no mother, this had to be difficult, seeing him with such a strong bond with both of his parents.

"I'll just leave you guys and start cleaning up." Josie eased her chair back and started reaching for the dishes. "I'll bring dessert in a few minutes."

"Don't clean up," Reese told her, but she was already stacking plates and carrying them away.

"You've got a good woman there," his father declared. "It's going to take a strong woman by your side to do the work we do."

Reese was well aware of that, but he hadn't thought of Josie by his side in that sense for the long term. They were friends…friends enjoying the hell out of each other and helping the other out during a difficult time.

Would his parents be disappointed when he told them he and Josie weren't actually going to get married? Maybe, but he would have to cross that bridge when they got to it.

And it wasn't like Josie was going anywhere, right? She would still be by his side as his friend. Her support was all he needed—the intimacy was just the fulfillment of something he'd been fantasizing about.

He had so many career goals to achieve before thinking of anything long-term with a woman. Besides, Josie never acted like she was ready for a commitment, either. So why was he stressing? Why was he feeling a heaviness, knowing the end of this farce was near?

"I was also thinking we could do a live timeline piece."

Josie had been taking diligent notes about the new spring options for her column. Even though they hadn't reached fall yet, the industry was always looking ahead at least one or two seasons. They had to stay ahead of other competing journalists, bloggers and magazines. The entire industry was one big race to see who could reveal the next season's hottest styles, fashions, dinner party themes and so much more.

"I'd like to document your journey to the aisle," Melissa stated with much more glee than Josie was feeling.

Josie stared down at the ruby. She couldn't stop staring at it. When she worked, there it was. When she drove, there it was. When she was sipping her morning coffee, there it was.

Always a reminder of this farce she'd started.

"I've got so much other material to cover," Josie stated. "I'm super excited about the fall spread I'm doing on various ciders and pairings. I think it will be great to incorporate those with a coastal feel since not everyone can have a bonfire and hoodies."

"Yes, yes," her editor agreed. "I love that idea, too, but I'd like to hand that one off and have you solely focus on this engagement."

Josie closed her eyes and took a deep breath. What could she say? Until the Manhattan opening, she and Reese were playing the part of lovers in love.

She had the lover part down, but she didn't know about the "in love" part.

Did she?

No. That would be silly. They weren't in love; they were just friends. Sure she loved him in that best-friend way, but what did she know about being in love with someone? She'd never experienced any such emotion.

She blew out her breath and attempted to relax. Once this was all over, she wouldn't be so anxious and have to take so many calming breaths…she hoped.

"That's fine," Josie reluctantly agreed.

She'd still get that fall piece back once Melissa realized there wasn't actually going to be a wedding, so there was nothing to worry about. Josie would just keep those notes saved on her computer and continue to work silently on that project.

"Would you be opposed to me sending a photographer with you when you look at dresses?" she asked. "Obviously, not taking shots when you find the one."

Dresses? Um, she wasn't going to go quite that far in this charade.

"I won't be looking at dresses for a while." Josie felt a little better about that true statement. "Reese is so busy with his opening in Manhattan, and we are taking a short trip to Tennessee before that. We can discuss the dress situation when I return."

And that would buy the time she needed to come clean.

"I can work with that time frame, but we'll need to post some things on the blog. Maybe you could share some of your favorite places where you'll be registering or we could do a fun poll on where viewers think you should honeymoon."

Registering and honeymoons were definitely not on her radar. Josie wanted out of this conversation and off the phone so she could start packing for her trip. She was both anxious and excited to go away with Reese. She wanted to meet Nick and Sam and she was more than ready to get away.

"Maybe a poll of favorite flowers?" Josie suggested. "Something simple, but not too much."

"Great idea. I'll get something put up tomorrow, but make sure you interact with the viewers." Her editor laughed. "Why did I tell you that? Of course you will. This is the happiest time of your life."

Josie glanced to the ring again. Maybe not the happiest, but definitely the most interesting.

"I'll be sure to hop on over the next few days," Josie promised.

She finally ended the call and sat back in her chair.

Pushing aside all the wedding talk and engagement whirlwind was going to be best for this trip. None of this was real, so letting it occupy space in her mind would only drive her crazy.

Josie came to her feet and shifted her focus to the trip. She needed to be Reese's support system for this. When he'd told his parents, Josie had been surprised at how well they took the news that Reese had discovered the truth. She'd been overcome with emotion at their precious bond, at the hurdles they faced as a team and conquered together.

She shouldn't feel sorry for herself. Maybe her entire life would've been different had her mother lived, but that was not the way things were meant to be. Josie knew her father loved her. He just had closed in on himself and become even more regimented since he'd retired from the military, and that was okay. She could look back now and see that he had struggled. Everyone dealt with loss differently.

Josie headed to the bedroom she had been sharing with Reese. The work on her house was almost done, but she wouldn't be staying there until she and Reese returned from New York. When they returned, the farce would be over, the engagement would end and they'd go back to being just friends.

The looming deadline weighed heavy on her. She didn't know why. They'd been friends before; they'd be friends again.

But now that she'd been intimate with him, how

could she give that up? They'd grown closer than she'd ever thought possible. But there was no future for them as an actual couple. There was no reason to be delusional about the truth.

Nope. Reese would go right back into that best-friend box and one day they would look back at this engagement and just laugh.

Right?

Thirteen

Reese slid his hand into Josie's as they made their way toward the entrance of Hawkins Distillery. This time walking in was no easier than the first, but at least now he had her by his side.

True, he'd already met the guys, but now there were more details to discuss and their lives would continue to intertwine.

Sam had arranged for a private dinner after closing hours so they would all have privacy and could freely talk. Apparently, Sam's and Nick's significant others were going to be here as well, so Reese was doubly glad he wouldn't be the fifth wheel.

"I've never heard you this quiet," she murmured as they neared the main entrance.

"How can you hear me being quiet?"

She laughed and slapped his arm. "You know what I mean."

He did and he appreciated her concern. Giving her hand a gentle squeeze, he stepped to the entrance and gripped the wrought iron door handle as he turned to face her.

"I know what you mean, but I'm fine. Nervous, but it helps that you're here." He tipped his head, his eyes darting to her lips. "You still haven't worn that red lipstick. Saving it for a special occasion?"

She rolled her eyes. "I can't just wear red lipstick, Reese."

"You can," he countered. "We all have to face our fears, Jo. Step out of our comfort zone sometimes to see what or who we can become."

Josie stared at him, then leaned in and gently kissed him before easing back. It took quite a bit to surprise Reese, but her spontaneous show of affection, when they didn't need to put on a show or weren't heading into the bedroom, surprised him.

"Since you're facing your fear, you looked like you needed it," she told him with a smile before he could question her.

Releasing the door, he framed her face and gave her a proper kiss. There was no gentleness, no lead-in. This woman was an addiction he couldn't let go of anytime soon.

When he eased back, still holding on to her, her eyes remained closed and her mouth open. He stroked his thumb across her lower lip.

"I always need that," he murmured.

Her lids slowly lifted as she refocused on him. "What's happening between us?"

A knot in his stomach tightened. He had no clue how to answer that because he wasn't quite sure himself. He knew she was his best friend, knew that they were more than compatible in the bedroom and knew she'd always stood by his side. But he wasn't sure beyond that. In his world right now, he had a mess that needed to be cleaned up before he could think too much about anything else.

"Let's curb this topic for later," he suggested.

She stared another minute before ultimately nodding. He kissed her once more before letting her go and opening the door. He gestured for her to go ahead of him and then he followed her in.

"Wow," she muttered as soon as they were inside.

Reese had to admit, the place was spectacularly done in an industrial, modern yet old-charm combination. The exposed brick walls, scarred wood floors, and leather-and-metal chairs in the lobby area were perfect. Definitely masculine, rustic, very Smoky Mountains and spot-on for a distillery.

"I've never been to a distillery," she told him. "I may just have to do an article on Hawkins because this place is amazing, and I only just walked in. Think I could get a guided tour?"

"Of course you can."

Reese turned to see Sam striding toward them. He reached out and shook Reese's hand, then turned his attention to Josie.

"I'm Sam Hawkins," he stated. "I'll give you a tour anytime you want. After dinner, if you have the time."

Josie's smile widened and nodded. "I'm Josie and I'd love that, but I should tell you I'm a journalist, so I ask all the questions."

Sam laughed and folded his arms across his chest.

"I'm aware of who you are, and you can ask all the questions you want."

Of course Sam had done his research. He'd invited virtual strangers into his space, strangers who were near family. Reese had done his share of looking into all parties in attendance as well.

Sam's fiancée, Maty Taylor, was an attorney. Actually, she had been Rusty's attorney, so Reese had to assume that's how Maty and Sam met.

Then there was Nick and his fiancée, Silvia Lane. Silvia was expecting a baby and the two were finishing up a spectacular resort in the mountains. Reese had every intention of booking their best suite once it opened.

"We'll discuss a possible article later," Josie promised.

Sam nodded. "Sounds good. Everyone is already in the back if you guys want to follow me."

Josie slid her hand into Reese's. The fact that he didn't even have to ask for her support just proved how in tune they were with each other. He might be a bundle of nerves on the inside, but having her with him during the most difficult, worrisome time in his life was absolutely invaluable.

They headed all the way into the back where a large enclosed dining area had been set up. The three exterior walls were all windows, providing a breathtaking view of the mountains.

"This is our main tasting room." Sam directed his comment to Josie. "I can set you up with a tasting after the tour, too, or you can try anything you want with your dinner."

Josie's smile beamed once again and Reese could

feel the excitement rolling off of her. This was why she excelled at her job. She truly loved what she did, and it showed through her enthusiasm and her research.

Reese turned his attention to the other three in the room. They stood in a group near the table all set up and he found that their smiling faces put his nerves at ease. Instinct had gotten him far in business and he had a good feeling about today, about the future.

"You must be Reese and Josie." A slender woman with long blond hair approached them and extended her hand. "I'm Maty Taylor, Sam's fiancée. We're really glad you both could join us."

The other two came around the table as well, and Reese felt the nerves slip away as all of the introductions were made. There was something so ironic that the three men were all broad and powerful and each of the women they were with appeared to be bold, confident. Reese wondered what other underlying similarities they all shared.

"I'm Nick Campbell and this is my fiancée, Silvia Lane."

Silvia had a small baby bump and Reese felt a twinge of jealousy. What would Josie look like pregnant with his child?

But immediately, he shut that question down. He wasn't ready for long-term with her or anyone else. He and Josie were forging their way through this new territory and the thought of a child terrified him.

That one-day-family idea he'd had wasn't coming anytime soon. He had too many plans he wanted to have in place before he started thinking about his legacy.

"I have to be honest," Maty said, leaning toward

Josie. "Silvia and I are giddy with excitement that you're here. We absolutely love your column."

Reese watched as Josie simply beamed. "Thank you so much. I love meeting readers one-on-one. Writing can be a lonely industry."

"And congratulations on the engagement," Silvia added. "Isn't it funny how life works? The guys all discover they're brothers and we all have recently become engaged."

Josie glanced to Reese and he literally saw the proverbial shield come down, masking her true emotions. Nobody knew her like he did, so her reaction wouldn't be noticeable. Still, he hated they were in a position to lie.

He also hated that he'd heard Chris had still been leaving notes and flowers on Josie's doorstep. His construction crew had kindly informed Reese of that fact, and Reese had sent Chris a not-so-subtle text telling the guy to move on or face harassment charges.

Hopefully that was the end of the issue.

The women seemed to shift and congregate discussing weddings and babies…neither topic appealed to Reese, so he moved toward Nick and Sam.

"Thanks for making the trip," Nick said. "I'm sure this is still a shock to you."

Reese tucked his thumbs through his belt loops and nodded. "I'm getting used to the idea. I spoke with my parents, so that was the toughest part."

"I can't imagine," Nick added. "Sam and I have a meeting set up with Rusty tomorrow evening at seven. We're actually meeting in his office."

Reese listened to the details about how the charges

of embezzlement were sticking, how Rusty was about to lose everything and how Sam had never revealed to Rusty that he was Sam's father.

"So Rusty only knows of you?" Reese asked Nick. Nick nodded.

"I didn't want anything from him," Sam chimed in. "I didn't want money or to merge our businesses, nothing. I didn't want to give him any inkling that I was his son, but after thinking it over, I don't care if he knows. He's tried to buy my distillery for years now and I'm more than happy to show him just how powerful I've become. He's got nothing on me."

Well, Rusty was in for one hell of a surprise when he discovered he had two more bouncing baby boys.

Laughter from the women filtered through the open space and Reese couldn't help but smile. Josie fit into every single aspect of his life. He wondered what that kiss meant earlier, the one just outside when she'd claimed it was because he needed it.

Was she developing stronger feelings? Was he?

He glanced over his shoulder and she happened to glance his way. She sent him a wink that packed a punch, but not of lust. There was something building between them, something he wasn't sure he was ready for.

Regardless of what happened once their two-week sham was over, Reese knew he would never be the same.

"That was so much fun," Josie exclaimed as she and Reese made their way into the cabin they'd rented. "I cannot believe I got a tour, a tasting and an invite to come back to watch firsthand production."

Reese unlocked the door and ushered her inside the

spacious mountainside cottage. Well, this particular cabin was called "Cozy Cottage" but there was nothing tiny about the four-thousand-square-foot space. Josie didn't realize how much she would love the mountains until she and Reese had driven up to this secluded rental. No wonder people always wanted to vacation here.

She might be a beach girl at heart, but she had a feeling the mountains would be calling her name again and again.

"And here I was worried you'd feel left out," Reese joked as he tossed his keys onto the table by the front door. "Sam seemed pretty anxious to let you interview him for a piece."

Josie smoothed her hair back and crossed her arms. "You're not jealous, are you?"

Reese held her gaze and cocked his head. "Should I be? Sam was named one of Tennessee's most eligible bachelors not that long ago."

Josie took a step closer. "Well, I think he's pretty in love with Maty and I'm—"

She stilled. No, she wasn't in love.

That was absurd. She was just getting caught up in all of this engagement fiasco.

"You're what?" Reese prompted.

Josie dropped her arms and squared her shoulders. "I'm not looking for a man," she told him.

Reese reached for her, his hands already working the zipper hidden on the side of her dress. "Is that so? Well, I wasn't looking for this, either, but here we are."

What did that mean? She wanted to ask, but his hands were moving on her, ridding her of all her clothes as he walked her backward.

"Have you checked out the deck?" he asked, a naughty gleam in his eye and a cocky smile to match.

"No. Should I?"

Her hands went to the buttons of his black dress shirt and she had him out of it before he could answer.

"There's a hot tub," he told her, firmly settling his hands at the dip in her waist. "There's also a flatbed swing. Both perfect for stargazing."

Josie smiled, raking her fingertip over the lines of his abs. "Is that what you're undressing me for? Stargazing?"

"You shouldn't get into the hot tub with your clothes on," he said.

Josie let him lead her outside, where she finished undressing him. The wide deck did provide a spacious hot tub and on the other end, a wide bed on a swing, perfect for lounging with your lover.

And that's the word she'd been looking for all this time. Reese had moved from best friend to lover, but she wasn't sure where his head was with all of this. What would happen once they decided to publicly call off the engagement? Would they still sneak a rendezvous here or there? Would he still want this physical intimacy? Because she wasn't sure she could give this up now that she'd experienced Reese.

"You're letting your mind take you away again," he accused.

Before she could defend herself, he picked her up and hauled her over his shoulder like she was nothing more than a blanket. Mercy, his strength was sexy.

He climbed into the hot tub and gently set her down. The warm water instantly had chill bumps popping up.

He reached over and tapped a button, instantly turning the jets on…as if she needed more stimulation to her already-aroused body.

When he turned back to her, he had that look again, the one that promised she was in for a good time.

"About that kiss earlier," he started as he reached for her. He sat down and pulled her onto his lap, giving her no choice but to straddle him. "Want to tell me why you're kissing me when nobody was looking?"

Yeah, about that. She'd told him he looked like he needed it, but in reality, she'd just wanted to. The pull toward him was growing stronger and stronger. She'd had to make up something quick because she didn't want to reveal her true feelings…basically because she wasn't even sure what her true feelings were.

"Maybe I like kissing you," she said, looping her arms around his neck. "Maybe I'm enjoying myself with you, despite all the chaos around us."

His hands eased up her thighs and around to cup her backside. "We do seem to draw the attention to us, don't we?"

She leaned into him, her breasts flattening against his chest. How could he keep carrying on a conversation? Her body was ready to go and he seemed to be taking his time.

Josie shifted a little more until she settled over him at the exact spot she ached to be. With her eyes locked onto his, she sank down, smiling when he moaned and closed his eyes.

Being in control where Reese was concerned wasn't an easy task. The man thrived on staying dominant at all times. But now his head dropped back against the edge of the hot tub and Josie braced her hands on his shoulders as she began to move.

Reese lifted his head and closed his mouth over her breast. She bit down on her lip to keep from crying out. Between his hands, his mouth and that rock-hard body moving beneath hers—oh, and those jets—Josie wasn't going to last.

When his lips traveled up to her neck, Josie dropped her head back and arched her body into his. He murmured her name over and over as she rocked against him.

All too soon, her body started climbing. As much as she wanted to make this moment last, she was fighting a losing battle.

Reese kept one hand on her backside and gripped her neck with the other, easing her down so he could claim her lips. She threaded her fingers through his hair and let every wave of emotion wash over her, through her.

His body tightened beneath hers as he joined her. Josie kept herself wrapped all around him, taking in the passionate kiss as her body came down from the high.

Reese's hold lessened as he nipped at her bottom lip, then rested his forehead against hers. The water continued to pulse around them, relaxing Josie even more. She didn't want to move, didn't want to face reality. She only wanted to stay in this moment that seemed so right because all too soon she would have to face the fact that she had to let Reese slip back into that friend box.

But for now, for tonight, she was in his arms.

Tomorrow he would meet his biological father and Josie wanted to give him as much comfort and peace as possible…and she prayed she could keep her heart from tumbling into love for her best friend.

Fourteen

"Are you ready for this?" Sam asked.

The three brothers stood outside the Lockwood Lightning Distillery. The sun was just starting to set behind the mountains, the tours had all ended, and the place was closed. Rusty was expecting them and Reese had a ball of nerves in his gut.

"Are you ready?" he countered to Sam. "Rusty isn't aware that you're his son, either."

Sam shrugged. "I honestly don't care if he ever finds out about me, but I'll stand with you guys as a united front."

Reese could understand and respect that. They were all at different places in their lives, but ultimately the deathbed confession of one woman had brought them all here. He also understood why Nick's mother had sent those letters. She hadn't wanted her son to have no family once she was gone.

"Let's get this over with," Nick stated. "I don't like spending any more time with this bastard than necessary."

Reese had dealt with some shady jerks in business before, but he hadn't imagined someone could be as terrible as Rusty was rumored to be. Clearly, he was getting ready to find out.

Sam reached up and pressed the intercom button next to the side door of the offices. Seconds later the door clicked and Nick reached for it.

He opened and gestured. "After you guys."

Reese stepped inside and the mixed scents of leather and alcohol hit him. The atmosphere was quite different from Sam's distillery. Here things seemed older, definitely a vibe from twenty years ago, where Sam's distillery seemed fresh and cutting-edge with the older themes complementing the decor.

"Gentlemen."

Reese turned toward the staircase and stared up at the landing, at Rusty Lockwood. He seemed older, heavier, in person than the photos Reese had seen online. Or maybe Rusty was just tired and run-down after being arrested and investigated regarding some serious charges.

Having your life and company on the brink of collapse would certainly wreak havoc.

Rusty's eyes scanned the guys, but ultimately landed on Reese.

"Recruiting new allies?" he asked. "I don't even know him, so I doubt he wants to see my demise."

Sam snorted. "You're about to know him. Are you coming down or standing there lording over us?"

"Are you staying long or will this meeting be short?" Rusty asked as he started to descend the steps.

Reese's first impression was that the man didn't like that he was being overrun. He didn't even bother with an introduction, as most people would when meeting someone new. He clearly didn't have any positive feelings toward Sam or Nick.

"Trust us, we don't want to be here any longer than necessary," Nick stated. "But there are some things we need to discuss."

Rusty came to the bottom of the steps and crossed his arms over his chest.

Reese couldn't stand it another second. "I'm Reese Conrad," he said, extending his hand.

Rusty stared for a second before giving a firm shake. "I've heard your name. You own those restaurants."

Those restaurants, like there was something wrong with being a restaurateur. Like people didn't have to book reservations at least a month in advance for a table, and even longer for the private lounge.

Rusty clearly had the mentality that he was above everyone else.

"I own eight restaurants and I'm opening my ninth in New York this coming weekend," Reese amended.

Rusty grunted and turned to Nick. "So what's this all about?"

"You recall my mother left me a letter about you being my biological father."

Rusty nodded. "And?"

"She sent letters to two of my brothers as well," Nick added.

Reese watched as Rusty processed that statement, then the man turned toward Sam, then Reese. His eyes showed absolutely no emotion. Nick might as well have told him the sky was blue for the lack of surprise on his face.

"So is this a family reunion?" Rusty asked. "And how do I know any of this is true?"

Sam took a step forward. "I don't give a damn if you believe us or not. We're just letting you know that you do have children. We want to clear the air and you can decide what to do from here. I don't believe any of us are looking for fatherly advice or holiday invites."

"I'm actually going to offer to buy Lockwood Lightning from you," Nick stated.

Reese jerked his attention to Nick, who only had his sights set on Rusty. From the way Sam reacted, he was just as surprised by Nick's offer.

"Buy me out?" Rusty scoffed. "When hell freezes over."

Nick shrugged and slid his hands into his pockets. "I knew that would be your first reaction, but that's why you're failing right now. You aren't thinking like a businessman. Instead, you're letting your emotions override common sense."

Rusty glanced at each of them. "Is that why you all came here? To gang up on me and get me to sell? You think I'm just passing down all I've built because I supposedly fathered you?"

"Bloodlines have nothing to do with this decision,"

Nick amended. "You don't need to answer me now, but I will own this distillery."

"What do you know about running a distillery?" Rusty mocked. "You renovate buildings and sell them off for others to run."

"He doesn't know about distilleries," Sam agreed. "But I do, and I'll be his partner."

"You think I'd sell to either of you?" Rusty asked. "After I tried to buy you out for years and you turned me down? I supposed your third crony is going to want in on this, too?"

Reese shrugged. "Always looking to expand. I'd go into business with them."

Rusty puffed up his chest as he pulled in a breath. The buttons on his shirt strained against the movement.

"If that's all you guys wanted, you wasted your time." Rusty started to turn back to the steps, but stopped himself. "I won't sell my distillery to any of you and I'm not really looking for children who will inherit my legacy. You can see yourselves out. The door will automatically lock, so don't come back."

And with that warm parting, Rusty went back up the steps to his lair or office or hellhole.

Nick and Sam both turned to Reese and he honestly didn't know what to say about the anticlimactic, not to mention fast, meeting they'd just had.

"Well, I guess that settles that," Reese said. "Clearly, he doesn't care about his sons, so I'm done here."

Nick glanced toward the empty steps and back to his brothers. "I meant what I said. I'm going to buy this place. It was something I'd thought about, but the minute I saw him, I knew. If you guys want to join me, we'd make a hell of a team."

Reese didn't make rash business decisions, but this was one thought that held merit. An already-established distillery run by three brothers who had all already made names for themselves in the hospitality and real estate industries was a no-brainer.

"We should discuss this elsewhere," Sam stated as he started toward the main door. "Let's head to my place where we can talk. I have a feeling this is going to take some strategic planning."

Reese followed, already pulling out his phone to text Josie and tell her what had happened and where he was heading. Odd that his first instinct had been to contact her and not his parents, but he would talk to them in person. He missed Josie when he wasn't with her and wanted to fill her in on everything going on in his life.

After last night, between the hot tub and then falling asleep holding her on the swinging bed under the stars, Reese couldn't help but wonder if maybe he was ready for more. Maybe the thought of commitment and long-term had always scared him in the past because the right person hadn't come into his life.

But she had.

She'd been there all along.

As things started to settle in his personal life, maybe long-term included Josie as well. Maybe she was settling right into the spot she was meant to be.

Reese had so much to think about regarding his brothers and Josie. There was a whole host of things he needed to weigh in his head before he made any life-changing decisions.

One thing was certain, though: the life he'd been living only a few weeks ago no longer existed. He was facing a new chapter and hell if all of this didn't scare him to death.

"I put an offer in on a house here."

Josie shifted and turned over in the swing bed, shocked by Reese's words. They swayed as she moved.

"In Green Valley?" she asked.

With one arm braced behind his head, he toyed with the ends of her hair with his other hand. His eyes held hers and she truly wished they could stay right here forever.

But that was a fantasy. They were friends, doing each other a favor, and they'd tumbled into bed in the process.

It was as simple and complex as that.

He grinned. "What do you think of this place?"

"You put an offer in on this cabin?"

Reese tucked her hair behind her ear, then rested his hand over hers, which was on his chest. "I love this outdoor setup overlooking the mountains. The interior would need to be updated to my tastes, but that's just cosmetic. I love the layout and the setting."

"Was it for sale?"

His brows drew in. "Did it need to be? I want a second home and for the right price, I bet the owners would be all too happy to find another cabin to buy and use as a rental."

That was Reese. Find something, make a plan, obtain it. He'd done the same with his Manhattan restaurant. He wanted to move on to a broader customer base and he'd done it without thinking twice.

"I don't know what's going to happen with Sam and Nick or even if this distillery of Rusty's is even going to be an option, but I want to be present when I'm needed and I'm growing to really love the mountains."

Yeah, she was, too. This was their third night here. They were flying to Manhattan in the morning, but they'd shared some special memories here... memories she'd have to keep locked away once all this was over.

"I invited the guys and their fiancées to the opening," Reese went on. "They said they'd be there."

Josie smiled. "You're really bonding with them. I'm glad. You all seem to really mesh well together."

"It's like we're old friends," Reese stated. "It's strange, really, but I'm comfortable around them."

"Have you talked to your parents about them?" she asked.

He nodded. "I called them earlier while you were in the shower. They're happy for me, that I'm forming a relationship with Nick and Sam. They apologized for how the meeting with Rusty went and I realized I had no expectations for that meeting, so it's not like I'm let down. I have the greatest parents of all time."

Josie couldn't argue there, but she didn't want to get swept up in thoughts about her late mom or her absent dad. She wanted to focus on the positive and the happiness that was stemming from all of this chaos.

Reese's finger slid over the ring on her hand. She cringed, feeling like a fraud every time she looked at it.

"Why did you marry Chris to begin with?" he asked.

The words hung between them and Josie didn't want to give him the truth. If she gave him the truth, that would just be another shove away from being "just friends."

Risking more terrified her. She'd rather have Reese back in that friend zone than to keep moving toward something that could crumble. She wasn't the best with relationships; she'd never had anything serious that lasted, so what did she truly know?

"Jo," he prompted.

She blinked her focus back to him. "It was a rash decision."

"Obviously, but what snapped inside that head of yours and made you rush to the courthouse? You had only dated him a few months."

Maybe she *should* be honest. Maybe that would be the best therapy and they could discuss what exactly was going on with all of these emotions. They'd talk and figure out why it was best that they just remain friends.

"You were engaged," she stated simply. "It made me realize that we were entering new chapters in our lives."

She stared down at him, wondering how he'd take her response. But that was the truth. She'd realized she might not be the only woman in his life forever. There would be someone else he'd share secrets or inside jokes with.

And she had gotten jealous.

There. Fine. She could admit it…to herself. She was human and she didn't like sharing, okay?

"Making a rush in judgment isn't like you," he told her. "You plan everything. Hell, you have an alarm to check your planner. But you married someone because I was engaged?"

"I made a mistake," she defended herself, sitting up a

little more. She crossed her legs in front of her, needing just a bit of distance between them in this small space. "I wasn't in love with Chris. He was a nice guy, I feel terrible that I hurt him, but honestly I don't think he loved me, either. He just wanted to be married because his family had been putting pressure on him."

Completely the truth.

"Why did you get engaged?" she retorted.

Reese shrugged and stared up at the starry sky. "I was taking over Conrad's full time and starting to wonder about my legacy and who I would share it with. I know I want a family someday, but once I got engaged, I realized I wasn't ready and she wasn't the one."

Josie placed her hand on his chest and smiled. "Sounds like we both dodged bigger mistakes."

"Speaking of, Chris has been leaving notes and stopping by your house," he told her. "My contractor informed me several days ago, so I reached out to Chris."

Josie stilled. "What? You should let me take care of this."

Reese's gaze came back to hers. "I let you try that, we ended up engaged and he still didn't back off. I told him if there was any further contact there would be harassment charges filed."

Josie didn't want a keeper. She didn't want anyone, especially Reese, fighting her battles.

"This engagement wasn't my doing," she informed him. "I told Chris I had moved on. You're the one who threw out I was your fiancée."

"He needed something stronger than just dating," Reese replied in that calm tone of his. "I could've said we'd already eloped."

Josie pulled in a deep breath and closed her eyes. The opening was in just a couple days and then they would go back to normal. Hopefully Chris would still keep his distance.

"I'm tired," she told Reese as she rolled off the side of the swing and came to her feet. "I'm going in to bed."

Reese continued to lie there, staring up at her. "We can stay out here," he suggested. "When I buy this place, I plan on staying out here as much as possible."

Josie smiled, but her heart was heavy.

She wanted things to go back to the way they were a few weeks ago. She wanted to ignore the way her heart shifted when Reese talked about lying with her, holding her or when he spoke of the future. They didn't have a future, not in the way they'd been playing house these past several days.

"You can stay out here," she told him. "I'll be fine."

She turned and stepped into the house, closing the patio door behind her. Maybe he'd come in and maybe he wouldn't. Right now, she needed time to think.

Reese had never acted like he wanted more with her. He seemed content with just the physical, which was fine. It had to be. If they tried this whole relationship for real, she didn't know how long that could or would last. If he tired of her and moved on...that would definitely ruin their friendship.

That was a risk she couldn't take, no matter how much she might be falling for her best friend.

Fifteen

Reese adjusted his tie, more out of nerves than anything else. The opening was due to kick off in less than thirty minutes, but that wasn't what had a ball of tension in his belly.

The restaurant business was in his blood; he wasn't worried in the slightest about failure or mishaps. Manhattan had been his main goal and here he was. Getting the building in the exact location he wanted had been the most difficult part. Everything from here on out was in his wheelhouse.

He stood on the second-floor balcony where he had a clear view of the first-floor entrance and one of the bars. For this location, he'd gone with old-world charm. Black and white, clean lines, clear bulbs suspended from the second floor to the first, a glossy mahogany bar. He'd wanted to keep this place upscale like the others, but really appeal to that classical era he associated with New York.

Josie had accompanied him from the penthouse he'd purchased a month ago. He wanted to keep a place in town because he planned on visiting quite often now. Their conversations had been a little strained since they'd left Green Valley a couple days ago. She was pulling back, and he was losing her.

The fear that continued to grow and develop inside him stemmed from that distance, from this fake engagement, from the fact that after tonight they wouldn't have to pretend anymore.

He'd just wanted to get through this opening, but now...well, he wasn't so sure he wanted things to end.

Oh, she wanted to go back to the friendship they'd once had, but that was impossible now. He knew her too intimately, had let her into that pocket of his heart he hadn't even known existed, and he'd seen her in a whole new light.

After being best friends for twenty years, Reese hadn't even known it was possible to still learn more about her, but he had. He'd actually discovered more about himself, too.

Like the fact that he wanted to give this relationship a go in every way that was real.

A flash of red caught his eye and he turned his attention to the bar area below. He knew that inky black hair and those killer curves.

But red?

When they'd arrived, she'd been wearing a long black gown with a high neck and an open back. This dress was...damn. This was the hottest thing he'd ever seen.

That dip in the back scooped dangerously low, and when she turned, he got an eyeful of a deep vee in the front as well. Classy, sexy and a hell of a shock to his entire system.

Hadn't he just thought that he'd finally seen all sides of Josie?

She glanced around the open space and he couldn't maintain the distance another minute. He made his way down the steps from the VIP area and crossed the tile floor.

"This is not the same woman who came with me," he stated.

Josie spun around, a wide smile on her face. Her dress wasn't the only thing red—she had her lips painted and it was all Reese could do to contain himself and not cover her mouth and mess that all up.

Damn, she was the sexiest thing he'd ever seen—and for the time being, fake or otherwise, she was his.

"I wanted to surprise you, so I had some things sent over so I could change here," she told him. "And I figured if I was going to go all out, I might as well do it all."

She gave a slow spin with her arms out wide. "What do you think? Can I pull off color?"

He took a step closer and reached for her hips. "I think I'm going to have to cut this night short and get you alone as soon as possible."

That red smile widened. "You can't mess me up, so keep those lips and hands to yourself. I have a dutiful hostess role to play as my fiancé is having a grand opening."

"He's a lucky bastard," Reese murmured as he leaned in and grazed his lips up the side of her neck.

She shivered beneath his touch and his grip on her hips tightened.

"We still have time," he whispered into her ear.

The waitstaff bustled around getting last-minute flutes of champagne and appetizers set out at various tables, but if they saw him and Josie in a passionate embrace, that would just make them look like more of a couple.

And right now, he didn't care who saw him doing what. He wanted her alone and he wanted her now.

"Other than the fact I want to rip that dress off and show you how much I need you, you do look so damn amazing, Jo."

She looped her arms around his neck. "I feel…good. I was worried once I got here I'd chicken out and keep on the black dress, but once I slid into this, it felt right."

He took a step back before he made a complete fool of himself and took her hands in his. His thumb slid over her ring.

"And it matches perfectly," he told her.

Her smile faltered a bit.

"What is it?" he asked.

Her eyes went from their joined hands back up to his face. "Have you seen the blog?" she asked. "It's up now. I just scanned through it when I was in the back."

"I haven't seen it," he told her. "Is something wrong with it?"

She pursed her lips for a moment before shaking her head. "No, nothing wrong. It just looks so real. Even I almost believe we're engaged."

Reese's breath caught, but he quickly recovered. Taking her hand, he ushered her off to the side where nobody could overhear. He kept his hands firmly locked with hers because he wanted to get this out; he wanted her to listen to everything he had to say.

Mercy, this was the riskiest move he'd ever made and he didn't care. If he let this moment, this woman, go without speaking his mind, then he'd regret it forever.

"You're scaring me with that look in your eye," she joked.

"What would you say to keeping the ring?" he asked.

Her brows drew in. "You insisted I keep it when I told you to return it. You claimed it could be my birthday gift, but it's a bit extravagant for that."

Reese swallowed the lump in his throat. "It's not extravagant if it's a real engagement ring," he suggested. "Keep it, keep me. Let's do this, Jo."

Her eyes widened on her gasp and she jerked her hands from his. "Do this? You mean, stay engaged?"

His delivery and proposal really needed work, but he was so damn nervous he hadn't really prepared his exact words.

"When we were talking the other night, it occurred to me that maybe we hadn't found the right people because we *are* the right people."

Josie continued to stare at him like he'd lost his mind, and maybe he had, but he still had to take this chance.

"Think about it," he went on. "We have always been there for each other. No matter what has happened, good or bad, we have each other's backs. Right? We trust each other. We're a hell of a team in bed and out."

"But you're my best friend," she countered, her voice holding no conviction. "We agreed…"

He took a step closer. "That was before everything changed. I love you, Josie."

"I love you, too," she said. "*As my best friend.* We can't do this, Reese. Just because we grew intimate doesn't mean we can build a life together."

"Your fear is showing," he murmured. "We've already built a life together."

"My fear?" she questioned. "It's common sense. We wouldn't know how to live together, to really forge our lives together like a husband and wife. Have you really thought about this or did you just get caught up in the role?"

"The only thing I've gotten caught up in is you. You can't believe I would ask if I wasn't serious. I want to try this with you."

Her eyes misted as she took another step back. "Trying leaves room for failure, and I love you too much to lose you as my friend, Reese. I'm sorry."

She turned and walked toward the back of the restaurant, leaving him completely confused and shattered.

He'd known before he'd asked that she'd be scared, but he'd had no clue she would completely shut him down. Did she really believe he'd let her get hurt? Didn't she trust him, trust *them*, more than that?

Chatter from the front doors pulled his attention back to the moment. Nick, Silvia, Sam and Maty were all smiles as they were the first to arrive. Right behind them, his parents.

This was his family. All of these people right here were here to support him on the most important night of his life.

Josie might have had to put distance between them, and that was fine, but he would regroup and stick around.

He wasn't going anywhere now that he knew exactly what he wanted...*who* he wanted.

Josie smiled and nodded, she shook hands and answered questions. Nobody knew the truth, that her insides were shaking, that her head was ready to explode with all the thoughts ramming together in there, and her heart was aching in a way she'd never known.

How dare Reese spring that on her? A real engagement? Was he out of his ever-loving mind?

"You look absolutely stunning."

Josie turned to see Silvia and Maty. The two women were beaming, which lightened Josie's mood somewhat. She needed a distraction and perhaps these were just the ladies she needed to chat with.

"I know you always wear black for your column and appearances," Maty stated, "but that red is gorgeous with your dark hair and skin tone."

"Thank you," Josie said, sipping her champagne. "I was worried it was too over-the-top, but I wanted to do something special for Reese. He's always on me about stepping out of my comfort zone."

Is that why he'd proposed for real? To get her out of that comfort zone? Because that wasn't just stepping out, that was jumping off a cliff without a parachute.

"I just saw the blog right before we came in." Silvia clutched her glass of sparkling water and leaned in to Josie. "Girl, you two are so adorably in love. I can't wait to see your journey to the aisle."

"I still can't believe we're all getting married," Maty said with a wide grin. "It's such an exciting time."

Josie wanted to correct them; she wanted to confide in someone that this was all a farce and there was no way she could marry Reese.

He didn't actually mean what he'd said. He'd gotten caught up, that's all. He would realize once he had time to come down from this high of the opening that they were better off as friends.

That nice, safe zone they'd lived in for so long was just waiting for them to return. Josie wanted that normalcy back because being in limbo with her emotions, her hormones, her heart…it was simply too much to bear.

She'd felt so brave wearing this red gown, but when it came to her feelings regarding Reese, she wasn't feeling so bold anymore. She'd tried. She wanted to be that daring woman. But…what if the risk was too great? What if they destroyed the life they'd built during all those years of friendship?

"I see the guys are talking with Reese's mom and dad." Josie nodded to the bar area. "I'm so glad this is all working out for him."

Silvia nodded. "Nick was worried if the third brother came forward that he would be like Rusty. I'm just grateful they've all found one another. Nick said he's going to do everything in his power to buy out Rusty, and Sam and Reese are joining forces."

Reese had mentioned that to Josie. She couldn't believe he was adding more business ventures to his plate, but that was Reese. He lived for success and to her knowledge, he'd never failed at anything.

Maybe that's why he didn't want to let her go. Would he see this public announcement calling off their engagement as a failure, like she had said at the start?

"Is everything all right?" Maty asked, placing a hand on Josie's arm.

Josie blinked back to the moment. "Oh, yes. Sorry about that. It's been a long couple of weeks."

Understatement.

"Would you two excuse me?" she asked.

The ladies nodded and Josie stepped aside to go get some fresh air or a moment to herself. Even with all the chaos of the successful opening, she was having a difficult time concentrating on anything other than this ring weighing so heavy on her hand.

The ring that Reese wanted to mean more than it could.

Josie made her way to the private office Reese kept in the back. Once inside, she closed the door and leaned back against it. She just needed a minute to compose herself, that's all. Then she could go back and play the dutiful, proud fiancée.

Because at midnight, this Cinderella story was over.

Sixteen

Reese stood on the second-floor balcony once again, staring down onto the empty first floor. The launch had been a huge success. The reservations were all booked up for the next three months and several reviewers were already talking about them during some prime spots on their social media accounts.

He wondered if Josie took mental notes or if she'd just checked out after he'd dropped that bomb on her.

Reese trusted her. He knew she'd still cover the event and make a good article for *Cocktails & Classy*.

Which reminded him, he still hadn't seen their post on the blog. Part of him didn't want to see it, if the images had impacted Josie so much. Was that why she'd been so scared? She'd seen the photos and realized what they had was real?

Reese pulled his cell from his pocket and quickly found the site. He skipped the dialogue; he knew exactly what they'd said during their interview. That had been the easy part.

The first image he came to was the one where Josie had her eyes closed, her head turned toward her shoulder and he had placed a kiss on her head. The tender, delicate picture made him smile.

He scrolled through more words and stopped when he came across the picture of when they had to lean in for the "almost" kiss. His fingertips splayed over her jawbone and neck as he tipped her head back. Josie's eyes were locked onto his, her lips slightly parted.

Even though he'd been right there in that moment, he'd had no clue what this shot had actually looked like. They definitely looked like they were in love, like they were literally half a breath away from closing that narrow gap between them. She'd been nervous, worried what this would do to them.

If only she'd let those fears go and see what she had right in front of her.

Heels clicked on the tile below and Reese glanced from his phone to see Josie step into view. She immediately glanced up and caught his gaze.

"I thought you took a ride back to the penthouse," he told her.

"I was going to, but I couldn't leave."

Reese glanced from the phone back to her. "I was just looking at the announcement online. We look good."

She crossed her arms over her chest, giving him a delicious view from this angle.

"We do," she agreed.

The tension in that vast gap between them was charged and Reese felt it best to keep a good distance. If he got too close, he'd want to touch her, hold her, tell her every reason why they should be together, but she had to come to that realization on her own.

"I know you think it's a good idea to keep going," she started. "But I can't marry you, Reese."

So they were still at that stalemate. Fine. He was a patient man and Josie was worth waiting for.

"You have to understand," she added.

"I understand you're afraid. I understand this isn't what you had planned, but you have to see that none of this is new."

She jerked like he'd surprised her. "Not new? We've only been faking this for two weeks and we've crammed quite a bit into that short time frame. It's all quite new."

He couldn't stand the distance anymore. Reese came down the steps and stood at the bottom of the landing, his eyes meeting hers across the way. She still wore that red dress, those red lips. She still took his breath away whether she had on black, red or nothing at all.

"None of this is new," he explained. "Everything between us has always been there. We are just now bringing it to the surface."

Her arms dropped to her sides as she shook her head. Her fear and hesitancy made him want to reach for her, but he also recognized he needed to give her some space.

She glanced down to her hand as she toyed with the ring. He stared, knowing what was coming, hoping he was wrong.

But she slid the ring off and held it out in her palm.

When her eyes came up to meet his, there was no way she could hide the unshed tears.

"I'm not taking it back," he told her. "I bought it for you."

"You never bought me something this expensive for my birthday before."

He stared at her for another minute, but knew which battle he wanted to fight. He didn't want to be a jerk about this, and she obviously needed time to think. Fine. He'd hold it for her until she was ready.

Sliding the ring into his pocket, he extended his hand.

"How about we head up to the rooftop, take a bottle of champagne and relax?" he suggested. "We've both had a rough few weeks and I could use some quiet."

She looked at his hand, then back to his face; her brows drew in as she cocked her head.

"That's it?" she asked. "We're just going to move past the fact that you wanted to marry me and now we're going back to being buddies that fast?"

Damn woman was confusing him…and herself, which was probably a good thing. If she was confused, then that meant her mind wasn't completely made up.

"Isn't that what you wanted?" he asked. "I still need my best friend. Do I want more? Of course. But I'm not pushing you out of my life simply because we don't agree on the future."

Her lips curved into a grin as she reached for his hand. "One glass," she told him. "And no sex."

She was killing him.

"That dress was made for sex," he informed her, leading her to the elevator.

As they stepped into the elevator, she slid her hand from his. "I can't, Reese. As much as I want you physically, I can't risk my heart. I need a clean break from this, or someone is going to end up hurt."

Too late. Her rejection stung, but he wasn't giving up and he had to believe she wanted more and was just too worried to grab hold of what was right in front of her.

Her actions said more than her words ever could.

She'd stepped out of her structured life to take a chance with him; she'd worn the red dress, the red lipstick...she did want to be bold and brave, but he knew she was afraid.

He respected her and knew she would realize what they had... eventually.

"Fine," he conceded. "Champagne on the rooftop with our clothes on to celebrate a successful night."

She nodded. "Deal."

Reese led her up to the rooftop with flutes and an unopened bottle. If she wanted to slide back into friend territory, then that's what they'd do. He hoped she realized he never backed down from a fight, and having Josie permanently in his life was the one fight he would never give up.

Josie stared at the blue bikini. Should she? She was home in her own element and going to her own private beach. Who would even care? Besides, she'd donned that red dress for everyone to see and she had to admit, she'd felt pretty damn good about it.

After flying back to Sandpiper Cove, Josie had moved back into her own home since the renovations were done. The crew had put everything back the way it had been before. Her spare closet needed to be reorganized, but at least the mess was completely gone and nothing had been ruined.

Josie needed to spend the day on the beach, to decompress after a whirlwind trip, meeting Reese's new family in Tennessee, his opening in New York and the proposal that never should've happened.

It shouldn't have…right?

Yes. She had made the right decision to save them further hurt down the road. Not only the hurt, but she was also saving them from destroying a friendship that she could never replace. He was her one constant. She needed him to always be there, and if they married and decided it didn't work or he grew tired of her, where would she be?

Alone with only her work to keep her company.

Josie stripped from her pajamas and pulled on the blue bikini. To hell with it. For two weeks she'd been so happy. Perhaps that was due to taking chances and being that bold woman she'd always thought she could be, a bold woman like her mother had been.

She grabbed the matching sheer cover and her straw hat. After sliding into a pair of gold sandals, she stepped from the closet and caught herself in the mirror. Well, she didn't look terrible, just different. But she was keeping it and spending the day in the sun, with a cold beverage and a good book.

Though with the way her mind was spinning, she wasn't sure any book could hold her attention.

The alarm from her driveway dinged. Who would be coming here? She wasn't expecting anybody.

Reese. Had to be.

She glanced at her reflection one more time, but decided not to change. He'd seen her in a bikini countless times over the years. Just because they'd been intimate didn't mean she had to do things differently. They were back to being just friends and a bikini was something she'd wear with a friend. Besides, this was her house. She could wear whatever she wanted without worrying about unexpected guests.

Josie headed down the hall and to the foyer just in time to see Chris pull his car up near the steps. On a sigh, she pulled her wrap around her and stepped onto the porch.

The second he got out of his car, he caught sight of her. Thankfully, he remained in the drive and didn't make his way to her.

"I'm not going to bother you," he promised with his hands up. "I just wanted to come by and tell you I'm happy for you."

Confused, Josie took another step until she was at the edge of the porch. "You couldn't text?"

"After all we've been through, I needed to see you one last time. I saw the blog and I realized that you and Reese have something I could never have with you. As much as I hate it and wish we were still together, I know you two belong together. Too bad we didn't realize that sooner."

She didn't know what to say, so she remained silent.

"Anyway, congratulations," he stated. "You deserve to be happy."

Josie could tell he truly meant it. "Thank you. I want you to be happy, too, Chris."

He offered her a smile and stared another moment

before he waved and got back into his car. She watched as he drove off and she wondered what he'd seen in those images that she hadn't. True, she'd stared at the blog longer than necessary; she'd even pulled it up again this morning.

She and Reese did look happy, but they *were* happy. They had a bond that was unmistakable. But they were going to have to discuss a mutual press release regarding their "breakup" and make it sound like they were still ridiculously happy and loved each other…they were just not in love.

The thought tugged at her heart and she pushed the emotion aside as she went back into her house. She reset the alarm and went to the kitchen to whip up a mai tai.

Just as she was pouring her blended drink into a large travel cup, her cell rang. Josie sat everything down and reached across the island to her phone.

Not Reese. How silly that she'd been expecting him to call or come by. True, they'd just gotten in yesterday, but it'd been over twelve hours since she'd seen him.

Her editor's name lit up the screen and Josie knew she still had to pretend the engagement was on.

"Hello."

"Jo, the blog is breaking records," Melissa squealed. "Have you seen? The comments are astounding and we are getting emails that we can't keep up with."

When she'd gotten online this morning, she hadn't even looked at the comments—she'd been too wrapped up in the photos.

"That's great news," Josie stated.

"We'd love to keep this momentum going," her editor tacked on. "Do you know when formal engagement pictures will be ready or when you will be dress shopping? If we could do a weekly wedding update, I think that would be best. There are so many details that we could easily make this work."

Josie rubbed her forehead. "Let me think about this, okay? Reese and I just got back last night and I'm still a bit fuzzy."

"Yes, of course. Oh, and honey, that red dress was fabulous," she praised. "Great move on your part to branch out at your fiancé's grand opening. You two looked absolutely perfect."

Guilt weighed heavy on her, but another emotion overrode the guilt. Regret.

Had she made the right decision turning Reese down? Since the moment she'd slid that ring off, everything had felt wrong, out of place.

"Thanks," Josie replied. "Let me think on weekly blogs and I'll be in touch."

"Sounds great. I'm just so happy for you guys. You really look like you're in love and that's so rare to find these days."

Unable to handle anymore, Josie said her goodbyes and hung up. She grabbed her drink, ignored her phone on the counter and slid her beach bag from the kitchen chair and onto her shoulder.

No phone, no uninvited guests at her door; she just needed peace and quiet and the ocean. That's all. The space in her head was filled to capacity.

And the man who occupied each and every thought was the man who claimed to love her, who wanted to spend his life with her.

Josie pulled in a deep breath and headed out to the

beach. She had so much thinking to do and serious decisions to make. Was she ready to take that leap? Was she ready to take the biggest risk of her life and create a brand-new box?

One where she and Reese were together forever?

Seventeen

A shadow came over her and Josie squealed.

"Good grief, Reese," she scolded as she jerked her legs over the side of her lounge chair. "You scared the hell out of me."

"Well, you scared me, because I've been texting and calling. Usually, you are glued to your phone."

She adjusted her hat and stared up at him. "I wanted some time alone and didn't want to be interrupted. What are you doing here?"

"I was going to see if you wanted to take the boat out?" he said. "Nick, Sam, Silvia and Maty are at my house."

"They are?" she exclaimed. "Did you know they were coming?"

"We had discussed it, but it was kind of a last-minute thing. I invited them yesterday before we left New York and they came this morning. Frisco is going to work up a shrimp and crab boil. I know how much you love that."

Josie came to her feet and reached for her cover-up, but too late. Reese's eyes raked over her barely clad body and every one of her nerve endings sizzled with arousal.

Well, clearly this was going to be a problem. Now that she'd had him, she couldn't simply turn off that need.

She slid her arms into the sheer material and stared back at him. "We aren't engaged anymore," she reminded him. "So how is this going to work?"

Reese shrugged. "I would have asked you as a friend even before we did this fake engagement. Nothing has changed there, Josie. I want my best friend by my side and I figured you'd enjoy the day out. You seemed to really hit it off with Maty and Silvia."

"I did. They're amazing."

Reese smiled and her heart ached. "So you'll come? I can take you over if you're ready now. It looks like you're all set for a day on the boat."

This was weird. He made no move to touch her. Except for that wandering gaze, she would swear he was right back in that friend zone.

Had he moved there so easily? Had he already forgotten that he'd told her he loved her?

Reese picked up her sunglasses and book and shoved them into her beach bag, then lifted it up.

"What do you say?" he asked.

What did she say? Josie shook her head, as if that would somehow put all these jumbled thoughts back into place.

Melissa thought she and Reese looked in love; her ex-husband had said the same. Reese professed his love and Josie…was confused.

"Something wrong?" he asked. "If you don't want to come, no pressure. We can tell them about this whole friend thing. Believe me, they're discreet with secrets, so they won't say anything until we can make an official statement."

Josie continued to stare at him. "That's it? Less than forty-eight hours ago you said you loved me and now you're good with being friends?"

"I do love you," he informed her without hesitation. "I also respect your decision. What do you want from me?"

The question was, what did she want from herself? She wanted to be able to trust her feelings, to trust that if she took this leap, he'd be holding her hand the entire way. She'd been slowly moving toward this moment, and now she was going to reach for the life she wanted…the life they deserved together.

"I want it all," she murmured before she could stop herself.

Her eyes dropped to her feet as a wave of fear coupled with relief washed over her.

She'd let out her true feelings, but now what?

Reese's fingertip slid beneath her chin as he forced her to meet his gaze. "Say that again, Jo. I didn't quite catch it."

She closed her eyes.

"No," he demanded. "Look at me. I've waited for this for a long time."

"How long?"

His smile softened. "Probably since I met you, but at least a few years."

Years? How had she taken so long to catch up?

"Tell me what you're thinking," he told her. "I don't want any confusion."

He still hadn't reached for her, so she reached for him. She placed her hands on either side of his face and stepped into him.

"As much as I love our friendship, I love you more," she told him. "All of you. I want to be with you, but I'm terrified."

"You think I'm not?" he asked with a laugh. "I just know that never having you again sounds like pure torture and I need you, Jo. I need you in my house, in my life, as more than a friend."

"What happens if we can't—"

He covered her lips with his. Her bag slipped to the ground, landing at her feet as he wrapped his arms around her and pulled her flush with his body.

"We don't fail," he murmured against her lips. "That's not who we are, and we love each other too much."

Her fear melted away little by little. He was right. They were both so strong, they'd always held each other up and she knew going into a deeper relationship would be no different.

"So do we get the ring back on this finger?" he asked.

Josie nodded. "Yes. Let's go back to your house since your family is waiting on you."

"Our family," he corrected. "They're our family now, Jo, because you're mine."

Epilogue

Six months seemed like a long time, but in the grand scheme of things regarding legal doings and commercial sales, it was lightning fast.

Reese smiled. Lockwood Lightning was now officially under new ownership. Sam, Nick and Reese were in the moonshine business.

"This has been a hell of a ride," Nick stated as he poured five glasses of moonshine and one glass of apple cider for his very pregnant fiancée.

The guys had signed papers yesterday and this morning they were making things official. Rusty had been so strapped for cash between the embezzlement, the lawyer fees and back taxes he'd "forgotten" that he'd had no choice but to sell. The guys offered more than anyone else would have and now they were all starting this new chapter as one unit.

"I'm glad I could be part of it," Reese said, sliding his arm around Josie's waist.

Since that day she'd come home with him six months ago, she hadn't left. She'd sent for her things, moved in and they were officially planning a wedding. The weekly blogs were getting to be exhausting, but she was loving every minute of it and he wanted nothing more than to see her happy.

Nick doled out all of the glasses as they stood in a circle in the main tasting area of Lockwood Lightning.

"To new beginnings," Sam declared as he raised his tumbler. "This is just the start of a new dynasty."

"And with the resort opening in a few weeks, we are slowly taking over Tennessee," Nick added.

"I'll drink to that," Sam laughed.

Silvia gasped. "Oh, no."

Everyone turned to see her holding her side.

"I think I'm having a contraction." She grimaced. "I mean, I think I've had them all morning, but this one seems strong."

"All morning?" Nick asked. "And you're just now telling me?"

She scrunched her face and handed over her glass. Josie quickly reached for it before it dropped.

"I knew this was such an important moment for you guys," she defended. "But I'm pretty sure I need to get to the hospital."

Reese nodded. "Go. We'll take care of things here."

Nick ushered Silvia out the door and Reese turned, catching Josie's eye. She smiled and something he didn't quite recognize glinted in her eye.

She tipped back the cider that had been Silvia's and handed him her moonshine.

"You might want to do another toast to new beginnings," she told him. "And I'll take another cider."

Her statement, her actions, finally hit him.

"Jo?"

Her smile widened and she nodded. "About ten weeks now."

"Ten weeks?"

"Surprise," she exclaimed.

Maty laughed and turned to Sam. "Don't look at me. I have no news, but I wouldn't mind getting a puppy."

"Deal," Sam agreed.

Reese took the empty glass from Josie and handed it to Sam. He pulled her against him and couldn't help the tears that clogged his throat. All these years he'd thought about a family, but never knew where to start.

Now he knew.

The woman he'd been waiting for had been in his life for so long. She'd agreed to marry him for real six months ago and now they were going to start a family. Nothing could have made him happier.

"I love you," he whispered into her ear.

"I love you, baby." She held on to him and he thought he heard a little sniff. "We're going to kill this parenting gig."

He eased back. "We are," he agreed. "But can we not tell your editor? I'm afraid of what she'll have us do next for the magazine."

Josie eased back, her eyes filled with unshed tears as she smiled. "We'll hold her off as long as possible."

Good, because Reese needed his family all to himself for now. He'd waited a long time and he finally had everything he'd ever wanted.

* * * * *

SINGLE DAD'S
HOLIDAY WEDDING

PATRICIA THAYER

To my Vine Street Sisters.
I've enjoyed our time together. Bless you all.

CHAPTER ONE

SHE still wasn't sure if coming here was a good idea.

Lorelei Hutchinson drove along First Street to the downtown area of the small community of Destiny, Colorado. She reached the historic square and parked her rental car in an angled spot by a huge three-tiered fountain. The centerpiece of the brick-lined plaza was trimmed with a hedge and benches for visitors. A pathway led to a park where children were playing.

She got out, wrapped her coat sweater tighter against the cold autumn temperature and walked closer to watch the water cascade over the marble structure. After nearly twenty years many of her memories had faded, but some were just as vivid as if they'd happened yesterday.

One Christmas she remembered the fountain water was red, the giant tree decorated with multicolored lights and ornaments and everyone singing carols. She had a family then.

A rush of emotions hit her when she recalled being in this exact spot, holding her father's hand as he took her to the park swings. One of the rare occasions she'd spent time with the man. He'd always been too busy building his empire. Too busy for his wife and daughter. So many times she had wanted just a little of his attention, his love. She never got it.

Now it was too late. Lyle Hutchinson was gone.

With a cleansing breath, she turned toward the rows of storefront buildings. She smiled. Not many towns had this step-back-into-the-nineteen-thirties look, but it seemed that Destiny was thriving.

The wind blew dried leaves as she crossed the two-lane street and strolled past Clark's Hardware Store and Save More Pharmacy, where her mother took her for candy and ice cream cones as a child. A good memory. She sure could use some of those right now.

There was a new addition to the block, a bridal shop called Rocky Mountain Bridal Shop. She kept walking, past an antiques store toward a law office with the name Paige Keenan Larkin, Attorney at Law, stenciled on the glass.

She paused at the door to the office. This was her father's town, not hers. Lyle Hutchinson had made sure of that. That was why she needed someone on her side. She pushed the door open and a bell tinkled as she walked into the reception area.

The light coming through the windows of the storefront office illuminated the high ceilings and hardwood floors that smelled of polish and age, but also gave off a homey feeling.

She heard the sound of high heels against the bare floors as a petite woman came down the long hall. She had dark brown hair worn in a blunt cut that brushed her shoulders. A white tailored blouse tucked into a black shirt gave her a professional look.

A bright smile appeared. "Lorelei Hutchinson? I'm Paige Larkin. Welcome home."

* * *

After exchanging pleasantries, Lori was ushered into a small conference room to find a middle-aged man seated at the head of the table, going through a folder. No doubt, her father's attorney.

He saw her and stood. "Lorelei Hutchinson, I'm Dennis Bradley."

She shook his offered hand. "Mr. Bradley."

When the lawyer phoned her last week, and told her of her father's sudden death and that she'd been mentioned in his will, she was shocked about both. She hadn't seen or talked with her father since she'd been seven years old.

All Lori was hoping for now was that she could come into town today, sign any papers for Lyle's will and leave tomorrow.

The middle-aged attorney began, "First of all, Lorelei, I want to express my condolences for your loss. Lyle wasn't only my business associate, but my friend, too." He glanced at Paige and back at her. "I agreed to see you today knowing your reluctance. Your father wanted the formal reading of his will at Hutchinson House tomorrow."

Great. Not the plans she had. "Mr. Bradley, as you know, I haven't seen my father in years. I'm not sure why you insisted I come here." He'd sent her the airline ticket and reserved a rental car. "If Lyle Hutchinson left me anything, couldn't you have sent it to me?"

The man frowned. "As I explained on the phone, Ms. Hutchinson, you're Lyle's sole heir." He shook his head. "And that's all I'm at liberty to say until tomorrow at the reading of the will. Please just stay until then. Believe me, it will benefit not only you, but this town."

Before she could comprehend or react to the news,

the door opened and another man walked into the room. He looked her over and said, "So the prodigal daughter finally made it to town."

The big man had a rough edge to him, his dark hair a little on the shaggy side. He was dressed in charcoal trousers and a collared shirt, minus the tie. His hooded blue-eyed gaze fringed by spiky black lashes didn't waver from her.

Paige stood. "Jace, you shouldn't be here. This is a private meeting between me and my client."

He didn't retreat. "I just wanted to make sure she doesn't take the money and run. Lyle had obligations he needed to fulfill before that happens."

Lori wasn't sure how to handle this—Jace's attack. But having heard of her father's shrewd business deals, she wasn't surprised by the man's anger.

"I'm Lorelei Hutchinson, Mr…."

He stepped closer. "Yeager. Jace Yeager. Your father and I were partners on a construction project until I realized Lyle pulled one over on me."

"Jace," Bradley warned. "Work stopped because of Lyle's death."

The man made a snorting sound. "It wouldn't have if Lyle had put his share of money into the business account in the first place." He glared at Lori. "Sorry if my impatience bothers you, but I've been waiting nearly three weeks and so have my men."

"Be patient a little while longer," Bradley told him. "Everything should be resolved tomorrow."

That didn't appease Mr. Yeager. "You don't understand. I can't keep the project site shut down indefinitely, or I go broke." He turned that heated look on her and she oddly felt a stirring. "It seems tomorrow you're coming into all the money. I want you to know that a chunk of that belongs to me."

Lori fought a gasp. "Look, Mr. Yeager, I don't know anything about your partnership with Lyle, but I'll have Paige look into it."

Jace Yeager had to work hard to keep himself under control. Okay, so he wasn't doing a very good job. When he'd heard that Lorelei Hutchinson was coming today, he only saw red. Was she going to stroll in here, grab her daddy's money and take off? He wasn't going to be on the losing end with a woman again.

Not when his business was on the chopping block, along with his and Cassie's future. Just about every dime he had was wrapped up in this project. And it was already coming to the end of October as it was, with only bad weather on the horizon. It needed to be completed without any more delays.

Jace looked over Lyle's daughter. The pretty blonde with big brown eyes stared back at him. She had a clean-scrubbed look with a dusting of freckles across her nose, and very little makeup.

Okay, she wasn't what he expected, but he'd been wrong about women before. And the last thing he wanted to do was work for her. After his ex-wife, he wasn't going to let another woman have all the control.

He looked at Bradley. "What does Lyle's will say?"

"It won't be read until tomorrow."

Lori saw Jace Yeager's frustration, and felt obligated to say, "Maybe then we'll have some news about the project."

He glared. "There's no doubt I will. I might not have your father's money, Ms. Hutchinson, but I'll fight to keep what's mine."

Jace Yeager turned and stormed out right past a tall redheaded woman who was rushing in. "Oh, dear," she said, "I was hoping I could get here in time." Her green eyes lit up when she saw Lori. "Hi, I'm Morgan Keenan Hilliard."

"Lori Hutchinson," Lori said as she went to shake Morgan's hand.

"It's nice to meet you. As mayor, I wanted to be here to welcome you back to town, and to try and slow down Jace. Not an easy job."

Since Paige and Bradley had their heads together going over papers, they walked out into the hall. "I'm not sure if you remember me."

"I remember a lot about Destiny. Like you and your sisters. You were a little older than I was in school, but everyone knew about the Keenan girls."

Morgan smiled. "And of course being Lyle's daughter, everyone knew of you, too. I hope you have good memories of our town."

Except for her parents' marriage falling apart, along with her childhood. "Mostly, especially the decorated Christmas tree in the square. Do you still do that?"

Morgan smiled. "Oh, yes and it's grown bigger and better every year." She paused. "Our mom said you have a reservation at the inn for tonight."

She nodded. "I don't feel right about staying at the house."

The redhead gripped her hand. "You don't have to explain. I only want your visit here to be as pleasant as possible. If there is anything else, any details about your father's funeral."

Lori quickly shook her head. "Not now."

Morgan quickly changed the subject. "Look, I know

Jace isn't giving you a very good impression at the moment, but he's having some trouble with the Mountain Heritage complex."

"I take it my father was involved in it, too."

Morgan waved her hand. "We can save that discussion for another time. You need to rest after your trip. Be warned, Mom will ask you to dinner…with the family."

Lori wasn't really up to it. She wanted a room and a bed, and to make a quick call back home to her sister.

Morgan must have sensed it. "It's only the family and no business, or probing questions. We'll probably bore you to death talking about kids."

Lori relaxed. She truly didn't want to think about what would happen tomorrow.

"You're right. That's what I need tonight."

That evening as Jace was driving to the Keenan Inn, he came to the conclusion that he'd blown his chance earlier today. He tapped his fist against the steering wheel, angry about the entire mess.

"Daaad, you're not listening."

Jace looked in the rearview mirror to the backseat. "What, sweetie?"

"Do I look all right?"

He glanced over his shoulder. His daughter, Cassandra Marie Yeager, was a pretty girl. She had on stretchy jean pants that covered coltish long legs and a pink sweater that had ruffles around the hem. Her long blond hair had curled around her face with a few tiny braids. Something she'd talked him into helping with.

"You look nice. But you always do."

"We're going to Ellie's grandmother's house. Ellie Larkin is my best friend."

"I think she'll like your outfit."

"What about my hair?"

"Honey, I've always loved your blond curls. The braids are a nice touch."

That brought a big smile to her face and a tightening in his throat. All he ever wanted was for her to be happy.

When they'd moved here six months ago, it hadn't been easy for her. He still only had temporary custody of his daughter. It was supposed to be only during the time when her mother remarried a guy from England. Jace had different plans. He wanted to make Cassie's life here with him permanent. Optimistic that could happen, he went out and bought a run-down house with horse property. Although it needed a lot of work, it felt like the perfect home for them. A couple horses helped coax his seven-year-old daughter into adjusting a little faster to their new life.

A life away from a mother who'd planned to take his Cassie off to Europe. He was so afraid that his little girl would end up in boarding school and he'd only get to see her on holidays.

No, he wouldn't let that happen. A product of the foster care system himself, he'd always longed for a home and family. It hadn't worked out with ex-wife Shelly, and that mistake cost him dearly—a big divorce settlement that had nearly wiped him out. Jace hadn't cared about the money, not if he got his daughter. He only hoped they weren't going to be homeless anytime soon.

His thoughts turned to Lorelei Hutchinson. He didn't like how he reacted to her. Why had she angered him so much? He knew why. She had nothing to do with Lyle's business dealings. But she was due to inherit a lot of money tomorrow, and he could be handed the shaft at the same time. It could cost him everything that mattered. His daughter. No, he wouldn't let that happen.

He pulled up in front of the beautiful three-story Victorian home painted dove-gray with white shutters and trim. The Keenan Inn was a historical landmark, a bed-and-breakfast that was also the home of Tim and Claire Keenan. Jace had heard the story about how three tiny girls had been left with them to raise as their own. That would be Morgan, Paige and Leah. After college all three returned to Destiny to marry and raise their own families.

Right now there was someone else staying in the inn—Lorelei Hutchinson. Somehow he had to convince her that this downtown project needed to move forward. Not only for him, but also for Destiny.

Just then Tim Keenan came out the front door, followed closely by some of their grandkids, Corey, Ellie and Kate.

His daughter grabbed her overnight bag and was out of the car before he could say anything. He climbed out, too.

Tim Keenan waved from the porch. "Hello, Jace."

"Hi, Tim." He walked toward him. "Thank you for inviting Cassie to the sleepover. I think she's getting tired of her father's bad company."

"You have a lot on your mind."

Tim was in his early sixties, but he looked a lot younger. His wife was also attractive, and one of the best cooks in town. He knew that because the Keenans had been the first to stop by when he and Cassie moved into their house. They'd brought enough food for a week.

"Hey, why don't you stay for supper, too?"

He wasn't surprised by the invitation. "Probably not a good idea. I don't think I made much of an impression on Ms. Hutchinson."

The big Irishman grinned. "Have faith, son, and use a little charm. Give Paige a chance to help resolve this." They started toward the door, as Tim continued, "I'm concerned about Lorelei. She wasn't very old, maybe seven, when her parents divorced. Lyle wrote them off, both his ex-wife and his daughter. As far as I know, he never visited her. Now, she has to deal with her estranged father's mess."

Jace felt his chest tighten because this woman's scenario hit too close to home. "That's the trouble with divorce, it's the kids who lose."

They stepped through a wide front door with an etched glass oval that read Keenan Inn and into the lobby. The walls were an ecru color that highlighted the heavy oak wainscoting. A staircase with a hand-carved banister was open all the way to the second floor. All the wood, including the hardwood floors, were polished to a high gloss. He suspected he wasn't the only one who was an expert at restoration.

"This house still amazes me," he said.

"Thanks," Tim acknowledged. "It's been a lot of work over the years, but so worth it. The bed-and-breakfast has allowed me to spend more time with Claire and my girls."

Jace shook his head. "I can't imagine having three daughters."

Keenan's smile brightened. "You have one who gives you joy. I'm a lucky man, I tripled that joy." Tim sobered. "Too bad Lyle didn't feel the same about his child. Maybe we wouldn't be having this conversation tonight."

The sound of laughter drifted in from the back of the house. "That sounds encouraging," Tim said. "Come on, son. Let's go enjoy the evening."

They walked through a large dining room with several small tables covered in white tablecloths for the inn's guests. They continued through a pantry and into a huge kitchen.

Okay, Jace was impressed. There was a large working area with an eight-burner cooktop and industrial-sized oven and refrigerator, and all stainless steel counters, including the prep station. On one side a bank of windows showed the vast lawn and wooded area out back and, of course, a view of the San Juan Mountains. A group of women were gathered at the large round table. He recognized all of them. Morgan because she was married to his good friend Justin Hilliard, another business owner in town. Paige he'd met briefly before today. The petite blonde was Leah Keenan Rawlins. She lived outside of town with her rancher husband, Holt.

And Lorelei.

Tonight, she seemed different, more approachable. She was dressed in nice-fitting jeans, a light blue sweater and a pair of sneakers on her feet. Her hair was pulled back into a ponytail and it brushed her shoulders when she turned her head. She looked about eighteen, which meant whatever he was feeling about her was totally inappropriate.

Those rich, chocolate-brown eyes turned toward him and her smile faded. "Mr. Yeager?"

He went to the group. "It's Jace."

"And I go by Lori," she told him.

He didn't want to like her. He couldn't afford to, not with his future in the balance. "Okay."

"Oh, Jace." Claire Keenan came up to them. "Good, you're able to stay for dinner. We don't get to see enough of you." She smiled. "I get to see your daughter when I volunteer at school."

He nodded. "And I'm happy Ellie and Cassie are friends. Thank you for including her in the kids' sleepovers." He glanced out the window to see his daughter running around with the other children. Happy. "Your granddaughter Ellie helped Cassie adjust to the move here."

Claire's smile was warm. "We all want to make sure you both got settled in and are happy."

That all depended on so many things, he thought. "You've certainly done that."

The older woman turned to Lori. "I wish I could talk you into staying longer. One day isn't much time." Claire looked back at Jace. "Lori is a second grade teacher in Colorado Springs."

Lori didn't want to correct Claire Keenan. She *had* been a second grade teacher before she'd been laid off last month. So she didn't mind that her dear father had decided to leave her a little something. It would be greatly appreciated.

But, no, she couldn't stay. Only long enough to finish up Lyle's unfinished business. She hoped that would be concluded by tomorrow.

Claire excused herself. Tim arrived, handed them both glasses of wine and wandered off, too, leaving them alone.

Lori took a sip of wine, trying not to be too obvious

as she glanced at the large-built man with the broad shoulders and narrow waist. No flab there. He definitely did physical work for a living.

"How long have you lived in Destiny, Mr.… Jace?"

"About six months, and I'm hoping to make it permanent."

She didn't look away. "I'm sure things will be straightened out tomorrow."

"I'm glad someone is optimistic."

She sighed. "Look, can't we put this away for the evening? I've had a long day."

He studied her with those deep blue eyes. "If you'd rather I leave, I will. I was only planning to drop my daughter off."

In the past few hours Lori had learned more about Jace Yeager. She knew that Lyle probably had the upper hand with the partnership. "As long as you don't try to pin me down on something I know nothing about. It isn't going to get us anywhere except frustrated."

He raised his glass in salute. "And I'm way beyond that."

CHAPTER TWO

Two hours later, after a delicious pot roast dinner, Lori stood on the back deck at the Keenan Inn. She'd said her goodbyes to everyone at the front door, but wasn't ready to go upstairs to bed yet.

She looked up at the full moon over the mountain peak and wondered what she was doing here. Couldn't she have had a lawyer back in Colorado Springs handle this? First of all, she didn't have the extra money to spend on an attorney when she didn't have a job and very little savings. She needed every penny.

So this was the last place she needed to be, especially with someone like Jace Yeager. She didn't want to deal with him. She only planned to come here, sign any papers to her father's estate and leave.

Now there was another complication, the Mountain Heritage complex. She had to make sure the project moved forward before she left town. She didn't need to be told again that the project would mean employment for several dozen people in Destiny.

"Why, Dad? Why are you doing this?" He hadn't wanted her all those years, now suddenly his daughter needed to return to his town. How many years had she ached for him to come and visit her, or to send for her.

Even a phone call would have been nice. The scars he'd caused made it hard for his daughter to trust. Anyone.

She felt a warm tear on her cold cheek and brushed it away. No. She refused to cry over a man who couldn't give her his time.

"Are you sad?"

Hearing the child's voice, Lori turned around to find Jace Yeager's daughter, Cassie.

Lori put on a smile. "A little. It's been a long time since I've been here. A lot of memories."

The young girl stood under the porch light. "I cried, too, when my daddy made me come here."

"It's hard to move to a new place."

"At first I didn't like it 'cause our house was ugly. When it rained, the ceiling had holes in it." She giggled. "Daddy had to put pans out to catch all the water. My bedroom needed the walls fixed, too. So I had to sleep downstairs by the fireplace while some men put on a new roof."

"So your dad fixed everything?"

She nodded. "He painted my room pink and made me a princess bed like he promised. And I have a horse named Dixie, and Ellie is my best friend."

Her opinion of Jace Yeager just went up several notches. "Sounds like you're a very lucky girl."

The smile disappeared. "But my mommy might come and make me go away."

Jace Yeager didn't have custody of his daughter? "Does your mom live close?"

The child shook her head. "No, she's gonna live in England, but I don't want to live there. I miss her, but I like it here with Daddy, too."

It sounded familiar. "I'm sure they'll work it out."

The girl studied her with the same piercing blue eyes as her father. "Are you going to live here and teach second grade? My school already has Mrs. Miller."

"And I bet you like her, too. No, I'm not going to teach in town, I'm only here for a visit. My dad died not too long ago, and I have to take care of some things."

"Is that why you were crying, because you're sad?"

"Cassie…"

They both turned around and saw Jace.

"Oh, Daddy," Cassie said.

Jace Yeager didn't look happy as he came up the steps. "Ellie's been looking for you." He studied Lori. "The rest of the girls took the party upstairs."

"Oh, I gotta go." She reached up as her father leaned over and kissed her. "'Bye, Daddy, 'bye, Miss Lori." The child took off.

Jace looked at Lori Hutchinson as his gaze locked on her dark eyes.

Finally Lori broke the connection. "I thought you'd left."

"I'd planned to, but I got caught up at the front porch with the Keenans."

He had wanted to speak to Paige, hoping she could give him some encouragement. She'd said she'd work to find a solution to help everyone. Then she rounded up her husband, Sheriff Reed Larkin, leaving her daughters Ellie and Rachel for Grandma Claire's sleepover.

The other sisters, Morgan and Leah, kissed their parents and thanked them for keeping the kids. He caught the look exchanged between the couples, knowing they had a rare night alone. The shared intimacy had him envious, and he turned away. He, too, planned to leave when he spotted his daughter on the back deck with Lori.

"And I was finishing my coffee." He'd had two glasses of wine at dinner. He had to be extra careful, not wanting to give his ex-wife any ammunition. "Well, I should head home."

She nodded. "Your daughter is adorable."

"Thank you. I think so." Jace had to cool it with Lori Hutchinson. "I just wanted to say something before tomorrow...."

She raised a hand. "I told you, I'll do everything I can to get your project operational again."

He just looked at her.

"Whether you believe it or not, I don't plan to cause any more delays than necessary."

"I wish I could believe that."

"After the meeting, how about I come by the building site and tell you what happened?"

He shook his head. "The site's been shut down. Until this matter is settled, I can't afford to pay the subcontractors. So you see there's a lot at stake for me."

"And I understand that. But I still have no idea what's going to happen tomorrow, or what Lyle Hutchinson's plans are. It's not a secret that I haven't seen the man in years." She blinked several times, fighting tears. "He's dead now." Her voice was hoarse. "And I feel nothing."

Jace was learning quickly that Lyle Hutchinson was a piece of work. "Okay, we can both agree your father was a bastard."

She turned toward the railing. "The worst thing is, you probably knew the man better than I did." She glanced over her shoulder. "So you tell me, Jace Yeager, what is my father planning for me? For his town."

* * *

Tim Keenan stood at the big picture window at the inn as he waved at the last of dinner guests left.

He was a lucky man. He loved his wife and his family. He'd been blessed with a great life running the inn for the past thirty-plus years. Mostly he enjoyed people and prided himself on being able to read body language.

For example, Jace and Lori had been dancing around each other all night. Not too close, but never out of eye sight. And the looks shared between them…oh, my.

Claire came down the steps and toward him, slipping into his arms. "I got the girls settled down for now, but I have a feeling they're plotting against me."

He kissed her cheek. "Not those little angels."

She smiled. "Seems you thought the same about your daughters, too."

"They are angels." He thought about the years raising his girls. And the grandchildren. "And we're truly blessed." He glanced out to see the lonely-looking woman on the porch. Not everyone was as lucky.

Lori watched from the inn's porch as Jace walked to his truck. He was strong and a little cocky. She had to like that about him. She also liked the way he interacted with his daughter. Clearly they loved each other. What about his ex-wife? She seemed to have moved on, in Europe. Who broke it off? She couldn't help but wonder what woman in her right mind would leave a man like Jace Yeager. She straightened. There could be a lot of reasons. Reasons she didn't need to think about. Even though she'd seen his intensity over the project, she'd also seen the gentleness in those work-roughened hands when he touched his daughter.

She shivered. One thing was, he wasn't going to be

put off about the project. And she couldn't wait for this mess to be settled. Then she could put her past behind her and move on.

She walked inside and up to the second floor. Overhead she heard the muffled voices of the kids. Her room was at the front of the house. A large canopy bed had an overstuffed print comforter opposite a brick fireplace. She took out her cell phone and checked her messages. Two missed calls.

Fear hit her as she listened to the message from Gina. She could hear the panic in her half sister's voice, but it had been like that since childhood.

Lori's mother had remarried shortly after moving to Colorado Springs. Not her best idea, losing Lyle's alimony, but Jocelyn was the type of woman who needed a man. She just hadn't been good at picking the right ones. Her short union with Dave Williams had produced a daughter, Regina. Lori had been the one who raised her, until big sister had gone off to college.

Without Lori around, and given the neglect of their mother, Gina had run wild and ended up pregnant and married to her boyfriend, Eric Lowell, at barely eighteen. Except for Gina's son, Zack, her life had been a mess ever since. It became worse when her husband became abusive, though the marriage ended with the man going to jail. Now Lori was tangled up in this mess, too.

She punched in the number. "Gina, what happened?"

"Oh, Lori, I think Eric found us."

Over a year ago, Lori had moved her sister into her apartment while Eric served a jail sentence for drug possession and spousal abuse. This hadn't been the first time he'd smacked Gina around, but the first conviction. That was the reason they'd planned to move out of state when Lori had been notified about Lyle's death.

"No, Gina, he doesn't get out until the first of the month."

"Maybe he got an early release."

"Detective Rogers would have called you. You still have a few weeks."

"What about you? Are you flying home soon?"

She knew this delay would worry Gina more. "I can't yet. I still need to meet with the lawyer tomorrow."

She heard a sigh. "I'm sorry, Lori. You've done so much for us. You have a life of your own."

"No, Gina. You're my sister. Zack is my nephew. I told you, I won't let Eric hurt you again. But I still need a day or so to get things straightened out. Then hopefully we'll have some money to start over and get away from Eric." She prayed that her father had left her something. Since their mother had died a few years ago, there wasn't anything holding them in Colorado Springs. They could go anywhere. "Think about where you and Zack want to move to." Preferably somewhere they needed a second grade teacher.

"No, you decide, Lori. We'll go anywhere you want. We just can't stay here. I won't survive it."

Lori could hear the fear in her voice. "I promise I'll do whatever it takes to keep you safe. Now go get some sleep and give my special guy a kiss from me."

Lori hung up the phone and hoped everything she said was true. Unlike Lyle Hutchinson, she didn't walk away from family.

The next morning, Lori was up early. She was used to being at school ahead of her students to plan the day.

Not anymore. Not since she'd gotten her pink slip at the start of the school year. She'd been told it was because of cutbacks and low enrollment, but she wondered if it was due to the trouble Eric had caused her at the up-scale private school where she taught.

No, she couldn't think about that now. She needed to have a clear head for the meeting. Was Lyle Hutchinson as wealthy as people said? Normally she wouldn't care, but it could help both her and Gina relocate to another part of the country. Somewhere Gina could raise Zack without the fear of her ex-husband coming after her again. Enough money so Lori had time to find a job.

She drove her car to the end of First Street. A six-foot, wrought-iron fence circled the property that had belonged to the Hutchinsons for over the past hundred years. Her heart raced as she raised her eyes and saw the majestic, three-story white house perched on the hilltop surrounded by trees. Memories bombarded her as she eased past the stone pillars at the gate entrance. The gold plaque read Hutchinson House.

She drove along the hedge-lined circular drive to-ward the house. She looked over the vast manicured lawn and remembered running through the thick grass, and a swing hanging from a tree out back. She parked in front of the house behind a familiar truck of Jace Yeager. Oh, no. Was the man following her?

Then she saw him standing on the porch leaning against the ornate wrought-iron railing. He was dressed in jeans and a denim shirt and heavy work boots. Without any effort, this man managed to conjure up all sorts of fantasies that had nothing to do with business.

She pulled herself out of her daydream. What was he doing here?

He came down the steps to meet her.

She got out of her car. "Jace, is there a problem?"

He raised a hand in defense. "Mr. Bradley called me this morning. Said he needed me here for after the reading."

Lori was confused. "Why?"

"I hope it's to tell me it's a go-ahead on the Mountain Heritage project."

They started up the steps when she saw a man in a khaki work uniform come around the side porch. He looked to be in his late sixties, maybe seventies. When he got closer she saw something familiar.

"Uncle Charlie?"

The man's weathered face brightened as he smiled. "You remember me, Miss Lorelei?"

"Of course I do. You built me my tree swing." She felt tears sting her eyes. "You let me help plant flowers, too."

He nodded and gripped her hands in his. "That was a lot of years ago, missy. You were a tiny bit of a thing." His tired eyes locked on hers. "You've turned into a beautiful young lady." His grip tightened. "I'm so sorry about your father."

Before Lori could say anything more, another car pulled up. Paige Larkin stepped out of her SUV. Briefcase in hand, she walked up the steps toward them.

They shook hands and Paige spoke briefly to Charlie before the man walked off. Paige turned to Jace. "So you've been summoned, too."

"I got a call from Bradley first thing this morning."

Paige frowned. "Dennis must have a reason for wanting you here." She turned back to her client. "Let's not speculate until we hear what's in Lyle's will."

Lori nodded and together they walked up to the large porch, where greenery filled the pots on either side of the wide door with the leaded glass panels.

She knew that her great-great-grandfather had built this house during the height of the mining era. It was said that Raymond Hutchinson never trusted banks. That was why he didn't lose much during the Great Depression.

They went inside the huge entry with high-gloss hardwood floors. A crystal chandelier hung from the high ceiling and underneath was a round table adorned with a large vase of fresh-cut flowers. The winding staircase circled up to the second story, the banister of hand-carved oak. Cream and deep maroon brocade wallpaper added a formality to the space.

Lori released a breath. "Oh, my."

She was reminded of Jace's presence when he let out a low whistle. "Nice."

"Do you remember this house?" Paige asked.

"Not much. I spent most of my time in the sunroom off the kitchen."

Paige shook her head. "Well, I wouldn't be surprised if this becomes yours. And then you can go anywhere in it you want."

Lori started to tell her she didn't want any part of this house when a thin woman came rushing into the room. Her gray hair was pulled back into a bun. She looked familiar as she smiled and her hazel eyes sparkled. Lori suddenly recognized her.

"Maggie?" she managed to say.

The woman nodded with watery eyes. "Miss Lorelei."

"I can't believe it." Lori didn't hesitate, and went

and hugged the woman. It felt good to be wrapped in the housekeeper's arms again. Years ago, Maggie had been her nanny.

"It's good to have you home." The older woman stepped back and her gaze searched Lori's face. "How pretty you are."

Lori felt herself blush. She wasn't used to all this attention. "Thank you, Maggie."

The housekeeper turned sad. "I'm so sorry about your father." Then squeezed her hands tighter. "I want you to know he went in his sleep. They said a heart attack. Maybe if we would have been there…"

Lori could only nod. "No. He couldn't be helped." She had no idea this would be so hard.

Dennis Bradley walked down the hall. "Good. You made it." He turned and nodded toward Jace. "Mr. Yeager, would you mind waiting a few minutes until I've gone over the will with Ms. Hutchinson?"

"Not a problem." He looked at Maggie and smiled. "I wonder if you could find a cup of coffee for me."

"I'll bring some out."

Once she left, the lawyer said, "We should get started."

He motioned them down the hall and into an office. Lori paused at the doorway. The walls were a deep green with dark stained wainscoting. The plush carpet was slate-gray. Bradley sat down behind the huge desk that already had a folder open.

After they were seated, the lawyer began, "I'll read through Lyle's requests. His first was that the will be read here at the family home." He handed Paige and her copies. "We can go over any details later."

The lawyer slipped on his glasses. "I don't know if

you knew that Lyle had remarried for a short time about ten years ago."

Nothing about her father surprised her. She shook her head.

"There was a prenuptial agreement, then two years later a divorce." He glanced down at the paper. "Lyle did have one other relative, a distant cousin who lives back in Ohio." He read off the generous sum left to Adam Johnson. Also he read the amount given to the household staff, which included Maggie and Charlie.

"I'm glad my father remembered them," Lori said.

Bradley smiled. "They were loyal to him for a lot of years." He sighed. "Now, let's move on to the main part of the will.

"Lyle Hutchinson has bequeathed to his only living child, Lorelei Marie Hutchinson, all his holdings in Hutchinson Corp." He read off the businesses, including Destiny Community Bank, two silver mines, Sunny Hill and Lucky Day. There were six buildings on First Street, and this house at 100 North Street along with all its contents, the furnishings and artwork.

Lori was stunned. "Are you sure this is right?" She looked down at Paige's copy to see the monetary amount stated. "My father was worth this much?"

Bradley nodded. "Lyle was a shrewd businessman. Maybe it was because your grandfather Billy lost nearly everything with his bad investments and eccentric living. Lyle spent years rebuilding the family name and recouping the money. And he also invested a lot into this town."

Bradley looked at her, then at Paige. "Are there any questions?"

Lori gave a sideways glance to her lawyer.

"I probably will once we go over everything."

Bradley nodded. "Call me whenever you need to. Now, for the rest I think Mr. Yeager should hear this. Do you have any objections, Lorelei?" With her agreement, he went to the door and had Jace come in.

He sat down in the chair next to Lori.

Bradley looked at Jace. "Whatever you thought, Mr. Yeager, Lyle went into the Heritage project honestly. The business complex was to promote more jobs and revenue for the town. He wasn't trying to swindle you. As we all know, his death was sudden and unexpected."

Jace nodded. "Of course I understand, but you have to see my side, too. I need to finish this job, get tenants in and paying rent."

Bradley nodded and looked at Lori. "And that will happen if Lorelei will agree to the terms."

"Of course I'll agree to finish this project."

"There is a stipulation in the will." Bradley paused. "You are the last living heir in the Hutchinson line, Lorelei. And this town was founded by your great-great-grandfather, Raymond William Hutchinson, after he struck it rich mining gold and silver. But other business has been coming to Destiny and your father invested wisely. He wants you to continue the tradition."

"And I will," she promised. "I plan to release money right away so the work on Mountain Heritage complex can resume."

Bradley exchanged a look with Paige, then continued on to say, "Everything your father left you is only yours if you take over as CEO of Hutchinson Corporation… and stay in Destiny for the next year."

CHAPTER THREE

LORI had trouble catching her breath. Why? Why would her father want her to stay here to run his company?

"Are you all right?" Jace asked.

She nodded, but it was a lie. "Excuse me." She got up and hurried from the room. Instead of going out the front door, she headed in the other direction.

She ended up in the large kitchen with rows of white cabinets and marble countertops. Of course it was different than she remembered. The old stove was gone, replaced with a huge stainless steel one with black grates.

Suddenly the smell of coffee assaulted her nose and she nearly gagged.

"Miss Lorelei, are you all right?"

She turned around to see a concerned Maggie. She managed a nod. "I just need some air." She fought to walk slowly to the back door and stepped out onto the porch. She drew in a long breath of the brisk air and released it, trying to slow her rapidly beating heart.

Two weeks ago, she couldn't say she even remembered her life here, or the father who hadn't had any time for her. Then the call came about Lyle's death, and she'd been swept up into a whirlwind of emotions and confusion. She couldn't even get herself to visit his grave site.

"Are you sure you're okay?"

She turned around and found Jace standing in the doorway. A shiver ran through her and she pulled her sweater coat tighter around her. "You were there. Would you be okay?"

He came to the railing. "Hell, with that kind of money, I could solve a lot of problems."

She caught a hint of his familiar scent, soap and just his own clean manly smell. She shifted away. She didn't need him distracting her, or his opinion.

"Easy for you to say, your life is here, and you wouldn't have to pull up and move." Lori stole a glance at him. "Or have Lyle Hutchinson running that life."

Jace didn't know the exact amount of money Lyle had left his daughter, but knew it had to be sizable from the investigation Jace had done before he'd entered into the Mountain Heritage project. And he needed that project to move ahead, no matter what he had to do. "It's only a year out of your life."

She glared at him. "That I have no control of."

He studied her face. She was pretty with her small straight nose and big brown eyes. His attention went to her mouth and her perfectly formed lips. He glanced away from the distraction.

Yet, how could he not worry about Lorelei Hutchinson when her decision could put his own livelihood in jeopardy? His other concern was having any more delays, especially when the weather could be a problem. This was business. Only.

"Look, I get it that you and your father had problems,

but you can't change that now. He put you in charge of his company. Surely you can't walk away."

She sent him another piercing look. "My father didn't have a problem walking away from his daughter."

He tried to tell himself she wasn't his problem. Then he remembered if she didn't take over the company, then that was exactly what he'd have to do. Walk away from Cassie. "Then don't walk away like he did. This town needs Hutchinson Corporation to exist."

"Don't you think I know that?"

He sat on the porch railing facing her. "I know it's a three-hundred-mile move from Colorado Springs, but you'll have a great income and a place to live." He nodded toward the house. Then he remembered. "I know you'll have to give up your teaching job."

She glanced out at the lawn. "That I don't have to worry about. I was laid off when the school year started. I have my résumé out in several places."

Jace felt bad for her, but at the same time was hopeful. "It's a bad time for teachers. So maybe it's time for a change. Why can't you take over your father's company?"

"There's so many reasons I can't even count them. First of all, I'm not qualified. I have limited business experience. I could lose everything by managing things badly."

He felt a twinge of hope. "You can learn. Besides, Lyle has lawyers and accountants for a lot of it. I'll be the person at the construction site. You can check out my credentials. I'm damn good at what I do."

This time she studied him.

"I can give you references in Denver," he offered.

Lori couldn't help but be curious. Her life had been

exposed, yet she knew nothing about him. "Why did you leave there? Denver."

"Divorce. I had to sell the business to divide the joint assets. Moving here was my best chance to make a good home for my daughter. Best chance at getting full custody."

She might not like the man's bad attitude toward her, but wanting to be a good father gave him a lot of points.

"Once I finish Mountain Heritage and the spaces are leased, I'll have some revenue coming in. It'll allow me to control my work hours. I can pick and choose construction jobs so I can spend more time with Cassie." His gaze met hers. "Best of all, Destiny is a great place to raise children."

She smiled. "That I remember about this town, and how they decorated at Christmas."

She watched conflict play across his face. "That's what I want Cassie to experience, too. I don't want her in some boarding school in Europe because her mother doesn't have time for her." He stood, and quickly changed the subject. "I also have several men that are depending on this job."

"I need to talk to my lawyer before I can make any decision." And she needed to speak to Gina. Her sister weighed heavily in this decision. She turned toward Jace. "I know you were hoping for more."

He nodded. "Of course I was, but I can't wait much longer. Just so you know, I'll be contacting my own lawyer. I have to protect my investment."

Lori tried not to act surprised as she nodded. Jace Yeager finally said his goodbye as he stepped off the porch and walked around the house to the driveway.

She heard his truck start up. Just one more problem to deal with.

"Thanks, Dad." She glanced skyward. "You couldn't give me the time of day when you were alive, but now that you're gone, you turn my life upside down."

She walked back inside the house and back into her father's office. Paige and Mr. Bradley had their heads together. They spent the next twenty minutes going over all the details. She could contest the will, but if she lost, she'd lose everything and so would this town.

Mr. Bradley checked his watch, gathered up his papers and put them in his briefcase. "Lorelei, if you need anything else from me, just call." He handed her a business card. "There's one other thing I didn't get a chance to tell you. You only have seventy-two hours to make your decision," he said then walked out the door.

Lori looked at Paige. "How can I make a life-changing decision in three days?"

"I know it's difficult, Lori, but there isn't a choice. What can I say? Lyle liked being in control." The brunette smiled. "Sorry, I hate to speak ill of the dead."

"No need to apologize. Over the years, my mother never had anything nice to say about the man. It doesn't seem as if he ever changed."

She thought about what Lyle had done to Jace Yeager. The man would lose everything he'd invested in this project if he couldn't complete it. She closed her eyes. "What should I do?"

"Are you asking me as your lawyer or as a citizen of Destiny?"

"Both."

"As your lawyer, if you turn down Lyle's bequest, the corporation and the partnerships would be dissolved and all moneys would be given to charity. You'd get nothing, Lori." Paige went on to add, "As a citizen of a town I love, I hope you accept. Hutchinson Corporation employs many of the people in this community."

She groaned. "Lyle really did own this town."

Paige shrugged. "A fair share of it. But remember, the Hutchinsons built this town with the money they got from mining." She smiled. "Times are changing, though. My brother-in-law Justin is moving at a pretty good pace to take that status. He has an extreme skiing business. And don't count out Jace Yeager. He's got some other projects in the works."

"And now he's tied up in this mess," Lori said. "Dear Lord, you all must have hated my father."

"Like I said there's always been a Hutchinson here to deal with. Your grandfather Billy was a piece of work, too. He'd done a few shady deals in his time. The family has done a lot of good for Destiny." She tried not to smile. "Maybe Lyle was a little arrogant about it."

"And now it looks like you all have me to continue the tradition."

Paige raised an eyebrow. "Does that mean you're staying?"

"Do I have a choice?" She knew it was all about Lyle protecting the Hutchinsons' legacy. Not about his daughter's needs or wants. He had never cared about that.

Well, she had to think about what was best for her family. She and Gina had planned to move away from Colorado, and her sister's ex-husband. Most important they had to be safe. Could Eric find them here in Destiny? Would he try? Of course he would if he had any idea where to look.

If Lori decided to stay, at least she could afford to hire a bodyguard. "I need to talk to my sister. She would have to move here, too."

Paige nodded. "I understand. So when you make your decision give me a call anytime. I need to get back to the office." Her lawyer walked out, leaving her alone.

Lori went to the desk, sat down and opened the file. She stared once again at the exorbitant amount of money her father was worth. Although she was far from comfortable taking anything from Lyle, how could she walk away from this? The money would help her sister and nephew so much. Not to mention the other people in Destiny.

But she'd have to be able to work with Jace Yeager, too. The man had his own anger issues when it came to a Hutchinson. Could she handle that, or him? No, she doubted any woman could, but if she stayed out of his way, they might be able to be partners.

She took her cell phone from her purse and punched in the familiar number. When Gina answered, she said, "How would you feel about moving into a big house in Destiny?"

The next morning, Jace took his daughter to school then drove to the site. He needed to do everything he could to save this project. That meant convince Lori Hutchinson to stay. And that was what he planned to do.

He unlocked the chain-link fence that surrounded the deserted construction site. After opening the gate, he climbed back into his truck, pulled inside and parked in front of the two-story structure. The outside was nearly completed, except for some facade work.

Yet, inside was a different story. The loft apartments

upstairs were still only framed in and the same with the retail stores/office spaces on the bottom floor. He got out as the cool wind caused him to shove his cowboy hat down on his head. Checking the sky overhead, he could feel the moisture in the air. They were predicting rain for later today. How soon before it turned to snow? He'd seen it snow in October, in Colorado.

He heard a car and looked toward the dirt road to see Lori pull in next to his truck and get out. Though tall and slender, she still didn't reach his chin. He glanced down at her booted feet, then did a slow gaze over those long legs encased in a pair of worn jeans. Even in the cold air, his body took notice.

Calm down, boy. She was off-limits.

His gaze shot to her face. "Good morning. Welcome to Mountain Heritage."

"Morning," Lori returned as she burrowed deeper in her coat. "I hope this tour is going to be on the inside," she said. "It's really cold."

He nodded. "Come on."

He led her along the makeshift path through the maze of building materials to the entry. He'd been surprised when he'd gotten the call last night from her, saying she wanted to see Mountain Heritage.

"As you can see, the outside is nearly completed, just a little work left on the trim." He unlocked the door, and let her inside.

"We're ready to blow in insulation and hang Sheetrock. The electricians have completed the rough wiring." He glanced at her, but couldn't read anything from her expression. "This is going to be a green building, totally energy efficient, from the solar panels on the roof, to the tankless water heaters. Best of all, the outside of the structure blends in with the surrounding buildings. But this complex will offer so much more."

He pushed open the double doors and allowed her to go in first. He followed as she walked into the main lobby. This was where it all looked so different. The open concept was what he loved the most about the business complex. He'd done most of the design himself and was proud of how well it was turning out.

The framework of a winding staircase to the second-story balcony still needed the wooden banister. He motioned for her to follow him across the subfloor to the back hall, finding the elevators. He explained about the hardwood floors and the large stone fireplace.

"It's so large."

"We need the space to entice our clients. These back elevators lead to the ten loft apartments upstairs. Both Lyle and I figured they'd rent pretty well to the winter skiers. Of course our ideal renter would be long-term. We were hoping to make it a great place to live, shop and dine all without leaving the premises.

"We have a tentative agreement to lease office spaces for a ski rental company from Justin Hilliard. He's planning on doing a line of custom skis and snowboards."

"How soon were you supposed to have this all completed?"

Was she going to stay? "We'd been on schedule for the end of November." Now he was hoping he still had a full crew. Some of the subcontractors he'd been working with had come up from Durango.

Lori felt ignorant. She'd never been to a construction site. Doubts filled her again as she wondered for the hundredth time if she'd be any good taking over for

Lyle. So many people were depending on her. "How are you at teaching, Jace?"

He looked confused, then said, "I guess that depends on the student and how willing they are to learn."

"She's very serious." She released a sigh. "It looks like we're going to be partners."

Damn. Jace had a woman for his partner, a woman who didn't know squat about construction. And he was even taking her to lunch. He'd do whatever it took to provide for his daughter.

He escorted Lori into a booth at the local coffee shop, the Silver Spoon. He hadn't expected her to accept his lunch invitation, but they'd spent the past two hours at the site, going over everything that would need to happen in the next seven weeks to meet completion. She took notes, a lot of notes.

He'd made a call to his project manager, Toby Edwards, and had asked him to get together a crew. Within an hour, his foreman had called back to tell him they got most of the people on board to start first thing in the morning.

So it seemed natural that he would take her to lunch to celebrate. He glanced across the table. She still looked a little shell-shocked from all the information she'd consumed this morning, but she hadn't complained once.

"This place is nice, homey," she said. "Reminds me of the café I worked in during college."

Okay, that surprised him. "It's your typical family-run restaurant that serves good home cooking, a hearty breakfast in the morning and steak for supper. Outside of a steak house, there isn't any fine dining in Destiny, and Durango is forty-eight miles away. We're hoping a restaurant will be added to our complex. Not only more revenue for us, but more choice when you want to go out."

He smiled and Lori felt a sudden rush go through her. No. No. No. She didn't want to think about Jace Yeager being a man. Well, he was a man, just not the man she needed to be interested in. He was far too handsome, too distracting, and they would be working together. Correction, he was doing the work, she would be watching…and learning.

"I hear from your daughter that you've been remodeling your house."

"Restoration," he corrected. "And yes, it's a lot of work, but I enjoy it. So many people just want to tear out and put in new. There is so much you can save. I'm refinishing the hardwood floors, and stripping the crown moldings and the built-in cabinet in the dining room. What I've replaced is an outdated furnace and water heater."

She smiled. "And the roof?"

He raised an eyebrow.

She went on to say, "Cassie told me that you had to put out pans when it rained."

She caught a hint of his smile, making him even more handsome. "Yeah, we had a few adventurous nights. We stayed dry, though."

She couldn't help but be curious about him, but no more personal questions. Focus on his profession. "I bet my father's house could use some updating, too."

"I wouldn't know. Yesterday was the first time I'd been there. I conducted all my business with Lyle in his office at the bank."

She didn't get the chance to comment as the middle-aged waitress came to the table carrying two mugs and a coffeepot. With their nods, she filled the cups.

"Hi, Jace. How's that little one of yours?"

"She keeps me on my toes." He smiled. "Helen, this is Lorelei Hutchinson. Lori, this is Helen Turner. She and her husband, Alan, are the owners of the Silver Spoon."

The woman smiled. "It's nice to meet you, Ms. Hutchinson. I'm sorry about your father."

"Thank you. And please, call me Lori."

"Will you be staying in town long?" the woman asked.

Lori glanced at Jace. "It looks that way."

She couldn't tell if Helen was happy about that or not. They placed their order and the woman walked away.

"I guess she hasn't decided if she's happy about me staying."

Jace leaned forward. "Everyone is curious about what you're going to do. Whether you'll change things at Hutchinson Corp." He shrugged. "These days everyone worries about their jobs."

"I don't want that to happen. That's one of the main reasons I'm staying in town."

Jace leaned back in the booth. "Of course it has nothing to do with the millions your father left you."

Lori felt the shock. "Money doesn't solve every problem."

"My ex-wife thought it did."

Before she could react to Jace's bitter words, Helen brought their food to the table. Their focus turned to their meal until a middle-aged man approached their booth.

"Excuse me, ma'am, sir," he began hesitantly. "Helen told me that you're Mr. Hutchinson's daughter."

Lori smiled. "I am Lori Hutchinson and you are...?"

"Mac Burleson."

She had a feeling that he wasn't just here to be neighborly. Had her father done something to him? "It's nice to meet you, Mr. Burleson."

Mr. Burleson looked to be in his early thirties. Dressed in faded jeans, a denim shirt and warm winter jacket, he held his battered cowboy hat in his hands. "I hope you'll pardon the intrusion, ma'am, but your father and I had business before his death. First, I'm sorry for your loss."

She nodded. "Thank you."

"I was also wondering if you'll be taking over his position at the bank."

She was startled by the question. "To be honest with you, Mr. Burleson, I haven't had much chance to decide what my involvement would be. Is there a problem?"

The man was nervous. "It's just that, Mr. Neal, in the loan department, is going to foreclose on my house next week." The man glanced at Jace, then back at her.

"I know I've been late on my payments, but I haven't been able to find work in a while. No one is hiring...." He stopped and gathered his emotions. "I have three kids, Miss Hutchinson. If I can have a little more time, I swear I'll catch up. Just don't make my family leave their home."

Lori was caught off guard. Her father planned to evict a family?

"Mac," Jace said, drawing the man's attention, "do you have any experience working construction?"

Hope lit up the man's tired eyes. "I've worked on a

few crews. I can hang drywall and do rough framing. Heck, I'll even clean up trash." He swallowed hard. "I'm not too proud to do anything to feed my family."

Lori felt an ache building in her stomach as Jace talked. "If you can report to the Mountain Heritage site tomorrow morning at seven, I'll give you a chance to prove yourself."

"I'll be there," Mac promised. "Thank you."

Jace nodded. "Report to the foreman, Toby."

Mac shook Jace's hand. "I won't let you down, Mr. Yeager." He turned back to Lori. "Could you tell Mr. Neal that I have a job now? And maybe give me a few months to catch up on my payments."

Lori's heart ached. She didn't even know her loan officer, but it seemed she needed to meet him right away. "Mac, I can't make any promises, but give me a few days and I'll get back to you."

He shook her hand. "That's all I can ask. Thank you, Ms. Hutchinson." He walked away.

Lori released a sigh. "I guess I have a lot more to do now than worry about one building."

"Your job as Hutchinson CEO covers a lot of areas."

Helen came over to the table, this time wearing a grin.

"I hoped you've enjoyed your lunch."

"Great as usual," Jace said.

The waitress started to turn away, then stopped and said, "By the way, it's on the house." She picked up the bill from the table. "Thank you both for what you did for Mac."

"I haven't done anything yet," Lori clarified, now afraid she'd spoken too soon.

"You both gave him hope. He's had a rough time of

late." Helen blinked. "A few years ago, he left the army and came back home a decorated war hero. At the very least, he deserves our respect, and a chance. So thank you for taking the time to listen to him." The woman turned and walked back toward the kitchen.

She looked at Jace, remembering what he said about her inheritance. She also wasn't sure she liked being compared to his ex. "I better go and stop by the bank." She pushed her plate away. "Who knows, maybe all those 'millions' just might do some good."

CHAPTER FOUR

LORI couldn't decide if she was hurt or angry over Jace's assumption about the inheritance. She'd lost her appetite and excused herself immediately after lunch.

She was glad when he didn't try to stop her, because she had a lot of thinking to do without the opinion of a man she'd be working with. And who seemed to have a lot of issues about women.

Was he like her father? What she'd learned from her mother about Lyle over the years had been his need to control, whether in business or his personal life. When Jocelyn Hutchinson couldn't take any more she'd gotten out of the marriage, but their child had still been trapped in the middle of her parents' feud. The scars they'd caused made it hard for Lori to trust.

But was coming back to Destiny worth putting her smack-dab into dealing with the past? All the childhood hurt and pain? It also put her in charge of Lyle's domain, and his business dealings, including the Mountain Heritage complex. And a lot more time with the handsome but irritating Jace Yeager.

The man had been right about something. She had a lot of money and it could do a lot of good. She recalled the look of hope on Mac Burleson's face and knew she needed to find an answer for the man.

She crossed the street to Destiny Community Bank. The two-story brick structure was probably from her grandfather's era. With renewed confidence she walked inside to a large open space with four teller windows. Along the wall were portraits of generations of the Hutchinson men—Raymond, William, Billy and Lyle. They were all strangers to her. She studied her handsome father's picture. This man especially.

She turned around and found several of the bank customers watching her. She put on a smile and they greeted her the same way as if they knew who she was.

She went to the reception desk and spoke to the young brunette woman seated there. "Is it possible to see Mr. Neal? Tell him Lorelei Hutchinson is here."

"Yes, Miss Hutchinson." The woman picked up the phone, and when she hung up said, "Mr. Neal said to have a seat and he'll be out…shortly."

Lori wasn't in the mood to wait. "Is he in a meeting?"

The girl shook her head.

"Then I'll just head to his office. Where is it?"

The receptionist stood and together they went toward a row of offices. "Actually, he's in Mr. Hutchinson's office."

Lori smiled. "Oh, is he? Excuse me, I didn't get your name."

"It's Erin Peters."

"Well, Erin, it's very nice to meet you. I'm Lori." She stuck out her hand. "Have you worked at the bank for long?"

"Three years. I've been taking college classes for my business degree."

"That's nice to know. I'm sure my father appreciated his employees continuing their education."

Erin only nodded as they walked toward the office at the end of the hall. Lori knocked right under the nameplate on the last door that read Lyle W. Hutchinson. She paused as she gathered courage, then turned the knob and walked in.

There was a balding man of about fifty seated behind her father's desk. He seemed busy trying to stack folders. When he saw her he froze, then quickly put on a smile.

"Well, you must be Lorelei Hutchinson." He rounded the desk. "I'm Gary Neal. It's a pleasure to finally meet you. Lyle talked about you often."

She shook his hand, seriously doubting Lyle said much about her. Her father hadn't taken the time to know her. Now, did she have to prove herself worthy of being his daughter?

"Hello, Mr. Neal."

"First off, I want to express my deepest sympathies for your loss. Lyle and I were not only colleagues, but friends. So if there is anything you need…"

"Thank you, I'm fine." She nodded. "I've only been in town a few days, but I wanted to stop by the bank. I'm sure you've already heard that I'm going to be staying in Destiny."

He nodded. "Dennis Bradley explained as much."

She hesitated. "Good. Do you have a few minutes to talk with me?"

"Of course."

Still feeling brave, she walked behind the desk and took the seat in her father's chair as if she belonged.

She didn't miss the surprise on the loan officer's face. "Where's your office, Mr. Neal?"

He blinked, then finally said, "It's two doors down the hall. Since your father's death, I've had to access some files from here. Lyle was hands-on when it came to bank business. I'm his assistant manager."

"Good. Then you're who I need to speak with." She motioned for him to sit down, but she was feeling a little shaky trying to pull this off. This man could be perfectly wonderful at his job, but she needed to trust him. "I take it you handle the mortgage loans." With his nod, she asked, "What do you know about the Mac Burleson mortgage?"

The man frowned. "Funny you should ask, I was just working on the Burleson file."

"Could I have a look?"

He hesitated, then relented. "It's a shame we're going to have to start foreclosure proceedings in a few days."

Neal dug through the stack, located the file and handed it to her. She looked over pages of delinquent notices, the huge late fees. And an interest rate that was nearly three points higher than the norm. No wonder the man was six months behind. "Has Mr. Burleson paid anything during all this time?"

"Yes, but it could barely cover the interest."

"Why didn't you help him by dropping the interest rate and lowering the payments?"

"It's not the bank's policy. Your father—"

"Well, my father is gone now, and he wanted me to take over in his place."

"I'm *sure* he did, but with your limited experience…"

"That may be, but I feel that given the state of the economy we need to help people, too. It's a rough time."

She knew firsthand. "I want to stop the foreclosure, or at least delay it."

"But Mr. Burleson isn't even employed."

"As of an hour ago, he's gotten a job offer." She looked at the remaining eight files. "Are these other homes to be foreclosed on, too?"

The loan officer looked reluctant to answer, but nodded. "Would you please halt all proceedings until I have a look at each case? I want to try everything to keep these families in their homes." She stood. "Maybe if we can set up a meeting next week and see what we can come up with."

Mr. Neal stood. "This isn't bank policy. If people aren't held accountable for their debts, we'd be out of business. I'm sure your father wouldn't agree with this, either."

For the first time in days, Lori felt as if she were doing the right thing. "As I said before, my father left me in charge. Do you have a problem with that, Mr. Neal?"

With the shaking of his head, she tossed out one more request. "Good. I also need money transferred into the escrow account for the Mountain Heritage project as soon as possible. Mr. Yeager will have his crew back to work first thing in the morning. And if you have any questions about my position here, talk to Mr. Bradley."

She walked out to the reception desk and found Jace standing there, talking with Erin. He was smiling at the pretty brunette woman. Why not? He was handsome and single. And why did she even care?

He finally saw her and walked over. "Hi, Lori."

"What are you doing here? I told you that I'd get the money for the project."

"I know you did, but that's not why I'm here—"

"I'm really busy now, Jace. Could we do this later?" She cut him off and turned to the receptionist. "Erin, would you schedule a meeting for all employees for nine o'clock tomorrow in the conference room?"

With Erin's agreement, Lori walked out of the bank, feeling Jace's gaze on her. She couldn't deal with him. She had more pressing things to do, like moving out of the inn and into her father's house, where she had to face more ghosts.

Jace was angry that he let Lori get to him. He'd wasted his afternoon chasing after a woman who didn't want to be found. At least not by him.

He hadn't blamed Lori for walking out on him at lunch. Okay, maybe he had no right to say what he did to her. Damn. He'd let his past dictate his feelings about women. Like it or not, Lori Hutchinson was his partner. More importantly, she had the money to keep the project going. If he wanted any chance of keeping Cassie he had to complete his job.

An apology was due to Lori. And he needed to deliver it in person. If only she'd give him a minute to listen to him. He also needed her to sign some papers that needed her authorization.

Jace left the bank to meet up with his foreman to finalize the crew for tomorrow. Then the search for Lori continued as he'd gone around town and ended up at the inn, where he finally got an answer as to her whereabouts.

He had to pick up Cassie from school, but went straight to the Hutchinson house after. He drove through the gates, hoping he could come up with something to say to her. The last thing he wanted was to start off on the wrong foot.

"Wow! Daddy, this is pretty. Does Ms. Lori really live here?"

He parked in the driveway and saw the rental car there. "Yes, she does. It was her father's, now it's hers."

He climbed out and helped Cassie from the backseat. They went up the steps as the front door opened and Maggie appeared. "This is a wonderful day. First, Ms. Lorelei comes home and now, Mr. Yeager and this beautiful child come to visit."

"Hi, Maggie," Jace said. "This is my daughter, Cassie. Cassie, this is Maggie."

They exchanged greetings then the housekeeper opened the door wider.

"I'd like to see Lori if she isn't too busy."

"Of course." Maggie motioned them inside the entry. "She's in her father's upstairs office." The housekeeper looked at Cassie. "Why don't I take you into the kitchen and see if there are some fresh baked cookies on my cooling rack? They're so good along with some milk." The housekeeper looked concerned. "Coming back here is hard for her."

"I expect it is. Are you sure it's okay?"

Maggie smiled. "I think that would be good. The office is the first door on the left."

Still he hesitated.

"You should go up," the woman said. "She could use a friend right about now."

Jace glanced up the curved staircase and murmured, "I'm not sure she'd call me 'friend' right now."

* * *

Lori had trouble deciding where to put her things. There were six bedrooms and a master suite. One had been turned into an office, and the one next to it was nondescript, with only a queen-size bed covered by a soft floral comforter. It had a connecting bath, so that was where she put her one bag.

She unpacked the few items she had, but went into her father's office. She couldn't get into his computer because she didn't have access.

"Okay, need to make a call to Dennis Bradley first thing tomorrow."

What she knew for sure was she needed to have someone to work with. Someone she trusted. As far as she knew her father had worked out of his office at the bank and from home. Did Lyle handle everything himself? Had he not trusted anyone? She rubbed her hands over her face. She didn't know the man. She stood up and walked out.

In the hall curiosity got the best of her and she began to look around. She peeked into the next room, then the next until she came to the master suite. She opened the door but didn't go inside.

The dark room had a big four-poster bed that dominated the space. The windows were covered with heavy brocade drapes and the bedspread was the same fabric. The furniture was also stained dark. Bits and pieces of childhood memories hit her. She pushed them aside and journeyed on to the next room. She paused at the door, feeling a little shaky, then she turned the knob and pushed it open.

She gasped, seeing the familiar pale pink walls. The double bed with the sheer white canopy and matching sheer curtains. There was a miniature table with stuffed animals seated in the matching chairs as if waiting for a tea party.

Oh, my God.

Nothing had been changed since she'd lived here. Lori crossed the room to the bed where a brown teddy bear was propped against the pillow.

"Buddy?" She picked up the furry toy, feeling a rush of emotions, along with the memory of her father bringing the stuffed animal home one night.

She hugged the bear close and fought tears. No, she didn't want to feel like this. She didn't want to care about the man who didn't want her. Yet, she couldn't stop the flood of tears. A sob tore from her throat as she sank down onto the mattress and cried.

"Lori?"

She heard Jace's voice and stiffened. She quickly walked to the window, wiping her eyes. She fought to compose herself before she had to face him.

He followed her, refusing to be ignored.

"It's okay to be sad," he said, his voice husky and soft.

She finally swung around. "Don't talk about what you know nothing about."

Jace was taken aback by her anger. "It seems that everything I've said to you today has been wrong. I won't bother you again."

She stopped him. "No, please, don't go."

She wiped the last of the tears off her face. "It's me who should apologize for my rudeness. You caught me at a bad moment. Why are you here?"

"Maggie sent me up to Lyle's office. I have some papers for you to sign, but they can wait. Believe it or not, Lori, I came to apologize for what I said to you at lunch. I had no right to judge your motivation."

Jace glanced around the bedroom and hated what he was feeling. What Lyle must have felt when his daughter left. Would this happen to him if his ex got Cassie back? "I take it you were about six or seven when you left here?"

She nodded. "It was so long ago, I feel silly for letting it upset me now."

"You were old enough to have memories. Your childhood affects you all your life. It was your father who chose not to spend time with you." It seemed odd, he thought, because Lyle had kept her room like a shrine.

Lori suddenly brightened as if all the pain went away. "Well, as you can see, I'll need to do some painting. My sister, Gina, is coming soon along with my nephew, Zack." She put on a smile. "I don't think he'd like a pink bedroom."

Before Jace could say anything, he heard his daughter calling for him. "I'm in here, Cassie. I picked her up from school, and I wanted to see you before work tomorrow. To make sure everything is okay…between us."

The expression on his seven-year-old's face was priceless as she stopped at the door. "Oh, it's so pretty." She looked at Lori. "Do you have a little girl, too?"

An hour later, with Cassie busy doing homework at the kitchen table, Jace and Lori went to do their work in Lyle's office.

"I hate that you have to keep going over everything again and again," Lori told him.

"It's not a problem. Better now, when I'm around to answer your questions. There aren't too many decisions to make right now. If you'd like to put in some input on finishes, like tile and countertops, you're more than welcome. A woman's touch." He held up a hand. "I didn't mean anything about that. A second opinion would be nice."

"I'd like that."

She smiled and he felt a tightening in his gut. Damn. He looked back at the work sheet.

"Well, the crew is showing up tomorrow to start the finish work on the outside. If we're lucky the weather will hold and we can complete everything before the snow comes."

"Will it affect the work inside?"

"Only if we can't get the materials to the site because the roads aren't passable."

She nodded, chewing her bottom lip. He found it hard to look away.

"What about Mac Burleson? Do you really have a job for him?"

Jace nodded. "If he can do the work."

"I wonder if Mac can paint," Lori said.

Jace looked at her to see a mischievous grin on her pretty face. She wasn't beautiful as much as striking. Those sparkling brown eyes and full mouth… "That was probably going to be one of his jobs—priming the walls once they're up. What were you thinking?"

"I doubt my father has done much work on this house in years." She shrugged. "I don't mind so much for myself, but Gina and Zack. I want this place…" She glanced around the dark room. "A little more homey. I want to talk to Charlie and see what he has to say about repairs."

"How soon are you expecting your family?"

"Next week. Gina is packing and putting most of the furniture in storage." She sighed. "I should go back to help her, but I want to make sure there won't be any holdup on the project."

Jace needed to remember that her entire life had been turned upside down by Lyle's death. "It's a shame you have to leave everything behind, like your friends. A boyfriend…?"

She looked surprised at his question. Not as much as he was. He stood and went to the window. "I only meant, Lyle had you make a tough choice."

"No, I don't have a boyfriend at the moment, and my sister is my best friend. So sometimes a fresh start is good." She turned the tables on him. "Isn't that why you came to Destiny?"

He didn't look at her, but that didn't mean he couldn't catch her scent, or wasn't aware of her closeness. He took a step back. "I came here to make a life for my daughter. She's everything to me."

Lori smiled at him and again his body took notice. "From what I've seen, Cassie feels the same way about you. You're a good father."

"Thank you. I'm not perfect. But I do try and want to make the job permanent."

His gaze went back to her. Darn. What was it about her that drew him? Suddenly he thought about his ex-wife, and the caution flag came out. He needed to stay focused on two things—business and his daughter.

A happy Cassie skipped into the room and rushed to him. "Maggie said to tell you that dinner is ready."

"Oh, honey. We should head home." He glanced at his watch. "Maybe another time."

"No, Daddy. We can't go. I helped Maggie make the biscuits, so we have to stay and eat them."

He was caught as he looked down at his daughter, then at Lori.

"I can't believe you're passing up a home-cooked meal, Jace Yeager," Lori said. "Maggie's biscuits are the best around, and probably even better with Cassie helping."

"Please, Daddy. I'll go to bed right on time. I won't argue or anything."

Jace looked back at Lori. It was her first night here, and would probably be a rough one.

Lori smiled. "Now that's a hard offer to turn down."

"You're no help," he told Lori.

"Sorry, us girls have to stick together."

That was what he was afraid of. He was losing more than just this round. He hated that he didn't mind one bit.

"Okay, but we can't stay long. We have a bedtime schedule."

"I promise, I'll go to bed right on time," Cassie said, then took off toward the kitchen.

He looked at a smiling Lori. "Okay, I'm a pushover."

"Buck up, Dad. It's only going to get worse before it gets better."

Suddenly their eyes locked and the amused look disappeared. Lori was the first to speak. "Please, I want you to stay for dinner. I think we both agree that eating alone isn't fun."

"Yes, we can agree on that."

He followed Lori into the kitchen, knowing this

woman could easily fill those lonely times. He just couldn't let that happen. No more women for a while, at least not over the age of seven.

CHAPTER FIVE

AT EIGHT-THIRTY the next morning, Lori was up and dressed, and grabbed a travel mug of coffee from Maggie, then she was out the door to the construction site. Not that she didn't think Jace could do his job, but she wanted to meet the crew and assure them that there wouldn't be any more delays with the project.

When she pulled through the gate and saw the buzz of activity, she was suddenly concerned about disturbing everyone.

She had every right to be here, she thought as she climbed out of her car and watched the men working on the trim work of the two-story structure. Jace hadn't wasted any time.

She walked carefully on the soggy ground. Okay, she needed more protection than her loafers. A good pair of sturdy boots was on her list. She headed up the plywood-covered path when a young man dressed in jeans, a denim work shirt and lace-up steel-toed boots came toward her.

He gave her a big smile and tipped back his hard hat. "Can I help you, ma'am?"

"I'm looking for Jace Yeager."

The man's smile grew bigger. "Aren't they all? I'm Mike Parker, maybe I can help you."

All? Lori couldn't help but wonder what that meant. She started to speak when she heard a familiar voice call out. They both turned to see Jace. He was dressed pretty much like the others, but he had on a leather vest over a black Henley shirt even though the temperature was in the low fifties.

Lori froze as he gave her a once-over. He didn't look happy to see her as he made his way toward them.

Jace ignored her as he looked at Mike. "Don't you have anything to do?"

"I was headed to my truck for some tools." He nodded to her. "And I ran across this nice lady. Sorry, I didn't catch your name."

"Lori Hutchinson."

Mike let out a low whistle. "So you're the big boss? I can't tell you how good it is to meet you, Ms. Hutchinson."

She tried not to cringe at the description. "It's Lori. I'm not anyone's boss. Jace is in charge of this project."

That was when Jace spoke up. "Mike, they've finished spraying the insulation up in the lofts, so I need you to get started hanging drywall."

"Right, I'll get on it." He tipped his hat to Lori. "Nice to meet you, ma'am."

"Nice to meet you, too, Mike."

She watched him hurry off, then turned back to Jace. "Good morning. Seems you've been busy. What time did you start?"

"I had a partial crew in at five."

"What about Cassie?"

He seemed surprised at her question. "I wasn't here,

but my foreman was. My daughter comes first, Lori. She always will."

"I didn't mean… I apologize."

That didn't ease the scowl on his face. "Were we supposed to meet this morning?"

She shook her head. "No."

"Did you come to work?" He looked over her attire. "You're not exactly dressed for a construction site."

She glanced down at her dark trousers and soft blue sweater under her coat. "I have an appointment at the bank later this morning. I wanted to stop here first to see if everything got off okay. Do you need anything?"

"No, it's fine. I know it looks a little chaotic, but things are running pretty smoothly for the first day back to work. It's most of the same crew so they know what I expect from them."

Lori had no doubt that Jace Yeager was good at his job. "So everything is on schedule?"

"If the weather holds." The wind picked up and brushed her hair back. "Come inside where it's a little warmer," he said. "I'll introduce you to the foreman."

"I don't want to disturb him."

"As you can see, it's a little late for that." He nodded toward the men who were watching.

She could feel a blush rising over her face as she followed Jace inside the building to a worktable that had blueprints spread out on top. A middle-aged man was talking with another workman.

"Hey, Toby," Jace called as he reached into a bin and pulled out a hard hat. He came to her and placed it on her head. "You need to wear this if you come here. Safety rules."

Their eyes met. "Thank you."

Toby walked up to them. "What, Jace?"

"This is Lori Hutchinson. Lori, this is my foreman, Toby Edwards."

The man smiled at her and tiny lines crinkled around his eyes. "So you're the one who saved this guy's as… sets."

Lori felt Jace tense. "I'd say I was just lucky to inherit some money," she told Toby. "Speaking of money…" She turned to Jace. "Were the funds transferred into the Mountain Heritage account?"

He nodded. "Yes. We're expecting materials to be delivered later today."

"Good." She glanced around, feeling a little excited about being a part of this. "It's nice to see all the work going on." It was a little noisy with the saws and nail guns.

Jace watched Lori. He wasn't expecting her here. Not that she didn't have a right, but she was a big distraction. He caught the guys watching her, too. Okay, they were curious about their attractive new boss. He hoped that was all it was. There could be a problem if she stopped by every day. And not only for his men, either. He eyed her pretty face and those big brown eyes that a man could get lost in.

No way. One woman had already cost him his career and future, and maybe his daughter. He wasn't going to get involved with another, especially in his workplace. Or any other place. He thought about the cozy dinner last night in the Hutchinson kitchen.

It was a little too cozy.

Enough reminiscing, he thought, and stuck his fingers in his mouth, letting go with a piercing whistle. "Let's get this over with so we can all get on with our day." All work stopped and the men came to the center of the main room.

"Everyone, this is Lorelei Hutchinson. Since Lyle Hutchinson's death, Lori will be taking over in her father's place. It's thanks to her we're all back to work on this project." The men let go with cheers and whistles. Jace forced a smile, knowing this was a means to get this project completed. But damn, being beholden to a woman stuck in his craw. "Okay, now back to work."

"Thank you," Lori said. "So many people in town have been looking at me like I have two heads."

"Has someone said anything to you?" he asked.

"No, but they're wondering what I'm going to do." She shrugged. "Maybe I should just make a big announcement in the town square. 'Hey, everyone, I'm not here to cause trouble.'"

A strange protective feeling came over him. "Now that the project has started up again, maybe they'll stop worrying."

"I hope so. I'm bringing my sister and nephew here to live. I want to be part of this community."

"What you did for Mac Burleson yesterday was a pretty good start."

"Oh, Mac. Is he here?"

Jace nodded. "Yeah, he was here waiting when Toby opened the gates."

She glanced around the area. "How is he doing?"

"Good so far."

She looked up at Jace. "There he is. Would you mind if I talked to him for a moment?"

"No, not a problem."

She walked across the large entry to the wall. Jace watched her acknowledge a lot of the workers before she got to Mac. She smiled and the man returned it. In fact he was smiling the whole time Lori was talking. Then he shook her hand and Lori walked back. "I just hired Mac to paint a couple of bedrooms at the house."

"Hey, are you stealing my help?"

"No. He's agreed to come over this weekend with his brother and paint the upstairs. I don't think my nephew wants to sleep in a pink room."

Jace nodded, knowing she would be erasing the last of her own memories of her childhood. "There are other bedrooms for him to sleep in."

"I know, but it should have been changed years ago."

"Maybe there was a reason why it hadn't been."

She looked at him. He saw pain, but also hope. "Lyle Hutchinson knew where I was since I left here twenty-two years ago. My father could have invited me back anytime. He chose not to."

Lori turned to walk out and he hurried to catch up with her. "Look, Lori. I don't know the situation."

She stopped abruptly. "That's right, you don't." She closed her eyes. "Look, it was a long time ago. My father is gone, and I'll never know why he never came to see me. And now, why in heaven's name does he want me to run his company?"

"I can't answer that, either."

"I've dealt with it. So now I move on and start my new life with Gina and Zack. I want them to have a fresh start here, in a new place, a new house and especially a new bedroom for my seven-year-old nephew."

Jace frowned. "I take it Zack is without his father."

Lori straightened. "His parents are divorced." She glanced around. "I should be going."

"I need to get back, too."

They started walking toward the door. "If there's anything you need," she offered, "just give me a call. You have my cell phone number. I'll be at the bank most of today."

He walked her out. "I can handle things here." Then he felt bad. "Maybe in a few days if you're available we could go over some samples of tiles and flooring."

She looked surprised at his request. "I'd like that. I want to be a part of this project."

Her steps slowed as she made her way over the uneven boards. He took Lori's arm, helping her along the path.

"What about the bank?"

"I doubt Mr. Neal will enjoy having me around." She stopped suddenly and nearly lost her balance. "Oh," she gasped.

"I got you." He caught her in his arms. Suddenly her trim body was plastered up against him. Even with her coat he wasn't immune to her soft curves. And he liked it. Too much. He finally got her back on her feet. "You need practical boots if you come to a construction site. Go to Travers's Outfitters and get some that are waterproof. You don't want to be caught in bad weather without protection."

She stopped next to her compact car. "I need a lot of things since I'll be living here awhile."

"Like a car that will get through the snow. This thing will put you in a ditch on the first bad day. Get something with bulk to it. You'll be driving your family around."

She nodded. "I guess I need to head down to Durango and visit a dealership next week when my sister flies in."

Before he could stop himself, he offered, "If you need any help, let me know."

She gave him a surprised look, mirroring his own feelings.

Two hours later, Lori glanced across the conference table at the Destiny Community Bank's loan officers, Gary Neal, Harold Brownlee and Larry McClain. The gentlemen's club. "I disagree. In this day and age, we need to work with people and help adjust their loans."

"In my experience," Neal said, "if we start giving handouts, people will take advantage. And no one will pay us."

She tried to remain calm, but she was so far out of her element it wasn't funny.

"I never said this is a handout, more like a hand up. All I suggested is we lower the interest rates on these loans." She pointed to the eight mortgages. "Two points. Waive the late fees and penalties. Just give these families a fighting chance to keep their homes. We'll get the money we loaned back." She paused to see their stunned looks and wondered if she were crazy, too.

She hurried on to say, "Mac Burleson has a job now, but he can't catch up on his mortgage if we don't help him."

"We've always done things this way," Larry McClain said. "Your father would never—"

Lori stiffened. "Well, I'm not my father, but he did put me in charge. In fact, I'm going to become more involved in day-to-day working here at the bank. I can see that there aren't any women in management positions. That needs to change, too."

The threesome gave each other panicked looks. "That's not true. Mary O'Brien manages the tellers."

Were these men from the Dark Ages? "I mean women in decision-making positions. It's a changing world out there and we need to keep up. I've seen the profit sheet for this bank. Over the years, it's done very well."

Neal spoke up again. "You can't come in here and just change everything. You're a schoolteacher."

Lori held her temper. "I became an expert when my father put me in charge of his company. Just so you know, not only am I a good teacher, but I also minored in business. So, gentlemen, whether you like it or not, I'm here."

She was feeling a little shaky. What if she was making a mistake? She glanced at her watch. "I think we've said about everything that needs to be said for now. Good morning." She took her purse and walked out.

She needed someone here on her side. She walked to Erin's desk.

The girl smiled when she approached. "Hello, Ms. Hutchinson. How was your meeting?"

"Not as productive as I would have liked." She sat down in the chair next to the desk. "Erin, could you help me?"

The girl nodded. "If I can."

"I'm looking for someone, a woman who is qualified for a managerial position. Could you give me some candidates?"

The pretty brunette looked surprised, but then answered. "That would be Mary O'Brien and Lisa Kramer. They've both worked for the bank for over five years.

I know Lisa has a college degree. I'm not sure Mary does, but she practically runs this bank."

"That's good to know, because I need someone to help me." She was going to need a lot of help. Since her father had never promoted a woman that was one of the things she needed to change. Immediately.

"Could you call a meeting with all the employees?" She looked at her watch. "And call the Silver Spoon and have them send over sandwiches and drinks."

Erin smiled. "This is going to be fun."

"We're going to need our strength to get this bank into the twenty-first century."

Two mornings later, Lori had been awakened by a call from a sick Claire Keenan, asking her for a favor. Would Lori like to take her place as a volunteer in the second grade classroom this afternoon?

There might have been several other things to do, but Lori found she wanted to check out the school. After her trip to the paint store and picking her colors for the bedroom, she had her purchase sent to the house.

She grabbed a quick lunch at the Silver Spoon, and after a friendly chat with Helen, she arrived at Destiny Elementary with time to spare. She went through the office then was taken down the hall to the second grade classroom.

Outside, she was greeted by the teacher. "It's good to meet you, I'm Julie Miller."

"Lori Hutchinson. I'm substituting for Claire Keenan. She's sick."

The young strawberry blonde smiled eagerly. "I'm glad you could make it. I've heard a lot about you."

"Well, I guess Lyle's long-lost daughter would be news in a small town."

Julie smiled. "No, I heard it all from Cassie Yeager. Seems you live in a castle and have a princess bedroom like hers."

That brought a smile to Lori's lips, too. "If only."

"I also heard you teach second grade."

"I did. I was laid off this year."

"I'm sorry to hear that, but you're welcome to come and help out in my class anytime. But it sounds like you've been pretty busy with other projects around town."

Lori blinked. "You must have a good source."

"My sister, Erin, works at the bank. You've really impressed her."

"Oh, Erin. She's been a big help showing me around. There do need to be some changes."

Julie smiled brightly. "I can't tell you how happy I am that you came to Destiny and I hope you stay."

"I'll be here for this year anyway. In fact, my sister and her son will be coming in next week. Zack will be in second grade."

"That's wonderful. Then you'll want to see how I run my class."

Julie Miller opened the door to a room that was buzzing with about twenty-five seven-year-olds. The room was divided in sections, half with desks, the other half with tables and a circle of chairs for reading time.

Suddenly two little blonde girls came up to her—Ellie Larkin and Cassie Yeager.

"Miss Lori, what are you doing here?" Cassie asked.

"Hi, girls. Ellie, your grandmother isn't feeling well today."

Both girls looked worried. "Really?" Ellie said.

"It's nothing serious, don't worry. But she asked if I'd come in her place."

They got excited again. "We're going to try out for our Christmas program today."

"That's wonderful," Lori said. This was what she missed about teaching, the children's enthusiasm.

"It's called Destiny's First Christmas," Cassie said as she clasped her hands together. "And everyone gets to be in it."

"But we want to be the angels," Ellie added.

Just then Mrs. Miller got their attention. "Okay, class, you need to return to your desks. We have a special guest today and we need to show her how well-behaved we are so she'll want to come back." A bright smile. "Maybe Miss Hutchinson will help us with our Christmas play."

CHAPTER SIX

LATER that evening, Jace finally headed home. He was beat to say the least. A twelve-hour day was usually nothing for him, but he'd been off for three weeks. He needed to oversee everything today to make sure that the schedule for tomorrow went off without a hitch. The one thing he knew, he didn't like to be away from Cassie that long. Luckily, he had good childcare.

He came up the road and the welcoming two-story clapboard house came into view. Although the sun had set an hour ago, he had installed plenty of lighting to illuminate the grounds, including the small barn. He had a lot of work yet to do on the place, but a new roof and paint job made the house livable for now.

The barn had been redone, plus he'd added stalls for his two horses, Rocky and Dixie. Maybe it was a luxury he couldn't afford right now, but it was something that had helped Cassie adjust to her move. Luckily he'd been able to hire the neighbor's teenage son to do the feeding and cleaning.

Jace frowned at the sight of a new SUV parked by the back door. Had Heather, the babysitter, gotten a new car? Then dread washed over him. Was it his ex-wife?

Panic surged through him as he got out of his truck

and hurried up the back steps into the mudroom. After shucking his boots, he walked into the kitchen. He froze, then almost with relief, he sagged against the counter when he saw his daughter at the kitchen table with Lori Hutchinson.

He took a moment and watched the interaction of the two. Their blond heads together, working on the math paper. Then Lori reached out and stroked Cassie's hair and it looked as natural as if they were mother and daughter. His throat suddenly went dry. His business partner had a whole new side to her, a very appealing side.

Too appealing. Lorelei Hutchinson was beginning to be more than a business partner and a pretty face. She had him thinking about the things he'd always wanted in his life. In his daughter's life.

Cassie finally turned to him. "Daddy." She got up and rushed over to him. "You're home."

He hugged her, but his gaze was on Lori. "Yes, sorry I'm so late."

"It's okay," she said. "Miss Lori drove me home." His daughter gave him a bright smile. "She's helping me with my homework."

"I thought Mrs. Keenan was going to do that." He'd made the arrangements with her yesterday.

Lori stood. "Claire would have, but she got sick. I took over for her this afternoon in Cassie's classroom, and I offered to bring her home. I knew you would be busy at the site."

Jace tensed. "My daughter is a priority. I'm never too busy to be here for her. At the very least I should have been called." He glanced around for the teenager who he depended on. "Where's Heather?"

"She had a 'mergency at her house," Cassie told him.

He turned to the jean-clad Lori. She didn't look much older than the high school babysitter.

"We tried to call you but I got your voice mail," Lori said. "It wasn't a problem for me to stay with Cassie until you got home."

Jace felt the air go out of him, remembering he hadn't had his phone on him. He wasn't sure where it was at the site. He looked at Lori. "Thank you. I guess I got wrapped up in getting things back on target at the job site."

"It's okay, Daddy." His daughter looked up at him. "'Cause we made supper."

Great. All he needed was for this woman to get involved in his personal life. "You didn't need to do that."

Lori caught on pretty quickly that Jace didn't want her here. She'd gotten rejection before, so why had his bothered her so much?

"Look, it's just some potato soup and corn bread." She checked her watch. "Oh, my, it's late, I should go."

"No!" Cassie said. "You have to stay. You said you'd help me practice my part in the play." She turned back to her father. "Daddy, Miss Lori has to stay."

Lori hated to put Jace on the spot. Whatever the issues he had about women, she didn't want to know. She had enough to deal with. "It's okay, Cassie, we'll work on it another time."

"But Miss Lori, you wanted to show Daddy your new car, too."

Lori picked up her coat and was slipping it on when Jace came after her.

"Cassie's right, Lori. Please stay."

His husky voice stopped her, but those blue eyes convinced her to change her mind about leaving.

His voice lowered when he continued. "I was rude. I should thank you for spending time with my daughter." He smiled. "Please, stay for supper and let me make it up to you."

Lori glanced away, knowing this man was trouble. She wasn't his type. Men like Jace Yeager didn't give her much notice. *Keep it light.* "We're getting an early start on the Christmas pageant. How are you at playing the part of an angel?"

Cassie giggled.

He smiled, too. "Maybe I'd do better playing a devil."

She had no doubt. "I guess I could write in that part."

She knew coming here would be crossing the line. They worked together, but it needed to stay business. Instead she was in Jace Yeager's home. And even with all the unfinished projects he had going on, it already felt like a real home. It set off a different kind of yearning inside her. That elusive traditional family she'd always wanted. Something all the money from her inheritance couldn't buy her.

Two hours later, Jace finished up the supper dishes, recalling the laughter he heard from his daughter and their guest.

It let him know how much Cassie missed having another female around. A mother. He tensed. Shelly Yeager—soon-to-be Layfield—had never been the typical mother. She'd only cared about money and her social status and her daughter ranked a poor second. More than anything he wanted to give Cassie a home and a life where she'd grow up happy and well-adjusted. He could only do that if she was with him. He'd do whatever it took to keep it that way.

In the past, money, mostly his, had pacified Shelly. Now, she'd landed another prospective husband, a rich one. So she had even more power to keep turning the screws on him, threatening to take Cassie back.

He climbed the steps to his daughter's bedroom and found her already dressed in pajamas. Lori was sitting with her on the canopy bed reading her a story.

His chest tightened at the domestic scene. They looked so much alike they could be mother and daughter. He quickly shook away the thought and walked in.

"The end," Lori said as she closed the book and Cassie yawned.

"I see a very sleepy little girl."

"No, Daddy." She yawned again. "I want another story."

He shook his head and looked at Lori. "The rule is only one bedtime story on a school night." He checked his watch. "Besides, we've taken up enough of Lori's time tonight."

Cassie looked at her. "I'm sorry."

"No, don't be sorry, Cassie." She hugged the girl. "I enjoyed every minute. I told you I read to my nephew."

Cassie's eyes brightened. "Daddy, Lori's nephew, Zack, is coming here to live. He's going to be in my class."

"That'll be nice. How about we talk about it tomorrow? Now, you go to sleep."

Jace watched Lori and his daughter exchange another hug, then she got up and left the room. After he kissed his daughter, he turned off the light and headed downstairs. He found Lori putting on her coat and heading for the back door.

"Trying to make your escape?"

She turned around. "I'm sure you're tired, too."

He walked to her. "I think you might win that contest. Spending four hours with my daughter, not counting the time at school, had to be exhausting."

She smiled. "Remember, I'm a trained professional."

His gut tightened at the teasing glint in her incredible eyes. "And I know my daughter. She can try anyone's patience, but she's the love of my life."

He saw Lori's expression turn a little sad. "She's a lucky little girl." She turned away. "I should get home."

Something made him go after her. Before she could make it to the back door, he reached for her and turned her around. "I wish things could have been different for you, Lori. I'm sorry that you had to suffer as a child."

She shook her head. "It was a long time ago and I've dealt with it."

"Hey, you can't fool a foster kid. I was in the system most of my life. We're experts on rejection."

Her gaze went to his, those brown eyes compelling. "What happened to your family?"

"My parents were in a car accident when I was eight. What relatives I had didn't want me, so I went into foster care."

"Oh, Jace," she whispered.

Her little breathless gasp caused a different kind of reaction from him. Then he saw the tears in her eyes.

His chest tightened. "Hey, don't. I survived. Look at me. A success story."

Jace reached out and touched her cheek. The next thing he knew he pulled her toward him, then wrapped her in his arms. He silenced a groan as he felt her sweet body tucked against his. It had been so long since he'd held a woman. So long since he'd felt the warmth, the glorious softness.

He pulled back trying to put some space between them, but couldn't seem to let her go. His gaze went to her face; her dark eyes mirrored the same desire. He was in big trouble.

He lowered his head and whispered, "This is probably a really bad idea." His mouth brushed over hers, once, then again. Each time she made a little breathy sound that ripped at his gut until he couldn't resist any longer and he captured her tempting mouth.

She wrapped her arms around his neck and leaned into him as her fingers played with the hair at his nape. He pushed his tongue into her mouth and found heaven. She was the sweetest woman he'd ever tasted, and the last thing he ever wanted to do was stop. He wanted so much more, but also knew he couldn't have it.

He tore his mouth away and took a step back. "Damn, woman. You pack a punch. I just can't…"

"It's okay." She pulled her coat tighter. "It would be crazy to start something."

He couldn't believe how badly he wanted to. "Right. Bad idea. We're business partners. Besides, I have room for only one female in my life. Cassie."

Her gaze wouldn't meet his. "I should go."

"Let me walk you out."

"No, you don't need to do that. It's too cold."

He tried to make light of the situation. "Right now, I could use a blast of cold air." He followed her out. Grabbing his coat off the hook, he slipped it on as they went through the mudroom. The frigid air hit him hard as they hurried out to the well-lit driveway and around to her side of the car.

"Nice ride." He glanced over the four-wheel-drive SUV. "You're ready for the snow." He held on to the door so she couldn't rush off. "Are you coming by the site tomorrow?"

"No." She paused. "Unless you need me for something."

He found he wanted to see her again. "I guess not."

"Okay then, good night, Jace."

"Thank you, Lori. Thank you for being there for Cassie."

"You're welcome. Goodbye." She shut her door and started the engine and was backing out of the drive before Jace could stop her. That was the last thing he needed to do. He didn't need to be involved with this woman.

Any woman.

It would be a long time before he could trust again. But if he let her, Lori Hutchinson could come close to melting his cold, cold heart.

Lori had spent the past two days at the bank where she'd been trying to familiarize herself with her father's business dealings. How many people expected her to fail at this?

She'd stayed far away from Jace Yeager, although that didn't change the fact that she'd been thinking about him.

Had he been thinking about her? No. If he had been, wouldn't he have called? Or maybe he'd resisted, knowing getting involved could create more problems.

Lori looked up from the desk as Erin walked into

the office. The receptionist had been such a big help to her, going through files and being the liaison between Lori and Dennis Bradley's office.

Erin sat down in the chair across from the desk. "I found this in an old personnel file, and it's kind of interesting. Kaley Sims did used to work for Mr. Hutchinson. It states that she managed his properties up until two years ago."

Lori had found this woman's notes on several contracts. "Why isn't she working for him now?"

Erin gave her a funny look and glanced away.

"You know something?"

"It's just some bank gossip, but there might have been something between Kaley and Mr. Hutchinson, beyond professional."

So her father had someone after his divorce. "I take it they were discreet."

"They went to business and social functions together, but no one saw any signs of affection between them."

Lori shrugged. "Maybe that's the reason Kaley left here. She wanted more from Lyle."

"If you want to talk to her, I could call her mother and see if she's available to come back to work here."

Lori needed the help. "I guess it wouldn't hurt to call. I sure could use the help, especially someone who already knows the business. I don't want to put in twelve-hour days."

Had Lyle Hutchinson become that much of a recluse that all he did was work? She was curious. Had her father driven off Kaley?

"Okay, I'll make the call tomorrow," Erin said as she stood. "Is there anything more you need today?"

Lori checked her watch. It was after five o'clock. "I'm sorry. You need to get home."

"Normally I'd stay, but I have a date tonight."

Lori smiled, feeling a little twinge of envy, and immediately thought about Jace. Since the kiss she hadn't heard a word from him in two days. *Stop.* She couldn't let one kiss affect her. She wasn't a teenager. "Well, you're great, Erin. I'm grateful to have all your help." She paused. "How would you like to be my assistant?"

"Really?"

"Really. But you have to promise to stay in college. We can schedule hours around your classes, and you'll get a pay raise."

"Oh, wow. Thank you. I'd love to be your assistant." Erin reached out and shook her hand. "And everyone thought you coming to town would be a bad thing."

"Oh, they did, huh?"

This time, Erin hesitated. "I think they thought that a lot of jobs might be lost." The pretty brunette beamed. "Instead, you've come here and come up with ideas so people can save their homes, and you're helping women advance, too."

Lori was happy she could do something. "So it's a good thing?"

"Very good." The girl turned and left the office.

Lori sank back into her father's overstuffed leather chair. "Lyle Hutchinson, you must have really been some kind of tyrant. What made you so unhappy?"

She thought about the sizable amount of money Lyle had acquired over the years. When the waiting period was over next year, she'd never be able to spend it all. She could give the money away. Right now, she received a large income just from his properties.

Sadness hit her hard. Seeing how her father lived, she realized he'd died a lonely man. Outside his few male friends, he didn't go out with anyone. "I was always there, Dad. Just a call away. Your daughter. I would have loved to spend time with you."

It might be too late for a family with her father, but there was a second chance, because she had a sister and nephew. Gina and Zack would always be her family.

A few days had passed and Jace hadn't been able to get Lori, or the kiss, out of his head. Even working nonstop at the site couldn't keep his mind from wandering back to Lori Hutchinson. Until work came to a sudden halt when problems with the staircase came up and didn't meet code. They had to make some changes in the design.

He needed Lori's okay to move ahead with the architect's revisions. He went by the bank, but discovered she was at home. So that was where he was headed when he realized he was looking forward to seeing her. Glad for the excuse.

He pulled up out front, sat there a moment to pull it together. Then he jerked open the door and got out of his truck. The early November day was cold. He looked up at the gray sky, glad that they'd finished the outside of the building. At the very least they would get some rain.

He walked up to the porch, but slowed his steps at the door, feeling his heart rate accelerate.

He hadn't seen Lori since the night at his house. When she had been in his arms. He released a breath. Even time away didn't change the fact that he was eager to see her.

Maggie opened the door with her usual smile. "Mr. Yeager. It's nice to see you again."

He stepped inside. "Hi, Maggie. Is Lori here?" He held up his folder. "I have more papers for her to sign," he said, suddenly hearing the noises coming from upstairs.

"Oh, she's here." Maggie grinned. "Been working all day trying to get things finished before her sister and nephew's arrival tomorrow. Charlie's helping." There was a big thud and Maggie looked concerned. "But maybe you should have a look."

Jace nodded. He headed for the stairs and took them two at a time to shorten the trip. He walked down the hall and was surprised when he found the source of the noise. It was coming from the room across from Lori's childhood bedroom.

He looked in the slightly open door and found Charlie and Lori kneeling on the floor with sections of wood spread out. The two were engrossed in reading a sheet of directions.

Lori brushed back a strand of hair, revealing her pretty face. Then his heart went soaring and his body heated up as she reached for something and her jeans pulled taut over her cute, rounded bottom.

"It says right here that *A* goes into *B*. Okay we got that, but I can't find the next piece." She held up the sheet of paper. "Do you see this one?"

Hiding his amusement, Jace stepped into the room. "Could you two use some help?"

They both swung around. "Mr. Yeager," Charlie said and got to his feet. "Oh, yes, we could use your expertise. And since you're here to help, I'll go do my work." The older man left, looking relieved.

Jace turned back at Lori. "What are you building?"

"Bunk beds," she offered.

Jace pulled off his jacket as he glanced over the stacks of boxes. "Why not buy it assembled?"

Lori stood. "I didn't have time to go to Durango, so I got them online. I didn't realize it would come in boxes."

"You should have called me. I would have sent Mac over." He took the paper from her. Their hands brushed, and he quickly busied himself by looking over the directions. "Okay, let's lay out the rails and the end pieces."

Lori took one end and he took the other. He set the bolts, then went to her end. He was close and could breathe in her scent, which distracted the hell out of him. He finally got the bolt tightened. He got up and went to the other side, away from temptation, but she followed him.

Over the next hour, they'd become engrossed in building the elaborate bunk-bed set. They stood back and looked over their accomplishment.

"Not bad work." He glanced at the woman beside him and saw her blink. "What's wrong?"

She shook her head. "Zack is going to love it. He's had to share a room with his mother the past few months. Thank you for this."

"Not a problem," he told her. "You helped me out with Cassie. I know how much you want to make a home for your sister and your nephew."

"They've had a rough time of it lately." She put on a smile. "It's going to be great for them to be here."

Jace looked around the freshly painted blue room. "I thought you were going to put Zack in your old bedroom."

She shrugged. "I tried, but I couldn't bring myself

to touch it." She looked at him and he saw the pain in her eyes. "I guess I'm still trying to figure out why my father kept it the same all these years. Crazy, huh?"

Unable to help himself, he draped his arm across her shoulders. "It's okay, Lori. You have a lot to work through. You've pulled up your roots and come back here. There's a lot to deal with."

She looked up. "But I have the funds now to take care of my family."

That was the one thing that kind of bothered him. He'd been pretty well-off financially before his divorce, but to have a woman with so much money when he was trying to scrape by hit him in his pride. But he truly thought it bothered her more.

"So how does it feel to have that kind of money?"

She scrunched up her nose. "Oddly strange," she admitted. "It's far too much. I'm the kind of girl who's had to work all my life, and when I lost my job a few months ago, I was really worried about what was going to happen, especially for Gina and Zack."

"They have you now."

She looked up at him, her eyes bright and rich in color. "And I have them. I wouldn't stay here in Destiny, money or no money, if they couldn't be with me. Their safety and well-being is the most important thing to me."

He frowned. "Why wouldn't they be safe here?"

She glanced away. "It's just a worry I have."

He touched her chin to get her to look at him. "Lori, what aren't you telling me? Is someone threatening you or your family?"

She finally looked at him. "It's Gina's ex-husband. He'll be getting out of jail soon."

"Why did he go to jail?"

"Look, Jace, I'm not sure Gina wants anyone to know her private business."

"I'm not a gossip. If your family needs protection then I want to help."

Lori was surprised at his offer. She wasn't used to anyone helping them. "Eric is in for drug possession and spousal abuse. He swore when he got out he'd make Gina pay for having him arrested."

She felt Jace tense. "So that's why you were headed out of state?"

She nodded.

"Does this Eric guy know where Gina is moving to?"

"No one knows. We haven't even told Zack. I want so badly for Gina to make a life here. She has full custody of her son, but we're still afraid of what the man might do."

"This house has a security system. I hope you're using it."

She nodded.

"And I think you should have protection for yourself, also. You're worth a lot of money and you could be a target for threats from this guy. Maybe a security guard isn't out of the question."

"I can't let my life be dictated by a coward."

Jace clenched his fists. "I don't care for a creep who gets his jollies by beating women, either, but you still need to take precautions. Not an armed guard, but maybe a security man disguised as a gardener or handyman."

She hesitated. "If Gina will agree."

"What about you? I'm sure you've had some run-ins with your brother-in-law."

Lori shivered, recalling Eric's threats.

Jace's eyes narrowed. "Did he hurt you, too?"

"Just a few shoves here and there, but I couldn't let him hurt Gina."

He cursed and walked away, then came back to her. He reached out and cupped her face. "He put his hands on you, Lori. No man ever has the right to do that unless the woman wants it."

She stared into his eyes. That was the problem. She wanted Jace's hands on her. Badly.

CHAPTER SEVEN

JACE had trouble letting go of Lori. He knew the minute he touched her again this would happen.

He cursed under his breath. "This isn't a good idea." His gaze searched her pretty face, those bedroom eyes, then he stopped at her perfect rosy mouth. He suddenly felt like a man dying of thirst. Especially when her tongue darted out over her lips. With a groan, he leaned down and brushed his mouth across hers, hearing her quick intake of breath.

"I swore I'd stay away from you. We shouldn't start something...." His mouth brushed over hers again and then again. "My life doesn't need to get any more complicated."

"Mine, either," she whispered.

He fought the smile, but it didn't stop the hunger, or the anticipation of the kiss he so desperately wanted more than his next breath.

Then Lori took the decision out of his hands as she rose up on her toes and pressed her mouth against his. That was all it took. His arms circled her waist and he pulled her against him, unable to tolerate the space between them any longer. Their bodies meshed so easily it was as if they were meant to be together. All he knew was he didn't want to let her go anytime soon.

His mouth slanted over hers, wanting to taste her, but all too quickly they were getting carried away.

He tore his mouth from hers, and trailed kisses along her jaw to her ear. "I could get drunk on you." Then he let his tongue trace her earlobe, feeling her shiver. He found her mouth again for another hungry kiss.

Then suddenly the sound of his cell phone brought him back to reality. He stepped back, and his gaze was drawn to Lori's thoroughly kissed mouth. Desire shot through him and he had to turn away.

"Yeager," he growled into the phone.

"Hey, Jace," Toby said. "What happened? I thought you were coming right back."

He glanced over his shoulder at Lori. "Sorry, something came up. I'm heading back now." He shut his phone. "I'm needed at the site."

"Of course," Lori said, wrapping honey-blond strands behind her ear. "I can't thank you enough for your help. I couldn't have done this on my own."

Unable to resist, he went back to her and stole another kiss. They were both breathless by the time he released her. "Your sister and nephew arrive tomorrow, right?"

She nodded.

"Okay, I'll have a security guy in place here before you get back from the airport." When Lori started to disagree, he put his finger over those very inviting lips. "He'll work with Charlie so Gina doesn't have to know. I want you and your family safe."

Lori smiled. "I wasn't going to disagree. I think it's a good idea."

He blinked. "You're agreeing with me? That's a first."

"Don't get used to it, Yeager."

The next afternoon, Lori had agreed to let Charlie drive her father's town car the 47 miles to the Durango airport to pick up Gina and Zack.

She couldn't hide her excitement as she watched her sister and nephew come out of the terminal. She gave them a big hug, then herded them into the backseat of the car while Charlie stowed the few belongings in the trunk.

They talked all the way to Destiny. It was as if they'd been apart for months instead of only two weeks.

Lori kept hugging her seven-year-old nephew beside her in the backseat. She'd missed him. "Zack. I was able to work in the second grade classroom last week and met your teacher, Mrs. Miller. I think you're going to like her."

The little dark-haired child didn't look happy. "But I don't know any kids."

"The class knows you're coming. And there's Ellie and Cassie, who will help you learn your way around the school."

"Girls?"

That brought a smile as Lori looked at her sister. Although beautiful, with her rich, dark brown hair and wide green eyes, Regina Williams Lowell looked a little pale and far too thin. Lori hoped she could erase her sister's fear once she knew she was safe living in Destiny. And her son would blossom here, too.

"It might take a little time, Zack, but I know you'll make lots of friends."

They drove through town, past the square and fountain, then down the row of storefronts. "Just wait. Soon they'll be putting up a big Christmas tree with colorful lights. The whole town will be decorated."

"Can we have a Christmas tree at your house?"

Suddenly Lori got excited. This was going to be a special holiday. And a new year that meant a fresh beginning for all of them. "You bet we can. And you can pick out a really big one."

Zack grinned as they pulled through the gate. "Wow!" The boy's eyes lit up. "Mom, are we really going to live here?"

"We sure are." Gina looked like a kid herself. "Although, I can hardly believe it myself."

Lori glanced at her sister's face. "That was my first reaction, too. Welcome to Hutchinson House."

Charlie drove up the long drive and stopped in front of the house. He opened the back door and helped them out, then sent them up the porch steps.

Maggie swung open the front door and opened her arms. "Welcome, welcome," the older woman said as she swept them inside the warm house. First, the older woman embraced Zack, then Gina.

"We're so happy you're here. Oh, my, and to have a child in this big house again is wonderful."

"It's so big," Zack said. "What if I get lost?"

"Don't worry. Charlie will show you around. The important thing to remember is there are two sets of stairs. One leads down here." Maggie pointed to the circular staircase. "Most important, the other one leads to the kitchen and I'm usually there."

Zack looked a little more comfortable after the quick explanation.

Maggie turned to Gina and smiled. "Goodness, my, you look so much like Lorelei and your mother. Your coloring might be different, but there's no doubt you're sisters. And both beautiful."

Her sister seemed embarrassed. "Thank you."

"How was your flight?"

"Not too bad, especially sitting in first class." Gina glanced at Lori. "It was a big treat for Zack and me."

"Well, we're planning on a lot of treats for Master Zack." The older woman placed her hands on the boy's shoulders. "After you go and see your new bedroom, come down to the kitchen so you can tell me all your favorite foods. And if it's okay with your mother you can sample some of my cookies." Maggie raised a hand and glanced at Gina. "I promise not to spoil his appetite for our special dinner tonight."

"The way my son eats, I doubt anything can." Gina smiled, which made Lori hopeful that her sister would start relaxing.

"We're also having a couple of guests for dinner," Maggie announced. "Mr. Yeager and his daughter, Cassie. And before you frown, Zack, the girl has a horse. That's a good friend to have."

Lori was surprised by the news, and a little too happy, feeling a stir of excitement. Maybe he was bringing the security guard they'd talked about.

Maggie gave her the answer. "Jace has something to discuss with you. So I invited them both to dinner."

Her nephew called to her. "Can I go see my new bedroom, Aunt Lori?"

"Sure. How about we all head up and see it?"

The child ran ahead of them, following Charlie up the steps with the bags.

Lori hung back with Gina. "Lori, you never said the place was a—" she looked around the huge entry, her eyes wide "—mansion."

"Okay, so the Hutchinson family liked things on the large size. Now that you and Zack are here, it's already starting to feel more like a home." She hugged her sister again. "I want you and Zack to think of this place as home. More important, I want you to feel safe here."

Gina looked a little panicked. "Just so long as Eric never finds us."

Another precaution had been for Gina to take back her maiden name, Williams.

"If he shows up in Destiny, you can believe he'll be arrested." Jace had convinced her to let Sheriff Reed Larkin in on the situation.

"Does everyone in town know?"

Lori shook her head. "No, only the people who work here at the house. And Jace Yeager, my business partner. He suggested that I hire some security." Lori raised a hand. "Only just as a precaution."

"That has to cost a lot of money."

Lori smiled. "Look at this place, Gina. Lyle Hutchinson might have been a lousy father, but he knew how to make money. And taking care of you and Zack is worth whatever it costs."

Tears filled her sister's eyes. "Thank you."

Before Lori started crying, too, she said, "Come on, I hope you like your bedroom. It's got a connecting bath with Zack's room."

They started up the steps arm in arm. "I can't imagine I wouldn't love it."

"If you don't like it, you can redo it. You're the one

with experience. In fact, I'd be happy if you would redo the entire place."

Gina turned to Lori. "Decorating a boutique window doesn't make me a professional." She looked around. "It's so grand as it is."

Lori knew what her sister had been thinking. There had been a lot of times when their living quarters hadn't been that great, especially when Gina was married. Being a school dropout, Eric hadn't been able to do much, and he spent his paycheck on alcohol instead of diapers.

"This is our fresh start, Gina. You don't have to worry about Eric anymore. I'm not going to let anything happen to either you or Zack."

Lori prayed that was a promise she could keep.

Three hours later, Jace walked up the steps to the Hutchinson home, carrying a bottle of wine and flowers. He normally didn't take Cassie out on a school night, but this was a special occasion and he knew how it was to be the new kid in town.

Okay, the truth was he wanted to see Lori. He'd tried to keep focused on work, but she was messing with his head. Last night he couldn't sleep, recalling their kisses, but he knew from now on that he had to keep his hands to himself. If Shelly got wind of any of this, she would make his life miserable just for the hell of it.

He had to focus on Cassie and getting the project completed on time. That was all. Once he had custody settled, he could think about a life for himself.

The front door opened and a little boy stuck his head out. "Hi," he said shyly.

His daughter answered back. "Hi. You're Zack. I'm Cassie Yeager. You're going to be in my class at school."

The boy looked up at Jace as if asking for help. His daughter never had a problem with being shy.

"I'm Jace. I think your aunt is expecting us."

Zack nodded. "You want to come in?"

"Sounds good. It's a little cold out here."

The door opened wider as another woman appeared. She smiled, showing off the resemblance to Lori.

"Hello, you must be Gina. I'm Jace Yeager. I'm Lori's business partner."

She took his hand. "It's nice to meet you."

"This is my daughter, Cassie."

His daughter beamed as she came up to Gina. "Hi, Miss Gina. My dad brought you flowers and for Miss Lori, wine. And I bought Zack a school sweatshirt." She held up the burgundy-colored shirt with Destiny Elementary School printed on it.

"Hello, Cassie. That's very nice."

Cassie turned to Zack. "My dad said you have a new bedroom."

"Yeah, it's cool."

"Can I see it?"

Zack looked at his mother for permission. With Gina's nod the two seven-year-olds took off upstairs.

"My son's a little shy," Gina admitted.

"Well, that won't last long if Cassie has anything to say about it."

He finally got a smile out of the pretty dark-haired woman with green eyes. There was definitely a strong resemblance between the two sisters, except for their coloring. Both women were lovely.

"Here, these are for you. Welcome to Destiny."

He watched her blush as she took the bouquet. "Thank you."

"It's rough having to pick up and move everything. I had to do it about six months ago, but it was worth it. Destiny is a wonderful place to raise kids. Cassie loves it here."

"I'm glad." Gina hesitated. "Lori said she told you about my...situation."

He watched her hesitation, maybe more embarrassment. "I assure you, Gina, no one else will know about your past. It's no one's business. Your sister only wants you safe. I agreed to help her take some precautions."

"I appreciate it, really. I'm sure Eric wouldn't think to look for us here. He knows nothing about Lori's father." She sighed. "But I wouldn't put anything past him. So I thank you for the extra security."

Jace was about to speak when Lori came down the steps. She was wearing a black turtleneck sweater and gray slacks. He was caught up in her grace as she descended the winding stairs. She smiled at him, and his insides went all haywire.

Lori felt Jace's gaze on her and it made her nervous, also a little warm. She'd missed seeing him. The last time had only been a little over twenty-four hours ago when he'd helped her with the bed, and they almost fell into it. A warm shiver moved up her spine. How did he feel about it?

She walked across the tiled floor, seeing her sister holding flowers. That was so nice of him. "Hi, Jace."

"Lori."

She went to him. "Sorry, I wasn't here when you arrived. I just saw Cassie upstairs."

"Has she reorganized Zack's bedroom yet?"

Lori couldn't help but laugh. "I think he's safe for the moment."

Gina spoke up. "Excuse me. I'll go put these in water, then go up and have the kids wash up for dinner." She turned and walked to the kitchen.

Jace looked at Lori. "I don't want to barge in on your family dinner."

"You're not at all. You're always welcome here," she told him, knowing that was probably admitting too much. "Maggie loves to have company. She hasn't been able to cook this much in a long time."

"Anytime she wants company tell her I'll be here." He held up the bottle. "I brought wine."

Lori smiled. "Why don't we open it?"

"Lead the way," he said and they started toward the dining room. Lori watched as he stared at the dark burgundy wallpaper, dark-stained wainscoting and long, long table with the upholstered chairs, also dark.

"It's pretty bad. This room is like a mausoleum. It's going to be my first redecorating project. In fact, I'll put Gina in charge. I hope you don't mind eating in the kitchen."

"I prefer the kitchen." He glanced down at his jeans and sweater pulled over a collared shirt. He followed Lori to the sideboard. In actuality, he preferred her over it all, but he tried to stay focused on the conversation. "As you can see, I'm not dressed for anything fancy."

Lori thought he was dressed perfectly. The man would look good in…nothing. Oh, no. *Don't think about that.* She busied herself by opening a drawer and searching for a corkscrew. Once she found it, she handed it to him, then crossed to the glass-front hutch and took out two crystal wineglasses.

"Gina won't drink, so we'll have to toast my sister and nephew's arrival on our own."

"I think I can handle that." He managed to uncork the bottle and when she brought over the glasses, he filled them with the rosy liquid.

He held out the stemmed glass to her. She brushed his hand and tried to remain calm. It was only a drink, she told herself.

Jace picked up his. "To yours, Gina's and Zack's new home," he said.

Lori took a slow sip, allowing herself to enjoy the sweet taste. She took another, and soon the alcohol went to her head, making her feel a little more relaxed. Then her eyes connected with Jace, and suddenly her heart was racing once again.

"This tastes nice," she said, unable to get her mouth to work. "I mean, I'm not much of a drinker, but I like this."

His deep sapphire gaze never left hers as he set his glass down on the sideboard. "Let me see." Then he leaned forward and touched his mouth to hers.

She froze, unable to do anything but feel as his firm mouth caressed her lips, coaxing her to open for him with a stroke of his tongue.

She whimpered as her hand rested against his chest, feeling his pounding heart. She only ached for more.

He pulled back a little. "You're right. Sweet." He took her glass from her and set it down beside his. "But I need another taste to be sure."

He bent down and took her mouth again. She went willingly as her arms circled his neck, and she wanted to close out the rest of the world. Just the two of them. She refused to think about how stupid it was to let this happen with Jace. When his tongue stroked against hers, and he drew her against his body, she lost all common sense.

Then it quickly returned when the sound of footsteps overhead alerted them to the fact that the kids were coming.

He broke off, and pressed his head against hers. "Damn, Lorelei Hutchinson, if you don't make me forget my own name."

She could only manage a nod. Then he leaned forward again. "Not that you don't look beautiful thoroughly kissed, but you might have to answer too many questions."

She smoothed her hair. "Tell everyone I'll be in shortly." She took off, knowing she was a fool when it came to this man. It had to stop before someone got hurt.

Jace had trouble concentrating on his pot roast dinner. Why couldn't he keep his hands off Lori? She wasn't even his type. Not that he had a type. He'd sworn off women for the time being. So why had he been trying to play tonsil hockey with her just thirty minutes ago?

"Daddy?"

He turned to his daughter. "What, Cassie?"

"Can Zack go riding with me tomorrow?"

Jace glanced at Gina and saw her concerned look. "Maybe it's a little cold right now, sweetheart. Let Zack and his mother get settled in first. Besides, you both have school all day."

Those pretty blue eyes blinked up at him. "I know, Daddy," she said. "I'm gonna help Zack get used to the class."

Jace fought a smile and stole a glance at Lori, then at the poor boy who'd become his daughter's newest project. "I'm sure Zack appreciates all your help, sweetheart, but remember, Miss Lori is a teacher. She can help, too."

The child looked deflated. "Oh."

"I can sure use your help," Lori said. "And we're all going to be working on the Christmas play together. I'm sure Zack would like to do that."

"I guess," he said. "Are there other boys in the play?"

Cassie nodded. "Everyone is in the play. Cody Peters and Owen Hansen and Willie Burns." She smiled. "And now, you."

Jace wasn't sure he liked how his daughter was smiling at Zack. *Oh, no, not her first crush.*

Maggie came in with dessert and after everyone enjoyed the chocolate cake, the kids were excused and went up to Zack's bedroom.

"Seems like they've become fast friends," Gina said. "I thank you, Jace. Your daughter is helping my son a lot." She glanced at her sister. "I hated that Zack had to go through all the pain of the last few years."

"You need to put that in the past. This is a new start."

Lori reached over and covered her sister's hand. "It's a new beginning, Gina. We're going to keep you safe."

"Lori's right," Jace told her. "The security guard is on duty as we speak. Wyatt McCray will be touring the grounds during the night. He's moved into the room behind the garage. His cover will be he's working with Charlie. No one is going to hurt you or your son again."

Tears formed in Gina's eyes. "Thank you."

Lori spoke up. "Has Eric been released yet?"

"Detective Rogers said he is scheduled to get out this Friday."

"Good." Jace nodded. "You and Zack were gone before he had a chance to know what your plans were. The fewer people who know the better. So we three, Maggie, Charlie, Wyatt and Sheriff Larkin are the only people who know about your situation. You're divorced, and your past life is private."

"I'm grateful, Jace. Thank you." Gina stood. "I think I'll go check on the kids."

Lori watched her sister leave. "She's still scared to death."

"I know," Jace said, hating that he couldn't do more. "And I almost wish the creep would show up here so I could get my hands on him."

"No, I don't want that man anywhere near them ever again. Zack still has nightmares." She put on a smile. "Thank you for all your help."

His gaze held hers for longer than necessary. "Hey, we're partners."

Problem was, he wanted to be so much more.

CHAPTER EIGHT

By the end of the week Gina and Zack had settled in and were getting into a routine. Her nephew had started school and was making new friends. Of course, Cassie was still taking charge of Zack's social schedule.

Life was great, Lori thought, as she arrived at the bank that cold, gray November morning. Thank goodness her car had seat warmers to ward off the near-freezing temperatures. She thought about the upcoming holidays and couldn't help but smile. Her family would all be together.

She also thought of Jace. She wanted to invite him and Cassie to Thanksgiving at the house. Would he come? The memory of the kisses they'd shared caused a shiver down her spine. She was crazy to think about a future with the man, especially when he'd been telling her all along he didn't want to get involved.

As she entered her office, she decided not to go to the construction site unless absolutely necessary. Besides, she had plenty to do at the bank to keep her busy for a long time. She looked down at the several stacks of files and paperwork covering the desktop. The last thing she wanted to do was spend all her time managing the number of properties, and the rest of the time at the bank. If only she could hire someone to oversee it all. And she didn't trust the "three amigos" loan officers to handle things on their own. They'd already thought she was in over her head. Maybe she was, but she wasn't going to let them see it.

She'd been working nearly two hours when there was a knock on the door. "Come in," Lori called.

Erin walked in. She wore a simple black A-line skirt and a pin-striped red-and-white blouse. She was carrying a coffee mug and a white paper sack. "Break time?"

"Thank you, I could use it. Everything is getting a little blurry."

"You should have more than coffee. Helen sent over some scones from the Silver Spoon. A thank-you for putting a six-month moratorium on foreclosures."

Lori thought of her own childhood after her mother remarried. They'd had some rough times over the years. "I refuse to let this bank play Scrooge especially with Christmas coming soon. The first thing on the agenda for the first of next year is reworking these loans."

Erin smiled. "You know, the other bank officers aren't happy with your decision."

Lori took a sip of her drink. "Yes. Mr. Neal has already decided to retire." She thought about the generous retirement package her father had given him. He wouldn't be giving up his lifestyle.

"Oh, I almost forgot," Erin said. "I located Kaley Sims. She's working for a management company in Durango. I have the phone number."

"Good. Would you put in a call to her and see if she's willing to talk with me?"

"Of course. Anything else?"

Erin was so efficient at her job, Lori wasn't sure what she would have done without her.

"There is one thing. In looking over my father's properties, I found a place called—" she searched through the list "—Hidden Hills Lodge. I'm not sure if it's a rental property, or what. It doesn't show any reported income."

"Maybe it was a place Mr. Hutchinson had for his personal use. Do you want me to find out more about it?"

Lori shook her head. "No, you have more than enough to do now." Maybe she would look into this herself. She had a great GPS in her new car. Surely she could find her way. She stood. "I'm going to be gone the rest of the afternoon. If you need me, call me on my cell phone."

Maybe it was time she delved a little further into her father's past and the opportunity was right in front of her.

Later that afternoon, Jace got out of his truck as snow flurries floated in the air, clinging to his coat and hat. He took a breath as he walked to the bank. Okay, he'd been avoiding going anywhere he might see Lori Hutchinson. He couldn't seem to keep his hands off the woman, but since he needed her signature on some changes in the project, he didn't have a choice.

He walked through the doors and Erin greeted him. "Is Miss Hutchinson in?"

"No, she's not. She left about noon."

"She go home?"

"No, I've tried to reach her there. I also tried her cell

phone, but it goes to voice mail." Erin frowned. "I'm worried about her, especially with this weather."

Suddenly Jace was concerned, too. "And she didn't say where she was going? A property? Out to the site?"

"That's what I'm worried about. I think she might have gone to the Hidden Hills Lodge."

"Where is this place?"

Erin sat down at her desk and printed out directions from the computer. Jace looked them over. He wasn't sure about this area, only that it was pretty rural.

He wrote down his number and handed it to Erin. "Give me a call if Lori gets in touch with you."

He left as he pulled out his cell phone and gave Claire Keenan a call, asking if she'd watch Cassie a little later, then he hung up and glanced up at the sky. An odd feeling came over him, and not a good one. "Where are you, Lori?"

An hour later, Lori had turned off the highway to a private road, just as her GPS had instructed her to do. She shifted her car into four-wheel drive and began to move slowly along the narrowing path.

It wasn't long before she realized coming today wasn't a good idea. Deciding to go back, she shifted her SUV into Reverse and pushed on the gas pedal, and all that happened was the tires began to spin.

"Great. Please, I don't need this." She glanced out her windshield as her wipers pushed away the blowing snow, which didn't look like it was going to stop anytime soon.

She took out her cell phone. No signal. The one thing that was working was her GPS and it showed her destination was a quarter mile up the road. What should she do? Stay in the car, or walk to Hidden Hills Lodge?

She buttoned her coat, wrapped her scarf around her neck and grabbed a flashlight. She turned on her emergency blinkers and climbed out as the blowing snow hit her. She started her trek up the dirt road and her fear rose. What if she got lost and froze to death? Her thoughts turned to Gina and Zack. And Jace. She cared more about the man than she even wanted to admit. And she wanted to see him again. She quickened her pace, keeping to the center of the dirt road.

Ten minutes later, cold and tired, she finally saw the structure through the blowing snow. It was almost like a mirage in the middle of the trees. She hurried up the steps to the porch and tried the door. Locked.

"Key, where are you?" she murmured, hating to break a window. It took a few minutes, but she found a metal box behind the log bench. After unlocking the dead bolt with nearly frozen fingers, she hurried into the dark structure and closed the door. She reached for the switch on the wall and light illuminated the huge main room. With a gasp, she glanced around. The walls were made out of rough logs and the open-beam ceiling showed off the loft area overhead. Below the upstairs were two doorways leading to bedrooms. The floors were high-gloss pine with large area rugs and overstuffed furniture was arranged in front of a massive fireplace. She found a thermostat on the wall and flipped it, immediately hearing the heater come on.

Shivering, Lori walked to the fireplace and added some logs. With the aid of the gas starter, flames shot over the wood. She sat on the hearth, feeling warmth begin to seep through her chilled body.

Once warmed, she got up and looked around. The kitchen was tucked in the back side of the structure, revealing granite counters and dark cabinets.

She checked out the two bedrooms and a bath on the main floor. Then she climbed up to the loft and found another bedroom. One of the walls was all windows with a view of the forest. She walked into the connecting bathroom. This one had a soaker tub and a huge walk-in shower.

"I guess if you have to be stranded in a snowstorm, a mountain retreat isn't a bad place to be." At least she'd stay warm until someone found her. When? Next spring?

She came back downstairs trying to think of a plan to get her back to town, when a sudden noise drew her attention. She froze as the door opened and Jace Yeager walked in.

"Jace!" she cried and leaped into his arms.

He held her close and whispered, "I take it you're happy to see me."

Jace didn't want to let Lori go. Thank God, she was safe. When he found her deserted car, he wasn't sure if she would find cover.

He pulled back. "Are you crazy, woman? Why did you go out in this weather?"

She blinked back the obvious tears in her eyes. "It wasn't this bad when I started out. Besides, I didn't think it was that far. I tried to go back when the weather turned, but my car got stuck. How did you know where I went?"

"I stopped by the bank. Erin was worried because she couldn't get ahold of you."

"No cell service."

Jace pulled out his phone and examined it. "I have a few bars." He walked toward the front door, where the signal seemed to be a little stronger. "I'll call the Keenans." He punched in the number and prayed he could get a message out. Tim answered.

"Tim. It's Jace." He went on to explain what had happened and that Lori was with him. Most importantly they were safe. He asked Tim to keep Cassie, then to call Lori's sister and let her know they wouldn't be back tonight. "Tell Cassie I love her and not to worry."

He flipped the phone closed and looked around the large room, then he turned back to Lori. "Tim will call Gina and let her know you're okay."

Lori's eyes widened. "We're not going back now?"

He shook his head. "Can't risk it. The storm is too bad so we're safer staying put." That was only partly true. He glanced around, knowing being alone with Lori wasn't safe anywhere. "I'd say this isn't a bad place to be stranded in." He looked at her. "This is one of your properties?"

She nodded. "I think my father came here...to get away."

Jace grinned. "So this was Lyle's secret hideaway?"

Lori frowned. "Please, I don't want that picture in my mind."

Jace looked around at the structure. "Well, whatever he used it for, it's well built. And it seems to have all the modern conveniences."

He went on a search, and found two bedrooms, then a utility room off the kitchen. There was a large generator and tankless water system. "Bingo," he called to Lori. "All the conveniences of home. In fact, it's better than back home." He nodded to the fire. "Propane gas for the kitchen stove and most importantly there's heat."

Lori looked at him. "You really think my father used this place for his own personal use?"

Jace shrugged. "Or he let clients use it. Come on, Lori, did you think your father lived like a monk?"

She shrugged. "Truthfully, I hadn't thought much about my father's personal business in a long time. So what if he came here." She walked to the kitchen. "Maybe we should look for something to eat." Opening the cabinets, she found some canned goods, soup, beans and tuna.

Jace opened the refrigerator. Empty, but the freezer was filled with different cuts of meat, steaks, chicken. "I'll say one thing about Lyle. He believed in being prepared." He pulled out two steaks. "Hungry?"

She arched an eyebrow. "Are you cooking?"

"Hey, I can cook." He took the meat from the package, put it on a plate and into the microwave to defrost. "I've been on my own for a long time."

Lori had wondered about his childhood since he'd mentioned that he'd been in foster care. "How old were you?"

"At eighteen they release you. So you're on your own," he told her as he found a can of green beans in another cabinet. "I got a job working construction and signed up for college classes."

Jace didn't have it much better than she did, Lori thought. "That had to be hard for you."

"Not too bad," Jace said. "I found out later, I had a small inheritance from my parents. It was in trust until I turned twenty-five." He turned on the broiler in the oven then washed his hands. "I used it to start my company. Yeager Construction."

Lori found she liked listening to Jace talk. He was a confident man, in his words and movements. Okay, so she more than liked him.

The microwave dinged and he took out the meat. "How about a little seasoning for your steak?" He held up a small jar.

"Sure."

He added the rub to the meat. She watched as he worked efficiently to prepare the meal. She couldn't help but wonder about how those broad hands and tapered fingers would feel against her skin.

She suddenly heard her name and looked at him. "What?"

He gave her an odd look. "How do you like your steak?"

"Any way you fix it is fine," she said, not really caring at all. Then he smiled and she couldn't find enough air to draw into her lungs.

He winked. "Medium rare it is," he said and slid the tray into the broiler.

Pull it together, girl, she told herself then went to the cupboard. She got out two plates and some flatware from the drawer, then set the table by the fire. No need for candles. She glanced around the room. It looked so intimate.

She went and found a can of pineapple and opened it, then heated the green beans just as the steaks came off the broiler.

Jace added another log to the fire, then they sat down to dinner. "Man, this looks good. Too bad we can't do a salad and some garlic bread."

"I find it amazing that there's so much food here."

"Your father struck me as well prepared. Hold on a minute." He got up, went into the utility room and came out with a bottle of wine. "In every way."

He opened the bottle and poured two glasses. He took them to the table, sat in his chair and began to cut his steak. "If he used this place, he wanted all the comforts money could buy," Jace said, nodding to the wine.

"I'm wondering who he shared all this with."

Jace took a drink. "You might never know. One thing for sure, Lyle had good taste."

She took a sip from her glass, too, and had to agree. Then she began to eat, discovering she was hungry. "I guess I'm still the daughter who wonders why he was such a loner, not even finding time for his only child."

"We can spend hours on that subject." Jace continued to eat. "Some people aren't cut out for the job of parenting."

She hated that her father's rejection still bothered her after all these years. She wanted to think she'd moved on. Maybe not.

She turned her attention back to the conversation. "Shelly hated anything to do with being a mother," Jace said. "That's why I can't let her have Cassie."

"Does Cassie want to live with her mother?"

"Cassie wants to be *loved* by her mother, but my ex is too selfish. She's been jealous of her daughter since her birth. And I'll do anything to prevent Cassie from taking a backseat to that. I know how it feels."

"Cassie's lucky she has you."

He smiled. "It's easy to love that little girl. I know I spoil her, but she's been so happy since she moved here. I have to make it permanent."

Lori put on a smile. "You're a good father, Jace Yeager." She placed her hand on his arm. "I'll help you in any way I can."

He stopped eating. "What do you mean? Help. I can afford to handle this custody battle on my own."

She shook her head. "I know that. I only meant that I know what it's like to not have a father in my life. I was offering moral support, nothing else. But don't be too bullheaded to take any and everything you can to keep your daughter. She needs you in her life, more than you know." Lori stood and carried her plate to the sink. Her appetite was gone.

He came to her. "I'm sorry, Lori."

She could feel his heat behind her. Good Lord, the man made his presence known. She wanted desperately to lean back into him. "For years Lyle Hutchinson never even acknowledged that I existed. I can't tell you how much that hurt."

She hated feeling needy. When Jace turned her around and touched her cheek, she couldn't deny she wanted his comfort.

"I can't imagine doing that to my child. I don't want to think about Cassie not being in my life. I know from experience that adults do dumb things, and in the end it's the kids that get hurt the most."

Lori felt a tear drop and he wiped it away. "It's not fair."

Jace leaned forward. "I wish I could change it." He brushed his mouth across hers. "I wish I could make you feel better."

She released a shaky breath. "What you're doing is nice."

His blue-eyed gaze searched her face. "Damn, Lori.

What I'm thinking about doing with you isn't nice." Then he pulled her close and captured her mouth. Desire burst within her, if possible more intense than ever before, pooling deep in her center. She could feel his heat even through their clothes as she arched into his body. She whimpered her need as his tongue danced against hers.

"You make me want so many things," he breathed as his tongue tormented her skin. He found his way to her collarbone. "I want you, Lorelei Hutchinson." His mouth closed over hers once again, giving her a hint of the pleasure this man offered her.

She arched against him, her fingers threading through his hair, holding him close. Mouths slanted, their tongues mated as his hands moved over her back and down to her bottom, pulling her closer to feel his desire.

Jace was on the edge. On hearing her soft moan, he drew back with his last ounce of sanity. Then he made the mistake of looking into her eyes and all good intentions flew out the window. "Tell me to stop now, Lori."

She swallowed. "I can't, Jace. I don't want you to stop."

His heart skipped a beat as he swung her up into his arms. With a quick glance around, he headed to one of the rooms under the loft, only caring there was a bed past the door.

The daylight was fading, but there was enough light from the main room. He set her down next to a four-poster bed. He captured her mouth in a long kiss, then reached behind her and threw back the thick comforter.

He returned to her. "I've dreamed of being with you

like this." He drew her into his arms. "So be sure you want the same."

She nodded.

He let out a frustrated breath. "You have to do better than that, Lori."

"I'm very sure, Jace."

Those big brown eyes looked up at him. He inhaled her soft scent and was lost, so lost that he couldn't think about anything except sharing this intimacy with this special woman.

His mouth descended to hers and the rest of the snowstorm and the world disappeared. There was only the two of them caught up in their own storm.

CHAPTER NINE

SOMETIME around dawn, Jace woke suddenly, aware he wasn't alone in bed. And it wasn't his bed. He blinked and raised his head from the pillow to find Lori beside him. He bit back a groan as images of last night came flooding into his mind.

He'd come looking for her, afraid she'd been stranded in the freak storm. He found her all right, and had given in to temptation. They'd made love last night. Right now her sweet body pressed against his had him aching again.

He lay his head back on the pillow. Why did she have to come into his life now? He didn't have anything to offer her. Not a future anyway. He couldn't let anyone distract him from getting custody of Cassie.

Lori stirred, then rolled over and peered at him through the dim light. Her soft yellow hair was mussed, but definitely added to her sex appeal.

"Hi," she said in a husky voice that had him thinking about forgetting everything and getting lost in her once again.

"Hi, yourself."

She pulled the sheet up to cover her breasts. "I guess

this is what they call the awkward morning-after moment."

He knew Lori well enough to know that she wasn't the type to jump into bed with just any man. That wasn't the type he needed right now. "The last thing I want to do is make you feel uncomfortable," he said, and leaned toward her. "It's just us, Lori."

She glanced away shyly. "I haven't had a relationship since college."

He found that made him happy. "That's hard to believe." He touched her face. "You're a very beautiful woman, Lorelei Hutchinson."

"Thank you." She glanced away. "I didn't have time for a personal life. Gina and Zack needed me."

"I take it Gina's ex has caused her and you a lot of trouble."

She nodded. "Sober Eric had a mean streak, but when drunk he was really scary. Even with his obvious abuse, it took a lot to convince Gina that the man would never change. Then one day he went after Zack and she finally realized how dangerous he was. That's what it took for her to go to court and testify against him. After that Eric threatened to come after her." Lori's large eyes met his. "That's why it was so hard for me to come to Destiny. When my father made the stipulation in the will about staying a year, I wasn't sure if I could."

"I'm glad you did," he told her, unable to stop touching her. His hand moved over her bare arm, her skin so soft.

She looked surprised. "Is that because I rescued your project?"

"No, it's because you're beautiful and generous." He decided not to fight whatever was going on between them any longer. He leaned down and brushed his mouth over hers, enjoying that she eagerly opened for him. He drew back and added, "You've also taken time with Cassie. Before we moved here she didn't have much female attention."

Lori wasn't sure what she'd expected this morning, but not this. "It's easy to be nice to her. Cassie's a sweet girl."

"Hey, what about me?"

She wrinkled her nose. "I wouldn't call you sweet. Not your disposition anyway."

"Maybe I can change your mind." He caressed her mouth again. "Is that any better?"

"Fishing for a compliment?"

He shifted against her. "How about we continue this without conversation?"

Though Lori wanted the same thing, they needed to get home. "Shouldn't we think about heading back?"

"It's barely dawn." He started working his magic as his mouth moved upward along her jawline. "What's your hurry?" His tongue circled her ear. "Are you trying to get rid of me?"

She gasped, unable to fight the sensation. "No, it's just that it's…" She forgot what she wanted to say as his lips continued along her neck. "Don't we need to leave?"

He raised his head and she could see the desire in his eyes. "I want to do one thing right and it only involves the two of us." He arched an eyebrow. "But if you'd rather go out in that cold weather and start digging out, I'll do it. Your choice."

Lori knew what she wanted, all right. This man. But the fear was that she could never really have him. Last night and these few early hours might be all she would ever have. She wrapped her arms around his neck and pulled his mouth down to hers. "I choose you."

Two hours later, Jace stood at the railing on the cabin porch, drinking coffee. The sun was bright, reflecting off the ten inches of snow covering the ground. The highways would be plowed by now, but not the private road that led to the cabin. He had four-wheel drive on his truck, so they could probably get out and make it to the main road. It better be sooner than later before he got in any deeper.

He had no regrets being with Lori. Making love with her had been incredible. He'd never felt anything like it in his life. Even the best times during his marriage hadn't come close to what he'd shared with Lori.

In just the past three weeks, he'd come to care about this woman more than he had any business doing. But he had strong feelings for Lori and that scared the hell out of him.

Worse, there was no guarantee and he couldn't even offer her a future. He had no extra money. Hell, he needed to rebuild his business. He had to get things settled with the custody issue before he could have a personal life. The question was, would he be able to walk away from Lori? Did he want to?

The front door opened and she stepped out. "I wondered where you went."

"Sorry." He pulled up the collar on her coat and kissed her. "I was just figuring out if we can make it back to town."

"I wouldn't mind getting stuck here a few more days," she admitted. "It's beautiful."

He wouldn't mind pushing reality away for a little

time with this woman. "That would be nice, but we both have jobs to do. Family to take care of."

"Oh, gosh. Gina. I bet she's going crazy with worry."

"Tim called her last night."

"She'll still worry, and be afraid."

Jace wondered who worried about Lori. Seemed she took care of everyone else. "Gina and Zack have Wyatt McCray, Lori. He'll protect them."

"I know," she said with a smile.

His heart began pounding in his chest. The effect she had on him could be a big distraction.

"Thank you for giving us that peace of mind. You've been so kind."

He wondered if she'd always think that. "I didn't do that much."

Those dark eyes locked with his. "You seem to be there whenever I need you."

He found he might not mind being that man. He leaned down to kiss her when he heard something and looked toward the road. "Looks like we're getting rescued."

Jace pointed to a large truck with a plow attached to the front. It stopped a few yards from the door and Toby and Joe climbed out.

Smiling brightly, his foreman called, "I hear someone here might need a ride back to town."

"Toby," Lori cried and hurried down the steps Jace had cleared earlier.

He watched as she ran through the snow to get to Toby. She hugged the big foreman. Jace felt a stab of jealousy stir inside him, but he didn't have any right to claim her. Not yet, maybe never.

* * *

After stopping to get Jace's truck, the ride back to town took about thirty minutes. He followed behind the plow truck until they reached the highway. After Lori gave Toby her car keys, she got into Jace's truck and drove to the Keenan Inn.

She knew she should probably go straight to the house but asked Toby to tow her car to the inn. Besides, she wasn't ready to leave Jace yet.

When they got to the porch, the door opened and they were immediately greeted by Claire and Tim.

"Well, you had yourself quite an adventure," Tim said.

Lori felt a blush rising up her neck as they crossed the threshold. "I guess I should pay better attention to the weather forecast before heading out into the countryside. I did discover my father has a lovely cabin. Thank goodness there was heat."

"Where's Cassie?" Jace asked, looking around.

Claire looked worried. "She's in the kitchen. She's with one of our new guests."

Lori caught Jace's frown. Then he took off and Lori followed him through the dining area and into the large kitchen.

She found Cassie at the counter with a tall, statuesque woman. Her hair was a glossy black in a blunt shoulder-length cut. Her face was flawless, her eyes an azure-blue. She was a beautiful woman until she flashed a hard look at Jace.

The child ran to him. "Daddy. Daddy, you're back."

"Yes, baby." He hugged his daughter. "I told you we got stuck in the snow."

Cassie looked at Lori. "Miss Lori, did you get stuck, too?"

"Yes, your daddy found me."

The child turned back to her father and whispered, "Daddy, don't let Mommy take me away."

Shelly Yeager stood and walked toward them. "Hello, Jace." She gave Lori a once-over. "It's nice to see that you could make it back to take care of our daughter."

"Shelly. What are you doing here?"

"I came to take my little girl home, of course."

An hour later, Lori's car had arrived and she got in and drove home to find a relieved Gina. She'd taken a long shower and gotten dressed in clean clothes, but couldn't push aside the memories from last night. The incredible night she'd shared with Jace, then reality hit them in the face with Shelly Yeager.

She couldn't stop thinking about Cassie and what her mother had said. Was she going to take the child back to Denver? No, Jace couldn't lose his daughter. She wished she could help him, like he'd helped her.

Lori came downstairs to find her sister in the dining room working with Wyatt. The security guard was a retired army man in his forties with buzz-cut hair. She smiled. He didn't look out of place pulling down twenty-year-old brocade drapes. No doubt this wasn't in the man's job description.

Standing back, Maggie was smiling at what was going on. "It's about time someone got rid of those awful things, don't you think?"

"The room does look brighter." Lori had put her sister in charge of making changes to the house. Gina had told her a few days ago about the plans for the dining room. This was good since it had taken her sister's mind off her ex-husband and any trouble he could cause.

Gina finally turned around. "Oh, yes, you look better now. Still a little tired, but better." She walked over as Maggie left the room. "You okay?"

Lori wasn't sure what she was. "I'm fine. We'll talk later." She sighed, not ready to share what had happened with Jace. "So what are you doing in here?"

Her sister smiled. "I hope you don't mind. I decided to take you up on your suggestion and redo the room. I'm going to order some sheer curtains and light-colored linen drapes. Then I'll plan to strip the wallpaper and paint." She went to the sideboard to find the paint chips. "I've narrowed it down to either shaker beige, or winter sunshine."

Lori tried to focus on her sister's selection and push Jace out of her head. It wasn't working. "You're the decorator, you decide."

"Well, since I'm going to keep the woodwork dark, I'm thinking shaker beige." She glanced at Wyatt. "What do you like?"

Lori found herself smiling. At least something was going well today.

"I can do anything I damn well please," Shelly told Jace as she paced her suite upstairs at the inn. Cassie stayed downstairs with the Keenans while her parents talked.

Jace knew better than to get into a fight with this woman. "I thought you wanted me to have Cassie until the first of next year. You were going to be on an extended honeymoon."

Shelly glanced away. "Plans change."

She was hiding something. "So you're going to just rip Cassie out of school and drag her back to Denver? Well, that's as far as you're going, Shelly. You can't take her out of state, and forget about out of the country." He glanced around the large room and into the connecting bedroom. "Where is your so-called duke?"

Shelly glared at him. "His name is Edmund. And he's not a duke." She raised her head as if she was better than everyone. That was always what Shelly wanted to be, but she had come from the same background he had. "He might not be a duke, but he's got money and a bloodline linked to the royal family. And he can take care of me."

That always got to him. He could never make enough money to satisfy her. "I'm happy for you, Shelly. So why are you here and not with…Edmund?"

"There's been a delay in our wedding plans. I might be having second thoughts. So I decided I'd come to see Cassie. And you. You were always good at calming me down."

Something was up with her, and Jace was going to find out what it was. First stop was to visit his lawyer, Paige Keenan Larkin. No one was taking Cassie away from him.

That afternoon, Lori went into her office at the bank. She had to do something to keep her mind off what had happened at the cabin. She also had to think realistically. She couldn't hold out hope about having a future with Jace. His ex-wife showing up in Destiny proved that.

The most important thing she had to remember was that a child was in the middle of this mess. That meant Cassie's welfare had to come first. She had to stay away from Jace Yeager.

A sudden knock brought her back to the present. "Come in."

Jace walked into her office and her breath caught in her throat. Would she ever stop reacting to this man? Her gaze roamed over Jace's six-foot-two frame, recalling how she'd clung to those broad shoulders.

"Lori."

"Jace. What are you doing here?"

"I needed to see you."

Once again she got caught up in his clean-shaven face. Suddenly the memory of his beard stubble moving against her skin caused her to shiver. The sensation had nearly driven her out of her mind.

He closed the door and went to her desk. "I thought we should talk."

She managed a smile, hoping she was covering her insecurities. "There's no need to. Cassie's mother is in town and you need to take care of them. I understand."

"There's nothing to understand except I don't want you caught up in this mess. I have no idea what Shelly is even doing in Destiny. She was supposed to be in England, married and heading off on her honeymoon."

Lori stood. "Did she give you any explanation?"

"Only that plans change," he told her as he crossed the room toward her.

Lori wanted to back away, to tell Jace to leave, that being together now could be dangerous. Instead, she rounded the desk and met him in the middle of the room.

It wasn't planned, but she didn't turn away when his head descended and his mouth captured hers. She surrendered to his eager assault and returned the kiss, hungry for this man. Finally she came to her senses and broke away. "We shouldn't be doing this."

"Are we breaking any laws?"

"But I don't think Shelly was happy when I walked into the inn with you today."

"It's none of her business."

"Jace, you need to get along with her. At least for Cassie's sake."

He pressed his head against hers. "It's funny. Shelly thinks I'm not worthy of her, but she has this need to interfere in my life."

Lori sighed. "I'm so sorry, Jace."

He drew back. "That's the reason I don't want you involved in this fight, Lori. Maybe it would be best if we cool it for a while. I have to think about Cassie."

Lori knew in her head this was the way it had to be, but her heart still ached. She was losing someone she truly cared about. She managed to nod. "Of course. Besides, we both have too much going on to think that far in the future, or at least to make any promises."

This time he looked surprised.

She moved away from him, or he might see how she truly felt. "Come on, Jace. We work together. Last night we gave in to an attraction. It might not have been the wisest thing to do, but it happened."

He studied her a moment. "Are you saying you regret it?"

"That's not the point."

Jace glared at her. The hell it wasn't. He wanted to reach for her, wanted her to admit more than she was. To tell him how incredible their night was. The worst of it was she couldn't do it any more than he could. "You're right."

She nodded. "Goodbye, Jace."

That was the last thing he wanted to hear, but he would only hurt her more if he stayed. He nodded and walked toward the door. It was a lot harder than he ever dreamed it would be, but he couldn't drag Lori into his fight.

CHAPTER TEN

OVER the next three days, Lori felt like she was walking around in a fog. After the incredible night with Jace, then his quick, easy dismissal of it, how could she not? It would be so easy to pull the covers over her head and just stay in bed. If she were living alone she might do just that. Instead she'd stayed home and gotten involved in Gina's redecorating projects. She tried to fill her time with other things, rather than thinking about a tall, dark and handsome contractor.

Then she'd gotten a call from Erin, telling her that Kaley Sims was in town and had agreed to see her. Anxious for the meeting, Lori arrived right at one o'clock and found an attractive woman with short, honey-blond hair and striking gray eyes waiting in her office.

"Ms. Sims. I'm Lori Hutchinson."

Kaley Sims stood up and they shook hands. "It's nice to meet you. And please call me Kaley." The woman studied her and smiled. "I see some resemblance. You have Lyle's eyes." The woman sobered. "I am sorry to hear of his passing."

"Thank you." Lori motioned for Kaley to sit in the chair across from the desk. "I can't tell you how happy

I am that you agreed to meet with me. I see in my files that you worked for my father a few years back."

Kaley nodded. "I was selling real estate in Destiny before he offered me a job as his property manager. I worked for Lyle about three years."

"You managed all his properties?

"I did."

"I'm impressed," Lori said with a smile. "He has a big operation. I can't handle it all, nor do I have the experience to deal with the properties."

Kaley seemed to relax. "I was a single mother, so I needed the money. And the market was different then. Now, property values are a lot lower. You'd lose a fortune selling in this market."

"See, that's something I don't know. You've probably heard that my father left me in charge of all this."

Kaley's eyes widened, then she smiled. "Lyle would be proud. He talked about you a few times."

Lori froze. "He did?" Why did she still want Lyle's approval?

Kaley looked thoughtful. "One day I came in and found him looking at pictures of you. I think you were about eight or nine in the photo. And of course, Destiny being a small town, everyone knew about your parents' divorce. I mentioned to Lyle how cute you were and he should have you come back for a visit. He said he blew his chance."

Lori felt her chest tighten as she fought tears. This wasn't the time to relive the past. She blinked rapidly at the flooding emotions.

Kaley looked panicked. "I'm sorry, I didn't mean to make you sad."

Lori put on a smile, finding she liked this woman.

"You didn't. I never heard anything from my father since the day I left Destiny."

Kaley sighed. "That was Lyle. The only family he had was his father. Poor Billy had lived to be ninety-two and ended up in the nursing home outside of town until his death a few years ago." Kaley studied her. "Do you remember your grandfather?"

Lori shook her head. "No, he wasn't around that I recall."

"You were probably lucky. Old Billy boy was what my mother called a hell-raiser. He was one of the last of the miners. Spent his gold as fast as he dug it out. Story has it that he loved gambling and women." Kaley raised an eyebrow. "His exploits were well-known around town. He was nearly broke when he suffered a stroke. It was Lyle who took over running what was left of the family fortune."

"Looks like he did a pretty good job," Lori said.

Kaley nodded in agreement. "I worked for the man, so I know how driven he was." She paused. "I also went with him to visit his father. Old Billy Hutchinson never had a good word to say to his son."

Lori didn't want to get her hopes up that there was something redeeming about Lyle Hutchinson.

Nor did she want to know about any personal relationship her father might have had with Kaley.

She quickly brought herself back to the present. "Well, I didn't ask you to come in to reminisce about my childhood. I was wondering if you'd be interested in coming back here and being my property manager." When Kaley started to speak, Lori stopped her. "I'll double whatever my father paid you."

The woman looked shocked to say the least. "You want me to work for you?"

Lori shook her head. "No, I want you to work *with* me. You have a good business sense, or my father wouldn't have trusted you. The one thing my father didn't offer, I will. There's a place in this company for advancement. Seems the women employees have been overlooked."

Kaley laughed. "I'm sure your father is somewhere cursing your words."

For the first time in two days, Lori laughed. It felt good. "So what do you say, Kaley?"

"I hear around town that you have to stay a year before you get your inheritance. Will you leave after that?"

Lori thought about her sister and nephew. How easily they had adapted to their new life. How Lori herself had, but could she be around Jace knowing she'd never have a life with the man?

She looked at Kaley. "News does travel fast, but no, I want to stay. I care about the residents of Destiny and I want to see the town prosper. Maybe it's my Hutchinson blood, but I can't let the town die away. That's why I need your help. I want to bring more businesses here and create more jobs."

The pretty woman studied her. "I'd like that, too, but there's one thing you need to know about your father and me—"

Lori raised her hand to stop her. "No, I don't need to know anything about your personal life. Makes no difference to me. I only care that you want to work for Hutchinson Corporation." Lori mentioned a yearly salary and benefits.

"Looks like you've got me on your team."

Lori smiled. "How soon can you start?"

"Give me a week to get moved back and get my daughter, Heather, settled in school."

"Let me know if there's anything I can do to help." The phone began to ring. She said goodbye to Kaley then answered.

"Lori Hutchinson."

"Hello, Lori. It's Claire Keenan. I hope I'm not interrupting you."

"Of course not, Claire. What can I do for you?"

"I need a big favor."

Tim Keenan eyed his wife of nearly forty years as she hung up the phone. He knew when she was planning something.

"Okay, what's going on, Claire?"

She turned those gorgeous green eyes toward him. She was also trying to distract him. "Whatever do you mean?"

"I thought you were looking forward to your afternoon volunteering in Ellie's class."

"I was," she admitted. "But I think Lori might need it more. She has to miss teaching. Besides, they're starting the Christmas pageant practice. She's volunteered to help."

Tim arched an eyebrow. "I'd say she has plenty to do taking over for Lyle. What's the real reason?"

"Did you happen to notice Lori and Jace when they were here the other day?"

"You mean after they'd been stranded at the cabin overnight? It was hard not to."

She nodded. "There were several looks exchanged between them." She sighed. "That only proves what

I've known from the moment I saw them together. They would be so perfect for each other, if only they got the chance."

He drew his wife into his arms. Besides her big emerald-green eyes, her loving heart was what drew him to her. The feel of her close still stirred him. "Playing matchmaker again?"

"It's just a little nudge. I'm hoping maybe they'll catch a glimpse of each other when Jace picks up Cassie."

"Sounds good in theory, but what about Shelly Yeager?" He raised his eyes toward the ceiling. The suite on the second floor was still occupied by the ex-wife. "She's been all but shadowing Jace's every move."

A mischievous smile appeared on his bride's lovely face. "I have plans for her."

About four-thirty that afternoon, Jace pulled up at the school and parked his truck. He was tired. More like exhausted ever since Shelly had arrived in town. And she showed no sign of leaving anytime soon. Something was up with her, but he couldn't figure out what it was.

He climbed out of his truck and started toward the auditorium. The last thing he wanted to do was anger his ex so much she'd walk away with Cassie. That was the only reason he'd put up with her dogging him everywhere, including several trips to the construction site. She even showed up at his house most evenings.

He hoped that Paige Larkin would get things in order, and fast, so he could finally go to the judge and stop Shelly's daily threats to take their daughter back to Denver. He liked the fact that Cassie got to spend time with her mother, but only if Shelly didn't end up hurting her.

No, he didn't trust Shelly one bit.

He opened the large door and walked into the theater-style room. Up on stage were several kids along with some teachers giving directions. That was when he caught sight of the petite blonde that haunted his dreams.

He froze as he took in Lori. She had on dark slacks and a gray sweater that revealed her curves and small waist. He closed his eyes and could see her lying naked on the big bed, her hair spread out on the pillow, her arms open wide to him.

He released a long breath. As much as he'd tried to forget Lori, she wouldn't leave his head, or his heart. All right, he'd come to care about her, but that didn't mean he could do anything about it.

The rehearsal ended and his daughter came running toward him. "Daddy! Daddy!" She ran into his arms and hugged him. "Did you see me practice?"

He loved seeing her enthusiasm. "I sure did."

Jace glanced up to see Lori coming toward them. His heart thudded in his chest as his gaze ate her up. Those dark eyes, her bright smile. His attention went to her mouth as he recalled how sweet she tasted. He quickly pulled himself back to the present, realizing the direction of his thoughts.

"Hello, Lori."

Her gaze avoided his. "Hi, Jace."

"Looks like you've got your hands full here."

"I don't mind at all. I love working with the kids. I gladly volunteered."

Why couldn't he have met this woman years ago?

Cassie drew his attention back to her. "Daddy, did you know that our play is called *Destiny's First Christmas?* It's about Lori's great-great grandfather Raymond Hutchinson. On Christmas Eve, he was working in his mine, 'The Lucky Strike,' and found gold. That night he made a promise to his wife to build a town."

Jace looked at Lori. "Not exactly the traditional Christmas story."

She shrugged. "Not my choice, but the kids voted to do this one. Probably because of my father's passing."

"No, I'd say because of you. You've made a lot of positive changes in the last month."

She shook her head. "Just trying to bring Lyle Hutchinson's business practices into the new century."

Jace found he didn't want to leave, but he couldn't keep staring at her and remembering how it was to hold her in his arms and make love to her.

Cassie tugged on his coat sleeve. "Daddy, I forgot to tell you, Miss Lori invited us to her house for Thanksgiving."

That surprised Jace.

"She's invited a whole bunch of people. It's going to be a big party. Can we go?"

The last thing he wanted to do was disappoint his daughter. "We'll talk about it. Why don't you go get your books." After he sent Cassie off, he turned back to Lori. "Please, don't feel you have to invite us."

"I don't. I wanted to invite you and Cassie, Jace. Besides, practically everyone else in town is coming. The Keenans and Erin and her family. A lot of the bank employees." She glanced away, not meeting his eyes. "And I plan to extend the invitation to Toby and the construction crew. There's going to be a lot of people at the house. I did it mainly for Gina and Zack so they could meet everyone. So you and Cassie are welcome."

Jace wanted so badly to reach out and touch her. He told himself that would be enough, but that was a lie. He wanted her like he'd never wanted a woman ever. "If you're sure."

She frowned. "Of course. We're business partners."

And that was all they could be, he thought. "Speaking of that, you need to come by the site. We're down to doing the finish trim work and adding fixtures. I'd like your opinion on how things are turning out."

She nodded. "How soon to completion?"

"Toby estimates two weeks."

"That's great. Then we can concentrate on getting the spaces rented. I can help with that since I've hired a property manager, Kaley Sims. If it's okay with you, I'd like her to come by and talk with you about listing the loft apartments."

Jace smiled. "So she's handling the rest of your properties?"

Lori nodded. "Yes, she worked for my father years ago, so she knows what she's doing. I convinced her to come back to work with me."

"Good, I'm ready to get this done."

She stiffened. "And you don't have to deal with a rookie partner."

He cursed. "Ah, Lori, I didn't mean it that way. It's just with all the delays we've had, I'm ready to be finished. You're a great partner. I'd work with you again."

She looked surprised. "You would?"

"In a heartbeat." He took a step toward her. There was so much he wanted to say, but he had no right to make promises when he wasn't sure what was in store for him and Cassie. He was in the middle of a messy custody battle. "Just come by the site tomorrow."

Lori started to speak when he heard his name called. He turned around to find Shelly coming toward him. Great. He didn't need this.

He turned back around but Lori had walked off. He wanted to go after her, but he couldn't, not until he got things settled. He'd better do it quickly, or he might lose one of the best things that ever happened to him.

The next week, Lori did what Jace asked and came by the site. She'd purposely stayed away from the project to avoid the man, so she was amazed at the difference.

The chain-link fence had been removed. They'd already started to do some stone landscape. Planters and retaining walls had been built, and a parking area.

"I'm impressed," Kaley said as she got out of the car and looked at the two-story wood-and-stone structure.

So was Lori. "Wait until you see the inside."

They headed up the path to the double-door entry. The door swung open and Toby greeted them with a big smile.

"Well, it's about time you showed up again."

Lori returned the smile. "Well, I knew you were in charge so I didn't worry about things getting done. Hello, Toby."

After a greeting, the foreman turned to Kaley and grinned. "Well, well, who's your friend, Lori?"

Lori made the introductions. "Kaley Sims, Hutchinson Corp's property manager, Toby Edwards."

"So you're not just a pretty face," Toby said.

"And you'd be wise to remember that, Mr. Edwards."

She took a step toward him, grinning. "Now, let's go see if this place looks as good as Lori says it does."

"Well, damn. You're making my day brighter and brighter."

Lori was surprised to see these two throw off sparks. "Go on ahead and don't mind me," she called as the two took off, not paying any attention to her.

She stepped through the entry and gasped as she looked around. The dark hardwood floors had been laid and the massive fireplace completed. She eyed the golden tones of the stacked stones that ran all the way from the hearth to the open-beam ceiling.

Then her attention went to the main attraction of the huge room. The arching staircase. The new design was an improvement from the old as the natural wood banister wrapped around the edge of the first floor, showing off the mezzanine. A front desk had been built for a receptionist for the tenants.

"So how do you like it so far?"

Lori swung around to see Jace. "It looks wonderful."

Then she took in the man. In his usual uniform of faded jeans and a dark Henley shirt, Jace also wore a carpenter's tool belt around his waist. Somehow that even looked sexy.

"Am I disturbing your work?"

He grinned. "Darlin', you've been disturbing a lot more than my work since the minute I met you."

Jace was in a good mood today. Although Shelly had no plans to leave town, he had talked to Paige first thing that morning. He now had a court date and also a preliminary injunction so Shelly couldn't run off with Cassie. At least not until after the custody hearing back in Denver.

"We butted heads a lot, too," she said.

He leaned forward and breathed, "And there were times when we couldn't keep our hands off each other." Before she could do more than gasp, he took her hand. "Come on, I want to show you around."

"I need to go with Toby and Kaley."

He led her up the staircase. "I think Toby can handle the job." He took her into the first loft apartment, showing off ebony-colored hardwood floors. The open kitchen had dark-colored cabinets, but the counters weren't installed yet. "Here are some granite samples for the countertops and tile for the backsplash."

He watched her study the light-colored granite, with the earth-toned contrasting tile. The other was a glossy black, with white subway tile. "I like the earth tone," she told him.

He smiled. "My choice, too. The next stop is the bathroom." He led her across the main living space, where the floor-to-ceiling windows stopped her.

"Oh, Jace. This is a wonderful view."

He stood behind her, careful not to touch her as they glanced out the window at the San Juan Mountains. He worked hard to concentrate on the snow-filled creases in the rock formations and evergreen trees dotting the landscape. "It's almost as beautiful as the view from the cabin."

She glanced up at him and he saw the longing in her dark eyes. "It was lovely there, wasn't it?"

"You were even more beautiful, Lori."

She shook her head. "Don't, Jace. We decided that we shouldn't be involved."

"What if I can't stay away from you?"

Lori closed her eyes. She didn't want to hope and be

hurt in the end. Then his mouth closed over hers and she lost all reasonable thoughts. With a whimper of need she moved her hands up his chest and around his neck and gave in to the feelings.

He broke off the kiss. "I've missed you, Lori. I missed holding you, touching you, kissing you."

"Jace..."

His mouth found hers again and again.

Finally the sound of voices broke them apart. His gaze searched her face. "Lucky for you we're not alone. I'm pretty close to losing control." He sighed. "And with you, Lorelei Hutchinson, that happens every time I get close." He pulled her against him so there was no doubt. "Please, say you'll come by the house tonight. There are so many things I want to tell you."

Lori wanted to hope that everything would work out with Jace. Yet, still Shelly Yeager lingered in town. The last thing Lori wanted was to jeopardize Jace getting custody of his daughter.

Yet, she wanted them both—Jace and Cassie—in her life. Question was, was she ready to fight for what she wanted? Yes. "What time?"

CHAPTER ELEVEN

AT THE site, Jace kept checking his watch, but it was only two o'clock. He had three more hours before he could call it a day and see Lori again.

He was crazy to add any more complications to his life, but he hadn't been able to get her out of his head. For weeks, he'd tried to deny his feelings, tried to convince himself that he didn't care about Lori, but he did care. A lot.

He hadn't been able to forget her or what happened between them. The night at the cabin, what they'd shared, made him think it was possible to have a relationship again. Tonight, when she came by the house, he planned to tell her. He only hoped she could be patient and hang in there a little while longer, until this custody mess was finally straightened out.

"Hey, are you listening?"

Jace turned toward his friend Justin Hilliard. "Sorry, what did you say?"

Justin smiled. "Seems you have something or someone else on your mind."

"Yeah, I do. But I can't do anything about it right now so I'd rather not talk about it."

"I understand. If you need a friend to talk later, I'm your guy. I'll even buy the beer."

Justin was the one who'd brought him to Destiny after Yeager Construction tanked following his divorce. He'd always be grateful. "I appreciate that."

His friend nodded. "Now, tell me when can I move in?" He motioned around the office space on the main floor at the Mountain Heritage complex.

"Is next week soon enough?"

"Great. I'll have Morgan go shopping for office furniture. And I'll need a loft apartment upstairs for out-of-town clients. Is there someone handling the loft rentals?"

Jace nodded. "Kaley Sims. I'll have her get in touch with you to negotiate the lease."

"Good. I'm available all this week." Justin studied Jace. "So what are your plans for your next project?"

"Not sure." That much was true. "I've been so wrapped up in getting this project completed, I haven't thought that far ahead." He had Lori on his mind. "I know I'd like to stay here, of course, but until I get this custody mess taken care of, I'm still in limbo."

"Like I said, let me know if I can help." Justin slapped him on the back. "Just don't let Shelly get away with anything."

"Believe me, I won't." She'd taken him to the cleaners once. No more. "Besides, Paige is handling it all for me."

Justin nodded. "Yeah, my sister-in-law is one of the best. She'll do everything she can to straighten this out."

God, he hoped so. Jace wanted nothing more than to end Shelly's threats.

They walked out of the office space and Justin said, "If you think you'd be ready to start another project by March, let me know."

Jace stopped. He was definitely interested. "What kind of project?"

"It's an idea I've had in the works awhile. I waited until I had the right partner in place, and now, it's in the designing stages."

Jace was more than intrigued. "So what is it?"

"A mountain bike racing school and trails. I bought several acres of land about five miles outside of town and plan to build a track. I'm bringing in a pro racer, Ryan Donnelly, to design it."

"I don't do landscaping."

Justin smiled. "I know. I want your company to handle the structures, cabins to house the students and instructors, including a main building to serve meals and a pro shop."

They walked through the main area of the building as Justin continued. "Eventually, I hope to work with Ryan to design bikes. I want the plant to be right here in Destiny." Justin arched an eyebrow. "I want you to handle it all, Jace."

This was a dream come true. "And I want the project, Justin. By early spring I could have the subs and crew in place to start." He worked to hold in his excitement. "But I'll need the plans by February."

Justin nodded. "Shouldn't be a problem."

Now if his personal life straightened out by then. With this new project he could move forward, make a fresh start. He thought about Lori. He couldn't wait to tell her. Tonight. This could be their new beginning.

* * *

By six o'clock, Lori had gathered her things and left the office. She went home, showered and changed into a nice pair of slacks and white angora sweater. Excited about spending the evening with Jace, she took extra time with her clothes and makeup.

Her pulse raced as she realized how badly she wanted to be with him. He was everything she'd ever dreamed the man she loved could be. Handsome, caring and a good father. What woman wouldn't dream about forever with him?

She walked back into the connecting bedroom to find Gina.

"Sorry, Lori, I didn't mean to disturb you. I know you plan to go out tonight."

"You never could disturb me," Lori assured her sister. "Is something wrong?"

Gina smiled. "No. For the first time in a very long time, everything is going right." She went to her sister. "Thanks to you. I never thought I could feel this happy again. And Zack…"

Lori hugged her, praying that continued. That Eric would leave them alone. "We're family, Gina. Besides, it's Lyle's money."

"No, you were there for us long before you inherited the Hutchinson money. You were always there for me."

"You're my sister and Zack is my nephew. Where else would I be?"

"Having a life?" Gina said. "And finding someone special."

Lori wanted to believe. "I think that has already happened."

Her sister smiled. "If Jace Yeager is as smart as I think he is, he'll snatch you up."

Of course, Lori hoped that tonight the man would make some kind of commitment, but she also knew he had to tread cautiously. They both did. "Let's just see what happens."

About eight o'clock that evening, Jace had put Cassie to bed, but she made him promise when Lori got there she would come up to say good-night. He was happy that his daughter got along with her.

He smiled, knowing he'd have Lori all to himself for the rest of the evening. There were so many things he wanted to tell Lori tonight. He wanted them to move ahead together.

He checked on the dinners he'd picked up from the Silver Spoon. Then he took the wine out of the refrigerator and got two glasses from the cupboard. He looked around his half-finished kitchen.

Okay, this place had been neglected too long. It was going to be his top priority. He could probably make some headway by Christmas. Thanksgiving at the Hutchinson house, and maybe, Christmas dinner at the Yeager house. That would be his goal.

He hoped to have the rest of his life in order by then, too. His daughter with him and Lori with them. He'd made a start with the custody hearing.

He saw the flash of headlights as a car pulled into the drive. His heart began to pound when he saw Lori climb out and walk up the steps to the back porch. He opened the door and greeted her with a smile.

"Hi, there."

She smiled. "Hi. Sorry I'm late."

Jace drew her into his arms because he couldn't go any longer without touching her, holding her. "Well, you're here now and that's all that matters. I missed you." He kissed her, a slow but intense meeting of their mouths, only making him hungry for more.

He didn't want to let go of her, but he promised himself he'd go slow. He tore his mouth away. "Maybe we should dial it down a little." He tugged at her heavy coat. "At least until I feed you."

She smiled. "I am a little hungry." She brushed her hair back and looked around. "Where's Cassie?"

"I'm losing out to the kid, huh? She's upstairs in bed." He led her into the kitchen. "I told her you'd come up and say good-night. I hope you don't mind."

"Of course not." Lori started off, but he brought her back to him for another intense kiss. "Just remember you're mine for the rest of the night."

"I'll be right back."

Jace's heart pounded as he watched the cute sway of her hips as she walked out of the kitchen and up the stairs.

He sighed and worked to get it together. "You got it bad, Yeager." He turned down the lights, and put on some music from the sound system, then lit the candles on the table. Back at the kitchen counter, he opened the chilled bottle of wine and filled the glasses at the two place settings.

It was impossible not to remember their dinner together at the cabin. He wanted nothing more than to have a repeat of that night. But that couldn't happen. Not with Cassie here. He blew out a breath. There was no doubt in his mind, they'd be together again. And soon.

Smiling, Lori walked down the steps and it turned into a grin when she saw Jace in the kitchen. "That's what I like about you, Yeager. You're just not a handsome face, you're domestic, too."

Jace turned around and tossed her a sexy smile. "I can be whatever you want."

Her heart shot off racing. *How about the man who loves me?* she asked silently as he came to her and drew her against him. She wanted nothing more than to stay wrapped in his arms, to close out the rest of the world.

She looked up at him. "Kiss me, Jace."

"My pleasure, ma'am." He lowered his head, brushing her mouth with his. She opened for him, but he was a little more playful and took nibbling bites out of her bottom lip.

With her whimper of need, he captured her mouth in a searing kiss. By the time he pulled back, her knees were weak and she had trouble catching her breath. "Wow."

He raised an eyebrow. "That was just an appetizer." He stepped back. "But before I go back to sampling you again, we better eat."

She was a little disappointed, but knew it was better to slow things down a little. She accepted the wine he offered her.

She sipped it and let the sweet taste linger in her mouth. She caught Jace watching her and smiled, then took another sip. "How was your day at the site?"

"Oh, I meant to tell you that Justin stopped by. Besides the office space, he wants to lease a loft apartment. I gave him Kaley's number."

"Good." She raised her glass. "The first of many, I hope."

"You and me both. Justin might want more than one apartment. I'm hoping Kaley can convince him of that.

Maybe give him a few incentives like a six-month reduction in the rent."

"That sounds good. Is that usually done in real estate?"

He nodded. "All the time." He walked her to the table and sat her down, then began filling their plates with roast chicken and mashed potatoes. "The Silver Spoon's Thursday night special."

Lori took a bite. "It's very good."

"Come spring," he began, "I'll barbecue us some steaks on the grill. That's my specialty."

She paused, her fork to her mouth. He was talking about the future. "I'd like that."

He winked and took a bite of food as they continued to talk about Mountain Heritage, then he told her about Justin's offer for the racing bike school.

"Oh, Jace, you have to be excited about that."

Jace wanted to be, but there were still problems looming overhead. Like getting permanent custody of his daughter. He prayed that Paige could pull this off. "There's still a lot to work out."

Lori nodded.

He didn't want to talk about it right now. This was just for them. No troubles, no worries, just them. Yet, he knew he couldn't make her any promises. He'd never thought he'd find someone like Lori, someone he'd want to dream about a future together.

The meal finished, they carried the dishes to the sink and left them. He offered her coffee, but she refused it.

A soft ballad came on the radio. He drew her into his arms and began slowly dancing her around the kitchen and into the family room, where soft flames in the fireplace added to the mood. He placed his hands against her back, pulling his swaying body against hers. "I want you, Lori," he whispered. "Never have I wanted a woman as much as you." His lips trailed along her jaw, feeling her shiver. He finally reached his destination. "Never." He closed his mouth over hers, and pushed his tongue inside tasting her, stroking her.

His hands were busy, too, reaching under her sweater, cupping her breasts.

"Jace," she moaned. "Please."

"I definitely want to please you." He kissed her again and was quickly getting to the point of no return.

"Well, well. Isn't this cozy?"

Jace jerked back and caught sight of Shelly standing in the doorway. He immediately turned Lori away from view. "What are you doing here?"

The tall brunette pushed away from the doorjamb and walked into the room as if she had every right to be there.

"Since no one was answering the phone, I came to see what the problem was." She gave Lori a once-over. "Now I know why. You're having a little party here while our daughter is asleep upstairs."

"That's my business, Shelly. And that doesn't give you the right to come into my house without an invitation. And you weren't invited."

"I don't need to be. I have custody of Cassie." She shot an angry look at Lori. "In fact I think I should remove her from here right now."

Lori gasped.

Jace got angry. "I wouldn't try it, Shelly."

"Try and stop me."

When she started to move past him, Jace stepped in

front of her. "You can't. I have an injunction that says she stays with me until the court hearing."

She glared. "I know. I got served today."

So that was why she showed up. "And this should be settled in court."

"I want my daughter. Now!"

"Stop it! Mommy, Daddy, don't fight!"

They all turned and saw Cassie standing at the bottom of the stairs.

Lori wanted to go to the child, but it wasn't her place.

Jace took over and went to his daughter's side. "Oh, baby. I'm sorry we woke you."

"You and Mommy were fighting again?"

"I'm sorry. We're trying to work something out and we got a little loud."

"Please, I don't want you to fight anymore."

Jace looked at Lori. "Will you take Cassie back to her room?" With her nod, he glanced down at his daughter. "I'll be up in a minute."

Shelly came over and kissed her daughter and sent her along.

Once they were alone, Jace took Shelly's arm and walked her out to the utility room. "I'm not going to let you come here and upset Cassie like that."

"You're just mad because I interrupted your rendezvous with little Miss Heiress."

"Leave Lori out of this. She's a respectable person in this town."

"And you're sleeping with her."

Jace had to hold his temper. "We've done nothing wrong. If you think so, then talk to the judge. I'll see you in court, Shelly."

Shelly's face reddened in anger. "Don't think you've

won, Jace Yeager. This is not going to end in your favor."

He held on to his temper. "Why, Shelly? Why are we arguing about this? You know Cassie is better off here. She's made friends and is doing great in school. I have a job that has me home every night." He stopped in front of the woman he once loved, but now he only felt sorry for. "When you get married, Shelly, I will let you see her anytime you want."

"That might not happen. So the game plan will change."

"Oh, Cassie."

Lori cradled the small form against her as they sat on the bed. She inhaled the soft powdery smell and realized how much Cassie had come to mean to her. She could easily become addicted to this nightly ritual.

She silently cursed Shelly Yeager. How could anyone drag a child into this mess? "I wish I could make it better, sweetheart."

The child's lip quivered as she looked up. "Nobody can. They always fight."

"I'm sorry. That doesn't mean they don't love you. They just have to work out what's best for you."

A tear ran down the girl's cheek. "I want to live here with Daddy, but if I do, Mommy will go away." Cassie's big blue eyes looked up at her, and Lori could feel her pain. "And she's gonna forget about me." She started to sob and Lori drew her into a tight embrace.

"Oh, sweetheart, have you told your father how you feel?"

The child pulled back, looking panicked. "No! I don't

want them to fight anymore." Her face crumpled again. "So please don't tell Daddy."

"Don't tell me what?"

They both looked toward the door to see Jace. "Nothing." Cassie wiped her eyes. "I'm just talking to Miss Lori."

Lori got up and Jace sat down to face his daughter. "Sweetheart, I'm sorry."

The little girl suddenly collapsed into her father's arms. Lori backed out of the room, not wanting to intrude. She realized right away how much this custody battle had affected the child.

And Cassie had to come first.

Lori couldn't help but wonder if they could get through this situation unscathed, or would Shelly follow through on her threats?

Lori's chest tightened. She'd never forget the heartache she'd felt when she had to leave her childhood home. Her father standing on the porch. That had been the last time she'd ever seen Lyle Hutchinson. Oh, God. She couldn't let that happen to this little girl. No matter what it cost her.

Cassie finally went to sleep and Jace walked out into the hall, but he didn't go downstairs yet. Heartsick over his daughter's distress, he needed some time to pull himself together. Cassie had been dealing with problems he and her mother had caused. No child should have to choose which parent to love, which parent to be loyal to.

He sighed, knowing he had to do something about it.

Jace made his way down the steps and found Lori standing in the kitchen. He went to her and pulled her into a tight embrace. "I guess we should talk." He released her and walked around the kitchen in a daze. "You want something to drink?"

"No," she said. "Is Cassie asleep?"

He nodded, feeling the rush of emotions as he went and poured himself a glass. "I'm so angry at Shelly for starting all this."

"Divorce isn't easy for anyone, kids especially." Lori closed her eyes momentarily. "Cassie needs constant re-assurance that her daddy's going to be around."

Jace tried to draw a breath, but it was hard. "And I have been right here for her. I've been doing everything possible to keep her with me."

He immediately realized the harshness of his words. "I'm sorry, Lori, that you had to witness this." He pulled her close, grateful that she didn't resist. "I'm so frus-trated." He held her tightly. "I've worked so hard to have a good relationship with my daughter."

Lori pulled back, knowing there wasn't any sim-ple solution. "I know, but Cassie is still caught in the middle."

"This is all a game to Shelly."

It wasn't for the rest of the people involved. "Well, she is here and you have to deal with her. For Cassie's sake."

"I've been doing that," he told her. "Paige has got-ten a court date for a custody hearing with a judge in Denver."

Lori was surprised by Jace's news. "That's good. When?"

"This coming Monday."

She told herself not to react, not to be hurt that he hadn't said anything before now. "So soon?"

He studied her with those intense blue eyes. "If we

don't do it now, the holidays are coming up. It could be delayed until January. By then Shelly might have taken Cassie to Europe." He paused. "I was going to tell you about it tonight."

That didn't take away the pain of his leaving. "How long will you be gone?"

"Probably just a few days. Don't worry, Toby has the project under control."

She shook her head. "You think I'm concerned about that when Cassie's future is in jeopardy?"

He shook his head. "Of course not, Lori. I know you care about her."

"I care about both of you. I want this to work, because she should be with you."

He looked at her, his blue eyes intense. "I'm going to see that happens no matter what the judge's decision is."

Lori felt her heart skip a beat. "Does that mean you'll move back to Denver?"

He nodded slowly. "I hope there's another way. I don't want to leave here, but if that's the end result of this hearing…there's no choice."

He might be going away, she thought, fighting tears. "Cassie's your daughter, so of course you have to go there. You have to fight for her."

"I care about you, Lori. A lot. I know you have a year commitment here, or I'd ask—"

"Then don't, Jace," she interrupted, forcing a smile. "Neither one of us is ready to jump into a relationship. Like you said, we both have other commitments."

His gaze locked on hers. "I want to say the hell with all of Shelly's games, but I can't. Bottom line is, I can't give you any promises."

And she couldn't beg him to. There was too much

at stake here. Most importantly, a little girl. Lori had once been that little girl whose father let her go. Cassie deserved better.

Lori couldn't meet his eyes. She fisted her hands so he wouldn't see her shaking. "It's too soon to make plans when we don't know the future."

"Is it? What about what happened between us at the cabin? Unless it didn't mean anything to you."

She swallowed hard. "Of course it did." She'd always have those incredible memories. "It was…special."

"Seems not as special for you as it was for me."

She had to get away from him. "I'm sorry, Jace. I need to go. I hope everything works out for you and Cassie." She headed toward the door and paused. She took one last look at the man she loved. "Goodbye, Jace."

When he didn't say anything to stop her, she hurried out the door and got into her car. Starting the engine, she headed for the highway. He hadn't even asked her to wait it out. Tears filled her eyes, blurring her vision, until she had to stop.

She cried for her loss, for letting this between her and Jace to get this far. She never should have let herself fall in love with this wonderful man. A man she couldn't have. She'd finally opened herself and let love in, only to be hurt again.

She brushed away more tears, praying that the pain would stop. That the loneliness would go away soon. This was what she got for starting to dream of that happy ending.

The only consolation was she wouldn't let another little girl go through the misery she had. She would never prevent Jace from having his daughter.

CHAPTER TWELVE

THAT night, sleep eluded Lori.

When she'd gotten home earlier she'd made up an excuse to go to her room. She hadn't been in the mood to talk about her evening with Jace. Not even with Gina. And what good would it do? Neither one of them had a choice in the matter. There was nothing to say except they couldn't be together.

But after several hours of tossing and turning, she got out of bed. Restless, she ended up wandering around the big house. She checked in on her sleeping nephew and pulled the covers around him, knowing Jace would do the same thing with Cassie. Smiling, she realized that had been one of the reasons she'd fallen in love with the man. His relationship with his daughter was part of that. She would miss them both so much if they couldn't come back here. What were Jace's chances of getting custody? Probably slim.

Lori walked down the hall, passing her childhood bedroom. She stopped, wanting nothing more than to shake the feeling of abandonment she'd had since her mother took her away from here.

She slipped inside, waiting as the moonlight coming through the window lit her path to the canopy bed.

Loneliness swept through her as more memories flooded back. Her absent father had been too busy for her. He'd been too busy making money and that meant he hadn't been home much.

Then long-forgotten images flashed though her mind. There had been some happy times. She remembered sitting at the dinner table, hearing her parents' laughter. Lyle wasn't very demonstrative, but she would always cherish the time he'd spent with her. Guess he'd been as loving as he was able to be.

She smiled, thinking of those good-night kisses she would treasure. She brushed away a tear as she turned on a bedside lamp and caught sight of the stuffed animals lined up on the windowsill.

Another memory hit her. "Oh, Daddy, you gave me all of these."

"Lorelei?"

Lori turned to find Maggie standing in the doorway. She was wearing her robe over a long gown. "Oh, Maggie, did I wake you?"

The housekeeper walked in. "No, I was up getting something to drink. This old house has a lot creaks and I know them all. When I heard someone walking around, I thought it might be the boy." The older woman eyed the stuffed animals. "Land sakes, child. You can't keep coming in here and getting all sad."

"No, Maggie. Really, I'm fine." She smiled as she wiped away the tears and held out one of her childhood animals. "Look. I remembered that Dad bought this for me." She reached for another. "He bought these, too." She gathered all them in her arms.

Maggie smiled. "I'm glad you remember those times."

And so much more. "Every time he went on a business trip, he came home with a toy for me." Another memory. "And when he was home he would come into my bedroom and kiss me good-night." Tears flooded her eyes. "He loved me, Maggie."

"Of course he loved you. You were his little girl, his pride and joy."

"Then why, Maggie? Why didn't he want me?"

The housekeeper shook her head. "It wasn't that." She hesitated, then said, "You never knew your grandfather Billy. If you had you might understand your father better."

"Kaley Sims mentioned him. She said he'd gone into a nursing home after a stroke."

Maggie made a huffing sound. "It was probably better than he deserved. That man was a terrible example as a parent. What Lyle went through as a child was... Let's just say, Billy wasn't much of a human being, so I won't go into his fathering skills."

"Wouldn't that make Lyle a better one?"

Maggie took hold of Lori's hands and they sank down to sit on the window seat. "I believe your dad did the best he could, honey. When Billy nearly lost all the family money, and that included the bank, this town almost didn't survive. Your father spent a lot of years rebuilding the family wealth, and trying to get Billy's approval."

Maggie continued, "Your mother didn't like being neglected, either. She wanted all of her husband's attention. I think she left hoping Lyle would come after both of you. Your father took it as another rejection and just shut down."

Lori had no doubt Jocelyn Hutchinson would do that to get attention. "But he had a daughter who loved him."

Maggie looked sad. "I know. I wish I had a better answer for you. I recall a few phone conversations between your mother and father. He asked Jocelyn to bring you here. She refused. When your mother remarried, he told me that you'd do better without him."

She felt a spark of hope. "He wanted me to come back here?"

Maggie nodded. "For Christmas that first year. He told me once how much you loved the tree lights in the town square."

A tear ran down Lori's cheek. She had no idea he would remember.

Maggie pulled her into a comforting embrace. "He kept this room the same, hoping to have you back here. So keep hanging on to the good memories, child. I know that was what your father did."

Lori pulled back. "How can I?"

The housekeeper brushed back Lori's hair. "Because your father knew he caused enough pain over the years." Maggie smiled through her own tears. "Think about it, Lorelei. Your father finally brought you home. No mistaking, he wanted you here."

Lori began to sob over the lost years that father and daughter would never get back. The tears were cleansing, and she had some answers.

"Lori?"

Lori looked at the open door to find her sister. "Oh, Gina. Sorry, did we wake you?"

"I was just checking on Zack."

Maggie hugged them both. "Share with your sister, Lorelei. It will get better each time." The older woman left.

"Should I be worried?" Gina asked once they were alone.

"Not any longer. I've learned a lot about my father. Lyle wasn't perfect, but he loved me in his way." Lori went on to explain about her discovery.

"I'm so glad," Gina agreed. "Every child needs those good memories." She hesitated. "That's what I hope for Zack."

"He'll have those good memories. I promise," Lori told her, thinking about Cassie, too.

Lori never wanted that child to go through what she had. So that meant she had to accept it. Accept she might not be able to have Jace Yeager.

Gina's voice broke into her thoughts.

Lori looked at her. "What?"

"Something else is bothering you. Would it have anything to do with Jace? Did you two have a fight?" Gina asked, frowning. "Oh, no, it's his ex-wife causing trouble, isn't it?"

Lori agreed. "Jace has to go back to Denver for the custody case. If he loses, he wants to live close by Cassie. That means he'll have to move back there."

"I wish I could hate the guy, but he's a great father." Gina suddenly grinned. "So move to Denver."

Lori would in a minute. "I can't until I fulfill Lyle's will. If I leave before the year is up, the town might not survive."

"That doesn't mean you can't go visit Jace for long weekends."

She could go for that. Would Jace want a long-distance relationship? "He hasn't asked me."

Gina jumped up. "Of course he hasn't. He doesn't know anything yet. Lori, I believe Jace Yeager loves you. And if he can, he'll do whatever it takes to get Cassie and come back here to you."

Lori was heartened with her sister's enthusiasm. "You sure seem to have a better outlook toward men these days."

Her sister shrugged. "Maybe they aren't all jerks like Eric. I've met a few here in town that seem really nice. Now, that doesn't mean I want to get involved with any of them. I'm happy concentrating on raising Zack."

If one good thing came out of returning to Destiny it was helping Gina and Zack have a chance at a new life. "And we have each other."

"Always." Gina nodded. "Now, we need something to do to keep you busy." She looked around what once had been a little girl's room. "This entire house, at the very least, needs a fresh coat of paint. We should redecorate the master suite, so you can move in there."

Lori knew Gina was trying to distract her, and she loved her for it. "The place is a little big for us, don't you think?"

"Of course it is. It's a mansion."

Lori turned to her sister. "What about moving into a smaller place?"

Her sister blinked. "Are you going to sell this house?"

She shook her head. "We have to live here for now. I think maybe Hutchinson House can be rented out for weddings and parties and the proceeds could go to the town." She couldn't help but wonder if Jace and Cassie would be living here in Destiny, too. "What do you think of that?"

"Lori, I think that's a wonderful idea." She hesitated.

"And you've been generous to Zack and me. But I feel I need to contribute, too. I know this mess with Eric still has me frightened, but thanks to you, I've felt safer than I have for years."

"I'm glad." Lori had already checked on her ex-brother-in-law. She'd contacted the police detective on the case. Eric had been staying with his family in Colorado Springs.

"I need a job," Gina blurted out. "It's not that I'm not grateful to you for everything, but I want to be more independent. I have to set a good example for my son. I don't want him to think he has an easy ride in life."

Lori hugged her, knowing the hell she'd gone through for years. "So you want a job. I just happen to have one."

Her sister frowned. "Lori, you can't make up a job for me."

"I hate to tell you, sis, but most of the people in Destiny work for Hutchinson Corp. And honestly, I'm not making this job up. Kaley Sims is going to advertise the Mountain Heritage spaces to rent and she needs to stage them. You're the perfect decorator to do it. So what do you say?"

Gina gave her a big smile. "I say, when do I start?"

"I'll talk to Kaley in the morning." Lori smiled, but inside she was hurting. Everyone was moving forward, but she couldn't, not knowing what her future held. "Come on, we both need to get some sleep."

They walked back to their rooms. Lori climbed in bed just as her cell phone rang. She reached for it off her nightstand.

She glanced at the familiar caller ID. "Jace," she answered. "Is something wrong?"

"No, nothing's wrong. I'm sorry I called so late. I just wanted to let you know that Cassie and I are leaving."

She already knew that. "When?"

"First thing in the morning."

So soon.

Jace went on. "Toby has everything under control at the site. There are only a few finishing touches before the last walk through. Kaley Sims is now handling the Heritage project. I'll pass on the news to her."

"I appreciate that," she told him. "Is there anything else?"

Lori begged silently that he'd ask her to wait for him. At least tell her he cared.

"I hated the way we left things last night," he finally said. "God, Lori, I wish it could be different."

She swallowed back the lump in her throat. "You're doing what's right, Jace."

"I know. I just needed to hear your voice," he told her and there was a long pause. "Goodbye, Lori." Then he hung up.

The silence was deafening. She lay back in her bed, pulling up the covers to protect her from the loneliness. It didn't help. Nothing would help but Jace.

"Why are you dead set on making my life hell?" Jace demanded as he stepped through the door into his one-time Denver home the next day. Something else that Shelly had gotten from their divorce.

He glanced around the spacious entry of the re-furbished Victorian. The hardwood floors he'd refin-ished himself, along with the plaster on the walls. He stopped the search when unpleasant memories of his marriage hit him. He turned back to Shelly to see her stubborn look.

"You're the one who had me served with papers."

"Because you came to Destiny and disrupted Cassie's life. I'm done with your games, Shelly. It's time we settle this."

"Well, that's too bad." She strolled across the room to the three windows that overlooked the street. "I'm Cassie's mother, and after today, the judge will see that I should have our child permanently. Where is our daughter?"

"She's in good hands." Paige had offered to watch her back at the hotel while he tried to straighten out a few things. "She's with Paige Larkin."

Shelly frowned. "So what are you willing to give up to spend time with Cassie? Your little girlfriend?"

"I'm not willing to give up anything. Besides, my personal life is none of your business." He prayed he still had one. Not only couldn't he make any promises to Lori, but he also couldn't even tell her his feelings.

"It is if you're living with her with our child. Maybe the judge should know, too."

"Stop with the threats, Shelly." He walked toward the front door. He opened the door and glanced out at the man on the porch and motioned to him to come inside.

Shelly looked at Jace suspiciously. "What are you up to?"

"You're the one who plays games, Shelly. So if I can't talk any sense into you, maybe he can." He prayed that all his hard work would pay off and not backfire in his face.

"Don't push me, Jace. You'll only lose." She gasped as Edmund Layfield stepped through the front door.

The distinguished gentleman was in his early fifties. He was dressed in a business suit and had thick gray hair. Jace had spent only an hour with the man and realized that he truly loved Shelly. Edmund also liked Cassie, but didn't particularly want to raise another child full-time, since his kids were grown.

Shelly came out of her trance. "Edmund, what are you doing here?"

"I came to see you, love. And I'm not leaving here until I convince you that we're meant to be together." He reached out and pulled her into his arms. That was when Jace made his exit.

For the first time in days, he realized that maybe they could come to a compromise. They all might get what they wanted. His thoughts turned to Lori. And that included him.

Tim parked the small SUV next to several other cars at Hutchinson House. It was Thanksgiving and half the town had been invited to have dinner here.

"Are you okay with this?" he asked Claire.

She smiled. "Normally no, but I can share this special day with Lori and Gina. It's important they feel a part of Destiny." She sighed. "Besides, all the kids and grandkids will be here." She smiled. "It's all about family being together. If only we would hear from Jace. You'd think our own daughter could give us some information."

He reached across the car and took his wife's hand. "Come on, Claire, you know Paige is Jace's lawyer."

"I know, I know, client/lawyer confidentiality." She frowned. "But I've seen how sad Lori is. If two people should be together, it's them."

"And if it's meant to be it will work out."

"I've been praying so hard for that."

It had been a week, and not a word from Jace. Lori had tried to stay positive—after all, it was Thanksgiving.

She looked around the festive dining room. The long table could seat twenty. There were two other tables set up in the entry to seat another twenty. And with the kids' table in the sunroom off the kitchen, everyone would have a place.

Maggie had cooked three turkeys and with Claire's two baked hams and many side dishes from everyone, she couldn't imagine not having enough food.

"Miss Hutchinson."

Lori turned to see Mac Burleson. "Mac, I asked you to call me Lori."

"Doesn't seem right," he told her.

"It seems very right to me. Unless you don't consider me a friend."

His eyes rounded. "You're a very good friend. I'm so grateful—"

"You did it," she interrupted. "You proved yourself at every job you've taken on. You make us all proud."

"Thank you...Lori." He smiled. "Is there anything else you want me to do?"

Some laughing kids ran by, chasing each other. She smiled at their antics. Her father would probably hate this. "Enjoy today. We have a lot to be thankful for." She knew she was so lucky, but two important people weren't here to share it with her.

"Hurry, Daddy, we're gonna be late for Thanksgiving."

Jace smiled, but it didn't relax him as he drove his

truck down First Street toward Hutchinson House. "We'll get there, sweetheart."

He glanced toward the backseat where his daughter was strapped in. They'd been gone a week, having stayed in Denver longer than planned. With the lawyers' help, they'd worked out the custody issue without a judge having to make the decision.

And in the end, it had been Cassie who'd told her mother that she wanted to live in Destiny with her daddy and all her friends and her horse. Shelly finally agreed, but wanted visitation in the summers and holidays. So Jace became the custodial parent. There was only one other thing that could make him happier. Lori.

"I just can't wait to see Ellie and Mrs. K. and Miss Lori, to tell everybody that I get to live here and be in the Christmas pageant."

"I can't wait, either," he told his daughter, praying that a certain pretty blonde felt the same about the news.

"Daddy, are you gonna ask Miss Lori today?"

On the flight home, Jace had told her how he felt about Lori and about her being a part of their lives. That was crazy, considering he hadn't even talked with Lori yet.

"Not sure. There's going to be a lot of people there today. It might have to wait, so you have to keep it a secret, okay?"

"Okay, but could I tell Ellie about Mommy's wedding? And that I'm going to go visit a real castle this summer?"

He smiled. "Yes, about the wedding, but the castle is only going to happen if I can get time off work." He was definitely going with her. He hoped Lori could go, too.

His heart began to race as he pulled up and climbed

out of the truck. He grabbed the wine and hurried after his daughter to the front door.

When they rang the bell, the door opened and Zack poked his head out. "Hi, Cassie. Hi, Mr. Jace."

"Hi, Zack. We came for Thanksgiving."

The boy grinned and opened the door wider and allowed them into the entryway filled with a long table decorated with colorful flowers and a paper turkey centerpiece. Cassie took off before he could stop her.

Jace was soon greeted by Justin and Morgan, then Tim Keenan and Paige and Reed Larkin joined them. He wanted to join in the conversation, but his eyes kept searching for a glimpse of Lori.

"She's in the kitchen."

He glanced at Justin. "Who?"

"As if you two are fooling anyone," his friend said. "You need to go to Lori before she comes out here and sees you."

Jace nodded and took off toward the kitchen. He knew his way around this house, but there were so many people here it was hard to maneuver. How was he going to be able to get her alone?

He saw Maggie at the counter. Without asking anything, she nodded toward the sunroom. He walked there as kids ran past him. Okay, so they weren't going to have any privacy.

Then he saw her and everyone else seemed to disappear from view. She was seated on the floor with some of the little kids. She was holding a toddler who'd been crying, and she managed to turn the tears into a smile before the child wandered off. Jace fell in love with her all over again.

Lori stood. Dressed in black slacks and a soft blue

sweater he ached to pull her close and just hold her. Tell her how much he'd missed her. How much he wanted her...

She finally turned in his direction. Her hair was in an array of curls that danced around her pretty face. Her chocolate eyes locked on his. "You're back."

That was a dumb thing to say, Lori thought as she looked up at Jace. So much for cool and calm.

"Hello, Lori."

"Hi, Jace." She didn't take a step toward him. "Is Cassie with you? Please tell me that she's with you."

He beamed. "Yes, she is." He glanced around. "I need to talk to you. There are so many things I have to tell you."

Just then Maggie broke in. "Sorry to interrupt but dinner is on the table. And Tim Keenan is ready to say the blessing."

Lori glanced back at Jace. "I'm sorry. Can we talk later?" Without waiting for an answer, Lori took off and headed toward the front of the house. She felt Jace following behind her as they reached the dining room. Hopeful, she added an extra place at the table for him.

She smiled at all her family and the new friends she was sharing today with. That included Jace and Cassie.

It grew quiet and someone handed her a champagne glass. "First of all, Gina, Zack and I want to thank you all for coming today. I hope this is the first of many visits to Hutchinson House. I want you all to feel welcome, so you'll come back here." She raised her glass. "To friends, and to Destiny." After everyone took a drink, she had Tim Keenan say the blessing.

The group broke up, and mothers went off to fill

their children's plates and settle them in the sunroom. Maggie stood by, watching for any emergencies. Lori ended up back at the head table, while Gina was seated at the entry table. Somehow Jace was seated at her table, but at the opposite end. Every so often, he'd smile at her.

She kept telling herself in a few hours they could be alone. After dinner, she went into the kitchen to check on dessert and finally saw Cassie.

"Miss Lori." The girl came and hugged her. "I got to come back."

"I know. Your daddy told me."

"Did he tell you about the wedding?" Cassie's tiny hand slapped over her mouth. "Oh, no, I wasn't supposed to tell you about that."

"Whose wedding? Your mommy's?" When Cassie didn't answer, she asked, "Your daddy's?"

The child giggled. "Both of 'em. But don't tell Daddy I told you. It's a surprise."

Lori could barely take her next breath. Was that why Jace said he got Cassie? He had to remarry Shelly?

She couldn't do this. She turned and found Jace behind her, holding her coat. "Okay, we need to get out of here and talk." He grinned. "I know just the place."

She gasped. "There's no need to tell me. I already heard from Cassie about the wedding. I hope you and Shelly will be happy."

He frowned. "What? You think that Shelly and I…" He cursed.

Lori held up her hand to stop him, but he took it in his.

"We're definitely going to talk about this," he began. "We need to get a few things straightened out. Now."

"I can't leave now."

"So we should just talk here. I'm sure all your guests would love to hear what I have to say," he said, and held out her coat.

"Why are you doing this?" she asked, keeping her voice low.

"I hate the fact that you even have to ask. I hope I can change that." When she hesitated, he asked, "Can't you even give me a few minutes to hear me out? To listen to what I have to say."

Lori wasn't sure what to do, only that she didn't want a scene here. She slipped on her coat and told Maggie she was leaving for a little while.

The housekeeper smiled and waved them on saying, "It's about time."

CHAPTER THIRTEEN

TWENTY minutes later, Jace was still furious as he pulled off the highway. The sun had already set, but he knew the way to the cabin.

"Why are you bringing me here?" Lori asked.

"So we can talk without anyone interrupting us." He glanced across the bench seat. "But if you want, I'll take you back home."

He watched her profile in the shadowed light. She closed her eyes then whispered, "No, it might be good if we talk. At least to clear the air."

"Oh, darlin', I plan to do more than clear the air."

Lori jerked her head around and even in the darkness he could see she was glaring. She opened her mouth but he stopped her words.

"Hold that thought. We're here." He pulled into the parking space and climbed out. No more snow had fallen since the last time he'd followed her here. It hadn't gotten any warmer, either.

He pulled his sheepskin coat together to ward off the cold as he went around to Lori's side. After helping her out, they hurried up to the lit porch. He took the key from his pocket and rushed on to explain, "I stopped by earlier." He unlocked the door, pushed it open and turned on the light inside the door.

"After you," he told her, watching surprise cross her pretty face. "Come on, let's get inside where it's warm."

Lori felt Jace's hand against her back, nudging her in. Once inside she stopped and looked around, trying not to think about the last time they'd been here. It didn't work. Memories flooded her head. How incredible it had been being in Jace's arms, making love with him.

"Just let me get a fire started." Jace went straight to the fireplace, where logs had been placed on the grate. He turned on the gas and the flames shot over the wood. He lit the candles that were lined up along the mantel, then turned to her. "You should be warm in a few minutes."

She recalled another time he hadn't waited for the fire to warm her. She pushed away the thought and walked to the table where she saw a vase of fresh flowers. Red roses. She faced him. "You bought these?"

He nodded.

"So you'd planned to bring me here?"

He pulled off his jacket and went to her. "I've been thinking about it since I left Denver. I want to be with you alone, to talk to you."

With her heart racing, she returned to the fire and held out her hands to warm them. Mostly, she wanted to gather her thoughts, but she was overwhelmed by this man. She wanted to be hopeful, but she also recalled what Jace had told her. He didn't want to get involved with another woman.

"Are you ready to listen to what I have to say?"

She stared into the fire. "So now you want to talk?

Why didn't you call me before? Let me know what was going on."

"Because I didn't know myself until recently. I was in mediation during the day with Shelly and her lawyers. At night, I was trying to ease my daughter's fears." His sapphire gaze met hers. "And I guess I've been so used to doing things on my own, I didn't know how to depend on someone else."

"You didn't have to be alone. I was here for you."

"I know that now. Yet, in the end, I had to make the decision based on my daughter's well-being. It was hard to know what was best for Cassie. Was I being selfish wanting her with me?"

Hearing his stress, she turned, but didn't go to him. "Oh, Jace. No, you weren't being selfish. You love Cassie enough to want to give her stability. I also believe that you love your daughter enough that if Shelly could give Cassie what she needed, you'd let her have custody."

He smiled. "It always amazes me how you seem to know me so well."

That wasn't true, she thought, praying he wanted the same thing she did. To be together. "Not so. I have no idea why you brought me here, especially since I haven't heard a word in the past week. And what about this wedding?"

This time he came to her. He stood so close, she could inhale his wonderful scent. The only sounds were the logs crackling in the fire as she waited for an explanation.

Then he took her hand. "I might have helped a little with a nudge to Edmund. He took it from there and went to see Shelly. They were married yesterday by the same judge who helped with the custody case. I escorted Cassie to her mother's wedding."

"Shelly got married?"

"Yes. I thought things would go smoother if I helped Shelly settle her problem with her now-husband. I contacted him the day I arrived, and got him to come with me to Shelly's place." He shrugged. "They took it from there, and now they're headed to England for their honeymoon and his family."

Jace met her dark eyes and nearly lost his concentration. "Before Shelly left we managed to sit down and decide what would be best for our daughter. In the end, Cassie told her mother she wanted to live with me in Destiny."

"That had to be hard on Shelly."

Jace nodded. "But she gets visitation, summers and holidays. She can't take Cassie out of the country until she's older." He studied Lori's pretty face and his stomach tightened. He wanted her desperately.

"It all finally got settled yesterday, and Cassie and I caught the first flight back here...and came to see you."

He reached for her hand and tugged her closer. "I want more, Lori. More than just having my daughter in my life. I also want you. No, not just want you, but need you."

Not giving her a chance to resist, his mouth came down on hers in an all-consuming kiss. He couldn't resist her, either. His hands moved over her back, going downward to her hips, drawing her against him.

With a gasp, she pulled back. "You're not playing fair," she accused.

"I want you, Lorelei Hutchinson. I'll use any means possible to have you."

"Wait." Lori pushed him away, not liking this. "What are you exactly talking about? Seduction?" She deserved more. "I won't be that secret woman in your life, Jace, that you pull out whenever it's convenient."

He frowned. "Whoa. Who said anything about that…" He stopped as if to regroup.

"First of all, I'm sorry that I ever made you feel that way. I asked a lot of you when I left here, and I know I should have called you. Believe me I wanted to, but I was so afraid that if I did, I'd confess how I felt about you. I didn't have a right yet. I needed all my concentration on Cassie. You and I both know what it's like to lose parents. I would do anything not to have that happen to my daughter." His gaze bore into hers. "No matter how much I care about you, Lori, I couldn't abandon my child and come to you." He swallowed. "No matter how much I wanted to. Not matter how much I love you."

She closed her eyes.

"No, look at me, Lori. I'm not your father. I'm never going to leave you, ever. How could I when I can't seem to be able to live without you. Even if I had to move back to Denver because of Cassie, I would have figured out a way to come and be with you, too."

"You love me?"

He drew her close and nodded. "From the top of your pretty blond hair, to your incredible brown eyes, down to your cute little ruby-red painted toes." He kissed her forehead, then brushed his lips against each eyelid. His mouth continued a journey to her cheek, then she shivered as he reached her ear. "I'll tell you about all your other delicious body parts later," he promised, then pulled back and looked down at her. "If you'll let me."

"Oh, Jace. I love you, too," she whispered.

"I was hoping you felt that way." He pulled her into his arms and kissed her deeply. By the time he released her they were both breathing hard.

"We better slow down a minute, or I'll forget what I was about to do." He went to his coat and pulled a small box out of his jacket pocket, then returned to Lori.

Her eyes grew round. "Jace?"

He felt a little shaky. "I want this to be perfect, but if I manage to mess up something, just remember how much I love you." He drew a breath. "Lorelei Hutchinson, I probably can't offer you a perfect life. I have a home that's still under construction. A business that isn't off the ground yet." His eyes met hers. "And a daughter that I'm going to ask you to be a mother to."

A tear ran down her cheek. "Oh, Jace, don't you know, those are assets. And I couldn't love Cassie any more than if she were my own."

"She loves you, too."

"So she's okay with me and you?"

He nodded. "She even approved of the ring." He opened the box and she gasped at the square-cut diamond solitaire with the platinum band.

"Oh, my. It's beautiful."

That was his cue. He got down on one knee. "Lorelei Hutchinson, you are my heart. Will you marry me?"

She touched his face with her hands and kissed him softly. "Yes, Jace, oh, yes."

With her mouth still against his, he rose and wrapped his arms around her as he deepened the kiss. He couldn't let her go. Ever.

He finally broke off the kiss, then slipped the ring on her finger. He kissed her softly, then pulled back. "Give me one second, then we'll have the rest of the night."

Lori nodded and looked down at her ring. She couldn't believe this was really happening. "Good, I'm going to need your full attention the rest of the night to convince me that this isn't a fairy tale." ·

He grinned, took out his cell phone and punched in a number. "You got it." He put it to his ear. "Hi, sweetheart," Jace said into the receiver. "She said yes." He looked at Lori and winked. "Yes, we'll celebrate tomorrow. I love you, too." He ended the call. "I hope you don't mind. Cassie wanted to know what your answer was."

"I don't mind at all. I think we have enough love that I can share it with your daughter." She wrapped her arms around his waist. "But maybe tonight, I'll let you show me."

"Not just tonight, Lori. Always. Forever."

EPILOGUE

It was nearly Christmas in Destiny.

This year, the town council had asked Lori to light the big tree in the town square. She was honored, to say the least. Of course, she didn't do it alone. She'd invited Zack and Cassie to help throw the switch that lit the fifty-foot ponderosa pine.

While enjoying the colorful light show and the children's choir singing carols, she recalled the first day she'd arrived in Destiny. She felt so alone, then she started meeting the people here. That included one stubborn contractor who made her heart race. Made her aware of what she'd been missing in life.

For Lori there were bittersweet memories, too. Her father was gone and she'd never had the chance to have a relationship with him. But with her new family, she wasn't going to be alone. Not only Gina and Zack, but also her future husband, Jace, and a stepdaughter, Cassie.

Suddenly she felt a pair of arms slip around her waist from behind. She smiled and leaned back against Jace's broad chest.

"So are you enjoying your big night?" he said against her ear.

"Oh, yes." She smiled, recalling the last time she'd been here with her father. She called them treasured memories now. "But I have to say, I'm glad the school play is over."

"Until next year," he reminded her.

"Very funny. I'm planning to be really busy."

"You do too much as it is," he said as they watched the children's choir singing beside the tree. He tightened his hold, his large body shielding her from the cold night. "Between the mortgage and college scholarship programs, you have no free time."

She and Jace had made the decision together about taking only a small part of the inheritance to put away for the kids; the rest would go back into the town. They both made an excellent income from Hutchinson Corp properties.

"I want to get the programs up and ready for when my father's money comes through next fall." She stole a glance over her shoulder at him. "You'd be proud of me. I've turned over my job on the mortgage committee to Erin. She'll go to all the meetings, and I'll work from her recommendations."

"However you get it done, you're a pretty special lady to be so generous to this town."

She turned in his arms. "I only want to be your special lady."

He grew serious. "You are, Lori, and will always be." He kissed her sweetly. "How about we ditch this place for something a little more private."

"Oh, I'd like that, but you know we can't. For one thing, Cassie and Zack are singing." They both looked at the children. "And we're all invited back to the Keenan Inn for a party and to finalize our wedding plans. It's going to be a big undertaking for Claire and Gina to pull this off, especially with the holidays."

"I know, the first wedding at Hutchinson House," he said.

"The first of many, I hope," she reminded him.

Jace had to smile. With the exception of Cassie's birth, he couldn't remember ever being this happy. Now he had it all, the woman he loved and his daughter permanently. "So I guess a wild night together is out of the question."

"Of course not. It's just postponed for a few weeks."

"Until New Year's Eve," he finished. The date they'd chosen for their wedding. "That's a long three weeks off." Even longer since they'd spent most of their time with Cassie trying to help her adjust to the new arrangement. He hated having to send Lori home every night.

"You sure we can't sneak off to the cabin tonight?"

She gave him a quick kiss. "Just hold that thought and I promise to make it worth your while after the wedding."

"You being here with me now has made my dreams come true."

Hutchinson House never looked so beautiful.

On New Year's Eve Lori stood at the window of the master suite. She could see over the wide yard toward the front of the property.

The ornate gates were covered with thousands of tiny silver lights and many more were strung along the hedges. It was only a prelude for what was to come as the wedding guests approached the end of the circular drive and the grand house on the hill.

The porch railings were draped in fresh garland, and

more lights were intermixed with the yards of greenery that smelled of Christmas. White poinsettias edged
the steps leading to the wide front door trimmed with
a huge fresh-cut wreath.

Lori smiled. The Hutchinson/Yeager wedding was
going to be the first of many parties in this house.

Gina came in dressed in a long dark green grown.
"Oh, Lori. You look so beautiful."

Lori glanced down at her wedding dress. She'd fallen
in love with the floor-length ivory gown the second
she'd seen it at Rocky Mountain Bridal Shop, from the
top of the sweetheart neckline, to the fitted jeweled
bodice with a drop waist and satin skirt. Her hair was
pulled back, adorned with a floral headband attached
to a long tulle veil.

"I hope Jace thinks so."

Gina handed her a deep red rose bouquet. "He will."

She felt tears forming. "I'm so lucky to have found
him, and Cassie."

Gina blinked, too. "They're lucky to have you." She
gripped Lori's hand. "I love you, sis. Thank you for always being there for us."

"Hey, you were there for me, too. And nothing will
change. We're still family. I'm only going to be a few
miles from your new place." Lori frowned, knowing
they had arranged to live in their own house. "You feel
okay about the move?"

Her sister nodded. "Zack and I are going to be fine."

Lori knew that. Her sister was working with Kaley,
having hours that enabled her to be home when Zack
got out of school. She still worried about Eric showing
up someday, but they'd all keep an eye out.

Gina straightened. "Okay, let's get your special day started."

They walked into the hall toward the head of the stairs where Charlie was waiting. She couldn't lie, every girl dreamed of walking down the aisle escorted by her father. She wasn't any different. At least now she'd been able to make peace with it all.

She whispered, "I'll always miss you, Dad."

Smiling, Charlie had tears in his eyes when she arrived. "Oh, Miss Lorelei, you are a vision. I'm so honored to escort you today."

She gripped his hands. "Thank you, Charlie."

The older man offered her his arm. "I know there's an anxious young man waiting for his bride."

The music began and Cassie and Zack, the flower girl and ring bearer, started down the petal-covered stairs. The banister entwined with more garland that wound down to the large entry. Next Gina began her descent. Once her sister reached the bottom the music swelled.

Holding tight on to Charlie, Lori's heart raced when she made her way down. Once she touched the bottom steps, she took it all in.

The room was filled with flowers: roses, carnations and poinsettias, all white. Rows of wooden chairs, filled with family and friends, lined either side of the runner that led through the entry and into the dining room and ended at a white trellis covered in greenery. And underneath stood Jace. The man who was going to share her life.

Jace's breath caught when his gaze met Lori's. She was beautiful. His heart swelled. He never knew he could love someone so much.

She made her way to him and he had to stop himself from going to her. Finally she arrived and he took her hand. When he locked on her big brown eyes, everything else seemed to fade away. There was only her. It was just the two of them exchanging vows, making the life commitment.

The minister began the ceremony and the vows were exchanged. Jace listened to her speak and was humbled by her words.

Then came his turn. He somehow managed to get the emotional words past his tight throat. Then Justin passed him the ring, and he slipped the platinum band on her finger. He held out his hand so she could do the same.

He gripped both her hands and the minister finally pronounced them husband and wife. Jace leaned down, took her in his arms and kissed her.

There were cheers as the minister announced, "It's my pleasure to introduce to you, Mr. and Mrs. Jace Yeager."

Jace held his bride close, never wanting to let her go. She was his heart, his life, the mother of his future children.

It had been a long journey but they had found each other. He pulled back and looked at his bride. "Hello, Mrs. Yeager."

With tears in her eyes, she answered, "Hello, Mr. Yeager."

Together they walked down the aisle hand in hand past the well-wishers toward their future together. It was their Destiny.

* * * * *

LET'S TALK

Romance

For exclusive extracts, competitions
and special offers, find us online:

f facebook.com/millsandboon

y @MillsandBoon

⊙ @MillsandBoonUK

Get in touch on 01413 063232

For all the latest titles coming soon, visit
millsandboon.co.uk/nextmonth

MILLS & BOON

THE HEART OF ROMANCE

A ROMANCE FOR EVERY READER

MODERN

Prepare to be swept off your feet by sophisticated, sexy and seductive heroes, in some of the world's most glamourous and romantic locations, where power and passion collide.

HISTORICAL

Escape with historical heroes from time gone by. Whether your passion is for wicked Regency Rakes, muscled Vikings or rugged Highlanders, await the romance of the past.

MEDICAL

Set your pulse racing with dedicated, delectable doctors in the high-pressure world of medicine, where emotions run high and passion, comfort and love are the best medicine.

True Love

Celebrate true love with tender stories of heartfelt romance, from the rush of falling in love to the joy a new baby can bring, and a focus on the emotional heart of a relationship.

Desire

Indulge in secrets and scandal, intense drama and plenty of sizzling hot action with powerful and passionate heroes who have it all: wealth, status, good looks…everything but the right woman.

HEROES

Experience all the excitement of a gripping thriller, with an intense romance at its heart. Resourceful, true-to-life women and strong, fearless men face danger and desire - a killer combination!

To see which titles are coming soon, please visit

millsandboon.co.uk/nextmonth

JOIN US ON SOCIAL MEDIA!

Stay up to date with our latest releases, author news and gossip, special offers and discounts, and all the behind-the-scenes action from Mills & Boon...

 @millsandboon

 @millsandboonuk

 facebook.com/millsandboon

 @millsandboonuk

It might just be true love...

GET YOUR ROMANCE FIX!

Get the latest romance news,
exclusive author interviews, story
extracts and much more!

MILLS & BOON

MODERN

Power and Passion

Prepare to be swept off your feet by sophisticated, sexy and seductive heroes, in some of the world's most glamourous and romantic locations, where power and passion collide.

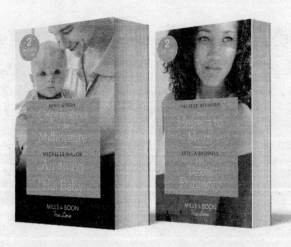